Also by Dan Simmons

SONG OF KALI
PHASES OF GRAVITY
CARRION COMFORT*
HYPERION
THE FALL OF HYPERION
ENTROPY'S BED AT MIDNIGHT
PRAYERS TO BROKEN STONES
SUMMER OF NIGHT*
THE HOLLOW MAN

*Published by
WARNER BOOKS

DAN SIMMONS

CHILDREN OF THE NIGHT

WARNER BOOKS

A Time Warner Company

WARNER BOOKS EDITION

Copyright © 1992 by Dan Simmons
All rights reserved.

This Warner Books Edition is published by arrangement with
G.P. Putnam's Sons, 200 Madison Avenue, New York, NY 10016.

Warner Books, Inc.
1271 Avenue of the Americas
New York, NY 10020

 A Time Warner Company

Printed in the United States of America

First Warner Books Printing: June, 1993

10 9 8 7 6 5 4 3 2 1

To the children

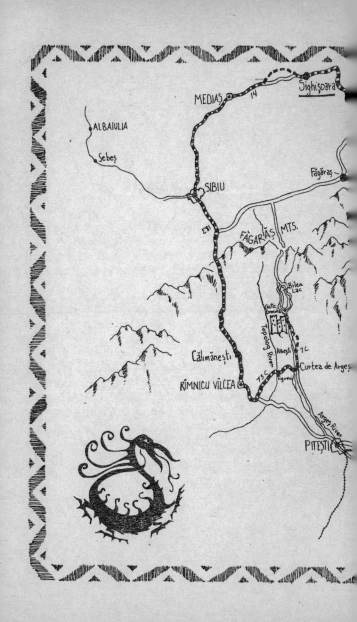

Chapter One

WE flew to Bucharest almost as soon as the shooting had stopped, landing at Otopeni Airport just after midnight on December 29, 1989. As the semiofficial "International Assessment Contingent," the six of us were met at my Lear jet, escorted through the confused milling that passed for Customs since Romania's revolution, and then herded aboard an Office of National Tourism VIP van for the nine-mile drive into town. They had brought a wheelchair to the bottom of the aircraft ramp for me, but I waved it away and made the walk to the van myself. It was not easy.

Donna Wexler, our U.S. Embassy liaison, pointed at two bullet holes in the wall near where the van was parked, but Dr. Aimslea topped that by simply pointing out the window as we drove around the lighted circular drive connecting the terminal to the highway.

Soviet-style tanks sat along the main thoroughfare where cabs normally would be waiting, their long muzzles pointed toward the entrance to the airport drive. Sandbagged emplacements lined the highway and airport rooftops, and the sodium-vapor lamps yellowly illuminated the helmets and rifles of soldiers on guard duty while throwing their faces into deep shadow. Other men, some in regular army uniforms and others in the ragtag clothing of the revolutionary militia, lay sleeping alongside the tanks. For a second the illusion of sidewalks littered with the bodies of Romania's dead was perfect and I held my breath, exhaling slowly only when I saw one of the bodies stir and another light a cigarette.

"They fought off several counterattacks by loyalist troops and *Securitate* forces last week," whispered Donna Wexler. Her tone suggested that it was an embarrassing topic, like sex.

Radu Fortuna, the little man who had been hurriedly introduced to us in the terminal as our guide and liaison with the transitional government, turned in his seat and grinned broadly as if he were not embarrassed by either sex or politics. "They kill many *Securitate*," he said loudly, his grin growing ever wider. "Three times Ceauşescu's people tried to take airport . . . three times they get killed."

Wexler nodded and smiled, obviously uncomfortable with the conversation, but Dr. Aimslea leaned into the aisle. Light from the last of the sodium-vapor lamps illuminated his bald head in the seconds before we entered the darkness of the empty highway. "So Ceauşescu's regime is really over?" he said to Fortuna.

I could see only the slightest gleam from the Romanian's grin in the sudden darkness. "Ceauşescu is over, yes, yes," he said. "They take him and that bitch-cow of a wife in Tîrgovişte, you know . . . have, how you call it . . . *trial*." Radu Fortuna laughed again, a sound which somehow sounded both childish and cruel. I found myself shivering a bit in the darkness. The bus was not heated.

"They have trial," continued Fortuna, "and prosecutor say, 'You both crazy?' You see, if Ceauşescu and Mrs. Ceauşescu crazy, then maybe the army just send them away in mental hospital for hundred years, like our Russian friends do. You know? But Ceauşescu say, 'What? What? Crazy . . . How dare you! That is obscene provocation!' And his wife, she say, 'How can you say this to the Mother of your nation?' So prosecutor say, 'OK, you neither one crazy. Your own mouth say.' And then the soldiers, they draw straws so many want to be the ones. Then the lucky ones, they take Ceauşescus out in courtyard and shoot them in heads many times."

Fortuna chuckled warmly, as if remembering a favorite anecdote. "Yes, regime over," he said to Dr. Aimslea. "Maybe a few thousand *Securitate*, they don't know it yet and still shooting peoples, but that will be over soon. Bigger problem is, what to do with one out of three peoples who spy for old government, heh?"

Fortuna chuckled again, and in the sudden glare from an oncoming army truck, I could see his silhouette as he shrugged. There was a thin layer of condensation turning to ice on the inside of the windows now. My fingers were stiff with the cold and I could barely feel my toes in the absurd Bally dress shoes I had put on that morning. I scraped at some of the ice on my window as we entered the city proper.

"I know that you are all very important peoples from the West," said Radu Fortuna, his breath creating a small fog that rose toward the roof of the bus like an escaping soul. "I know you are famous Western billionaire, Mr. Vernor Deacon Trent, who pay for this visit," he said, nodding at me, "but I am afraid I forget some other names."

Donna Wexler did the introductions. "Doctor Aimslea is with the World Health Organization . . . Father Michael O'Rourke is here representing both the Chicago Archdiocese and the Save the Children Foundation."

"Ah, good to have priest here," said Fortuna, and I heard something that may have been irony in his voice.

"Doctor Leonard Paxley, Professor Emeritus of Economics at Princeton University," continued Wexler. "Winner of the 1978 Nobel Prize in Economics."

Fortuna bowed toward the old academic. Paxley had not spoken at all during the flight from Frankfurt, and now he seemed lost in his oversized coat and folds of muffler: an old man in search of a park bench.

"We welcome you," said Fortuna, "even though our country have no economy at present moment."

"Goddamn, is it always this cold here?" came the voice from deep in the folds of wool. The Nobel Prize–winning Professor Emeritus stamped his small feet. "This is cold enough to freeze the nuts off a bronze bulldog."

"And Mr. Carl Berry, representing American Telegraph and Telephone," continued Wexler quickly.

The pudgy businessman next to me puffed his pipe, removed it, nodded in Fortuna's direction, and went back to smoking the thing as if it were a necessary source of heat. I had a moment's mad vision of the seven of us in the bus huddled around the glowing embers in Berry's pipe.

"And you say you remember our sponsor, Mr. Trent," finished Wexler.

"Yesss," said Radu Fortuna. His eyes glittered as he looked at me through Berry's pipe smoke and the fog of his own breath. I could almost see my image in those glistening eyes—one very old man, deep-set eyes sunken even deeper from the fatigue of the trip, body shriveled and shrunken in my expensive suit and overcoat. I am sure that I looked older than Paxley, older than Methuselah . . . older than God.

"You have been in Romania before, I believe?" continued Fortuna. I could see the guide's eyes glowing brighter as we reached the lighted part of the city. I spent time in Germany shortly after the war. The scene out the window behind Fortuna was like that. There were more tanks in Palace Square, black hulks which one would have thought deserted heaps of cold metal if the turret of one had not tracked us as our van passed by. There were the sooty corpses of burned-out autos and at least one armored personnel carrier that was now only a piece of scorched steel. We turned left and went past the Central University Library; its gold dome and ornate roof had collapsed between soot-streaked, pockmarked walls.

"Yes," I said. "I have been here before."

Fortuna leaned toward me. "And perhaps this time one of your corporations *will* open a plant here, yes?"

"Perhaps."

Fortuna's gaze did not leave me. "We work very cheap here," he whispered so softly that I doubt if anyone else except Carl Berry could hear him. "Very cheap. Labor is very cheap here. Life is very cheap here."

We had turned left off of the empty Calea Victoriei, right again on Bulevardul Nicolae Bălcescu, and now the van screeched to a halt in front of the tallest building in the city, the twenty-two-story Intercontinental Hotel.

"In the morning, gentlemens," said Fortuna, rising, gesturing the way toward the lighted foyer, "we will see the new Romania. I wish you dreamless sleeps."

Chapter Two

OUR group spent the next day meeting with "officials" in the interim government, mostly members of the recently cobbled-together National Salvation Front. The day was so dark that the automatic streetlights came on along the broad Bulevardul N. Bălcescu and Bulevardul Republicii. The buildings were not heated . . . or at least not perceptibly . . . and the men and women we spoke with looked all but identical in their oversized, drab wool coats. By the end of the day we had spoken to a Giurescu, two Tismaneanus, one Borosoiu, who turned out not to be a spokesman for the new government after all . . . he was arrested moments after we left him . . . several generals including Popascu, Lupoi, and Diurgiu, and finally the real leaders, which included Petre Roman, prime minister in the transitional government, and Ion Iliescu and Dumitru Mazilu, who had been President and Vice President in the Ceauşescu regime.

Their message was the same: we had the run of the nation and any recommendations we could make to our various constituencies for help would be eternally appreciated. The officials treated me with the most deference because they knew my name and because of how much money I represented, but even that polite attention was tinged with a distracted air. They were like men sleepwalking amidst chaos.

Returning to the Intercontinental that evening, we watched

as a crowd of people—most, it looked, office workers leaving the stone hives of the downtown for the day—beat and pummeled three men and a woman. Radu Fortuna smiled and pointed to the broad plaza in front of the hotel where the crowd was growing larger. "There . . . in University Square last week . . . when peoples come to demonstrate with singing, you know? Army tanks roll over persons, shoot more. Those probably be *Securitate* informers."

Before the van stopped in front of the hotel, we caught a glimpse of uniformed soldiers leading away the probable informers, encouraging them with the butts of their automatic weapons while the crowd continued to spit and strike them.

"Can't make an omelette without breaking a few eggs," muttered our Professor Emeritus, while Father O'Rourke glared at him and Radu Fortuna chuckled appreciatively.

"You'd think Ceauşescu would have been better prepared for a siege," Dr. Aimslea said after dinner that evening. We had stayed in the dining room because it seemed warmer than our own rooms. Waiters and a few military men moved aimlessly through the large space. The reporters had finished their dinner quickly, with a maximum of noise, and left soon after to wherever reporters go to drink and be cynical.

Radu Fortuna had joined us for coffee, and now he showed his patented, gap-toothed grin. "You want to see how prepared, Ceauşescu, he was?"

Aimslea, Father O'Rourke, and I agreed that we would like to see. Carl Berry decided to go to his room to get a call through to the States, and Dr. Paxley followed him, grumbling about getting to bed early. Fortuna led the three of us out into the cold and down shadowed streets to the soot-blackened shell of the presidential palace. A militiaman stepped out of the shadows, raised an AK-47, and barked a challenge, but Fortuna spoke quietly and we were allowed to pass.

There were no lights in the palace except for occasional fires in barrels where militiamen and regular soldiers slept or huddled to keep warm. Furniture was tossed everywhere,

drapes had been ripped from twenty-foot-tall windows, papers
littered the floor, and the formal tiles were smeared with dark
streaks. Fortuna led us down a narrow hall, through a series
of what appeared to be private residential rooms, and stopped
at what seemed to be an unmarked closet. Inside the four-
foot-square closet there was nothing but three lanterns on a
shelf. Fortuna lighted the lanterns, handed one to Aimslea
and one to me, and then touched the molding above the back
wall. A sliding panel opened to a stone staircase.

"Mr. Trent," began Fortuna, frowning at my walking stick
and shaking, old-man arms. The lantern light tossed unsteady
shadows on the walls. He held out his hand for the lantern.
"There are many stairs. Perhaps . . ."

"I can make it," I said through tensed jaws. I kept the
lantern.

Radu Fortuna shrugged and led us down.

The next half hour was dreamlike, almost hallucinatory.
The stairway led down to echoing chambers from which a
maze of stone tunnels and other stairways branched. Fortuna
led us deep into this maze, our lights reflecting off the curved
ceilings and slick stones.

"My God," muttered Dr. Aimslea after ten minutes of
this, "these go for miles."

"Yes, yes," smiled Radu Fortuna. "Many miles."

There were storerooms with automatic weapons on shelves,
gas masks hanging from hooks; there were command centers
with radios and television monitors sitting there in the dark,
some destroyed as if madmen with axes had vented their
wrath on them, some still covered with clear plastic and
waiting only for their operators to turn them on; there were
barracks with bunks and stoves and kerosene heating units
which we eyed with envy. Some of the barracks looked untouched, others obviously had been the site of panicked evac-
uation or equally panicked firefights. There was blood on the
walls and floors of one of these chambers, the streaks more
black than red in the light of our hissing lanterns.

There were still bodies in the farther reaches of the tunnels,
some lying in pools of water dripping from overhead hatches,

others tumbled behind hastily erected barricades at the junction of the underground avenues. The stone vaults smelled like a meat locker.

"*Securitate*," said Fortuna and spat on one of the brown-shirted men lying facedown in a frozen pool. "They fled like rats down here and we finished them like rats. You know?"

Father O'Rourke crouched next to one of the corpses for a long moment, head bowed. Then he crossed himself and rose. There was no shock or disgust on his face. I remember someone having said that the bearded priest had been in Vietnam.

Dr. Aimslea said, "But Ceauşescu did not retreat to this . . . redoubt?"

"No." Fortuna smiled.

The doctor looked around in the hissing white light. "For God's sake, why not? If he'd marshaled an organized resistance down here, he could have held out for months."

Fortuna shrugged. "Instead, the monster, he fled by helicopter. He flied . . . no? Flew, yes . . . he flew to Tîrovişte, seventy kilometers from here, you know? There other peoples see him and his bitch-cow wife get in car. They catch."

Dr. Aimslea held his lantern at the entrance to another tunnel from which a terrible stench now blew. The doctor quickly pulled back the light. "But I wonder why . . ."

Fortuna stepped closer and the harsh light illuminated an old scar on his neck that I had not noticed before. "They say his . . . advisor . . . the Dark Advisor . . . told him not to come here." He smiled.

Father O'Rourke stared at the Romanian. "The Dark Advisor. It sounds as if his counselor was the devil."

Radu Fortuna nodded.

Dr. Aimslea grunted. "Did this devil escape? Or was he one of those poor buggers we saw back there?"

Our guide did not answer but entered one of the four tunnels branching off there. A stone stairway led upward. "To the National Theater," he said softly, waving us ahead of him. "It was damaged but not destroyed. Your hotel is next door."

The priest, the doctor, and I started up, lantern light throwing our shadows fifteen feet high on the curved stone walls above. Father O'Rourke stopped and looked down at Fortuna. "Aren't you coming?"

The little guide smiled and shook his head. "Tomorrow, we take you where it all began. Tomorrow we go to Transylvania."

Dr. Aimslea gave the priest and me a smile. "Transylvania," he repeated. "Shades of Bela Lugosi." He turned back to say something to Fortuna but the little man was gone. Not even the echo of footfalls or shimmer of lantern light showed which tunnel he had taken.

Chapter Three

W
E flew to Timişoara, a city of about 300,000 in western Transylvania, suffering the flight in an old recycled Tupolev turboprop now belonging to Tarom, the state airline. The authorities would not allow my Lear to fly from city to city in the country. We were lucky; the daily flight was delayed only an hour and a half. We flew through cloud for most of the way, and there were no interior lights on the plane, but that did not matter because there were neither flight attendants nor the interruption of a meal or snack. Dr. Paxley grumbled most of the way, but the scream of the turboprops and the groaning of metal as we bounced and bucked our way through updrafts and storm clouds muffled most of his complaints.

Just as we took off, seconds before entering the clouds, Fortuna leaned across the aisle and pointed out the window to a snow-covered island on a lake that must have been about twenty miles north of Bucharest. "Şnagov," he said, watching my face.

I glanced down, caught a glimpse of a dark church on the island before the clouds obliterated the view, and looked back at Fortuna. "Yes?"

"Vlad Ţepeş buried there," said Fortuna, still watching me. He pronounced the last name as "Tsepesh."

I nodded. Fortuna went back to reading one of our *Time*

magazines in the dim light, although how someone could read or concentrate during that wild ride, I will never know. A minute later Carl Berry leaned forward from the seat behind me and whispered, "Who the hell is Vlad Ţepeş? Someone who died in the fighting?"

The cabin was so dark now that I could barely make out Berry's face inches from my own. "Dracula," I said to the AT&T executive.

Berry let out a discouraged sigh and leaned back in his seat, tightening his belt as we began to pitch and bounce in earnest.

"Vlad the Impaler," I whispered to no one at all.

The electricity had failed, so the morgue was cooled by the simple expediency of opening all of the tall windows. The light was still very thin, as if watered down by the dark green walls and grimy panes of glass and constant low clouds, but was adequate to illuminate the rows of corpses across the tabletops and filling almost every inch of the tiled floors. We had to walk a circuitous path, stepping carefully between bare legs and white faces and bulging bellies, just to join Fortuna and the Romanian doctor in the center of the room. There were at least three or four hundred bodies in the long room . . . not counting ourselves.

"Why haven't these people been buried?" demanded Father O'Rourke, his scarf raised to his face. His voice was angry. "It's been at least a week since the murders, correct?"

Fortuna translated for the Timişoaran doctor, who shrugged. Fortuna shrugged. "Eleven days since the *Securitate*, they do this," he said. "Funerals soon. The . . . how do you say . . . the authorities here, they want to show the Western reporters and such very important peoples as yourself. Look, look." Fortuna opened his arms to the room in a gesture that was almost proud, a chef showing off the banquet he had prepared.

On the table in front of us lay a corpse of an old man. His hands and feet had been amputated by something not very sharp. There were burns on his lower abdomen and genitals, and his chest showed open scars that reminded me of Viking photos of the rivers and craters of Mars.

The Romanian doctor spoke. Fortuna translated. "He say, the *Securitate*, they play with acid. You know? And here . . ."

The young woman lay on the floor, fully clothed except for the ripped clothing that extended from her breasts to pubic bone. What I first took for another layer of slashed, red rags, I now realized was the red-rimmed wall of her opened belly and abdomen. The seven-month fetus lay on her lap like a discarded doll. It would have been a boy.

"Here," commanded Fortuna, stepping through the maze of ankles and gesturing.

The boy must have been about ten. Death and a week or more of freezing cold had expanded and mottled flesh to the texture of bloated, marbled parchment, but the barbed wire around his ankles and wrists was still quite visible. His arms had been tied behind him with such force that the shoulder joints were totally out of their sockets. Flies had been at his eyes, and the layer of eggs there made it look as if the child were wearing white goggles.

Professor Emeritus Paxley made a noise and staggered from the room, almost tripping over the bodies set out for display there. One old man's gnarled hand seemed to tug at the professor's pant leg as he fled.

Father O'Rourke grabbed Fortuna by his coat front and almost lifted the little man from the floor. "Why in the hell are you showing us this?"

Fortuna grinned. "There is more, Father. Come."

"They called Ceauşescu 'the vampire,'" said Donna Wexler, who had flown up later to join us.

"And here in Timişoara is where it started," said Carl Berry, puffing on his pipe and looking around at the gray sky, gray buildings, gray slush on the street, and gray people moving through the dim light.

"Here in Timişoara is where the final explosion began," said Wexler. "The younger generation has been getting more and more restless for some time. In a real sense, Ceauşescu signed his own death warrant by creating that generation."

"Creating that generation," repeated Father O'Rourke, frowning. "Explain."

Wexler explained. In the mid-1960s Ceauşescu had outlawed abortion, discontinued the import of oral contraceptives and IUDs, and announced that it was a woman's obligation to the state to have many children. More importantly, his government had offered birth premiums and reduced taxes to those families who obeyed the government's call for increased births. Couples who had fewer than five children were actually fined as well as heavily taxed. Between 1966 and 1976, said Wexler, there had been a forty percent increase in babies born, along with a huge rise in infant mortality.

"It was this surplus of young people in their twenties by the late 1980s who provided the core of the revolution," said Donna Wexler. "They had no jobs, no chance for a college education . . . not even a chance for decent housing. They were the ones who began the protests in Timişoara and elsewhere."

Father O'Rourke nodded. "Ironic . . . but appropriate."

"Of course," said Wexler, pausing near the train station, "most of the peasant families could not afford to raise the extra children . . ." She stopped with that diplomat's tic of embarrassment.

"So what happened to those children?" I asked. It was only early afternoon, but the light had faded to a wintry twilight. There were no streetlights along this section of Timişoara's main boulevard. Somewhere far down the tracks, a locomotive screamed.

The embassy woman shook her head, but Radu Fortuna stepped closer. "We take train tonight to Sebeş, Sibiu, Copşa Mica, and Sighişoara," the smiling Romanian said. "You see where babies go."

Winter evening became winter night beyond the windows of our train. The train passed through mountains as jagged as rotten teeth—whether they were the Făgăraş Range or the

lower Bucegi Carpathians, I could not remember right then—
and the dismal sight of huddled villages and sagging farms
faded to blackness broken only by the occasional glow of oil
lamps through distant windows. For a second the illusion was
perfect and I thought I was traveling through these mountains
in the fifteenth century, traveling by coach to the castle on
the Argeş, hurrying through these mountain passes in a race
against enemies who would . . .

I realized with a start that I had almost dozed off. It was
New Year's Eve, the last night of 1989, and the dawn would
bring what was popularly thought of as the last decade of the
millennium. But the sight out the window remained a glimpse
of the fifteenth century. The only intrusion of the modern age
visible in the evening departure from Timişoara had been the
occasional military vehicle glimpsed on snow-packed roads
and the rare electric cables snaking above the trees. Then
those slim talismans had disappeared and there were only the
villages, the oil lamps, the cold, and an occasional rubber-
wheeled cart, pulled by horses who seemed more bone than
flesh, guided by men hidden in dark wool. Then even the
village streets were empty as the train rushed through, stopping nowhere. I realized that some of the villages were totally
dark, even though it was not yet ten P.M., and leaning closer,
wiping frost from the glass, I saw that the village we were
passing now was dead—buildings bulldozed, stone walls demolished, farm homes tumbled down.

"*Systematization,*" whispered Radu Fortuna, who had appeared silently next to me in the aisle. He was chewing on
an onion.

I did not ask for clarification, but our guide and liaison
smiled and provided it. "Ceauşescu wanted to destroy the
old. He break down villages, move thousands of peoples to
city places like Victory of Socialism Boulevard in Bucharest . . . kilometers and kilometers of tall apartment buildings. Only buildings, they not finished when he tear down
and move peoples there. No heat. No water. No electricity
. . . he sell electricity to other countries, you see. So village
peoples, they have little house out here, be in family three,

maybe four hundreds of years, but now live on ninth floor of bad brick building in strange city . . . no windows, cold wind blow in. Have to carry water a mile, then carry up nine flights of stairs.''

He took a deep bite of the onion and nodded as if satisfied. "*Systematization.*" He moved on down the smoky aisle.

The mountains passed in the night. I began to doze again . . . I had slept little the night before, dreamlessly or otherwise, and I had not slept on the plane the night before that . . . but awoke with a start to find that the Professor Emeritus had taken the seat next to me.

"No goddamn heat," he whispered, tugging his muffler tighter. "You'd think with all these goddamn peasant bodies and goats and chickens and what have you in this so-called first-class car, that they'd generate some body heat in here, but it's as cold as Madame Ceauşescu's dear dead tit."

I blinked at the simile.

"Actually," said Dr. Paxley in a conspiratorial whisper, "it's not as bad as they say."

"The cold?" I said.

"No, no. The economy. Ceauşescu may be the only national leader in this century who actually paid *off* his country's foreign debt. Of course, he had to divert food, electricity, and consumer goods to other countries to do it, but Romania has no foreign debt at all now. None."

"Mmmm," I said, trying to remember the fragments of the dream I'd had in my few moments of sleep. Something about blood and iron.

"A one-point-seven-billion-dollar trade surplus," muttered Paxley, leaning close enough that I could tell that he'd also had onion for dinner. "And they owe the West nothing and the Russians nothing. Incredible."

"But the people are starving," I said softly. Wexler and Father O'Rourke were asleep in the seat in front of us. The bearded priest mumbled slightly, as if battling a bad dream.

Paxley waved away my comment. "When German reunification comes, do you know how much the West Germans are going to have to invest just to retool the infrastructure in the East?'' Not waiting for my reply, he went on. ''A hundred *billion* Deutschmarks . . . and that's just to prime the pump. With Romania, the infrastructure is so pitiful that there's little to tear down. Just junk the industrial madness that Ceauşescu was so proud of, use the cheap labor . . . my God, man, they're almost *serfs* . . . and build whatever industrial infrastructure you want. The South Korean model, Mexico . . . it's wide open for the Western corporation that's willing to take the chance.''

I pretended to doze off again, and eventually the Professor Emeritus moved down the aisle to find someone else to explain the economic facts of life to. The villages passed in the darkness as we moved deeper into the Transylvanian mountains.

We arrived in Sebeş before dawn and there was some minor official there to take us to the orphanage.

No, orphanage is too kind a word. It was a warehouse, heated no better than the other meat lockers we had been in so far, undecorated except for grimy tile floors and flaking walls painted a vomitous green to eye height and a leprous gray above that. The main hall was at least a hundred meters across.

It was filled with cribs.

Again, the word is too generous. Not cribs, but low metal cages with no tops to them. In the cages were children. Children ranging in age from newborns to ten-year-olds. None seemed capable of walking. All were naked or dressed in filth-caked rags. Many were screaming or weeping silently, and the fog of their breath rose in the cold air. Stern-faced women in complicated nurse's caps stood smoking cigarettes on the periphery of this giant human stockyard, occasionally moving among the cages to brusquely hand a bottle to a child . . . sometimes a seven- or eight-year-old child . . . or more frequently to slap one into silence.

The official and the chain-smoking administrator of the

"orphanage" snapped a tirade at us which Fortuna did not deign to translate, and then they walked us through the room and slammed open tall doors.

Another room, a larger room, opened into the cold-shrouded distance. Thin morning light fell in shafts onto the cages and faces there. There must have been at least a thousand children in this room, none of them more than two years old. Some were crying, their infant wails echoing in the tiled space, but most seemed too weak and lethargic even to cry as they lay on the thin, excrement-smeared rags. Some lay in the foetal grip of near starvation. Some looked dead.

Radu Fortuna turned and folded his arms. He was smiling. "You see where the babies go, yes?"

Chapter Four

IN Sibiu we found the hidden children. There were four orphanages in this central Transylvanian city of 170,000, and each orphanage was larger and sadder than the one in Sebeş. Dr. Aimslea demanded, through Fortuna, that we be allowed to see the AIDS children.

The administrator of Strada Cetatii State Orphanage 319, a windowless old structure in the shadow of the sixteenth-century city walls, absolutely refused to acknowledge that there *were* any AIDS babies. He refused to acknowledge our right to enter the orphanage. He refused, at one point, to acknowledge that he was the administrator of Strada Cetatii State Orphanage 319, despite the stenciling on his office door and the plaque on his desk.

Fortuna showed him our travel papers and authorization forms, cosigned with a personal plea for cooperation from interim Prime Minister Roman, President Iliescu, and Vice President Mazilu.

The administrator sneered, took a drag on his short cigarette, shook his head, and said something dismissive. "My orders come from the Ministry of Health," Radu Fortuna translated.

It took almost an hour to get through to the capital, but Fortuna finally completed a call to the Prime Minister's office, who called the Ministry of Health, who promised to call

Strada Cetatii State Orphanage 319 immediately. A little over two hours later, the call came, the administrator snarled something at Fortuna, tossed his cigarette butt on dirty tiles littered with them, snapped something at an orderly, and handed a huge ring of keys to Fortuna.

The AIDS ward was behind four sets of locked doors. There were no nurses there, no doctors . . . no adults of any kind. Neither were there cribs; the infants and small children sat on the tile floor or competed to find space on one of half a dozen bare and excrement-stained mattresses thrown against the far wall. They were naked and their heads had been shaved. The windowless room was illuminated by a few naked 40-watt bulbs set thirty or forty feet apart. Some children congregated there in the pools of murky light, raising swollen eyes to them as if to the sun, but most lay in the deep shadows. Older children scuttled on all fours to escape the light as we opened the steel doors.

It was obvious that the floors were hosed down every few days—there were rivulets and streaks along the cracked tiles—and it was just as obvious that no other hygienic efforts had been made. Donna Wexler, Dr. Paxley, and Mr. Berry turned and fled from the stench. Dr. Aimslea cursed and pounded his fist against a stone wall. Father O'Rourke first stared, his Irish face mottling with rage, and then moved from infant to infant, touching their heads, whispering softly to them in a language they did not understand, lifting them. I had the distinct impression as I watched that most of these children had never been held, perhaps never been touched.

Radu Fortuna followed us into the room. He was not smiling. "Comrade Ceauşescu told us that AIDS is a capitalist disease," he whispered. "Romania has no official cases of AIDS. None."

"My God, my God," Dr. Aimslea was muttering as he moved from child to child. "Most of these are in advanced stages of AIDS-related complexes. And suffering from malnutrition and vitamin deficiencies." He looked up and there were tears gleaming behind his glasses. "How long have they been here?"

Fortuna shrugged. "Most maybe since little babies. Parents put here. Babies not go out of this room, that why so few know to walk. No one to hold them up when they try."

Dr. Aimslea unleashed a series of curses that seemed to smoke in the chill air. Fortuna nodded.

"But hasn't anyone documented these . . . this . . . tragedy?" said Dr. Aimslea in a constricted voice.

Now Fortuna smiled. "Oh, yes, yes. Doctor Patrascu from Stefan S. Nicolau Institute of Virology, he say this happening three . . . maybe four years ago. First child he test, was infected. I think six out of next fourteen also sick from AIDS. All cities, all state homes he went to, many, many sick childrens."

Dr. Aimslea rose from shining his penlight in a comatose infant's eyes. Aimslea grabbed Fortuna by the coat, and for a second I was sure that he was going to strike the little guide in the face. "For Christ's sake, man, didn't he *tell* anyone?"

Fortuna stared impassively at the doctor. "Oh, yes. Doctor Patrascu, he tell Ministry of Health. They say for him to stop immediately. They cancel AIDS seminar Doctor schedule . . . then they burn his minutes and . . . how do you say it? Like little guides for meeting . . . *programs*. They confiscate printed programs and burn them."

Father O'Rourke set down a child. The two-year-old's thin arms strained toward the priest as she made vague, imploring noises—a plea to be lifted again. He lifted her, laying her bald and scabrous head tight against his cheek. "Goddamn them," whispered the priest in a tone of benediction. "Goddamn the Ministry. Goddamn that sonofabitch downstairs. Goddamn Ceauşescu forever. May they all burn in Hell."

Dr. Aimslea stood from where he crouched near a toddler who seemed all ribs and extended belly. "This child is dead." He turned to Fortuna again. "How in the hell can this happen? There can't be that many cases of AIDS among the general population yet, can there? Or are these children of drug addicts?"

I could see the other question in the doctor's eyes: in a nation where the average family could not afford to buy food and where possession of a narcotic was punishable by death, how could there be so many children of drug users?

"Come," said Fortuna, and led the doctor and me out of that ward of death. Father O'Rourke remained, lifting and touching child after child.

In the "healthy ward" downstairs, differing from the Sebeş orphanage only in size—there must have been a thousand or more children in the endless sea of steel cribs—nurses were moving stolidly from child to child, giving them glass bottles of what looked to be formulized milk, and then, as each child sucked noisily, injecting him or her with a syringe. Then the nurse would wipe the syringe with a rag she carried on her belt, re-insert it in a large vial from her tray, and inject the next child.

"Mother of Christ," whispered Dr. Aimslea. "You don't have disposable syringes?"

Fortuna made a gesture with his hands. "A capitalist luxury."

Aimslea's face was so red that I thought capillaries were bursting there. "Then what about fucking autoclaves!"

Fortuna shrugged and asked the nearest nurse something. She snapped a reply and went back to her injections. "She say, the autoclave is broken. Has been broken. Sent to Ministry of Health to be fixed," translated Fortuna.

"How long?" grated Aimslea.

"It broken four years," said Fortuna after calling the question to the busy woman. She had not bothered to turn around while replying. "She say, that was four years *before* it sent to the Ministry for repair last year."

Dr. Aimslea stepped closer to a six- or seven-year-old lying in his crib, sucking on his bottle. The formula looked like gray water. "And these are vitamin shots they're administering?"

"Oh, no," said Fortuna. "Blood."

Dr. Aimslea froze, then turned slowly. "Blood?"

"Yes, yes. Adult's blood. It make little babies strong. Ministry of Health approve . . . they say it is very . . . how do you say . . . *advanced* medicine."

Aimslea took a step toward the nurse, then a step toward

Fortuna, and then wheeled toward me as if he would kill either of the first two if he got close to them. "*Adult's blood*, Trent. Jesus H. Christ. That was a theory that went out with gaslights and spats. My God, don't they realize . . ." He suddenly turned back toward our guide. "Fortuna, where do they get this . . . adult blood?"

"It donated . . . no, wrong word. Not donated, *bought*. Those peoples in big cities who have no money at all, they sell blood for babies. Fifteen *lei* each time."

Dr. Aimslea made a rough sound in his throat, a noise that soon turned to chuckles. He shaded his eyes with his hand and staggered backward, leaning against a tray filled with bottles of dark liquid. "Paid blood donors," he whispered to himself. "Street people . . . drug addicts . . . prostitutes . . . and they administer it to infants in the state homes with reusable, nonsterile needles." The chuckles continued, grew louder. Dr. Aimslea lowered himself to a sitting position on the dirty towels, the hand still over his eyes, laughter coming from deep in his throat. "How many . . ." he started to ask Fortuna. He cleared his throat and tried again. "How many did this Doctor Patrascu estimate were infected with AIDS?"

Fortuna frowned as he tried to remember. "I think maybe he find eight hundred of the first two thousand. More higher number after that."

From beneath the visor of his hand, Dr. Aimslea said, "Forty percent. And how many . . . orphanage children . . . are there?"

Our guide shrugged. "Ministry of Health say maybe two hundred thousands. I think more . . . maybe a million. Maybe more."

Dr. Aimslea did not look up or speak again. The deep chuckles grew louder and deeper, and I realized then that they were not chuckles at all, but sobs.

Chapter Five

S IX of us took the train north through late-afternoon light toward Sighişoara. Father O'Rourke stayed behind in the Sibiu orphanage. Fortuna had planned one stop in a small town along the way.

"Mr. Trent, you like Copşa Mica," he said. "It is for you we see it."

I did not turn to look at him, but kept my gaze on the demolished villages we were passing. "More orphanages?" I said.

"No, no. I mean, yes . . . there is orphanage in Copşa Mica, but we don't go there. It is small town . . . six thousand peoples. But it is reason you come to our country, yes?"

I did turn to stare. "Industry?"

Fortuna laughed. "Ah, yes . . . Copşa Mica is most industrious. Like so many of our towns. And this one so close to Sighişoara, where Comrade Ceauşescu's Dark Advisor was born."

"Dark Advisor," I snapped. "What the hell are you saying? That Ceauşescu's advisor was Vlad Ţepeş?" The guide did not answer.

Sighişoara is a perfectly preserved medieval town where even the presence of the few autos on the narrow, cobblestoned streets seems an anachronism. The hills surrounding Sighişoara are studded with tumble-down towers and keeps, none of them as cinematic as the half-dozen intact castles in Transylvania which advertise themselves as Dracula's castle for impressionable travelers with hard currency. But the old house on Piaţa Muzeului had truly been Vlad Dracula's birthplace and home from 1431 to 1435. The last time I had seen it, many years earlier, the upstairs had been a restaurant and the basement a wine cellar.

Fortuna stretched and went off in search of something to eat. Dr. Aimslea had overheard the conversation and dropped into the seat next to me. "Do you believe that man?" he whispered. "Now he's ready to tell you ghost stories about Dracula. *Christ!*"

I nodded and looked out at the mountains and valleys sliding by in gray monotone. There was a wildness here that I had not seen elsewhere in the world, and I have traveled in more nations than there are in the U.N. The mountainside, deep ravines, and trees seemed malformed, gnarled, like something struggling to escape from an Hieronymus Bosch painting.

"I wish it were Dracula we had to deal with here," continued the good doctor. "Think of it, Trent . . . if our contingent announced that Vlad the Impaler were alive and preying on people in Transylvania, well . . . hell . . . there'd be ten thousand reporters up here. Satellite trucks parked in Sibiu's town square to bounce back InstaCam reports to every Channel 7 and Channel 4 hometown news market in America. One monster biting a few dozen people, and the world would be galvanized with interest . . . but as it is, tens of thousands of men and women dead, hundreds of thousands of children warehoused and facing . . . *goddammit.*"

I nodded without turning. "The banality of evil," I whispered.

"What?"

"The banality of evil." I turned and smiled grimly at the physician. "Dracula would be a story. The plight of hundreds of thousands of victims of political madness, bureaucracy, stupidity . . . this is just an . . . inconvenience."

* * *

We arrived at Copşa Mica just before nightfall, and I realized at once why it was "my" town. Wexler, Aimslea, and Paxley stayed on the train for the half-hour layover; only Carl Berry and I had business there. Fortuna led the way.

The village—it was too small to call a town—lay in a broad valley between old mountains. There was snow on the hillsides, but the snow was black. The icicles which hung from the dark eaves of the buildings were black. Underfoot, the slush along the unpaved roads was a gray and black mixture, and over everything hung a visible pall of black air, as if a million microscopic moths were fluttering in the dying light. Men and women in black coats and shawls moved past us, dragging their heavy carts or leading children by the hand, and the faces of these people were soot black. As we approached the center of the village, I realized that the three of us were wading through a layer of ash and soot at least three inches deep. I have seen active volcanoes in South America and elsewhere, and the ash and midnight skies were the same.

"It is a . . . how do you say it . . . auto-tire plant," said Radu Fortuna, gesturing toward the black industrial complex that filled the end of the valley like some grounded dragon. "It makes black powder for rubber products . . . works twenty-four hours a day. Sky is always like this . . ." He gestured proudly toward the black haze that settled down on everything.

Carl Berry was coughing. "Good Lord, how can people live in this?"

"They not live long," said Fortuna. "Most old peoples, like you and me, they have lead poisoning. Little children have . . . what is word? Always coughing?"

"Asthma," said Berry.

"Yes, little childrens have ashthma. Babies born with hearts which are . . . how do you say, badformed?"

"Malformed," said Berry.

I stopped a hundred yards from the black fences and black walls of the plant. The village behind us was a sketch of blacks against grays. Even the lamplight did not truly penetrate the soot-blackened windows. "Why is this 'my town,' Fortuna?" I said.

He held his hand out toward the factory. The lines in his palm were already black with soot, the cuff of his white shirt a dark gray. "Ceauşescu gone now. Factory no longer have to turn out rubber things for East Germany, Poland, U.S.S.R. . . . you want? Make things your company want? No . . . how do you say . . . no environmental impactment states, no regulations against making things the way you want, throwing away things where you want. So, you want?"

I stood there in the black snow for a long moment and might have stood there longer if the train had not shrieked its two-minute warning. "Perhaps," I said. "Just perhaps."

We trudged back through ash.

Chapter Six

DONNA Wexler, Dr. Aimslea, Carl Berry, and our Professor Emeritus, Dr. Leonard Paxley, took the waiting VIP van back to Bucharest from Sighişoara. I stayed behind. The morning was dark, with heavy clouds that moved up the valley and shrouded the surrounding ridges in shifting haze. The city walls with their eleven stone towers seemed to blend their gray stones with the gray skies, sealing the medieval town under a solid dome of gloom. After a late breakfast, I filled my Thermos, left the old town square, and climbed the old steps to the house on Piaţa Muzeului. The iron doors to the wine cellar were closed, the narrow doors to the first floor sealed with heavy shutters. An old man sitting on a bench across the street told me that the restaurant had been closed for several years, that the state had considered turning the house into a museum but then decided that foreign guests would not pay hard currency to see a run-down house . . . not even one where Vlad Dracula had lived five centuries before. The tourists preferred the large old castles a hundred miles closer to Bucharest; castles which had been erected centuries after Vlad Ţepeş had abdicated.

I went back across the street, waited until the old man had fed his pigeons and left, and then I tugged off the heavy bar holding the shutters in place. The panes on the doors were as black as the soul of Copşa Mica. The doors were locked, but I scratched at the centuries-old glass.

Fortuna opened the door and led me in. Most of the tables and chairs had been stacked on a rough bar, cobwebs running from them to the smoke-blackened rafters, but Fortuna had pulled one table down and set it in the middle of the stone floor. He dusted off the two chairs before we sat.

"Did you enjoy the tour?" he asked in Romanian.

"*Da,*" I said, and continued in the same language, "but I felt that you overdid it a bit."

Fortuna shrugged. He went behind the bar, dusted off two pewter tankards, and brought them back to the table.

I cleared my throat. "Would you have recognized me at the airport as a member of the Family if you had not known me?" I said.

My erstwhile guide showed his grin. "Of course."

I frowned at this. "How? I have no accent and I have lived as an American for many years."

"Your manners," said Fortuna, letting the Romanian word roll off his tongue. "Your manners are much too good for an American."

I sighed. Fortuna reached below the table and brought forth a wineskin, but I made a gesture and lifted the Thermos from my overcoat pocket. I poured for both of us and Radu Fortuna nodded, as serious as I had seen him during the past three days. We toasted.

"*Skoal,*" I said. The drink was very good, fresh, still at body temperature and nowhere near that point of coagulation where a certain bitterness sets in.

Fortuna drained his tankard, wiped his mustache, and nodded his appreciation. "Your company will buy the plant in Copşa Mica?" he asked.

"Yes."

"And the other plants . . . in other Copşa Micas?"

"Yes," I said. "Or our consortium will underwrite European investment in it."

Fortuna smiled. "The investors in the Family will be

happy. It will be twenty-five years before this country will be able to afford the luxury of worrying about the environment . . . and the people's health.''

"Ten years," I said. "Environmental awareness is contagious."

Fortuna made a gesture with his hands and shoulders . . . a peculiarly Transylvanian gesture which I had not seen in years.

"Speaking of contagious," I said, "the orphanage situation seems insane."

The small man nodded. Dim light from the door behind me lighted his brow. Beyond him there was only blackness. "We do not have the luxury of your American plasma or private bloodbanks. The state had to provide a reservoir."

"But the AIDS . . ." I began.

"Will be contained," said Fortuna. "Thanks to the humanitarian impulses of your Doctor Aimslea and Father O'Rourke. In the next few months your American television will air 'specials' on *60 Minutes* and *20/20* and whatever other programs you have created since I visited last. Americans are sentimental. There will be a public outcry. Aid will flow from all those groups and from rich people who have nothing better to do with their time. Families will adopt, pay a fortune for sick children to be flown to the States, and local television stations will interview mothers weeping with happiness."

I nodded.

"Your American health workers . . . and British . . . and West German . . . will flock to the Carpathians, and the Bucegis, and the Făgăraş . . . and we will 'discover' many other orphanages and hospitals, many other of these isolation wards. Within two years it will be contained."

I nodded again. "But they're liable to take a sizable amount of your . . . reservoir . . . with them," I said softly.

Fortuna smiled and shrugged again. "There are more. Always more. Even you know that in your land of teenage runaways and missing children's photos on milk cartons, no?"

I finished my drink, got up, and paced toward the light.

"Those days are over," I said. "Survival equals moderation. All of the Family must learn that someday." I turned back toward Fortuna and my voice held more anger than I had expected. "Otherwise, what? The contagion again? A growth of the family more rapid than cancer, more virulent than AIDS? Contained, we are in balance. Left to . . . propagate . . . there will be only the hunters with no prey, as doomed to starvation as those rabbits on Easter Island years ago."

Fortuna held up both hands, palms outward. "We must not argue. We know that. It is why Ceauşescu had to go. It is why we overthrew him. It is why you advised him not to go into his tunnels, to reach the triggers that would have brought Bucharest down."

For a moment I could only stare at the little man. When I spoke, my voice was very tired. "You will obey me then? After all these years?"

Fortuna's eyes were very bright. "Oh, yes."

"And you know why I returned?"

Fortuna rose, walked to the dark hall where a darker stairway waited. He gestured upward and led the way into the dark, my guide one final time.

The bedroom had been one of the larger storerooms above the tourist restaurant. Five centuries ago it had been a bedroom. My bedroom.

Others were waiting there, members of the Family whom I had not seen for decades or centuries. They were dressed in the dark robes we used only for the most sacred Family ceremonies.

The bed was waiting. My portrait hung above it: the one painted during my imprisonment in Visegrad in 1465. I paused a moment to stare at the image—a Hungarian nobleman stared back, a sable collar topped by gold brocade, gold buttons closing the mantle, a silk cap in the style of the times ringed by nine rows of pearls, the whole headpiece held in place by a star-shaped brooch with a large topaz in its center. The face was both intimately familiar and shockingly strange: nose long and aquiline, green eyes so large as to appear grotesque, thick eyebrows and thicker mustache, an oversized underlip on a prognathous shelf of jaw and cheek . . . altogether an arrogant and disturbing visage.

Fortuna had recognized me. Despite the years, despite the ravages of age and revisions of surgery, despite everything.

"Father," whispered one of the old men standing near the window.

I blinked tiredly at him. I could not quite remember his name . . . one of my Dobrin brothers' cousins perhaps. I had last seen him during the ceremony before I migrated to America more than a century and a half earlier.

He came forward and touched my hand gingerly. I nodded, removed the ring from my pocket, and set it on my finger.

The men in the room knelt. I could hear the creaking and popping of ancient joints.

The Dobrin cousin rose and lifted a heavy medallion into the light.

I knew the medallion. It represented the Order of the Dragon, a secret society first formed in 1387 and reorganized in 1408. The gold medallion on the gold chain was in the shape of a dragon: a dragon curled into a circle, jaws open, legs outstretched, wings raised, its tail curled around to its head and the entire form entwined with a double cross. On the cross were the Order's two mottos: "*O quam misericors est Deus*" (Oh, how merciful is God) and "*Justus et Pius*" (Just and Faithful).

My father had been invested in the Order of the Dragon on February 8, 1431 . . . the year I was born. As a Draconist . . . a follower of *draco*, dragon in Latin . . . my father carried this insignia on his shield and had it inscribed on his coins. Thus he became Vlad Dracul, *dracul* meaning both dragon and devil in my native language.

Dracula meant simply Son of the Dragon.

The Dobrin brother set the medallion around my neck. I felt the weight of gold trying to drag me down. The dozen or so men in the room chanted a short hymn, then filed forward one after the other to kiss my ring and return to their places.

"I am tired," I said. My voice was the rustle of ancient parchment.

They moved around me then, removing the medallion and my expensive suit. They dressed me carefully in a linen nightshirt and Dobrin pulled back the linen bedclothes. Gratefully, I got into bed and lay back on the high pillows.

Radu Fortuna moved closer. "You've come home to die then, Father." It was not a question. I had neither the need nor energy to nod.

An old man who may have been one of the other surviving Dobrin brothers came closer, went to one knee, kissed my ring again, and said, "Then, Father, is it time to begin thinking about the birth and investiture of the new Prince?"

I looked at the man, thinking how the Vlad Ţepeş in the portrait above me would have had him impaled or disemboweled for the inelegance of that question.

Instead, I nodded.

"It will be done," said Radu Fortuna. "The woman and her midwife have been chosen."

I closed my eyes and resisted a smile. The sperm had been collected many decades ago and declared viable. I could only assume that they had preserved it well in this inefficient, hapless nation where even hope had trouble surviving. I did not want to know the crass details of the selection and insemination.

"We will begin preparations for the Investiture," said an old man I had known once as the young Prince Mihnea.

There was no urgency in his voice and I understood the lack of it. Even my dying was to be a slow thing. This disease that I had embraced so very, very long ago would not release me lightly. Even now, riddled and made rotten by old age, the disease ruled my life and resisted the sweet imperative of death.

I will not drink blood after this day. This is my decision and it is irrevocable. Having entered this house again, this bed, I will not leave either willingly.

But even fasting, my body's relentless ability to heal itself, to prolong itself, will struggle with my urge to die. This deathbed may hold me for a year or two or even longer before my spirit and the insidious, cell-deep compulsion to *continue* must surrender to the inevitable need to *cease*.

I am determined that I shall live until the new Prince is born and until his Investiture, no matter how many months or years may intervene until then.

But by then I will no longer be the aged but vital Vernor Deacon Trent; I will be only a mummified caricature of the man with the strange face in the portrait above my bed.

I lay back deeper into the pillows, my yellowed fingers frail above the bedclothes. I do not open my eyes as—one by one—the eldest Family members in the room file by to kiss my ring a final time and then to stand, whispering and murmuring like peasants at a funeral, in the hall outside.

Below, on the ancient stairs of the home where I was born, I hear the soft creaking and shuffling as other Family members—long lines of Family members—ascend in reverent silence to view me like some museum mummy, like a waxwork Lenin all hollowed and yellowed in his tomb, and to kiss the ring and medallion of The Order of the Dragon.

I close my eyes and allow myself to slip away to dreams.

I feel them hovering above me, these dreams of past times, dreams of sometimes happier times, and all too frequently these dreams of terrible times. I feel their weight, these dreams of blood, and of iron.

I close my eyes and surrender to them, dreaming fitfully while my final days file through my mind, shuffling past like the curious and mourning members of my Family of Night.

Chapter Seven

D R. Kate Neuman had reached the point where she could not take it anymore. She left the children's ward, passed the isolation ward where her eight hepatitis B cases were recovering, stopped outside the unnamed, dying infant's room just long enough to peer through the window and slam her fist into the doorframe, and then she strode quickly toward the doctors' lounge.

The halls of Bucharest's District One Hospital reminded Kate of an old Massachusetts binding factory she had worked in one summer while saving money to put herself through Harvard; the hallways here had the same grimy green paint, the same cracked and filthy linoleum tile floor, the same lousy fluorescent lighting that left long stretches of darkness between the pools of sick light, and the same kind of men wandering the hall with their stubbled faces and swaggering gait and smug, sexist, sidelong glances.

Kate Neuman had had enough. It had been six weeks since she had come to Romania for a "brief advisory tour"; it had been forty-eight hours since she had slept and almost twenty-four since she had taken a shower; it had been countless days since she had been outside in the sunlight; it had been only minutes since she had seen her last baby die, and Kate Neuman had had enough.

She swept through the door to the doctors' lounge and

stood breathing hard, surveying the startled faces looking up at her from the sprung couch and long table. The doctors were mostly men, sallow-faced, many with soiled surgical fatigues and scraggly mustaches. They looked sleepy, but Kate knew that it was not from long hours in the wards; most of these physicians put in banker's hours and lost sleep only in what passed for nightlife in post-revolution Bucharest. Kate caught a glimpse of blue jeans far down the couch and for a second she felt a surge of relief that her Romanian friend and translator Lucian was back, but the man leaned forward, she saw that it was not Lucian but only the American priest whom the children called "Father Mike," and Kate's anger flowed back over her like a black tide.

She noticed the hospital administrator, Mr. Popescu, standing by the hot water dispenser and she rounded on him. "We lost another infant this afternoon. Another baby dead. Dead for no reason, Mr. Popescu."

The chubby administrator blinked at her and stirred his tea. Kate knew that he understood her.

"Don't you want to know why she died?" Kate asked the little man.

Two of the pediatricians began moving toward the door, but Kate stepped into the doorway and held one hand up like a traffic cop. "Everybody should hear this," she said softly. Her gaze had not left Mr. Popescu. "Doesn't anyone want to know why we lost another child today?"

The administrator licked his lips. "Doctor Neuman . . . you are . . . perhaps . . . very tired, yes?"

Kate fixed him in her gaze. "We lost the little girl in Ward Nine," she said, her voice as flat as her gaze. "She died because someone was careless in setting up an IV . . . a goddamn simple everyday fucking IV . . . and the fat nurse with the garlic breath injected a bubble straight into the child's heart."

"*Îmi pare foarte rău*," muttered Mr. Popescu, "*nu am înţeles.*"

"The hell you don't understand," snapped Kate, feeling

her anger mold itself into something sharp and finely edged. "You understand perfectly well." She turned to look at the dozen or so medics standing and sitting and staring at her. "You all understand. The words are easy to understand . . . malpractice . . . professional carelessness . . . slovenliness. That's the third child we've lost this month to sheer bullshit incompetence." She looked directly at the closest pediatricians. "Where *were* you?"

The taller man turned to his companion, smirked, and said something in whispered Romanian. The words *tiganesc* and *corcitura* were clearly audible.

Kate took a step toward him, resisting the impulse to punch him right above his bushy mustache. "I *know* the child was a Gypsy halfbreed, you miserable piece of shit." She took another step toward him and, despite the fact that she was five inches shorter and seventy pounds lighter than the Romanian, the pediatrician backed against the wall.

"I also know that you've been selling the babies that survive to the dipshit Americans wandering around here," she said to the pediatrician, raising a finger as if she were going to stab it through his chest. At the last second she turned away from him as if repelled by his smell. "And I know the business dealings the rest of you have, too," Kate said, her voice so weary and filled with disgust that she hardly recognized it as her own. "The least you could do is *save* more of them . . ."

The two pediatricians by the door went through it in some haste. The other doctors at the table and on the couch abandoned their tea and left the room. Mr. Popescu came closer and made as if to touch her arm, then thought better of it. "You are very tired, Mrs. Neuman . . ."

"*Doctor* Neuman," said Kate, not raising her gaze. "And if there isn't better supervision in the wards, Popescu, if one more child dies for no reason, I swear to Christ that I'll turn in a report to UNICEF and Adoption Option and Save the Children and all the other organizations that are feathering your nest . . . a report so strong that you'll never see another

American cent and your greedy friends downtown will send you to whatever passes for a gulag in Romania these days.''

Mr. Popescu had turned red and then pale and then red again as he backed away, slid backwards along the side of the table toward the door, set his teacup behind him, missed the table with it, hissed something in Romanian, and stalked out the door.

Kate Neuman waited a moment, her eyes still lowered, and then went over, lifted his cup off the floor, wiped it with a rag from the counter, and set it back in its niche above the hot water dispenser. She closed her eyes, feeling the fatigue move beneath her like long, slow waves under a small ship.

"Your tour here almost over then?" asked an American voice.

Kate snapped upright. The bearded priest was still seated on the couch, his blue jeans, gray sweatshirt, and Reeboks looking incongruous and a bit absurd. Kate formed a snappish reply and then let it slide away. "Yes," she said. "Another week and I'm gone no matter what.''

The priest nodded, finished his tea, and set the chipped mug away. "I've been watching you," he said softly.

Kate glared at him. She'd never liked religious people very much and celibate clerics grated on her more than most. Priests seemed like a useless anachronism to her—witch doctors who had exchanged their fright masks for Roman collars, dispensers of false care, carrion crows hovering around the sick and dying.

Kate realized how tired she was. "I haven't been watching you," she said softly. "But I have noticed you with the new children and working in the wards. The children like you."

The priest nodded. "And you save their lives." He went over to the window and shoved back thick drapes. Rich evening sunlight flooded the room, possibly for the first time in decades.

Kate blinked and rubbed her eyes.

"It's time to call it a day, Doctor Neuman," said the priest. "I'd like to walk with you.''

"There's no need . . ." began Kate, trying to feel anger

again at the man's presumption, but mustering nothing. She felt her emotions grinding like a dead battery. "All right," she said.

He walked with her out of the hospital and into the Bucharest evening.

Chapter Eight

USUALLY Kate had a cab take her home to her apartment in the dark, but this evening they walked. Kate blinked at the thick evening light painted on the sides of buildings. It was as if she had never seen Bucharest before.

"So you're not staying at one of the hotels?" said the priest.

Kate shook herself out of her reverie. "No, the Foundation rented a small apartment for me on Ştirbei Vodă." She gave the address.

"Ah," said Father O'Rourke, "that's right near Cişmigiu."

"Near what?" said Kate. The last word had sounded much like a sneeze.

"Cişmigiu Gardens. One of my favorite places in the city."

Kate shook her head. "I haven't seen it." She twitched a smile. "I haven't seen much since I got here. I've had three days off from the hospital, but I slept those away."

"When did you get here?" he asked. Kate noticed his limp as they hurried across busy Bălcescu Boulevard. Here on the sidestreets by the university, the shade was deeper, the air cooler.

"Hmmm . . . April four. God."

"I know," said Father O'Rourke. "A day seems like a week at the hospital. A week is an eternity."

They had just reached the large plaza on Calea Victoriei when Kate stopped and frowned. "What's the date today?"

"May fifteenth," said the priest. "Wednesday."

Kate rubbed her face and blinked. Her skin felt anaesthetized. "I'd promised CDC that I'd be back by the twentieth. They sent me tickets. I'd sort of forgotten just how close . . ." She shook her head again and looked around at the plaza, still busy with evening traffic. Behind them, Crețulescu Church was a mass of scaffolding, but the bullet holes were still visible on the sooty façade. The Palace of the Republic across the *piața* had been even more heavily damaged. Long red and white banners hung over the columned entrance, but the doors and shattered windows were boarded up. To their right, the Athenée Palace Hotel was open but with vacant windows and stitcheries of bullet holes like fresh scars on a heroin addict's skin.

"CDC," said Father O'Rourke. "You're out of Atlanta?"

"Boulder, Colorado," said Kate. "The big brass still hang out in Atlanta, but it's been the *Centers* for Disease Control for several years. The Boulder facility's fairly new."

They crossed Calea Victoriei at the light and headed down Strada Ştirbei Vodă, but not before three Gypsy beggars in front of the Hotel Bucureşti saw them and came swooping toward them, thrusting babies at them, kissing their own hands, tapping Kate's shoulders, and saying, "*Por la bambina . . . por la bambina . . .*"

Kate raised a tired hand but Father O'Rourke dug out change for each of them. The Gypsy women grimaced at the coins, snapped something in dialect, and hurried back to their places in front of the hotel. The blue-jeaned and leather-coated money changers in front of the hotel watched impassively.

Ştirbei Vodă was a narrower street but still busy with cheap Dacias and the moneychangers' Mercedes and BMWs rumbling past over brick and worn asphalt. Kate noticed the priest's slight limp again but decided not to ask him about it. Instead, she said, "Where do you call home base?" She had considered adding the *Father*, but it did not come naturally to her.

The priest was smiling slightly. "Well, the order I work for is based in Chicago, and on this trip I take my instructions from the Chicago Archdiocese, but it's been awhile since I was there. In recent years I've spent a lot of time in South and Central America. Before that, Africa."

Kate glanced to her left, recognized the street called 13 Decembrie, and knew that she was just a block or two from her apartment. The avenue seemed different in daylight, and on foot. "So you're sort of a Third World expert," she said, too tired to concentrate on the conversation but enjoying the sound of English.

"Sort of," said Father O'Rourke.

"And do you specialize in orphanages around the world?"

"Not really. If I have a specialty, it's children. One just tends to find them in orphanages and hospitals."

Kate made a noise of agreement. A few chestnut trees along the avenue here caught the last reflected light from the buildings on the east side of the street and seemed to glow with a gold-orange corona. The air was thick with the smells of any Eastern European city—undiluted car exhausts, raw sewage, rotting garbage—but there was also a scent of greenery and fresh blooms on the soft evening breeze.

"Has it been this pleasant the whole time I've been here? I seem to remember it being cold and rainy," Kate said softly.

Father O'Rourke smiled. "It's been like summer since the first of May," he said. "The trees along the avenues north of here are fantastic."

Kate stopped. "Number five," she said. "This is my apartment complex." She extended her hand. "Well, thanks for the walk and the conversation . . . uh, Father."

The priest looked at her without shaking her hand. His expression seemed a bit quizzical, not directed at her but almost as if he were debating something with himself. Kate noticed for the first time how strikingly clear his gray eyes were.

"The park is right there," said Father O'Rourke, pointing down Ştirbei Vodă. "Less than a block away. The entrance is sort of hard to notice if you're not aware of it already. I know you're exhausted, but . . .''

Kate *was* exhausted and in a lousy mood and not the least bit tempted by this celibate cleric in Reeboks, despite his startlingly beautiful eyes. Still, this was the first non-medical conversation she'd had in weeks and she was surprised to find herself reluctant to end it. "Sure," she said. "Show me."

Cişmigiu Gardens reminded Kate of what she had imagined New York's Central Park to have been like decades ago, before it surrendered its nights to violence and its days to noise: Cişmigiu was a true urban oasis, a hidden vale of trees and water and leaf shade and flowers.

They entered through a narrow gate in a high fence that Kate had never noticed, descended stairs between tall boulders, and emerged into a maze of paved paths and stone walkways. The park was large, but all of its vistas were intimate: a waterway here threading its way under an arched stone bridge to widen into a shaded lagoon there, a long meadow—unkempt and seemingly untouched by a gardener's blade or shears—but strewn with a riot of wild flowers, a playground abuzz with children still dressed for the winter just past, long benches filled with grandparents watching the children play, stone tables and benches where huddles of men watched other men play chess, an island restaurant bedecked with colored lights, the sound of laughter across water.

"It's wonderful," said Kate. They had strolled around the east side of the lagoon past the noise of the playground, crossed a bridge made of cement logs and twigs, and paused to watch couples rowing in the connecting waterway below.

Father O'Rourke nodded and leaned on the railing. "It's always too easy to see just one side of a place. Bucharest can be a difficult city to love, but it has its attractions."

Kate watched a young couple pass below, the young man wrestling with the heavy oars while trying to make it seem easy, his young lady reclining languorously—or what she thought was languorously—in the bow. The rowboat seemed to be the size of one of the *QE2*'s lifeboats, and appeared to be just about as easy to handle. The couple rowed out of sight around the bend in the channel, the young man sweating and swearing as he leaned on the oars to avoid a paddle-boat coming the other way.

"The Ceauşescus and the revolution seem very far away, don't they?" said Kate. "It's hard to imagine that these people had to live for so many years under one of the planet's worst dictators."

The priest nodded. "Have you seen the new presidential palace and his Victory of Socialism Boulevard?"

Kate tried to force her tired mind into gear. "I don't think so," she said.

"You should see it before you go," said Father O'Rourke. His gray eyes seemed absorbed with some inner dialogue.

"That's the new section of Bucharest he had built?"

The priest nodded again. "It reminds me of architectural models Albert Speer had made up for Hitler," he said, his voice very soft. "Berlin the way it was supposed to look after the ultimate triumph of the Third Reich. The presidential palace may be the largest inhabited structure on earth . . . only it's not inhabited now. The new regime doesn't know what the hell to do with it. And the Boulevard is a mass of gleaming white office and apartment complexes—part Third Reich, part Korean Gothic, part Roman Imperial. They march across what used to be the most beautiful section of the city like so many Martian war machines. The old neighborhoods are gone forever . . . as dead as Ceauşescu." He rubbed his cheek. "Do you mind if we sit down a moment?"

Kate walked with him to a bench. The sunset had faded in all but the highest clouds, but the twilight was the slow, warm melting of a late spring evening. A few gas lamps were coming on down the long curve of path. "Your leg's bothering you," she said.

Father O'Rourke smiled. "This leg can't bother me," he said, lifting his left pant leg above the athletic sock. He rapped the pink plastic of a prosthesis. "Just to the knee," he added. "Above that, it can hurt like hell."

Kate chewed her lip. "Automobile accident?"

"In a manner of speaking. Sort of a national auto accident. Vietnam."

Kate was surprised. She had still been in high school during the war, and she assumed that the priest was her age or younger. Now she looked carefully at his face above the dark beard, seeing the webwork of laugh lines around the eyes, really *seeing* the man for the first time, and realized that he was probably a few years older than she, perhaps in his early forties. "I'm sorry about your leg," she said.

"Me too," laughed the priest.

"Was it a land mine?" Kate had interned with a brilliant doctor who had specialized in VA cases.

"Not exactly," said Father O'Rourke. His voice was free of the self-consciousness and hesitance she had heard from some Vietnam veterans. *Whatever demons the war and the wound brought him,* she thought, *he's free of them now.* "I was a tunnel rat," he said. "Found an NVA down there that was more booby trap than corpse."

Kate was not sure what a tunnel rat was, but she did not ask.

"You're doing wonderful things with the children at the hospital," said the priest. "The survival rate on the hepatitis cases has doubled since your arrival."

"It's still not good enough," snapped Kate. She heard the edge in her tone and took a breath. When she spoke again, her voice was softer. "How long have you been in Romania . . . uh . . ."

He scratched his beard. "Why don't you call me Mike?"

Kate started to speak, then hesitated. "Father" was wrong; "Mike" didn't seem quite right.

The priest grinned at her. "Okay, how about 'O'Rourke'? It worked fine in the army."

"All right—O'Rourke," said Kate. She extended her hand. "I'm Neuman."

His handshake was firm but Kate perceived a great gentleness behind it. "Well, Neuman," he said, "to answer your question . . . I've been in and out of Romania for quite a bit of the last year and a half."

Kate was surprised. "Working with the children all that time?"

"Mostly." He leaned forward, idly rubbing his knee. Another rowboat passed by. Rock music, the lyrics indecipherable, drifted across the lagoon from the island restaurant. "The first year or so . . . well, you know about the conditions of the state orphanages. The first task was to get the sickest children transferred to hospitals."

Kate touched her tired eyelids. Amazingly, the sick-feeling fatigue was retreating a bit, allowing a simple tiredness to fill her. "The hospitals aren't much better," she said.

Father O'Rourke did not look at her. "The hospitals for the Party elite are better. Have you seen them?"

"No."

"They're not on the official Ministry of Health list. They don't have signs out front. But the medical care and equipment is light-years ahead of the district hospitals you've been working in."

Kate turned her head to watch a couple strolling by hand in hand. The sky was darkening between the branches above the walkway. "But there are no children in these Party-elite hospitals, are there, O'Rourke?"

"No abandoned children. Just a few well-fed kids in for tonsillectomies."

The couple had strolled out of sight around the curved path, but Kate continued to stare in that direction. The pleasing park sounds seemed to fade into the distance. "God damn," she whispered softly. "What are we going to do? Six hundred-some of these state institutions . . . two hundred thousand or more kids we know of out there . . . fifty percent of those exposed to hepatitis B . . . almost as many testing positive for HIV in some of those hellholes. What are we going to do, O'Rourke?"

The priest was looking at her in the fading light. "The money and attention from the West has helped some."

Kate made a rude sound.

"It has," said Father O'Rourke. "The children aren't penned up in cages the way they were when I first arrived on the tour Vernor Deacon Trent arranged."

"No," agreed Kate. "Now they're left to rock and grow retarded in clean iron cribs."

"And there's always hope for the adoption process . . ." began the priest.

Kate rounded on him. "Are you part of that fucking circus? Do you round up healthy Romanian kids for these beef-fed born-again American yahoos to buy? Is that your role in all this?"

Father O'Rourke sat silently in the face of her anger. His face showed no retreat. His voice was soft. "Do you want to see my role in all this, Neuman?"

Kate hesitated only a second. She felt the fury rising in her again like heated bile. Children were suffering and dying by the thousands . . . by the tens of thousands . . . and this Roman-collared anachronism was part of the Great Baby Bazaar, the strictly-for-profit sideshow being run by the thugs and former informers that were the greasy Mafia of this country.

"Yeah," she said at last, allowing the anger to emerge as a verbal sneer. "Show me."

Without another word, Father O'Rourke rose from the bench and led her out of the park and into the dark city.

Chapter Nine

P ITEŞTI was a wall of flame in the night. A solid wall of refinery towers, tanks, cooling towers, and silhouetted scaffoldings spread for miles across the northeastern horizon, flame rising from a thousand valves, dark domes, and black buildings. It was a refinery town, Kate knew, but it looked like Hell to her as they approached.

O'Rourke had stopped by his room in the UNICEF building on Ştirbei Vodă Street and changed into what he'd called his mutant ninja priest suit: black shirt, black coat, black trousers, Roman collar. He had led Kate to the small Dacia sedan parked behind the gothic building and they had rattled across bricks and cobblestones to the Hotel Lido on Magheru Boulevard. Instead of stopping, O'Rourke had turned down Strada C. A. Rosetti and driven around the block, slowing each time he passed the darkened hotel.

"What are we—" began Kate the third time they inched past the hotel.

"Wait . . . *there*," O'Rourke had said and pointed. A couple dressed in Western clothes had come out of the hotel, chatted with a tall man in a leather coat, and then all three got in the rear seat of a Mercedes waiting in the no-parking zone at the curb. O'Rourke had pulled the Dacia into the darkness under the trees on Strada Franklin and turned the lights out. A moment later, when the Mercedes pulled out into the thinning traffic, he followed.

"Friends of yours?" asked Kate, a little put off by this cloak-and-dagger nonsense.

O'Rourke's teeth looked very white between the dark lines of his well-groomed beard. "Americans, of course. I knew they were meeting this guy about now."

"Adoption?"

"Sure."

"Are you involved in it?"

O'Rourke glanced at her. "Not yet."

They had followed the Mercedes down Bulevardul Magheru until the street became Bulevardul Nicolae Bălcescu, swung west behind the Mercedes at the traffic circle in Plaza Universitatii, and followed it until the broad avenue of Bulevardul Republicii became Gheorghe Gheorghiu-Dej. Once across the cement-trenched canal that once had been the Dimbovița River, they drove west through a section of Stalinist apartment buildings and electronics factories. The streets here were wide, littered with deep potholes, and largely empty except for clots of dark-garbed pedestrians, the occasional rushing taxi, and rattling trollies. The posted speed limit was fifty kilometers per hour, but the Mercedes soon accelerated to a hundred and O'Rourke flogged the Dacia to keep up.

"You're going to get stopped by a traffic cop," said Kate.

The priest nodded toward the glove compartment. "Four cartons of Kents in there if I do," he said, swerving to avoid a group of pedestrians standing in the middle of the boulevard. The avenue was illuminated by the sick yellow glow of occasional sodium-vapor lamps that were very far apart.

Suddenly the ghastly apartment complexes grew fewer, then disappeared altogether, and they were suddenly out in the country, accelerating even faster to keep up with the Mercedes' taillights. Kate saw a road sign flash by: A-1, AUTOSTRADA BUCUREŞTI-PITEŞTI, PITEŞTI, 113 KM.

The ride took a little more than an hour, and she and the priest spoke very little during it: Kate because she was so exhausted that she found it hard to form words, O'Rourke apparently because of a preoccupation with his own thoughts. The road was a shoulderless, potholed version of an American Interstate, although the countryside passing on either side was much darker than farmland Kate remembered in the States. Only the occasional village was visible in the distance from the highway, and even those glowed feebly, as if from a few kerosene lamps rather than electricity.

Piteşti was that much more of a shock with its wall of flame rising into the night.

The Mercedes took the first exit off the main highway into Piteşti and O'Rourke followed, accelerating now to close the distance. The access road soon took them to a dim avenue, then to a narrower street without streetlights. The apartment complexes here seemed grimmer than those in Bucharest; it was not yet ten P.M. but only a few lights glowed through curtains. The raw-cement buildings were backlighted by the pulsing orange glow reflected from low clouds. Kate and O'Rourke had rolled up the Dacia's windows, but acrid fumes from the refineries still entered the car and made their eyes water and throats burn. Kate thought again of Hell.

The Mercedes pulled down an even narrower street and stopped. O'Rourke pulled the Dacia to the curb just beyond an intersection.

"What now?" said Kate.

"You can stay here or come into the building with me," said O'Rourke.

Kate got out of the car and followed him around the corner, across the street to the hulk of the apartment complex. The sound of a few radios or televisions came from the darkened upper stories. The spring air was chilly here, despite the hellish glow above them. The elevator inside was out of order; they heard footsteps echoing on the stairs above them. The priest gestured for her to hurry and Kate followed him up the steps in a half-jog. They could hear the heavy scrape of four people above them, but O'Rourke's footfalls were almost inaudible. She noticed that he had kept his Reeboks on and she smiled a bit even as she began to pant with the exertion.

They paused on the sixth floor, what would have been the seventh floor in America. O'Rourke opened the door from the stairway and they were assaulted by old cooking smells almost as abrasive as the chemical stink outside. Voices echoed down the narrow corridor.

O'Rourke held up one hand, motioning her to stay in the pool of darkness by the stairway, and then he moved silently down the hall. Kate thought that "mutant ninja priest suit" was about right; the tall man blended into the shadows between the dim lights.

Despite his command to stay behind—or perhaps because of it—Kate followed him down the hallway, staying near the walls where it was darkest. She had a premonition of the scene she would see when she reached the open apartment door, and she was not disappointed.

Two Romanian men in leather jackets were standing with the American couple, translating and arguing with the man and woman who lived in the apartment. Three young children clung to their mother's legs, and there was the cry of a baby from an open bedroom door. The apartment was small, cluttered, and dirty, with a threadbare carpet littered with pots and pans, as if toddlers had been playing with them on the floor a moment before. The air was thick with the odor of fried food and dirty diapers.

Kate glanced around the edge of the door again. O'Rourke actually stood in the shadows just inside the apartment, as yet unnoticed by the arguing adults in the lighted room. The two Romanian men who had brought the Americans here were the usual mafioso, money-changer type: greasy hair, one with a bandido mustache, the other with a three-day stubble, dressed in designer jeans and silk shirts under their leather jackets, both with a bullying, condescending attitude that Kate had seen on three continents.

The Romanian couple whose apartment it was were shorter, sallower, the wife hollow-eyed and frantic looking, the husband chattering away, his frequent smile little more than a facial tic. Amidst all of this, the American couple—young, blond, pink-cheeked and dressed in Lands' End casual clothes—looked overwhelmed. The American woman kept crouching to hug or smile at the toddlers, none of whom were very clean, but the children kept slipping behind their parents or sliding away into the dark bedroom.

"How much for this one?" asked the American man, reaching out to tousle the hair of the three- or four-year-old clinging to his mother's skirt. The boy pulled back quickly. The taller of the Romanian guides snapped a question, then cut the Romanian father off in mid babble.

"He says one hundred thousand *lei* and a Turbo," said the tall guide, smirking.

"A Turbo?" said the American woman, blinking rapidly.

"Turbo automobile," said the shorter and swarthier of the two guides. When he grinned, a gold tooth caught the light.

The American man pulled out a notebook calculator and tapped at it. "A hundred thousand *lei* would be about sixteen hundred and sixty-six dollars at the official exchange rate, honey," he said to his wife. "Mmmm . . . but just about five hundred bucks at the black market rate. But the car . . . I don't know . . ."

The taller guide smirked. "No, no, no," he said. "They all ask for hundred thousand *lei*. No pay. These Gypsies . . . see? Very greedy people. Gypsy baby is not worth hundred thousand *lei*. Their little childrens worth even less. We offer thirty thousand, tell them that if they say no, we go somewhere else." He turned and tapped the Romanian father on the chest, none too gently. The little man twitched a smile and listened to the barked flow of Romanian.

Kate understood only a few words—America, dollars, fool, authorities.

The young American wife had moved to the doorway of the darkened bedroom and was trying to coax the two-year-old girl out into the light. The husband was busy with his calculator; his forehead glistened with sweat under the bare bulb.

"Ahhh," grinned the tall guide. "The little girl, very healthy, they agree to forty-five thousand *lei*. Can leave tonight. At once."

The American woman closed her eyes and whispered, "Praise the Lord." Her husband blinked and moistened his lips. The shorter of the two guides grinned at his colleague.

"This is illegal," said O'Rourke, stepping into the apartment.

The Americans jumped and looked sheepish. The guides scowled and stepped forward. The Gypsy husband looked at his wife, and both of their faces showed the pure panic of loss.

"It's illegal and it's unnecessary," said the priest, standing between the guides and the American couple. "There are orphanages where you can carry out a legitimate adoption."

"*Cine sînteţi dumneavoastră?*" demanded the taller guide angrily. "*Ce este aceasta?*"

O'Rourke ignored him and spoke directly to the American wife. "None of these children are being put up for adoption or need to be adopted. The father and mother both work at the refinery. These two . . ." He gestured toward the guides with a dismissive wave of his left hand, as if too disgusted to look at them. "They're punks . . . informers . . . thugs. They chose this family because others in this same building have been intimidated into selling their children. Please consider what you're doing."

"Well . . ." began the American man, licking his lips again and holding on to his calculator with both hands. "We didn't mean . . ."

His wife appeared to be on the verge of tears. "It's just so *hard* to get visas for the sick children," she said. Her accent sounded like Oklahoma or Texas.

"Shut *up!*" shouted the taller of the guides. He was yelling at O'Rourke, not the couple. The guide took three fast steps forward and raised his fist as if he were going to hammer the priest into the floor.

Kate watched as O'Rourke turned slowly and then moved very quickly, catching the guide's raised arm at the wrist, and slowly lowering it. The guide shifted his left hand to grip O'Rourke's wrist, but his arm continued downward. She could see the Romanian's face growing redder as he struggled, could hear his heavy boots scraping the floor as he shifted for better leverage, but the captured wrist continued descending until O'Rourke held the arm and still-clenched fist immobile at the man's side. The guide's face had gone from red to something approaching purple; his entire body was shaking from the strain of attempting to break free. The priest's face had never changed expression.

The smaller guide reached into his jacket and came out with a switchblade. The blade flicked out and he took a step forward.

The taller man snapped something even as the Romanian parents began shouting and the American wife began crying. O'Rourke released the first guide's wrist and Kate saw the big man gasp and flex his fingers. He snarled something else and his shorter companion put away the knife and herded the confused Americans out of the apartment, the procession brushing past Kate in the doorway as if she didn't exist. The children in the apartment were crying, as was the Gypsy woman. The father stood rubbing his stubbled cheek as if he had been slapped.

"*Îmi pare foarte rău,*" O'Rourke said to the Gypsy couple, and Kate understood it as *I'm very sorry.* "*Noapte bună,*" he said, backing out of the apartment. *Good night.*

The door slammed and he looked at Kate standing there.

"Don't you want to catch the Americans?" she said. "Get them to ride back to Bucharest with us?"

"Why?"

"They'll just go somewhere else with those . . . those creeps. They'll end up stealing another child out of its bed."

O'Rourke shook his head. "Not tonight, I don't think. This sort of messed up the rhythm of their evening. I'll call the Americans tomorrow at the Lido."

Kate glanced at the dark stairwell. "Aren't you afraid that one or the other of those two thugs will be waiting for you?"

She had the sense that the priest could not stop the smile of pure pleasure at the thought. She watched as he rubbed the smile away. "I don't think so," he said softly, with only a hint of regret audible. "They'll be too busy herding their pigeons home, trying to calm them and set up another buying spree.''

Kate shook her head and walked down the stairs with him, out of the building smelling of garlic and urine and hopelessness.

Despite her exhaustion, they talked more on the ride back to Bucharest. The Dacia was an accumulation of gear rumbles, mechanical moans, and spring creakings, the air whistled in even through closed windows, but they raised their voices and talked.

"I knew that most of the American couples ended up paying for healthy children," said Kate. "I didn't know that the shopping trips were this cynical."

O'Rourke nodded, his eyes still on the dark road. Piteşti was a receding wall of flame behind them. "You should see it when they take them to one of the poorer Gypsy villages," he said softly. "It turns into an auction . . . a real riot."

"Do they concentrate on Gypsies then?" Kate heard the thickness of pure tiredness in her own voice. She found herself longing for a cigarette even though she had not smoked since she was a teenager.

"Frequently. The people are poor enough, desperate enough, less willing to go to the authorities when bullied."

Kate looked sideways at the sparse lights in a village a kilometer or two from the highway. Road flares flickered alongside the frequent vehicles broken down in the weeds alongside the road. She had counted at least one disabled truck or car every kilometer or two during the ride west. "Do these born-again Americans ever adopt from the orphanages?"

"Occasionally," said the priest. "But you know the difficulties."

Kate nodded. "Half of the children are sick. Most of the rest are retarded or emotionally crippled. The American Embassy won't allow the sick ones a visa." She laughed and was shocked by the harshness of the sound. "What a fuck-up."

"Yes," said O'Rourke.

Suddenly Kate found herself telling the priest about the children she had been trying to help, the children who had died through lack of appropriate medical care, or lack of supplies, or lack of compassion and competence on the part of the Romanian hospital staff. She found herself telling him about the baby in the isolation ward in District Hospital One; the abandoned, nameless, helpless little boy who responded to transfusions but who soon began wasting away again from some immune disorder that Kate could not isolate or diagnose with the primitive equipment available to her here.

"It's not AIDS," she said. "Not simple anemia or hepatitis, not any of the blood-related immune disorders that I'm familiar with—not even the rare ones. I'm convinced that in the States, with the equipment and people I have at Boulder CDC, I could isolate it, find it, and fix it. But this child has no family and this country would never pay for his transfer to Stateside, or even allow a visa if I paid for it." She rubbed harshly at her cheek. "He's seven months old and he's depending on me and he's dying . . . and there's not a damn thing I can do about it." She was amazed to find her cheek moist with tears. She turned her face farther from the priest.

"Why don't you adopt him?" O'Rourke said softly.

She turned to stare at him in shock. He looked at her but said nothing more. Nor did she. They drove into darkened Bucharest in silence.

Chapter Ten

THE Romanians did not refer to their unnamed and unidentified male patients as John Doe. The abandoned seven-month-old in the isolation ward of District Hospital One was called—in the notes Lucian had translated for Kate—Unidentified Juvenile Patient #2613. Most abandoned children had notes in their file telling who the parents had been, or who had dropped them off at orphanages or hospitals, or at least where they had been discovered, but the file on Unidentified Juvenile Patient #2613 was empty of all such information.

Kate had gone through those notes the night before after returning from Piteşti with Father O'Rourke. She had thanked him for the ride when getting out of the Dacia in front of her apartment after midnight. They had said nothing else about his suggestion—if it had been a suggestion. Kate still wondered if the priest might have been making a joke.

But she had gone through her notes before collapsing onto her bed.

Unidentified Juvenile Patient #2613 had been brought to Bucharest's District Hospital One after doctors in a pediatric hospital in Tîrgovişte had failed to make a diagnosis of the boy's obviously life-threatening condition. Symptoms included loss of weight, listlessness, vomiting, refusal to take formula, and some sort of immune-system disorder that made every cold or flu virus potentially deadly to the infant. Blood tests showed no hepatitis or other liver dysfunction, nor anemia, but the white cell count was far too low. Transfusions beginning when the baby was five months old had seemed to offer a miraculous recovery—for almost weeks the boy had drunk from the bottle and put on weight, his reaction to a patch test had shown a positive immune-system response—but then the immune problem began again and the cycle started over. More recent transfusions had brought about shorter and shorter remissions. The Tîrgovişte hospital had transferred the child to Bucharest five weeks ago and Kate Neuman had spent most of that time just struggling to keep him alive.

Now she entered the isolation ward. The fat nurse with the harelip was standing at the infant's cribside, feeding him; or rather, she was smoking a cigarette and staring the opposite direction while holding a bottle through the crib bars, pressing the nipple against the baby's cheek. He was crying feebly and ignoring it.

"Get out," said Kate. She repeated it in Romanian. The nurse slid the bottle into the grimy pocket of her smock, gave Kate a malevolent smile, flicked ashes from her cigarette, and waddled out.

Kate lifted the baby and looked around for the rocker she had requisitioned for the room. It was missing again. Kate sat on the cold radiator under the window and cradled the baby, rocking him softly. *I'll authorize the intravenous feeding at once,* she thought. The last transfusion had offered remission for only five days.

The tiny baby in her arms focused his eyes on her and quit crying. He was so small that he could have been seven weeks old rather than seven months. The flesh of his little hands and tiny feet was pink and almost translucent. His eyes were very large. He stared intently at Kate, as if awaiting an answer to an old question.

Kate removed the bottle of formula she had heated before coming in and sought his small mouth with the nipple. He turned away, repeatedly refusing, but each time his gaze came back to her. Kate set the bottle on the window ledge and just rocked him. The baby's eyes slowly closed and his rapid breathing slowed into sleep.

She rocked him softly and hummed a lullabye her mother had sung to her.

Hush little baby don't say a word,
Mama's gonna buy you a mockingbird.
And if that mockingbird won't sing,
Mama's gonna buy you a diamond ring . . ."

Suddenly Kate stopped and lifted the child's face to hers. She smelled the infant scent of his skin, felt the infinite baby softness of what little dark hair he had. His breath was warm and fast against her cheek; she could hear the slight rasp and squeak when he inhaled.

"Don't worry, Joshua," she whispered, still rocking him. "Don't worry, little Joshua. I'm not going to let anything bad happen to you. I'm not going to let you go."

The next morning, after a sixteen-hour shift and only three hours' sleep, Kate went to the proper Ministry building downtown to begin the endless paperwork for adoption.

Lucian Forsea, her young friend and translator, met her on the steps of the hospital when she returned that afternoon. He came down the stairs with open arms, hugged her fiercely, kissed her firmly on the cheek, and stepped back. "It is true then?" he asked. "You are adopting the child in Isolation Three?"

Kate could only stare. She had told no one at the hospital. She had told no one but the officials at the Ministry that morning. But she had seen this before in Bucharest: everyone seemed to know everything as soon as it happened. "It's true," she said.

Lucian grinned and hugged her again.

Kate had to smile. The Romanian medical student was in his mid-twenties, but she would never have taken him for either a Romanian or a med student. Today Lucian was wearing a Reyn Spooner Hawaiian shirt with huge, pink flowers on it, stone-washed Calvin Klein jeans, and Nike running shoes. His hair was well cut in a style just short of punk, and there was an expensive but not gaudy Rolex chronometer on his wrist. Lucian's face was too tanned for any medical student, his eyes too clear and outgoing for any Romanian, and his English was smooth and idiomatic. Kate often thought that if she were fifteen years younger, even ten, that Lucian would hold a powerful attraction for her. As it was now, he was her one firm friend in this strange, sad land.

"Great!" he said, still grinning at the news of her imminent parenthood.

"If you and I marry, that way we have a child without all the work and waiting. I always said that Polaroid should get involved in the baby business."

Kate hit him on the chest with the heel of her hand. "Be quiet," she said. "How were your finals?"

"My finals are finally finalized," said Lucian. He took her arm in his and started up the stairs. "Tell me your experience at the Ministry. Did they keep you waiting for hours?"

"Of course." They went through the tall door into the dim and echoing main hall of District Hospital One. Waiting patients-to-be lined the benches down the long corridor. Gurneys with sleeping or comatose patients sat ignored, like double-parked vehicles. The air smelled of ether and mingled medicines.

"And once they had you fill out the papers, they kept you waiting hours more?" Lucian's blue eyes looked at her with what might have been a combination of merriment and . . . what? . . . affection? Love? Kate shook the thought away.

"Actually, no," she said, stopping with the realization of it. "Once I filled out the forms, they were very efficient. I dealt with just one man. He said he would expedite everything and I realized now that he did. Strange, isn't it?"

Lucian made a funny face. Kate sometimes thought that the young man would make a better comedian than doctor, his wit was so quick and face so flexible. "Strange!" he cried. "It is unprecedented! Unheard of! An efficient bureaucrat in Bucharest . . . my God! The next thing you will be telling me is that there is a real patriot in the National Salvation Front!''

Lucian had not lowered his voice, and two hospital administrators down the corridor turned to stare and scowl.

"Seriously," said Lucian, patting her hand. "What is this bureaucrat's name? I, too, may need an efficient man someday.''

Kate had met Lucian's father, a well-known poet, intellectual, and critic of the regime; while, somewhat ironically, his mother was connected with the *Nomenclature* . . . the Party elite that could shop at Command stores and which always received special privileges. Bucharest had almost two and a half million inhabitants, and sometimes Kate thought that Lucian knew all of them personally. As connected as he was to the *Nomenclature* and a life of privilege, Lucian was openly contemptuous of both the Ceauşescu and post-Ceauşescu regimes.

"The man's name was Stancu, I think," said Kate. "Yes, Stancu."

"Ahhh," said Lucian, "like the novelist who died seventeen years ago. No wonder he is a good man. He has large socks to fill with a name like Stancu."

"Large shoes to fill," Kate corrected absently. She was remembering just how efficient the bureaucrat had been, making calls, cutting through paperwork, assuring her that the child's Romanian exit visa would be completed by eight-thirty the next morning. When she had brought up the ticklish subject of Joshua's health—she thought of the infant only as Joshua now, although she was not sure why that name had occurred to her—Mr. Stancu had waved away the detail, saying that it might be a problem only with the American Embassy.

"Shoes, yeah," said Lucian, still teasing her. "But what kind of slob would wear black wing-tipped bureaucrat shoes without socks? He must fill novelist Stancu's socks before he can fill his shoes. And speaking of socks . . ."

They had taken the elevator to the third floor, gotten clean smocks and masks from the supply closet, and now Lucian

was gesturing toward the oversized socks that hospital workers wore over their shoes in the isolation wards. "Just
masks," said Kate. Joshua's white cell count had been moderately low in this morning's charts.

"Hi ho, Silver," said Lucian, tying his mask in place.

Kate shook her head. Lucian had told her that he had visited
America once with his father. But that had been for only a
few days. How would he know about the Lone Ranger?

Lucian seemed to read her mind. She could see his cheeks
crinkle into a grin under the mask. "Tapes of the old radio
show," he said. "I picked some up when I was in New York
a few years ago."

"When you were a child," said Kate. Whenever she began
to find Lucian irresistible, she reminded herself that the boy
had not been born when President Kennedy was assassinated
. . . that he was only three years old when Robert Kennedy
and Martin Luther King were killed. The fact made Kate feel
very old indeed, although she herself had been just ten when
the President had been killed and still in high school when
Bobby had been shot.

Lucian shrugged. "OK, Gramma. Touché. Now are we
going to look at your baby here or what?"

Kate led the way inside, her heart suddenly frozen with the
premonition that Joshua would be lying dead and cold in the
crib.

The baby was alive. He lay on his back and looked up at
them with wide eyes, his little hands clenching and unclenching. Naked except for his bulky diaper, the flimsy
blanket having been kicked off and not set back in place,
Unidentified Juvenile Male Patient #2613—soon to be
Joshua Arthur Neuman—looked a little like a bruised baby
bird dropped prematurely out of its nest: distended belly, ribs
sharp against pale, pink skin, tiny fingers flexing, and the
obscenity of the tape and needle holding the clumsy umbilicus
of the i.v.-drip in place.

Kate moved to check the i.v. but Lucian was already doing
it, adjusting the flow with a practiced hand.

Kate leaned over the high crib rails and lowered her face

to the infant's, kissing him softly on the cheek. "A few more days, Little One."

The baby screwed up his face as if to cry, then sighed instead. His eyes shifted to Lucian's face, now hanging over the crib.

"Hey, kid," said Lucian in a stage whisper, "it's Neil Diamond time." Lucian hummed a few bars of "Coming to America."

Kate had picked up the metal clipboard hanging on a nail at the foot of the crib and was frowning at the lab notes added since she had stopped by that morning before heading down to the Ministry. "Well, they finally got around to completing the extra blood analysis I asked for three weeks ago," she said. "I would have done it myself if this goddamn place had a centrifuge or decent microscope."

"What did it show?" asked Lucian, using his finger to poke ribs and play with the baby's belly button.

"The same low T-cell count we're finding now," said Kate. "Also, it confirmed a critical shortage of adenosine deaminase."

Lucian suddenly stood at mock attention, closed his eyes, and spoke in a rapid clip, as if answering questions in his oral final exams. "Adenosine deaminase . . . a critical enzyme required to break down toxic by-products of normal metabolism . . . missing in such rare disorders as adenosine deaminase deficiency." Lucian opened his eyes and when he spoke, his voice was serious. "I'm sorry, Kate. That's not treatable, is it?"

"Yes, it is," snapped Kate, slamming the clipboard down on the radiator so hard that the clash of metal on metal echoed in the small room. "It's an extremely rare disorder . . . perhaps fewer than thirty children worldwide . . . but it's treatable. In the States we use—"

"A synthetic enzyme called PEG-ADA," Lucian finished for her. "But I doubt if there is any PEG-ADA in Romania. Perhaps not in Eastern Europe."

"Not even in the Party hospitals?"

Lucian slowly shook his head. Kate noticed how strong his

chin was, how smooth the skin of his cheek. He had put on a pair of round tortoise-shell spectacles to read the lab report, but they just made him look more boyish rather than older or more serious.

"I can requisition the enzyme from America or the Red Cross," she said, "but by the time they get the shipment through all the red tape, a month or more will have passed and Joshua will be dead from some virus or the other. No, it'll be faster for me to take him to the States." She paused. "Lucian, you *are* good to know about the adenosine deaminase deficiency. Most GPs in the States wouldn't have heard of it. What did you get on your finals?"

"Four point oh, oh, oh," he said. "Outstanding in all areas, just like my lovemaking." He bent over the crib again. "And you, you little homunculus. You'd better get your tiny little Transylvanian ass to Boulder, Colorado, with Doctor Mama Neuman here so they can puncture it with a shot of PEG-ADA."

In his crib, Joshua seemed to ponder the statement a moment before he clenched his fists tighter, screwed up his face, and began crying loudly.

Chapter Eleven

KATE went to the American Embassy the next morning, walking down Bulevardul Bǎlcescu to the landmark of the Intercontinental Hotel, then up Strada Bastiştei a block to Strada Tudor Arghezi. It was not yet nine A.M., but already there was a long line of Romanians crowding the narrow street. Feeling guilty but knowing that she did not have the hours or days to queue up with these people, she walked to the head of the line. The Romanian soldiers peered at her passport and waved her to the gate; the Marine inside nodded and spoke into a black telephone.

Kate looked across the street to where several protesters stood against a brick wall. The banner on the wall read: A.V.C. WE ARE WAITING FOR IMMIGRATION VISAS 1982–1987. The signs they carried said HUNGER STRIKE FOR IMMIGRATION VISA and WHERE IS THE FAIR PLAY and STOP THE INJUSTICE and WASHINGTON SAID *YES* WHY ROMA SAID *NO* WHAT DOES AMERICAN CONSULATE *SAY*?

The Marine returned, the Romanian soldier opened the black iron gate, and Kate walked into the embassy courtyard, nodding her apologies to the stoic people left in line.

Inside, she passed through an airport-style metal detector, handed her purse over for a search, and then submitted to an inspection performed by a bored guard carrying a hand-held metal detector. Her purse was returned and she was buzzed through a doorway into the first floor of the embassy.

The once-grand hall here had been partitioned into a waiting room and a dozen office cubicles. People stood in lines everywhere: Romanians seeking visas standing in the longest line at the far end of the room, Americans in shorter lines at every cubicle window. There were eight rows of chairs in the main waiting room and most of these were filled with American women holding Romanian babies and toddlers. The cacophony was disturbing. As Kate waited in the first line to check in with the watch duty officer, she felt her heart sink with the hopelessness of it all.

Two and a half hours later, that hopelessness was confirmed. Kate had spoken to four people on the embassy staff and had threatened to scream unless she was allowed to speak to a higher-ranking official. Someone from the Ambassador's office had come downstairs, pulled a folding metal chair out and straddled it backward, smiled, and slowly explained exactly what the first four functionaries had explained.

"We simply cannot allow these AIDS children in the States," the man said slowly. His teeth were perfect, his haircut perfect, the crease in his gray trousers perfect. He had introduced himself as Cully or Cawley or Crawley. "The United States has a serious enough AIDS problem of its own. Surely you can understand this, Mrs. . . . ah . . . Neuman."

"*Doctor* Neuman," Kate corrected for the fifth time. "And this child does not have AIDS. I am a *specialist* in blood diseases. I can attest to this."

The embassy man pursed his lips and nodded slowly, as if assessing some complicated data. "And has the Trojan Clinic verified this?"

Kate snorted. The Trojan Clinic was a knock-off, walk-in doc-in-the-box place that had won the lottery when the American Embassy chose it to do all of its pre-visa hepatitis B and AIDS testing. Kate would have as soon consulted an astrologer as trusted the Trojan Clinic's lab tests. "*I* have verified it," she said. "We ran the HIV procedures at District Hospital One five weeks ago. And we eliminated the possibil-

ity of all the hepatitis strains at the same time. I have the tests
. . . confirmed and verified in writing by Doctors Ragrevscu
and Grigorescu, chief and assistant pathologists at District
Hospital One.''

The embassy man—Curly? Cally? *Crawley*—pursed his
lips, nodded again, and said, "But we would, of course, have
to have Trojan Clinic's confirmation that the child is healthy.
And, of course, written permission for adoption from one or
both of the birth parents.''

"God *damn* it," Kate said, leaning forward so quickly
that Mr. Crawley almost fell backwards off his straddled
chair. "First, I will repeat for the tenth time: the infant has
no record of birth parents, neither father nor mother. No
records whatsoever. He was abandoned. Deserted. Left to
die. Even the orphanage in Tîrgovişte has no records on who
brought him in. Second, the child is *not* healthy—that is
one reason I'm bringing him to the States. I've explained
this fifteen times. But he's also not contagious. No hepatitis
B. No AIDS. No contagious disease of any sort. As far as
we can tell, the infant has an immune-deficiency disorder
that is almost certainly genetic and will be almost certainly
fatal if *you don't allow me to get him somewhere I can help
him.*''

The embassy man nodded, pursed his lips again, tapped a
pencil against the desk, nodded toward the lower-echelon
embassy man, folded his arms, and said, "Well, Mrs. Neuman, we'd certainly like to help you, but it would take at
least a month to process the paperwork for a . . . ah . . .
unusual child like this, and in all likelihood the visa application would be disallowed without written permission from the
child's birth mother and a clean bill of health from the Trojan
Clinic. Have you considered adopting a healthy child?''

Kate's scream could be heard on the street outside. If she
allowed herself to scream.

A Marine security guard was escorting her to the door of
the embassy when she saw the mutant ninja priest suit in the
waiting room, a black silhouette amidst the riot of American
summer pastels and Romanian grays.

"O'Rourke!"

The priest turned, started to smile, saw her face, and came quickly across the crowded room to her. He waved the security guard away, and the Marine hesitated only a second before releasing her arm. Father O'Rourke led her to a chair in the least-crowded corner of the room and kicked a stack of papers off for her to sit. She almost cried out his name when he turned and left her, but he was back a few seconds later with a paper cone filled with cool water. Kate drank it gratefully.

"What's going on, Neuman?" His voice was soft. His gray eyes never left her face.

She told him everything, and even as she spoke a detached part of her mind was thinking, *Is this what confession is like? Is this the feeling that religion brings . . . this turning over all your problems to someone else*? She didn't think so.

When she was finished, O'Rourke nodded once. "And you're sure the Romanian officials will expedite the release of the child by your departure date, even if the Americans won't?"

Kate nodded vigorously. When she looked down she was surprised to see that she was still clutching the paper cone with both hands.

"And how much baksheesh?" he asked. "The Romanian official, I mean."

Kate frowned. "None. I mean, I was expecting some . . . expecting to pay up to five or six thousand dollars, American . . . but, none. Mr. Stancu . . . the man at the Ministry . . . he never asked for any and I . . . none."

Father O'Rourke paused a minute at this news. She could see the disbelief in his eyes.

Kate pulled a sheaf of documents from her purse. "They were ready this morning, O'Rourke. Look. Lucian says that they're official and complete. I tried to show them to the embassy people here . . . *our* people . . . but these stupid sons of bitches have their heads stuck so far up their asses that—"

"All right, Neuman. All right." The priest's hand was gentle but firm on her arm.

Kate stopped, took a breath, nodded.

"Just wait here a minute, would you?" he asked. He brought her another cone of water and touched the top of her head when she bent to drink from it.

Kate felt the anger surge in her like nausea. It had been years since she had been so out of control of a situation.

Father O'Rourke leaned into the nearest cubicle. "Donna, can I use your office for a moment? Yeah, just a few minutes, honest. I'll answer the phone if His Highness buzzes. Thanks, Donna, you're a sweetheart."

Kate realized that she was blinking through tears as she watched the young woman leave. Father O'Rourke winked at her and slipped into the cubicle. She heard him asking the switchboard operator for a Stateside satellite line. Kate recognized the 202 as a District of Columbia area code.

The conversation could not have lasted two minutes and she caught only snatches of it as her mind kept veering back to what she *should* have said to Mr. Crawley from the embassy.

"Hello, Jim . . . yeah, Mike O'Rourke, right . . . great, great, how are you? No, not Lima or Santiago this time . . . Bucharest. Yep."

Kate closed her eyes. She was one of the fifteen top hematologists in the Western hemisphere and she was listening to some parish priest chew the fat with somebody on his Old Boy network, probably another priest at Georgetown University or somewhere . . . some pissant Jesuit with an in-law in the State Department.

No, she corrected herself, *priest don't have in-laws. Do they*?

"That's it exactly," O'Rourke was saying on the phone. Kate realized that she had heard him summarize her visa problems in a dozen words or less. "That's it, Jim . . . no moss growing on your brain since the Bike Patrol days. She's one of the few Americans I've seen in the year and a half I've been here who's trying to adopt one of the real orphanage cases . . . a very sick child . . . sick but not contagious in any way . . . right . . . and this putz in Visa section is making it impossible. Yeah . . . I agree, it amounts to a sentence of death.''

Kate felt her skin go clammy when she heard someone else say that. *Joshua. Dead.* She thought of the tiny fingers, the trusting eyes. She thought of the scores and scores of small, unmarked graves she had seen behind the orphanages and pediatric hospitals she had toured in Bucharest and beyond.

"OK, Jimmy. Same to you, kid. No, Kev's still in Houston, I think . . . NASA . . . and Dale's working on his next book up in the Grand Tetons or wherever. No, uh-uh, that was Lawrence's *third* wedding. No, he invited me as a *guest*. They had some sort of Grand Prix driver who moonlights as a Zen guru do the actual ceremony. You too, amigo. Talk to you later.''

He came out and touched her knee the way a father would pat the leg of a child who had been crying. Kate choked back her anger at herself and the situation. She was trying to think of the blood specialists, CDC administrators, media people, print reporters, and medical lobbyists she knew. Certainly, among them there must be somebody with more clout than O'Rourke's Georgetown buddy. She would begin calling that afternoon. Somebody would put pressure on the State Department for her. *In three days?*

"I'll walk you back to the hospital," said the priest.

"All right," she said. Before they got to the embassy's inner doors, she squeezed his arm through the black coat. "Thanks, O'Rourke. Thanks for trying."

"You're welcome, Neuman."

They were just out the doors when Mr. Crawley from upstairs came hurrying down the steps, almost sliding across the marble floor in his haste. His tie was askew. His hair was mussed. His face was flushed except where it was pale around the mouth, and there was a look in his eyes that made Kate think that some civil servant with a forgettable name had just had a preview of his career ox being royally and terminally gored.

"Mrs. . . . ah . . . *Doctor* Neuman!" cried the embassy man, relief visible on his features. "I'm glad I caught you. There's been a mixup . . . I'm afraid I may have misspoke myself." He thrust a sheaf of documents at her. "We'll have the visa application processed by tomorrow morning. This temporary visa should satisfy the Romanian authorities if there are any questions on their part about—"

Later, during the walk back to the hospital, Kate said to O'Rourke, "And what were you doing at the embassy, anyway?"

"My job takes me there."

"Intercepting more inappropriate adoptions?"

He shrugged. Kate thought, irrelevantly, that the man looked very trim, very handsome, and very Irish in his black suit and white collar. "Sometimes," said the priest, "I expedite as well as interdict."

"You certainly expedited this situation. You may have expedited Joshua's last chance to survive." She paused to watch the traffic pass on the busy Bulevardul Bălcescu. "Can you tell me your friend Jim's last name?"

Father O'Rourke scratched his chin through the short beard. "Why not? It's Harlen."

"*Senator* Harlen? Senator *James* Harlen? The senator who's head of the Foreign Affairs Committee? The one who Secretary of State Baker wanted as his number-two guy even though he was from the wrong party? The senator that Dukakis almost picked as a running mate in '88 rather than Lloyd Bentsen?"

The priest smiled. "Jimmy was right to think that *that* wouldn't have been a smart move. I wanted him to run, which shows how naive I am. But he's going to wait until '96 to get into national politics . . . and that won't be for a vice-presidential slot. He and Cuomo are the only Democrats left with real presidential timber . . . and I think Jimmy has the energy and new ideas to go with it."

"And you're friends," said Kate, realizing how dumb that statement was.

"Were friends. A long time ago." Father O'Rourke was

staring at the ONT tourist offices across the boulevard, but his eyes were seeing something else.

"Well, if I believed in miracles, I'd say that the last couple of days have been full of them," said Kate. She felt a strange sensation as she said this. *It's real. It's happening. I am going to have a child*. Kate felt the way she had as a young girl, taking a dare, standing at the edge of the fifteen-foot-high diving board at Kenmore Municipal Pool: too scared to jump, too proud to retreat.

"The only miracle was a Romanian ministry official doing someone a favor without major baksheesh," said O'Rourke. When he saw her trembling he started to touch her arm again, then dropped his hand. Kate felt the force of his gaze on her. "Neuman, if the boy is going to survive, you'll have to provide the miracles."

"I know," said Kate. Then, realizing that she may not have spoken aloud, she said, firmly and clearly, "I know."

Chapter Twelve

KATE and Joshua were set to fly to the United States on Monday, May 20, and by the evening of Sunday the nineteenth, she was sure that they would never be allowed out of the country.

UNICEF, the co-sponsor, along with the CDC International Relief Fund, of her six weeks of medical aid in Romania, had sent the PanAm ticket weeks ago, and since Otopeni Airport did not allow telephone confirmations of flights, she called the Office of National Tourism almost hourly to confirm her reservations. Not satisfied with that, she had Lucian drive out to the airport twice on Saturday and three times on Sunday to confirm that the flight was still scheduled and that she had a seat reserved. Joshua would fly in her arms and needed no separate ticket. She also had Lucian confirm this.

Mr. Stancu at the Ministry had been as good as his word— he was a short, red-cheeked, cheerful man, the exact opposite of the stereotype of an Eastern European bureaucrat as well as the opposite of all the other bureaucrats Kate had met in the country—confirmed that Joshua's exit visa was complete and cleared. They had waived the usual requirement for the signature of one of the birth parents. The Romanian end of the adoption process was amazingly simple.

The American Embassy was slower, but by Saturday after-noon Mr. Crawley had expedited Joshua's exit visa . . . Lucian had brought a Nikon to the hospital to shoot the infant's photo, but it turned out that no photo was necessary . . . and the U.S. part of the adoption was begun through their liaison with Rocky Mountain Adoption Option Services. Their American headquarters was Denver, so Kate had no problems in completing the process once she got home.

Mr. Popescu, the chief administrator of District Hospital One, was at first displeased that their fiery American visitor was taking one of the children out of their wards—especially without paying him for the privilege—but phone calls from the Ministry of Health and reassurances from the Romanian pediatricians that the child had almost no chance of survival and was a drain on hospital resources evidently reassured the little man to the point he merely smirked at Kate during her last day on the job.

All paperwork was in place. Pan American had been notified that a very sick child was being transported to the States and had extra medical equipment standing by in Frankfurt. Kate was bringing her own medical bag aboard the aircraft, replenished as it was by Red Cross supplies and even bootlegged syringes, i.v.-drips, and antibiotics somehow scrounged by Lucian from the medical school. The syringes were the Western disposable type, still in their sterile pacs. The antibiotics were from West Germany. Kate was deeply touched, knowing how much money such contraband would have brought on the black market.

And while a part of her mind thought that these supplies should stay in Romania to help a few of the thousands of children in hospitals there, a greater part of her mind and heart knew that she would do anything, steal anything, deny anyone anything in order to keep Joshua alive. It was a shock to Kate after almost two decades of service to medical ethics to realize that there were higher imperatives.

She had been trying to call Tom, her ex-husband, since Thursday, but his answering machine in Boulder had rattled off an announcement in his deep, happy, little-boy voice that he was off leading a rafting trip down the Arkansas River and would be back when he got back. Leave a message if you're so inclined. Kate left four messages, each one a bit more coherent than the last.

Her breakup with Tom six years earlier had been quiet rather than melodramatic, resigned rather than angry. As is true of that one percent or so of marriages, she and her ex-husband became closer friends *after* the divorce and often had meals or drinks together after work. Tom, just turned forty but as strong as a proverbial ox and handsome in a Tom Sawyerish sort of way, could finally acknowledge that it was true—he had never grown up. His Boulder-based job as river guide, part-time mountaineer, part-time bicycle racer, part-time Himalayan trekking guide, part-time nature photographer, and full-time adventure-seeker had given him—he now admitted—the perfect excuse not to grow up.

As for Kate, she had been able to admit to him in recent months that perhaps she had grown up too much, that her adult-adult medical persona had pushed out whatever child-like fun she had shared with him in the early days. There was no talk of a reconciliation between them—Kate was sure that neither could imagine living together again—but their conversation had become more relaxed in recent years, their sharing of small problems and large confidences less constrained.

And now Kate was bringing home a baby. After reassuring each other for years, each for his or her own reasons, that neither wanted a child in their lives, Dr. Kate Neuman, at age thirty-eight, was bringing home a baby.

Tom caught her at her Strada Ştirbei Vodă apartment on Sunday evening. His raft trip had been a success. He could not believe her message. His voice was the usual blend of boyish energy and Boulderish enthusiasm. It made Kate want to cry.

"I'm scared it won't happen," she said. The connection was terrible, suffering from all the echoes, delays, and hollownesses common to most transatlantic calls, with the added fuzz, rasp, clunk, and echoes of Romanian telephonic service.

Still, Tom heard her. "What do you mean it's not going to happen? Didn't you say that you had all the paperwork licked? The baby . . . Joshua . . . didn't you say he's OK right now?''

"He's stable, yes.''

"Then what . . .''

"I don't *know*,'' said Kate. She realized that if it was seven o'clock on Sunday evening where she was . . . the rich May light lay heavy on the chestnut tree outside her apartment window . . . then it must be ten o'clock Sunday morning in Boulder. She took a breath. "I just have this terrible fear that it's not going to happen. That something's going to . . . stop us.''

Tom's voice was as serious as she ever remembered hearing it. "This isn't like you, Kat. What happened to the Iron Lady I used to know and love? The woman who was going to cure the world, whether it wanted to be cured or not?'' The gentleness of his tone belied the words.

Kate winced at the "Kat.'' It had been the name he called her during their lovemaking early in their marriage. "It's this place,'' she said. "It makes you paranoid. Somebody told me that every third or fourth person was a paid informer during the Ceauşescu years.'' The phone clunked and whistled. Distance hummed in the wires. "Which reminds me,'' she said, "we shouldn't be talking on the phone.''

"Eavesdroppers? Wiretappers? KGB or whatever the Romanian equivalent is?'' came Tom's voice through the static. "Fuck 'em. Fuck *you*, whoever's listening. Not you, Kat.''

"Not *Securitate*,'' said Kate, trying to smile. "The phone bill.''

"Well, fuck AT&T too. Or MCI. Or whoever the hell I signed up with.''

Kate did smile. She always had to pay the bills when they were married; Tom had rarely known whom they were paying for what. She wondered who was paying his bills now.

"When do you get into Stapleton tomorrow?'' asked Tom. His voice was barely audible over the line noise.

Kate closed her eyes and recited her itinerary. "Out of Bucharest on PanAm Ten-seventy to Frankfurt via Warsaw at seven-ten A.M. PanAm Flight Sixty-seven out of Frankfurt at ten-thirty in the morning, arriving JFK at one-oh-five P.M. Then PanAm Five Ninety-seven out of JFK, arriving Denver at seven fifty-eight P.M.''

"Wow," said Tom. "Hell of a day for the kid. The mother too." There was a moment of silence except for line noise. "I'll be down at Stapleton to pick you up, Kate."

"There's no need . . ."

"I'll *be* there."

Kate did not argue further. "Thank you, Tom," she said. "Oh . . . and bring a car seat."

"A what?"

"An infant-carrier car seat."

There was the muted sound of laughter and then cursing. "Great," said Tom at last. "I get to spend my day off hunting for a freaking baby's car seat. You got it, Kat. Love you, kid. See you tomorrow night." He hung up with the abruptness that used to take Kate by surprise.

The sudden silence after the conversation was difficult. Kate paced her room a hundredth time, checked her luggage—all packed except for her pajamas and toilet kit—for the fiftieth time, and went through the papers in her Banana Republic safari jacket for the five hundredth time: passport, her visa, Joshua's visa, adoption papers—stamped by the Ministry and the U.S. Embassy—record of inoculation, record of testing for contagious diseases, a letter of request for expedited treatment from Mr. Stancu's office and a similar letter from Mr. Crawley at the American Embassy. Everything there. Everything stamped, counterstamped, approved, sealed, and completed.

Something was going to go wrong. She knew it. Every footstep in the hallway or the apartment courtyard was some official with the word—Joshua had died in the hour since she had seen him, sleeping peacefully in his hospital crib. Or the Ministry had revoked its permission. Or . . .

Something would go wrong.

Lucian had offered to drive her to the airport and she had accepted. Father O'Rourke had business Monday morning in Tîrgovişte, fifty miles north of the capital, but he had insisted on coming by the hospital at six when she was scheduled to pick Joshua up. Everything was timed, arranged, and packaged . . . she had even had Lucian help her figure out schedules on the Orient Express to Budapest in case PanAm and Tarom Airlines suddenly quit serving Bucharest . . . but Kate was sure something was going to go wrong.

At ten P.M., Kate got into her pajamas, brushed her teeth, set her alarm clock for 4:45, and got into bed, knowing that she would not sleep. She stared at the ceiling, thought of Joshua sleeping on his stomach or lying on his back, the i.v. still attached to give him that final strength for tomorrow's ordeal, and Kate began the vigil of the long night of waiting.

Dreams of Blood and Iron

I watched from these windows . . . these small windows which shed such thin light upon me now . . . I watched from these windows as a child of three or four as they led the thieves, brigands, murderers, and tax dodgers from the cramped jail in Councilmen's Square across the street to their place of execution in the Jewelers' Donjon. I remember their faces, these prisoners, these condemned men: unwashed, eyes red-rimmed, faces gaunt, bearded and wild, casting their gaze about them in desperation as the knowledge descended on each man that he had only minutes left before the rope would be set around his neck and the executioner would tumble him from the platform. Once I remember there were three women who had been kept separate in the Councilmen's Tower lockup, and I watched on a brisk autumn morning as they were led in chains out of the Tower and across the square, from the square to the street, and then down the cobblestoned hill out of sight of my eager eyes. But oh, those seconds of pure sight as I knelt here on the couch in my father's room which passed as both court and private chamber . . . oh, those endless moments of ecstasy!

The women were dressed in filthy rags, like the men. I saw their breasts through the tatters of rotted brown. The women were streaked with dirt from the Tower's jail and with blood from the guards' rough treatment of them. But their breasts were pale, white, defenseless. I saw glimpses of their streaked legs and pale thighs; I saw the darkness between those thighs when the oldest of the three women fell, legs spread and sliding on cobblestones as the jailer dragged them squealing and wailing on the long length of chain. But it is their eyes that I remember most . . . as terrified as those of the male prisoners I had seen, so wide that the whites showed around the dark irises, like the sliding eyes of mares being forced forward after smelling fresh blood or the presence of a stallion.

That was the first time I felt the excitement—the rise of thrill in my chest as I watched the sure knowledge of death descend on these men and women—the excitement and the throbbing purity of sensation. I remember falling, legs too weak to support me, on my father's couch at this very window, heart pounding, the images of those straining, doomed men and women burning fresh in my consciousness even as their actual cries echoed and diminished on the cool air wafting in through Father's open windows.

My father, Vlad Dracul, had sentenced those people to hang. Or rather, he had confirmed the sentence with no more than a nod or flicker of his hand to a subordinate. Father had created and now enforced the laws which had condemned those women, those men. It was Father who had brought that great terror down upon these people, Father who had summoned that palpable throbbing of Death's wings in the square below.

I remember lying there on the couch, feeling my heart slowly return to normal, feeling the first flush of embarrassment at the strange excitement . . . I remember lying in this room and thinking, Someday I shall have that power.

It was in this room when I was four that I first drank from the Chalice. I remember every detail. My mother was not present. Only Father and five other men I had never seen before, all robed and cowled in their green-over-red Draconist ceremonial garb, were in attendance that night. I remember the bright tapestry behind Father's throne, set out for this night only—the great dragon curling in a circle of gold scales, its terrifying mouth open, its wings widespread, its mighty claws curved into grasping talons. I remember the torchlight and muttered ritual of the Order of the Dragon. I remember the presentation of the Chalice. I remember my first taste of blood. I remember the dreams it brought me that night.

It was in this room when I was five, in the Year of Our Lord 1436, that I heard my father declare his intention to the court of seizing the land and title of his dying half-brother Alexander Aldea, thus making Father the first full prince of Wallachia. I remember the sound of horses' shod hooves on the winter air beyond my nursery window, the creak of leather and death-hollow clank of iron against iron as the cavalry passed our windows that December night. I remember how I loved the richness of the imperial city of Tîgovişte, I remember the sensuous feel of the Italian, Hungarian, and Latin words I learned there, each new syllable as rich as the taste of blood in my mouth, and I remember the excitement behind the dry history taught to me by my boyar tutor and the old monks there. And I remember how short that wonderful time was to be.

I was twelve years old when my father gave me and my younger half-brother Radu as hostages to the Turkish Sultan Murad. Perhaps he had not planned to do it as we rode to Gallipoli to meet the Sultan, for Father was also seized by the Sultan's men only minutes after we had reached the city gates. But Father later swore an oath on the Bible and Koran not to oppose the Sultan's will, and our continued role as hostages was part of that oath. Radu was only eight and I remember his tears as the escorted wagon bore us away from Gallipoli toward the fortress of Egrigoz in the province of Karaman in western Anatolia.

I did not weep.

I remember how cold that winter was, how strange the food, and how the manservants who looked after our wants also locked the door to our apartments when the early twilight settled on that mountain city. I remember the shock of the Sultan's people when the Ceremony of the Chalice was ex-

plained to them, but they accepted it as just another barbarism of the Christian faith. Their jails were filled with criminals, slaves, and prisoners of war waiting to be disposed of; so finding donors was not difficult. Later we were taken to Tokat, and later still, to Adrianople, where we lived, ate, traveled, and grew into manhood in the Sultan's company.

The Sultan Murad was a cruel man, but less cruel, I think, than Father had been. He treated us more like sons than Father ever had. I remember once the Sultan touching my cheek after I had excitedly shown him the sweep and soaring pounce of a falcon I had helped train. His surprisingly gentle touch lingered.

By the end of my six years there, I was thinking in Turkish more often than in my own language, and even now, as strength ebbs and consciousness dims, it is in Turkish that I form my half-waking thoughts.

Radu was always handsome, even as a young child, and was beautiful by the time he showed the earliest signs of manhood. I remained ugly. Radu licked up to the philosophers and scholars who tutored us. I resisted their efforts to instruct us in Byzantine culture. Radu abandoned the Chalice even while I found need to drink from it weekly rather than monthly, then daily rather than weekly. Radu gained the awards and caresses of our jailors and tutors; I suffered their whippings. By the time he was thirteen, Radu had learned how to please both the women in the seraglio and the male courtiers who came to our apartments late at night.

I hated my half-brother, and he returned the hatred with added contempt. Each of us knew that if we survived—and each of us, in our own way, was filled with full determination to survive—that someday we would be enemies and rivals for our father's throne.

Radu followed his path to the throne by becoming the minion of Sultan Murad II and harem boy to his successor, Mehmed. He stayed in Turkey until 1462; at twenty-seven, Radu was still beautiful, but could no longer be considered a harem boy. Promised my father's title by the Sultan, he found it claimed by someone more daring and resourceful. He found it claimed by me.

I remember the day—I was sixteen—when word of my father's death reached us at the Sultan's court. It was in the late autumn of 1447. Cazan, my father's most faithful chancellor, had ridden five days to Adrianople with the news. The details were few but painful. The boyars and citizens of Tîrgovişte had revolted, urged on by Hungary's rapacious King Hunyadi and his Wallachian ally, the boyar Vladislav II. Mircea, my full brother, had been captured in Tîrgovişte and buried alive. Vlad Dracul, my father, had been hunted down and murdered in the marshes of Balteni, near Bucharest. Cazan informed us that Father's body had been returned to a hidden chapel near Tîrgovişte.

Cazan, his old man's rheumy eyes moistening more than usual, then presented me with two objects Father had asked him—asked as they fled toward the Danube with the assassins on their trail—to give to me as my legacy. This legacy consisted of a beautiful Toledo-forged sword presented to Father by Emperor Sigismund in Nuremberg on the year that I was born, and also the gold Dragon Pendant that my father had received upon entering the Order of the Dragon.

Setting the Dragon Pendant about my neck and holding the sword high above my head, the bright blade catching the torchlight, I swore my oath in front of Cazan and Cazan alone. "I swear upon the Blood of Christ and the Blood of the Chalice," I cried, my voice not breaking, "that Vlad Dracul will be avenged, that I will personally drain and drink the blood of Vladislav, and that those who planned and committed this treachery will lament the day when they murdered Vlad Dracul and earned the enmity of Vlad Dracula, Son of the Dragon. They have not known true terror until this day. So I swear upon the Blood of Christ and the Blood of the Chalice, and may all the forces of Heaven or Hell come to my aid in this solemn purpose."

I sheathed the sword, patted the weeping chancellor on his shoulder, and returned to my quarters to lie awake and plot my escape from the Sultan, my vengeance on Vladislav and Hunyadi.

I lie awake now, realizing that as blades of Toledo steel are forged in the furnaces and crucibles of flame, so are men forged in the crucibles of such pain, loss, and fear. And, as with a fine sword, such human blades take centuries to lose their terrible edge.

The light has failed. I will pretend to sleep.

Chapter Thirteen

THE Colorado extension of the Centers for Disease Control occupied a structure set in the foothills above Boulder on the greenbelt just below the geological formation known as the Flatirons. Locals still referred to the complex as NCAR—pronounced En-Car—because of its twenty-five-year stint as the National Center for Atmospheric Research. When NCAR had finally outgrown the complex the year before and moved into its new headquarters in the town below, CDC had been quick to recycle the center for its own use.

The building had been designed by I. M. Pei out of the same dark red Pennsylvanian and Permian conglomerates that had formed the great, titled slabs of the Flatirons which dominated the foothills above Boulder. His theory had been that the sandstone-like material of the structure would weather at the same rate as the Flatirons themselves, thus allowing the building to "disappear" into the environment. For the most part, Pei's theory had worked. Although the lights of the CDC were quite visible at night against the dark mass of the greenbelt forest and foothills, in the daytime a casual glance often left tourists thinking that the building was just another strange sandstone outcropping along this dramatic stretch of the Front Range.

Kate Neuman loved her office at CDC Boulder, and her return from Bucharest made her appreciate the aesthetics of the place almost as if she had never seen it before. Her office was on the northwest corner of the modern structure—Pei had designed it as a series of vertical slabs and overhanging shale-and-sandstone boxes with large windows—and from her desk she could see the great wall of the first three Flatirons to the north, the undulating meadows and pine forests at the foot of the Flatirons, the hogback ridges of Fountain sandstone formations poking up through the thin soil of the meadows like a stegosaur's plates, and even the plains themselves, starting at Boulder and stretching away to the north and east as far as the eye could see. Her ex-husband, Tom, had taught her that the Flatirons had once been layers of sediment beneath an ancient inland sea, upthrust some sixty million years ago by the ferocious mountain-building going on in the Rockies to the west. Now Kate could never look at the Flatirons without thinking of cement sidewalk slabs upended by roots.

A trail began immediately outside the back door of the CDC, the larger Mesa Trail was visible beyond the next ridge, deer came down to graze immediately below her window, and her co-workers had informed Kate that a mountain lion had been seen that summer in the trees not a hundred feet from the building.

Kate was thinking of none of this. She ignored the stacks of papers on her desk and the blinking cursor on her computer screen, and she thought about her son. She thought about Joshua.

Unable to sleep that last night in Bucharest, she had taken all her bags, found a cab in the dark and rainy streets, and gone to the hospital to sit by Joshua's side until it was time to go to the airport. The elevator was out of order at the hospital and she had run up the stairs, suddenly sure that the crib in Isolation Ward Three would be empty.

Joshua was sleeping. The final unit of whole blood Kate had ordered for him the day before had brought him back to the appearance of rigorous health. Kate had sat on the cold radiator, her fist under her chin, and watched her adopted son sleep until the first light of dawn seeped through the dirty windows.

Lucian picked them up at the hospital. The last volley of paperwork there was less than Kate had feared. Father O'Rourke met them as promised. As she and the priest were shaking hands on the front steps, Kate surrendered to impulse and kissed him on the cheek. O'Rourke smiled, held her face in his hands for a long moment, and then—before Kate could think or protest—blessed Joshua with a gentle touch of his thumb to the baby's forehead and a quick sign of the cross.

"I'll be thinking about you," O'Rourke said softly and held the front door of the Dacia open for Kate and the baby. The priest looked at Lucian. "You drive carefully, hear?" Lucian had only smiled.

The highway to the airport was almost empty. Joshua woke during the drive but did not cry, merely stared up from the cradle of Kate's arms with his large, dark, questioning eyes. Lucian seemed to sense Kate's uneasiness. "Would you like to hear another Ceauşescu joke I used to tell?"

Kate smiled wanly. The dilapidated wipers scraped tiredly at the rain. "Aren't you afraid there are microphones in your car?" she asked.

Lucian grinned. "They wouldn't work any better than the rest of this junkheap," he said. "Besides, the National Salvation Front doesn't mind Ceauşescu jokes. They just shit bricks when we tell NSF jokes."

"Okay," said Kate, tucking the baby deeper in his light blanket. "Let's hear your old Ceauşescu joke."

"Okay. Well, not long before the revolution, the Big C wakes one morning in a good mood and goes out on his balcony to greet the sun. 'Good morning, sun,' he says. Imagine his surprise when the sun says. 'Good morning, Mr. President.' Ceauşescu rushes back inside and wakes up Elena. 'Wake up!' he says. 'Even the sun respects me now.' 'That's nice,' says the wife of our Supreme Leader. And she goes back to sleep. Ceauşescu thinks maybe he's going a little crazy, so at noon he goes out on the balcony again. 'Good day, sun,' he says. Again the sun answers in a respectful voice. 'Good day, Mr. President . . .' ''

"Does this have an ending?" asked Kate. She could see the exit for the airport less than a kilometer ahead of them. The rain was falling more heavily now. She wondered if the PanAm flight to Warsaw might be canceled.

" 'Good day, Mr. President,' the sun said at noon," continued Lucian. He tapped the turn signal but there was no click, no blinking light. He ignored it and took the exit into the long airport drive. "Ceauşescu is so excited, he tries to get Elena out on the balcony, but she is busy putting on her makeup. Finally, at sunset, he convinces her to come out on the balcony. 'Watch. Listen,' he says to his wife, who is also the Chairman of the National Science and Technology Council. 'The sun respects me.' He turns toward the beautiful sunset. 'Good evening, sun,' he says. 'Fuck you, asshole,' says the sun. Ceauşescu is upset. He demands an explanation. 'This morning and at noon you addressed me with respect,' he splutters. 'Now you insult me. Why?' ''

Kate saw a parking place along the row of cars and cabs lining the curved drive to the terminal, but before she could point to it, Lucian stopped and parallel parked with some skill. He did not break the rhythm of his story.

" 'Why do you insult me now?' Our Leader demands. 'You dumb shit,' answers the sun, 'I'm in the West now.' ''

He came around to the passenger side and held an umbrella above them while she and the baby got out. Kate smiled her appreciation—more of his kindness than of the joke. They walked toward the terminal together, Lucian carrying one of her suitcases and holding the umbrella in place, Kate carrying her lighter carry-on bag and the baby.

"The Transylvanians have a proverb about jokes like mine," said Lucian. "*Rîdem noi rîdem, dar purceaua e moartă în coşar.*"

"Which means?" Kate blinked in the dimness as they came in under the heavy concrete overhang of the terminal. Gray-uniformed guards with automatic weapons stared impassively at them.

"Which means . . . we are all laughing, but the pig is dead in the basket." Lucian lowered the umbrella, shook it, folded it, and opened the door to the terminal with his shoulder.

The place was as dismal as Kate remembered it from her arrival in the country: a cavernous, concrete, echoing space, rimmed with dirt and debris, guarded by soldiers. To her left, the long, scarred tables and inoperable conveyer belts of incoming Customs lay empty. There were no incoming flights. Straight ahead, security checkpoints and curtained booths marked the beginning of the gauntlet she and Joshua would have to run before boarding the PanAm plane.

Lucian set her bags on the first inspection table and turned toward her. Non-passengers were not allowed beyond this point.

"Well . . ." he began and stopped.

Kate had never seen her young friend and translator at a loss for words. She threw her free arm around his neck and kissed him. He blinked and then touched her back gently, tentatively. An official behind the counter marked CONTROLUL PASAPOARTERLOR snapped something and Lucian pulled away, still looking at her. Kate thought that there was a question in Lucian's eyes and that those eyes looked strangely like Joshua's for that moment.

The official said something more loudly. Lucian finally broke the gaze and snapped back at the man. "*Lasă-ma in pace!*"

For an instant the man behind the passport control counter stared as if in shock at Lucian's insolence. Then he recovered and snapped his fingers; three uniformed thugs moved quickly across the concrete floor.

Kate thought she saw something like wildness in Lucian's eyes. She hugged him again, putting her body and the baby's body between Lucian and the guards. At the same time she had fumbled out her American passport and held it toward the guards as if it were a magic amulet.

The magic worked . . . at least temporarily. The guards hesitated. The passport control officer snarled something at

Lucian and crossed his arms. The guards looked at him and then back at Lucian and Kate.

"I'm sorry," Kate said to the guards. "But my fiancé gets very emotional. We hate being separated. Lucian, tell the gentleman that we have something for him . . ."

Lucian was glaring at the passport control officer but he snapped out of it when Kate pinched his forearm. "What? Oh, . . . *aveţi dreptate, îmi pare rău . . . Avem ceva pentru dumnneavocestră.*"

Kate heard Lucian's apology and the phrase that meant "I've been thinking of you," which was the polite precursor to bribery, baksheesh, the universal Romanian game of paying off those in authority. She fumbled three cartons of Kents out of her carry-on baggage and handed them to Lucian, who handed them to the passport control man.

The guard blinked and scowled, but whisked the cartons out of sight, dismissed the three security men, gave Kate's luggage a cursory inspection while he snapped questions at her, and then tossed her bags on a battered luggage cart and waved her through. She automatically took a step forward and was startled when a barrier slammed shut behind her.

Kate turned toward Lucian and found herself suddenly too filled with emotion to speak. Joshua stirred and fretted in her arms, his face reddening in preparation for tears. "I . . ." she began and had to stop. She felt like an idiot but did not try to hide the tears. Kate could not remember the last time she had cried in public.

"Hey, it's all right, babe," said Lucian in his best imitation of Southern California surfer-speak. "I'll catch you and Josh when I come to the States to do my residency. 'Later, dudes . . ." He reached across the barrier and touched his fingertips to hers.

The passport control officer snapped something and Lucian nodded without taking his eyes off Kate and the baby. Then Lucian turned and walked across the empty terminal space without looking back.

Kate carried Joshua through the security aisles, down a

narrow corridor, and into the arrival and departure area. Hidden speakers carried recordings of what may have been children singing traditional Romanian folk songs, but the voices were so shrill, the recording so scratched and distorted, that the effect was far from quaint or pleasant; Kate thought of choruses of torture victims screeching. There were a dozen other passengers waiting for the boarding call, and Kate could tell from their ill-fitting clothes that they were either Romanian officials traveling to Warsaw or Poles returning home. She saw no Americans, no Germans, no Brits—no tourists other than herself.

She stood a little apart from the group and glanced nervously around the terminal. The space was huge, designed for hundreds of people, the arched ceiling rising sixty feet or more overhead, and every squeak of shoes or cough echoed mercilessly. There were a few booths against the north wall—a counter to change money at the official rate, a dusty sign for the National Tourist Office—but they were empty. Most of the waiting passengers were smoking and glancing furtively at the armed guards who stood by the stairway to the lower level, by the security gates, and by the Customs counters. More guards wandered across the cavernous space in teams of two, their automatic weapons slung under their arms.

Joshua was still fretting but Kate rocked him rapidly, cooed to him, and offered him a pacifier. He sucked on the plastic and held off the tears. Kate wished that she had a pacifier herself to calm her nerves, and in that second of silliness she had a very real insight into why so many people in East European police states were chain-smokers.

She wandered over to one of the tall strips of window. There were two aircraft on the tarmac near the terminal: the smaller one obviously an official government jet of some sort; the other plane, the one resembling a DC-9, waiting to take Joshua and her to Warsaw, where they would continue on to Frankfurt. Several armored personnel carriers lumbered between the jets, their thick exhaust rising in the steaming air. Kate could see tanks parked along the edge of the runway and made out artillery pieces under camouflage netting near a line of trees. Gray-uniformed soldiers huddled by their trucks or around a fire in a barrel.

Much farther away, a line of Tarom airline jets sat along a weed-infested taxi strip. These jets looked like crude Boeing 727s that had seen better days before being abandoned: they were rusted, there were patches on the wings and fuselage, and one had two flat tires. Kate suddenly noticed the armed guards pacing beneath the planes—the bored men trying to keep out of the heavy rain—and she realized with a start that these aircraft were almost certainly still in service.

She was very glad that she had paid almost twice as much to fly PanAm to Warsaw and Frankfurt rather than take the Romanian national airline.

"Mrs. Neuman?"

She whirled to find two security men in black leather coats standing behind her. Three soldiers with automatic weapons stood nearby. "Mrs. Neuman?" the taller of the two security men said again.

Kate nodded. She found it impossible not to think of old war movies where the Gestapo interdicted travelers. She shivered inwardly as she thought of traveling in such a society with a yellow Star of David on one's coat, the word *Juden* stamped in one's passport. She expected these latter-day Gestapo types to ask for her papers.

"Your passport," snapped the tall man. His face showed the cratered terrain of a smallpox survivor. His teeth were brown.

She handed him her passport and tried not to flinch with anxiety when he put it in his jacket pocket without glancing at it.

"This way," he said, and gestured her toward a curtained alcove in the security area she had just passed through.

"What is this . . ." began Kate and then broke off as the other security man touched her elbow. She pulled her arm away and followed the taller man across the littered floor. The other passengers watched passively, smoke rising from their cigarettes.

There was a woman security guard waiting in the curtained alcove. Kate thought that the woman looked like a humorless version of Martina Navratilova with a bad haircut. Then all flippant comparisons fled as Kate was overcome with the certainty that this butch monstrosity was going to strip-search her.

The pockmarked security man pulled her passport out, inspected it for a long moment—taking care to look at the seams where the document was stitched—and then snapped something in Romanian to the other two guards. He turned toward Kate. "You are adopted child, yes?"

Kate was puzzled for a moment, not certain if the man was making a bizarre joke or not. Then she said, "I have adopted this child, yes. He is my son now."

Both men peered at the passport and the wad of papers and carbons that were tucked into it. Finally the tall, pockmarked one looked up and stared at her. "There is no parent sign."

Parent signature, Kate realized he was saying. New Romanian laws demanded the signature of at least one of the biological parents whenever a Romanian child was adopted. Kate had wholeheartedly agreed with the law. "No, there is no signature," she said, speaking slowly and enunciating carefully, "but that is only because no biological parents were ever found. He is a child of an orphanage. Abandoned."

The pockmarked security man squinted at her. "For baby to adopt, you must have parent sign."

Kate nodded and smiled, using all of her will to keep from screaming. "Yes, normally," she said, "but it is believed that this child has no parents. No parents." She reached out and touched the documents. "You see, there is a waiver here saying that no parent signature is required in this case. It is signed . . . here . . . by the Deputy Minister of the Interior. And here by the Minister of Health . . . you see, here." She pointed to the pink form. "And here it is signed by both the administrator of the original orphanage where Joshua was found . . . and here by the Commissioner of District Hospital One."

The security man scowled and riffled through the documents almost contemptuously. Kate sensed the dirt-deep stupidity under the thug's arrogant demeanor. *Oh, God*, she thought, *I wish Lucian were here*. Or someone from the embassy . . . or Father O'Rourke. *Now why did I think of O'Rourke?* She shook her head and stared at the three security people, showing a calm defiance but no provocation. "*Alles ist in Ordnung*," she said, not even realizing that she had slipped into German. Somehow it seemed appropriate to the moment.

The female guard held out her hands and said something.

"The baby," said the pockmarked man. "Give her the baby."

"No," Kate said calmly but firmly. She felt anything but calm. Saying no to *Securitate* thugs was still an invitation to violence, even in post-Ceauşescu Romania.

The two male guards scowled and stared. The woman snapped her fingers with impatience and extended her arms again.

"No," Kate said firmly. She had the image of the female guard carrying Joshua through the doorway while the other two restrained her. She realized how easy it would be for her never to see her son again. "No," Kate said again. Her insides were quaking but her voice remained firm and calm. She smiled at the two men and nodded toward Joshua. "You see, he's sleeping. I don't want to wake him. Tell me what you need and I'll do it, but I'll keep holding him."

The taller guard shook his head and said something to the female. She folded her arms and snapped something at him. The tall man responded harshly, tapped Kate's passport, rustled her other documents, and said, "Take baby's blanket and clothes off."

Kate blinked, felt the anger hanging in the air like charged ions before a storm, and said nothing. She removed Joshua's blanket and unsnapped his terrycloth jumper.

The baby awoke and began to cry.

"Shhhh," whispered Kate. With her free hand she set the blanket and jumper on the filthy counter.

The woman guard said something. "Diapers off," translated the security man.

Kate looked from face to face, trying to find a smile. There were none. Her fingers trembled ever so slightly as she undid the safety pins—even the embassy had not been able to provide her with disposable diapers—and lifted Joshua free. The baby looked even more frail without his clothes, his skin pale, ribs visible. There were bruises on his skinny arms where the i.v.-drip and transfusion needles had been. His tiny penis and scrotum were shrunken in the cold, and as Kate watched, goosebumps broke out on his arms and upper chest.

Kate hugged him close and glared at the woman. "All right? Satisfied that we aren't smuggling any state secrets or gold bullion?"

The female guard gave Kate a blank look, pawed through the jumper and blanket, carefully avoided the diaper, said something to the pockmarked man, and left the booth.

"It's cold," said Kate. "I'm going to put his clothes back on." She did so quickly. Beyond the curtained alcove, the shrill public address system announced her flight in a burst of static. She heard the other passengers clattering down the stairs to the boarding area.

"Wait," said the pockmarked guard. He set Kate's passport and papers on the counter and left with the other man.

Kate rocked Joshua and peered out through the curtain. The departure area was empty. The single clock above the door read 7:04 A.M. The flight was scheduled to leave at 7:10. None of the three security guards who had been with her in the booth were visible.

Kate took a ragged breath and patted the baby. His breathing was rapid and liquid, as if he were catching another cold. "Sshhh," whispered Kate. "It's all right, Little One." She knew that the tractor that pulled the passenger trailer out to the aircraft would be leaving in a moment. As if to confirm that, an unintelligible but urgent announcement echoed out of the terminal speakers.

Without looking back, Kate grabbed her papers, held the

baby tightly, left the booth, and walked across the endless expanse of terminal with her head high and eyes forward. Two lounging guards at the head of the stairs squinted through cigarette smoke as she approached.

Briskly, but not as if she had to hurry, Kate flashed her passport and boarding pass. The young guard waved her by.

At the bottom of the stairs there was another counter, another security guard. Kate could see the last of the passengers boarding the transfer jitney outside. The tractor engine started in a rush of smoke. Kate focused on the outside door and started to walk past the guard.

"Stop!"

She stopped, turned slowly, and forced a smile on her face. Joshua squirmed but did not cry.

The guard had a fat face and small eyes. His pudgy fingers tapped the counter. "Passport."

Kate set it down without comment and tried not to fidget while the fat man looked it over carefully. There were footsteps and voices just out of sight up the stairs.

Outside, the last of the passengers and baggage had been loaded on the two trailers. The tractors roared their engines. "We'll be late," Kate said quietly to the guard.

He lifted his pig eyes and scowled at her and the baby.

She held his gaze in silence for the better part of a minute. The baggage jitney pulled away. The passenger jitney waited to follow it the hundred yards out to the aircraft.

When she had been a practicing surgeon, Kate had often commanded colleagues or nurses to hurry with nothing more than the strength of her gaze above the surgical mask. She did so now, putting every once of authority she had earned in her life and career into the look she gave the guard.

The fat man looked down, stamped the passport a final time, and brusquely handed it to her. Kate forced herself not to run with Joshua in her arms. The jitney had already begun rolling toward the aircraft, but it stopped and waited while she caught up and stepped aboard. The Polish and Romanian passengers stared at her.

They were on the aircraft twelve minutes before it taxied

to the head of the runway, but Kate was sure that her watch had stopped. It seemed like hours, days. She watched out the streaked window as two security men in leather jackets joked and smoked at the foot of the stairs. They were not the two men from the terminal. But they carried hand-held radios. Kate closed her eyes and came as close to praying as she had since she was ten.

Three airport workers rolled away the stairs. The plane taxied to the end of the deserted runway. No aircraft had taken off or landed since they had boarded. The plane accelerated down the patched runway.

Kate did not breathe deeply until the landing gear was up and Bucharest was a scatter of white buildings rising above chestnut trees behind them. Her hands continued to tremble until she knew they must be out of Romanian airspace. Even at the Warsaw airport she felt her heart pounding until they changed crews and lifted off for Frankfurt.

Finally the pilot's voice came over the intercom. He had an American accent. "Ladies and Gentlemen, we've just leveled off at our cruising altitude of twenty-three thousand feet. We've just passed over the city of Lodz and should be coming up on the German border in . . . oh . . . five minutes or so. We've had a bit of rough weather, as I'm sure you noticed, but we've just passed the tail end of that front and Frankfurt informs us that it's sunny and very warm there, temperature thirty-one degrees Centigrade, winds out of the west at eight miles per hour. We hope you enjoy the rest of the flight."

Sunlight had suddenly streamed through the small window. Kate kissed Joshua and allowed herself to cry.

Kate Neuman blinked away the glare from the sunlight that had made its way through Boulder CDC's tinted windows and answered the phone. She honestly could not have said how long it had been buzzing. She vaguely remembered her secretary sticking her head in the office to announce she was running down to the cafeteria for lunch.

"Doctor Neuman," said Kate.

"Kate, this is Alan down in Imaging. I have the newest pictures from your son's last workup."

"Yes?" Kate realized that she had been doodling circles within circles until her memo pad was almost black. She set the pen down. "How do they look, Alan?"

There was the briefest hesitation and Kate could imagine the red-headed technician sitting in the glare of his multiple display monitors, a half-eaten corned beef sandwich on the terminal in front of him.

"I think you'd better come down, Kate. You should see this yourself."

There were six video monitors set into the long console and each of them displayed a slightly different view of nine-month-old Joshua Neuman's internal organs. These were not X rays but complex images built up by Alan's magnetic resonance imaging equipment. Kate was able to make out her child's spleen, liver, the sinuous curves of the upper small intestine, the lower curve of his stomach. . . .

"What is that?" she asked and stabbed a finger at the center monitor.

"Exactly," said Alan, pushing his thick glasses up and taking a bite of his corned beef sandwich. "Now, watch when we run the sequence with the CT data from three weeks ago."

Kate watched the primary VDT as the images coalesced, rotated in three dimensions, zoomed in for a closer look on the lower curve of the stomach, differentiated layers of stomach lining with false colors, and then ran a time-lapse sequence with digital enhancement.

A small appendix or abscess seemed to grow in the wall of Joshua's stomach.

"Ulcer?" said Kate, knowing that it was not one even as she said the word. The magnetic resonance imaging showed solid structure in the anomaly. She felt her heart sink.

"No," said Alan, taking a sip of cold coffee. Suddenly he saw Kate's face and he jumped to his feet and slid a chair under her. "Sit down," he said. "It's not a tumor either."

"It's not?" Kate felt the vertigo lessen. "But it has to be."

"It's not," said Alan. "Trust me. Watch. This is the CT-enhanced series from this week's MR imaging."

The lower curve of stomach was normal again. Colored layers proliferated, the abscess or whatever it was appeared, grew as substantial as an appendix, and then began to shrink.

"A separate growth?" said Kate.

"Same phenomenon, different time period." Alan pointed to the data column to the right of the image. "Notice the correspondence?"

For a moment Kate did not. Then she leaned closer and rubbed her upper lip. "The same day that Josh received the plasma . . ." She wheeled her chair over to the monitor where the previous cycle had been frozen on the screen. Running her finger down the screen, she said, "And the same date three weeks ago that he had a transfusion. These images show some change in the baby's gut whenever he receives blood?"

Alan took a healthy bite of sandwich and nodded. "Not just a change, Kate, but some sort of basic adaptive process. That structure is there at other times, it just becomes more visible when it's absorbing blood . . ."

"Absorbing blood!" Kate's shout surprised even herself. She modulated her voice. "He's not absorbing blood through the stomach wall, Alan. We give Joshua intravenous injections . . . we don't give him a baby bottle with blood in it!"

Alan missed the irony. He nodded and finished chewing. "Of course, but the adaptation . . . organ . . . whatever it is *does* absorb blood, there's no doubt about it. Look here." He touched buttons and all six of the monitors blinked red near the abnormal swelling. "The gut wall there is rich with veins and arteries. It's one of the reasons an ulcer is such a problem there. But *this*"—he touched the image of the tumor-like structure—"this thing is fed by a larger arterial network than I've ever seen. And it *is* absorbing blood, there's no doubt about that."

Kate pushed her chair back. "My God," she whispered. Alan was not listening. He shoved his glasses higher on his nose. "But look at the other data, Kate. It's not the absorption of blood that's interesting. Look at the most recent MR series. What happens next is unbelievable."

Kate watched the new series of MR images and flickering data columns with eyes that did not blink. When it was finished she sat in silence for a full minute.

"Kate," whispered Alan. His voice was almost reverent. "What's going on here?"

Kate's eyes never left the screen. "I don't know," she said at last. "I honest to God do not know." But somewhere, deep in the creative subconscious that had made her one of CDC's finest diagnosticians, Kate Neuman *did* know. And the knowledge both scared her to death and filled her with a strange exhilaration.

Chapter Fourteen

KATE Neuman's home was in a high meadow six miles up Sunshine Canyon above Boulder. Kate had always disliked canyons—she hated the lack of sunshine, especially in winter, and being at what she considered the mercy of gravity if any boulders decided to dislodge—but the road climbed out of the broad swale of Sunshine Canyon and ran along high ridgelines miles before it reached the turnoff to her home. She considered the location of her home almost perfect: high meadows laced with aspen and pine trees swept away on either side, the snow-capped summits of the Indian Peaks section of the Continental Divide loomed up ten miles to the west, and at night she could look out the gaps in the Front Range south of the Flatirons and see the lights of Boulder and Denver.

She and Tom had bought the home the year before their breakup, and while they had used her income to secure the mortgage and pay the down payment, Kate would always be grateful to Tom for suggesting they look in that particular area for a house. The structure itself was large and modern but it blended into the rocks and trees of the ridgeline, its windows framed views in all four directions, there was a wonderful patio from which she could look downhill toward the Flatirons, and while there was only a handful of houses in the six-hundred-acre residential ranch, the area was guarded by a security gate which could be unlocked only by the residents after a visitor contacted them via intercom. These visitors were usually shocked by the roughness of the gravel road beyond that security gate. The year-round residents there all owned four-wheel-drive vehicles to cope with winter snows at the seven-thousand-foot level.

On this July morning one week after her discussion with Alan, Kate rose, jogged her usual three-quarters of a mile on the loop trail behind her home, showered, dressed in her usual casual outfit of jeans, sneakers, and a man's white shirt for CDC—she wore a suit or dress only when a VIP visit or travel was inflicted on her—and had breakfast with Julie and Joshua. Julie Strickland was a twenty-three-year-old graduate student who was currently working on her PhD dissertation on the effects of pollution on three species of flowers found only on the alpine tundra. Kate had met Julie three years earlier through Tom; the younger woman had traveled with Tom's Mountain Challenge Tours for an entire summer of hiking and camping above treeline in some of Colorado's most inaccessible regions. Kate was fairly certain that Julie and Tom had enjoyed a brief fling that summer, but for some reason the fact never bothered her. The two had become friends soon after meeting each other. Julie was quiet but enthusiastic, competent and funny. In exchange for watching Joshua five days a week, Julie had her own section of Kate's five-thousand-square-foot house, was free to use Kate's 386e PC with its CD-ROM memory for her thesis when Kate was at work, had weekends free for her field trips, and received a token salary that allowed her to buy gas for her ancient Jeep.

Both women enjoyed the arrangement, and Kate was already worrying about the winter when Julie would be finished with her dissertation. Always sympathetic to the plight of working mothers forced to scramble for daycare, Kate now had nightmares about finding adequate care for Joshua. But on this beautiful summer morning, the sun already high above the plains and free of the rim of foothills to the east, Kate put the worry out of her mind as she ate her bran flakes and fed Joshua his cereal.

Julie looked up from her section of *The Denver Post*. "Are you taking the Cherokee or the Miata to work this morning?"

Kate resisted a smile. She had planned to take the red Miata, but she knew how much Julie loved to drive the roadster down the canyon. "Mmmm . . . the Jeep, I think. Did you have any shopping to do before you dropped Josh off at CDC?"

At the mention of his name, the baby smiled and banged a spoon on his tray. Kate wiped a bit of excess cereal from his chin.

"I thought I'd stop by the King Soopers on Table Mesa. You sure you don't mind me driving the Miata?"

"Just be sure to use the baby seat," said Kate.

Julie made a face as if to say, *Of course I will.*

"Sorry," smiled Kate. "Maternal instinct." She said it as a joke but instantly realized that this was precisely what prompted such obvious comments.

"Josh loves the convertible," said Julie. She took her own spoon and pretended to eat some of the baby's cereal. Joshua beamed his appreciation. Julie looked at Kate. "You want him there right at eleven?"

"Approximately," said Kate, glancing at her watch and clearing her dishes. "We have the MR equipment reserved until one, so it's all right if it's a few minutes after. . . ." She gestured toward Joshua's unfinished cereal. "Do you mind . . ."

"Uh-uh," said Julie, exchanging goofy expressions with the baby. "We like to eat together, *don't* we, Pooh?" She looked back at Kate, oblivious to the drop of milk on her nose. "This MR stuff won't hurt him, will it?"

Kate paused by the door. "No. It's the same procedure as before. Just pictures." *Pictures of what?* she asked herself for the hundredth time. "I'll have him home in time for his nap."

* * *

It was less fun driving the Cherokee down the winding canyon road than double-shifting the Miata through the turns, but this morning Kate was so lost in thought she did not notice the difference. Once in her office she asked her secretary to hold all calls and put a call through herself to the Trudeau Institute in Saranac, New York. It was a small research facility, but Kate knew that it did some of the best work on effector mechanisms of cell-mediated immunity relating to lymphocyte physiology. More than that, she knew its director, Paul Sampson.

"Paul," she said when she had got past receptionists and secretaries, "Kate Neuman. I've got a riddle for you." She knew that Paul was a sucker for puzzles. It was a trait that he shared with quite a few of the best medical researchers.

"Shoot," said Paul Sampson.

"We have an eight-and-a-half-month-old infant found in a Romanian orphanage. Physically the child looks about five months old. Mental and emotional development seem normal. Physically we see intermittent bouts of chronic diarrhea, persistent thrush, failure to thrive, chronic bacterial infections as well as otitis media. Diagnosis?"

There was only the slightest hesitation. "Well, Kate, you said it was a riddle, so AIDS is out. And that would be too obvious given the Romanian orphanage. Something interesting, you say."

"Yep," said Kate. On the greenbelt below her CDC window, a family of white-tailed deer had come out to graze.

"Was the workup done in Romania or here?"

"Both places," said Kate.

"OK, then we have some chance of reliability." There was a pause and Kate could hear the soft sound of Paul chewing on his pipe. He had given up smoking the thing almost two years earlier, but still played with it when he was thinking. "What was the T- and B-cell count?"

"T-cell, B-cell, and gammaglobulin levels almost did not register," said Kate. The data was in the file on her desk but she did not have to refer to them. "Serum IgA and IgM were markedly decreased. . . ."

"Hmmm," said Paul. "Sounds like Swiss-type SCID. Sad . . . and rare . . . but not too much of a riddle, Kate."

She watched the deer freeze as a car came up the winding road to the CDC parking lot. The car passed; the deer returned to grazing. "There's more, Paul. I agree the symptoms seem to suggest Swiss-type severe combined immunodeficiency, but the white blood cell count is also low . . ."

"What is the WBC count?"

"Less than three hundred lymphocytes/mu-one," she said.

Paul whistled. "That is strange. I mean, he makes the so-called 'boy-in-the-bubble' case of SCID look tame. According to your description, this poor Romanian kid has three of the four types of SCID—Swiss type, SCID with B lymphocytes, and reticular dysgenesis. I don't think I've ever seen a child with more than one of the manifestations. Of course, SCID itself is rare, no more than twenty-five or so kids world-wide . . ." His voice trailed off from stating the obvious to silence. "Is there more, Kate?"

She resisted the urge to sigh. "I'm afraid so. The child shows severe adenosine deaminase deficiency."

"ADA too?" interrupted the doctor on the other end of the line. She heard his teeth click on the stem of his pipe and imagined the pained expression on his face. "The poor little bastard has all four types of SCID. The symptoms usually manifest themselves between the third and sixth month. How old did you say he was?"

"Almost nine months." Kate thought of the "birthday cake" Julie would be shopping for at King Soopers. They celebrated Joshua's "birthday" every month. She wished she had taken time to shop for the cake herself.

"Nine months," came Paul's voice, obviously musing to himself. "I don't know how the little guy got that far . . . he won't be getting much older."

Kate winced. "That's your prognosis, Paul?"

She heard fumbling sounds at the other end of the line and could almost see the rumpled researcher sitting up, setting his pipe on the desk. "You know I wouldn't make a prognosis without seeing the patient and the tests in person, Kate. But . . . my God . . . signs of all four of the SCID variations. I mean, if it were just the ADA it would be bad enough . . . Has there been a haploidentical bone-marrow transplant?''

"There's no twin," Kate said softly. "No siblings at all. The orphanage couldn't find even the parents. Obviously no histocompatibility is possible."

There was silence for a moment. "Well, you could still try ADA injections to restore some of the immune function. Also shots of transfer factor and thymic extracts. And there's the human-gene-therapy work that Mulligan, Grosveld and the others are working on. They're having some real success in building some ADA-delivering retroviruses . . ." His voice trailed off.

Kate said what her friend would not. "But with all four types of SCID present, the chance of avoiding a killer germ while the gene therapy was building resistance would be . . . what, Paul? Too small to count?"

"My God, Kate," said the researcher, "you know as well as I do that all it takes to bushwhack a SCID's kid is one infection . . . generalized chicken pox, measles with Hecht's giant-cell pneumonia, cytomegalovirus or adenovirus infections, or our old buddy *Pneumocystosis carinii* . . . one good head cold and the child is gone. Their own protein-losing enteropathy adds to the problem. It's like greasing a slide and then going down it on waxed paper." He paused for breath, obviously upset.

Kate spoke softly. "I know, Paul. And I used to do that too."

"Do what?"

"Grease the slide on the playground and go down it on waxed paper."

She heard him chewing on his pipe again. "Kate, are you working with this child . . . personally, I mean?"

"Yes."

"Well, I'd put my hope on the gene-therapy work being done and hope for the best. There's a lot of energy going into solving the ADA problem these days, and if you lick that, the Swiss type, B lymph, and reticular dysgenesis malfunctions can be attacked with more conventional immunological reconstructive techniques. I'll fax you everything we have on Mulligan's work.''

"Thank you, Paul,'' said Kate. The deer had gone back into the pine forest when she was not looking. "Paul, what would you say if I told you that this child's symptoms were periodic?''

"Periodic? You mean varying in severity?''

"No, I mean literally periodic. That they appeared, grew critical, and then were beaten back by the child's own rebuilt system?''

This time the silence extended for almost a minute. "Auto-immunological reconstruction? WBCs rebuilt from zero? T- and B-cell levels up? Gammaglobulin levels returned to normal? From a SCID child with three hundred lymphs/mu-one as a starting point? With no histocompatible marrow transfusions, no ADA retrovirus gene therapy?''

"Correct,'' said Kate. She took a breath. "With nothing but blood transfusions.''

"*Blood transfusions*?'' His voice was almost shrill. "Before or after diagnosis?''

"Before.''

"Bullshit,'' said the researcher. Kate had never heard him use a curse word or vulgarity before. "Absolute bullshit. One, auto-immune reconstruction doesn't happen outside the comic strips. Two, any live vaccines or non-irradiated transfusions for this child prior to diagnosis would have almost certainly *killed* him . . . not brought about some miracle cure. You know the problems an allogenic transfusion would cause, Kate—fatal graft-versus-host disease, progressive generalized vaccinia—hell, you *know* what the result would be. There's something wrong with this picture . . . either a misdiagnosis on the Romanian end or a total screw-up in the T-cell study or something.''

"Yes,'' agreed Kate, knowing that the data was valid.

"I'm sorry to take up your time on this, Paul. It's just that things seem a bit muddled."

"That's an understatement," came her friend's voice. "But if anyone can straighten it out, you can, Kate."

"Thank you, Paul, I'll talk to you soon." She set the phone in its cradle and stared out at the empty meadow.

She was still staring two hours later when her secretary buzzed to tell her that Julie was there with the baby.

Even after fifteen years as a physician, Kate thought that the saddest sight on earth was a small child surrounded by modern medical equipment. Now, as a mother watching her own child submit to sharp needles and frightening equipment, she found it twice as sad.

Julie had shown up weeping and apologizing. It took several minutes for Kate to understand that the girl had set Joshua loose in his baby seat for a moment in the front seat of the Miata—"just while I put his birthday cake in that dinky little trunk"—and the child had tumbled out, hitting his forehead against the center console. There had been little bleeding, Joshua had already stopped crying, but Julie was still upset.

Kate had calmed her, shown her how slight the abrasion was—although there was going to be a serious goose egg—and then led a small parade of Josh, Julie, Kate's secretary Arleen, her office neighbor Bob Underhill—one of the world's top men on hereditary nospherocytic hemolytic anemia—and his secretary Calvin on a search for some antiseptic and a Band-Aid. Kate found it amusing, and even Julie began chuckling through her tears that there they were in the Rocky Mountain Region Center for Disease Control, a six-hundred-million-dollar research center containing state-of-the-art medical laboratories and diagnostic equipment . . . and no Mercurochrome or Band-Aid.

Finally they found some spray-on antiseptic and adhesive strips in the chief administrator's office—he was a fanatic jogger who tended to fall down a lot—Calvin brought a lollipop for Joshua, Julie left in a better mood, and Kate brought her baby down to the basement Imaging Center.

When the Center was being moved to the NCAR complex, Dr. Mauberly—chief administrator and a PhD doctor in epidemiology, *not* a medical doctor—had opposed the presence of the magnetic resonance imagers in the same complex as CDC's pride and joy, the twin Cray computers on the second floor. Mauberly and the others knew that in the early days of MR-imaging, faults in shielding had ruined wristwatches and stopped automobiles on the street outside. Or so the tales went. Dr. Mauberly wanted to take no chances with the Crays that represented a sizable chunk of RM-CDC's budget.

Alan Stevens and the other technicians had convinced the administrator that the Crays' brains and cojones were in no danger from the MR and CT scanners; Alan had shown how the basement imaging complex would be electromagnetically isolated from the rest of the world, literally a room within a room. When Dr. Mauberly had still hesitated, Alan brought in the pathologists and Class-VI Biolab glamour boys. The MR and CT equipment might not be necessary for *living* patients, they pointed out, but it was absolutely vital for the corpses—both human and animal—that were the *raison d'être* of Pathology and Biolab's daily toil. Mauberly had agreed.

Alan met Kate in the basement hallway between the imaging and sealed lab centers. Joshua had been here before and was not afraid of it, although this time there was a nasty surprise as RN Teri Halloway was waiting in the imaging room with an i.v. tube and needle. Joshua wailed as the needle was inserted on the inside of his skinny arm. Kate tried not to wince. She would have handled the transfusion herself, but Teri had a gentler touch. Sure enough, Joshua quit crying after only a *Pro forma* protest and lay back blinking. Alan and Kate helped set him onto the imaging palette, setting his head firmly in place with pillows and strips of broad tape, also taping his wrists to the pillows. It was disturbing to see, but they could not run the risk of the baby turning and moving during the imaging sequence. Not only would it ruin the CT pictures, but it would dislodge the bio-sensors Teri was setting in place so they would monitor real-time physiological changes. Kate leaned over and cooed to Joshua during the entire preparation, having his favorite stuffed animal—a Pooh bear with one eye missing—talk and play with him. He barely seemed to notice when Teri pricked his finger for the first of many blood tests. The nurse nodded at Kate, smiled at Joshua, and hurried off to the adjoining lab.

Finally Kate tucked Pooh in next to her son and left the room. Airlock-style doors slid shut behind her. She joined Alan at the bank of video monitors.

"Is his runny nose just from crying or have the flu symptoms returned?" asked Alan.

"The last three or four days," said Kate. "The diarrhea's back, too."

Alan nodded and pointed toward the bio-sensor readout. "His temperature is closing in on a hundred. And look at the results of the first test Teri took."

Kate was looking. Data from the lab was fed directly through to the MR/CT control room. According to the first test, Joshua was showing the characteristic SCID shortage of white blood cells—the WBC count was at 930 lymphocyte/μl—as well as the classic dropoff in T-cell, B-cell, and gammaglobulin levels. More than that, liver enzymes were elevated and there were indications of an electrolyte imbalance.

"Look like GVH problems to me," said Alan.

Kate tapped a pencil against her teeth. "Yes, except it's been almost a month since the last transfusion, and he showed no graft-versus-host rejection *then*. It's not the new blood his body has trouble with . . . it's his own system he seems to want to reject." She glanced at the monitor. Joshua seemed frail and insignificant strapped into his imaging cradle. She could see his mouth move as he cried, but there was no sound. Kate switched on the audio pickup and keyed the microphone so that he could hear her. "It's all right . . . Mama's right here . . . It's all right."

She nodded at Alan. "Let's do it and get him out of there."

Alan's fingers played the console as if it were a Wurlitzer keyboard. Joshua's imaging palette slid him into the CT torus, and Kate had the surreal sense that he was a tiny, human artillery shell being loaded into the breech of a plastic cannon. She watched as the display showed that the i.v.-drip had been opened to the whole blood, then as the bio-sensors began to relay Joshua's body's response to it. Three-dimensional images of his liver, spleen, and abdominal lymph nodes began to build up on the monitors.

"To do this right," said Alan, his eyes moving from monitor to monitor, "we should scan his spleen using ^{99m}Tc colloid or heat-damaged red blood cells so we could get a detailed fix on any functioning splenic tissue."

"Too invasive," snapped Kate. Her eyes stayed glued to the bio-sensor columns. "We'll stick to the CT, MR, and ultrasound," she added, her voice softer. "I don't want him to go through any more than he absolutely has to."

Alan nodded agreement. "OK," he said, "coming up to the scan of stomach wall . . . right . . . *here*."

Kate leaned over, stared at the central monitor, and frowned. "I don't see the abnormality we found last time."

"The CT can't pick up anything less than two centimeters," said Alan. "At this point we're dealing with a slightly fibrous mass, smaller and less dense than most tumors. Ultrasound isotopic imaging with ^{67}Ga- and ^{111}In-labeled leukocytes would show it was something worth worrying about, but the CT just gives us the slightest indication of an abscess . . . there, see that shadow?"

Kate did, but only because Alan's finger tapped the monitor at the precise spot. It was the shadow of a shadow. She looked back at the bio-sensor columns.

"My God," she whispered, "his temperature is at a hundred and three and rising. Stop the sequence, I've got to get in there."

Alan grasped her forearm. "No, wait . . . I've got a hunch on this, Kate. We weren't monitoring his temperature last time, just taking pictures. My guess is that whatever's going on with the redistribution of blood to that shadow organ in his stomach wall, it's burning up lots of energy."

"It's burning *him* up," said Kate. "Abort the sequence."

Alan set his hand above the red master switch, but then raised it and pointed. "Look."

Joshua's temperature now hovered at 103.5, but the other sensors showed near chaos. His blood pressure spiked, normalized, then spiked again. His heart rate was fifty percent over normal. Skin resistance traced a mountain range of changes.

Kate leaned over the console, her mouth open. "What's happening?"

Alan pushed his glasses higher on his snub nose and pointed to the primary monitor.

The shadow on Joshua's stomach wall had materialized into a vein-and-capillary-rich mass. The CT scan showed a nexus of nerves that was almost three centimeters across and growing.

"He's stabilizing," said Alan, voice tense.

Kate saw that he was right. Temperature, blood pressure, heart rate, and the other vitals were dropping back into the normal range.

"We're finished with the first sequence," said Alan. The monitor showed the palette sliding out. Joshua was squirming a bit within his restraints, but showed no signs of trauma or discomfort. He was not crying. Alan looked at Kate over the tops of his glasses. "Do you want to go in with Teri for the next round of blood and pictures or shall we scrub this right now?"

Kate hesitated only a second. The mother in her wanted to lift her son out of that torture device *now* . . . take him home *now*. The doctor in her wanted to find out what was trying to kill him, and find out *now*.

"Call Teri," she said, already heading for the airlock. "Tell her I'll help her draw the next blood sample."

The three imaging sequences took less than fifty minutes. Joshua had wet his diaper—they'd had a catheter rigged for urine samples but it had overflowed—but other than that and a lot of rage at being restrained for so long, the baby seemed fine as Kate lifted him out and rocked him while Teri and

Alan helped detach the bio-sensors. Teri took the last blood sample, pricking Joshua's big toe again, and the small room echoed to his wails.

As they left the imaging complex, Alan said, "I'll program the entire sequence to deal with different variables and have the enhanced videotapes ready to roll by eight A.M. Shall I start with T-cell rate or the adenosine deaminase curve?"

"Do the AD," said Kate. "But I want it visually all cross-referenced."

Alan nodded and made a note on a small pad.

"We'll have all the lab data back by six P.M.," said Teri. "I'll make sure McPherson handles it personally."

Kate used her free hand to pat the nurse's shoulder.

"Oops," said Teri. Joshua's Band-Aid had been loosened from rubbing against his head restraints. Teri pulled it free. "Well, I guess we don't need this old thing, do we, sweetums?"

Alan caught Kate's hesitation and sudden attention. "What?" he said, some concern in his voice.

Kate made sure that her voice was calm and level. "Nothing. I was just hoping that this doesn't screw up his nap schedule."

Swinging him around slightly, bringing out the first smile of the afternoon, Kate brought her son's forehead closer to the overhead light. She leaned closer and kissed him, her eyes only inches away from the sweet-smelling skin of his scalp.

The nasty bruise and abrasion he'd received less than two hours before were gone. No pooled blood under the skin, no sign of swelling or lingering hematoma, not the slightest sign of the raspberry rash that should have taken a week or two to fade.

The wound was *gone*. As if it never existed.

"This should be fascinating stuff," said Alan, returning to his console. "I can hardly wait."

"Me too," said Kate, looking into the baby's eyes and realizing that her heart was pounding wildly against her rib cage. "Me too."

Chapter Fifteen

ON Saturday morning Tom drove his Land Rover to
Kate's house, she loaded picnic things in her backpack, Tom
stowed Joshua in the backpack carrier, and they hiked the
easy mile to Bald Mountain. Technically, Bald Mountain was
part of the Boulder city park system, but it was far enough
away from the town not to get too many hikers and picnickers.
Kate had always loved it for its view; it was just that much
higher than her home to open up a wider vista of high peaks
and plains.

The July sun was hot and they paused several times while
climbing the hill to let the breeze cool them. At one of these
times Kate had the out-of-body view of the three of them,
Joshua well and happy on Tom's broad back, her ex-husband
grinning and not the least out of breath, the breeze ruffling
her own hair and the sunlight hot on her bare legs. She could
not help but feel a pang of loss at this snapshot of their family
that could have been.

The summit of Bald Mountain was almost devoid of trees,
which made the view that much more impressive. Kate spread
the blanket she had packed up, they set Joshua down to play,
and Tom began setting out picnic things. The sky was a
faultless arch of blue. Heat shimmered on the plains to the
east and Kate could see sunlight glimmering off windshields
on the narrow ribbon of the Boulder Turnpike to Denver.

Only the smallest pockets of snow remained on the Indian Peaks to the west.

"Deviled eggs," said Tom. "You sweet thing."

Kate hated deviled eggs, but she had remembered Tom's fondness for them. She cut a slice from the roll of French bread and folded it around some turkey. Joshua ignored the food and crawled over Tom's knee to get off the blanket and onto the grass.

Kate started an old game that she and Tom used to play on their outings. "What's that tree over there?" she asked.

Tom did not even glance behind him. "Ponderosa pine."

"I knew that," said Kate.

"Then give me a hard one."

She scooped up some of the sandy, pebbly soil they were sitting on. "What do you call this stuff?"

"Dirt," said Tom. He was building a gargantuan sandwich.

"Come on now, Balboa," she said, "be pacific." It was an old, dumb joke of theirs.

Tom used his free hand to lift a bit of the soil. "This is called gruss," he said. "It's just a worn-down version of the granite that makes up these hills."

"What wears it down?" Kate rarely grew tired of this game. Most of what she knew about nature came from talking to Tom.

"The granite?" he said and took a big bite of his sandwich. "Ice expanding and contracting. The plant roots. The acid from fungi hyphae in those lichens. Given time, living things will chew the crap out of any mountain. Then the organic stuff decomposes, we get critters burrowing in it and enriching it further when *they* decompose, and *voilà!* . . . dirt." He took another bite.

Kate ran her hand across the sparse grass and low weeds where Joshua was crawling. "And what's this?"

"Blanketflower," said Tom around his sandwich. "That jagged thing you don't want Josh to tumble into is prickly gilia. Those sharp little jobbies are mistletoe stems and the involucral bracts of gumweed. That scabby stuff on the rock is crustose lichen. That other stuff we have a sort of technical name for—''

''Which is?''

''Grass,'' said Tom and took another big bite.

Kate sighed and leaned back on the blanket, feeling the fierce sun on her skin. The breeze stirred the high grass, cooled her, and then died, allowing the sun to fill her senses again. Kate knew that she should not feel so totally content with her ex-husband and a sick child, but at the moment everything was perfect.

She opened one eye and looked at Tom. His blond hair, always thin on top, had thinned a bit more, allowing his eternal sunburn to creep higher on his forehead, but other than that detail he looked just like the overgrown boy she had met and fallen in love with fifteen years ago. He was still fit and almost obscenely healthy looking, his forearms sculpted in the muscled symmetry only rock-climbers could develop. His face, pink-skinned and unlined, fell into the pleasant, unselfconscious smile lines of someone pleased with not only where he was, but who he was. Tom greeted every day as if he had just arrived on planet earth, fresh and rested, and had too much to do and see that day to cram into twenty-four hours. On the other hand, Kate admitted, he never seemed rushed or in a hurry. Living with him had been like hiking up a mountain with him—steady, unforced, taking time to see and know the names of all the flowers, but never turning back short of the goal.

It was just, Kate realized now, that they had never agreed on a goal.

Joshua's arms slipped and he went facedown into the grass. Tom lifted him and set him down on a softer surface. The baby sat for a minute, balancing, and then teetered sideways. He began moving again, pausing only to check the taste of the soil he was creeping across. He did not like it.

Tom watched him. ''Shouldn't this guy be walking pretty soon?''

Kate pulled a strand of grass and chewed on it. ''He could be already if his development had been normal. As it is, he's still several months behind. We'll be lucky if he walks by the time he's fourteen months old.''

Tom poured them each coffee from the Thermos. "OK, why don't you tell me what the tests showed. I've been waiting all week."

Kate held the plastic cup under her chin so she could inhale the rich scent of the coffee. "The results were crazy," she said.

Tom arched an eyebrow. "You mean screwed up?"

"No, the data is accurate. It's just that the results are crazy."

"Explain." He leaned back on one elbow. His blue eyes were clear and attentive.

Kate concentrated on keeping it in layman's terms. For all of Tom's interest in the natural world, medicine—at least above the first-aid level—had never been something he spent time trying to understand.

"You remember," said Kate, "that I told you about the cyclical nature of Josh's immune deficiency problem and how it seemed to relate to the transfusion he was receiving?"

"Yeah. But you said that that shouldn't be the case. Wasn't it bone marrow, not blood, that would help the kid's immune system?"

"Right. Well, I've seen the results of our last test, and there's no doubt that the blood transfusion has brought about an amazing recovery in his immune system. Within an hour of the injection of whole blood, Joshua's WBCs were back to normal—''

"What's WBC?" asked Tom. He was watching the child crawl while he listened.

"White blood cells." Kate took another sip of coffee. "More than that, his T-cell and B-cell count shot back up to normal. Above normal, actually. His gammaglobulin levels peaked. And the weirdest part is, the enzyme I told you about—the one that's totally lacking in his system?"

"Adenosine something," said Tom.

"Adenosine deaminase. Right. Well, his ADA count had returned to normal within an hour of the transfusion."

Tom frowned. "But that's good . . . isn't it?"

"It's great," said Kate, trying not to get emotional, "but it's *impossible*."

"Why?"

Kate lifted a twig and drew a circle in the pebbly soil as if she could explain it all with diagrams. "ADA deficiency is a *genetic* failure," she said. "The gene for ADA is on chromosome 20. We know how it works, although we're not sure *why* it's so important. I mean, the reason for toxicity of adenosine metabolites isn't totally resolved, but we know it has something to do with inhibition of nucleotide reductase by deoxyadenosine triphosphate—"

"Whoa!" said Tom and held up one hand. "Back to why it's impossible."

"Sorry." Kate rubbed out the circle and squiggles in the soil. "It's a *genetic* defect, Tom. The gene is either there or it isn't. We can look at one of Joshua's red blood cells and see whether ADA is being produced or not."

"Is it?"

Kate chewed her lip. "No. I mean, no it's not being produced naturally. But, after a transfusion, his immune system suddenly comes up to snuff and he produces ADA like it's going out of style."

Tom nodded. "But you don't see *how* he's getting this new ability to create the stuff. I mean, you can't borrow a gene from somebody's blood, right?"

"Exactly. The only way we can get that ADA-producing gene into children with SCID—this immune problem—is either to have a bone-marrow transplant from a twin or via a newfangled gene-therapy program that's just been developed where you splice the human gene into the patient by using a virus—"

Tom blinked. "A *virus*? Wouldn't that make the patient sicker?"

Kate shook her head. "Viruses don't have to be harmful. In fact, most are harmless. And for the gene therapy, retroviruses are perfect."

Tom whistled. "Retroviruses. We're in AIDS territory here, aren't we, Kate?"

Still almost lost in thought, Kate nodded. "That's what makes this kind of gene therapy so interesting. The HIV retrovirus really shook us up because it's so lethal, but the cloned retroviruses the gene therapists use are harmless. Retroviruses don't even screw up the cell they're invading. They just break into the cell, insert their own genetic programming there, and let the cell go about its business."

Tom sat up and poured more coffee for each of them. Joshua had crawled in a full circle and now returned to play with Tom's shoelaces. He managed to tug one until it was untied. Tom grinned and untied the other one for him. "So you're saying that this gene therapy could save Joshua's life by getting some harmless retrovirus in there to fake out the cells into producing ADA."

"We could," said Kate, sipping at her coffee, gaze unfocused, "but we don't *have* to. Somehow Josh uses the blood we inject to do the same thing. Somehow his body breaks down the genetic structure of that blood, finds the cellular building blocks it needs to overcome his own body's immune deficiency, and trucks it around his system within an hour."

"How?" said Tom. He ruffled the dark fuzz on Joshua's head.

"We have no idea. Oh, we've found what Alan calls a 'shadow organ'—a thickening of the stomach wall that might be the site where blood is absorbed and deconstructed for its constituent genetic parts—and my guess is that Joshua's body carries its own neutral virus to disseminate the new genetic information around his body, but the actual mechanism is unknown to us."

Tom lifted the child high. Joshua's face showed a second of alarm and then filled with pure pleasure. Tom swung him around in an airplane and set him back on the grass. "Kate," he said, "are you saying that your child is a mutant of some sort?"

Kate paused in the act of getting out jars of the baby's

applesauce and strained carrots. "Yes," she said at last, "that's exactly what I seem to be saying."

Tom leaned over and touched her wrist. "But if his mutation allows his body to overcome its own whatchamacallit deficiency, beat the immune-system problem, then it may hold the cure for—"

"For AIDS," finished Kate, her voice raw. "And for cancer. And for God knows how many other scourges we've had to suffer throughout the whole history of humankind."

"Jesus Christ," whispered Tom, looking at Joshua in a strange way.

"Yes," said Kate, and opened the jar of applesauce to feed her baby.

Kate had not planned for it to happen that night. She and Tom had come close to making love several times in the years after their divorce, but each time one or the other or both of them had thought better of it. In the past couple of years, their new relationship as friends had seemed too important to jeopardize by resuming a sexual relationship which each knew to be an emotional dead end.

But this Saturday night had been different. It was just the two of them and Joshua in the house; Julie was off on an alpine-flower collecting tour somewhere near Lake City. They had barbecued chicken out on the patio, moved around to the terrace on the west side to watch the sun set north of Long's Peak, and sat drinking wine and talking until the sky was strewn with stars. It had seemed natural when Tom had finally set down her wineglass, taken her hand, and led her into the bedroom they had shared until six years ago.

Their lovemaking had been urgent but gentle, heightened by the unselfconsciousness that only an intimate familiarity with the other person's body can bring, and tinged a bit with sadness as they lay in each other's arms afterward.

"Would it be better if I left?" Tom had whispered sometime after midnight.

Kate had stirred against him, set her hand on his chest. Tom no longer lived near Boulder, but in a renovated cabin near Rollins Pass, an hour's drive away up Boulder Canyon and south along the Peak to Peak Highway. The thought of him driving it so late at night made her heart sad. "No," she whispered, "it's all right. Julie won't be back until late tomorrow evening. I have some bagels in the freezer and Toby's going to deliver the *Times* when he comes up to work on the satellite dish tomorrow morning."

Tom had touched her head gently. One of the few rituals of their marriage that each had enjoyed had been a slow Sunday morning with bagels, coffee, and *The New York Times*.

He kissed her on the lips. "Thanks, Kat. Sleep well."

"Same to you," Kate had mumbled, already sliding into a contented sleep.

She awoke suddenly and completely. The alarm clock dial read 3:48 A.M. Kate was sure that she had heard something. For a relieved second she remembered that Tom had stayed and assumed she had heard him padding around in the bathroom, but when she sat up in bed she realized that he also was sitting up in bed, listening. There came a second sound from down the hall.

Tom put his hand on her mouth and whispered "Shhh" in her ear. Another soft sound came from the dining room.

Tom leaned close again and whispered, "Would Julie be up here if she came back early?"

Kate shook her head. She could hardly hear her own answering whisper for the pounding of her heart. "Her rooms are downstairs. She never comes up at night."

She could see Tom's head silhouetted against the faint starlight from the patio. A chair in the dining room was bumped softly. Kate heard the loose floorboard squeak at the far end of the hall.

Tom slid noiselessly out of bed but leaned close to whisper in her ear again. "Is the twelve-gauge where I left it?"

For a second the question did not register, but then Kate remembered the argument about the shotgun that Tom had insisted she keep if she was going to live alone out here. They had compromised when he had put it far back in the unused corner of her closet. She'd meant to get rid of the thing, but after a while she had just forgotten about it. She nodded.

"Did you load it the way I told you to?" he whispered.

There was another squeak in the hallway. Heart pounding, Kate shook her head.

"Shit," whispered Tom. He was crouched by the side of the bed. His lips touched her ear again. "Is the box of shells still on the top shelf?"

"I think so," whispered Kate. Her mouth was terribly dry. She strained to hear any sound. Suddenly a door creaked and she swung herself out of bed. "The baby's room!" she said aloud.

Tom moved incredibly fast. The closet door slid open with a bang that almost made Kate scream, he flicked the light on, came out with the pump shotgun and a yellow box of shells, stopped Kate from running down the hall by pressing his hand flat against her chest before she could get out the bedroom door, and shouted, "We have a gun!" as he fed three shells into the magazine.

They both heard Joshua's door slamming open.

Tom was out the door and down the hall in an instant, slapping light switches as he ran. Kate was a half-second behind him. She froze as she stumbled through the doorway into Joshua's room.

A tall man dressed in black was bending over Joshua's crib. In the second before Tom hit the light switch in the room, Kate saw only the black shape looming over her baby, the man's thin face illuminated by the night-light next to the crib. His fingers were long, gloved, and reaching for her son.

Tom snapped on the light and crouched with the shotgun pointed. "Don't move a fucking muscle!" he shouted, his voice strong and in command. He was still naked; his body looked tanned and powerful to Kate rather than made vulnerable by the nudity.

The intruder was wearing some sort of black balaclava, but his face was uncovered. He had a wide gash of a mouth, long nose, heavy brows, and eyes that looked like black pits to

Kate. *This is a nightmare*, she thought through the frenzied pounding of her heart.

Kate was sure the intruder would use the baby as a shield, but the man stared at Tom from the black pits of his eyes and then lifted his spidery hands and stepped away from the crib. Tom shifted to his left to keep the field of fire away from the baby, and Kate slid along the wall behind him.

"Freeze," Tom commanded and pumped a shell into the chamber.

The man in black seemed to nod, and then everything happened very fast.

Kate had seen Tom's reflexes in action before—catching a rafter who had gone over the side in heavy rapids, going on belay to arrest her fall while teaching her to rock-climb, once leaping to stop Kate from a nasty collision with a rock while glissading down a snowfield—but the man in black moved so quickly that even Tom did not have time to react. One second the intruder was ten feet across the room, arms extended, and the next instant the black form was hurling across the carpet in a tuck and roll, then exploding upright under the shotgun, hands going for Tom's throat.

Tom was the strongest man Kate had ever known, but the intruder lifted him like a child and tossed him across the room. A mobile came crashing down, Tom slammed into the framed N.C. Wyeth print on the far wall, and then he bounced and rolled while the man in black leaped after him. Somehow Tom had held on to the shotgun.

"Down, Kate!"

She had run toward the crib but dropped to the floor on Tom's command. Kate saw a glimmer against the black gloves and realized that the man had a blade in his hand and that the hand was rising above where Tom was sprawled . . .

Kate's scream and the shotgun blast were simultaneous.

The intruder's downward leap suddenly reversed itself as if a film were being run backward; he flew up and back, slammed against the wall where Kate had been standing a moment earlier, and slid to the floor. He left a trail of blood and black wool on the ducks-and-airplanes wallpaper.

Kate ran to the crib and lifted Joshua out. The baby was screaming, face red with terror at the sudden sounds, but he looked unharmed.

Tom got to his feet, his left arm obviously injured, and approached the fallen man carefully. The knife the man had held now lay on the carpet. Kate had never seen anything so short and deadly. It had no handle, no hilt, merely a flat knob that she guessed would fit in the palm of his hand. Both sides of the blade were obviously razor sharp.

"Careful!" began Kate as Tom turned the slumped form over with his foot. She caught her breath. The shotgun blast had torn a foot-wide hole in the man's chest and upper abdomen, while some of the pellets had struck his throat and face. There was much blood. Kate stared for a long second before her medical training took over. She kissed Joshua, set him back in his crib, and crouched next to the man. Blood wicked onto the hem of her silk nightgown and she brusquely flipped it out of the way, tore the remnants of the man's black sweater open, and felt for a pulse at the base of his neck. There was none. The intruder's eyes were slightly open but the pupils had rolled up until only the whites showed.

"Call 911 and tell them to have an ambulance dispatched from Community," she said. She arched the man's head back and opened his mouth to clear it of blood and tissue fragments.

"Oh, Jesus, Kate . . . don't give that asshole mouth-to-mouth. Besides, he's dead."

"I know," said Kate, bending closer, "but we have to try."

Tom cursed and set the shotgun against the wall. Lifting Joshua, he stepped toward the door. Kate fought down a sudden surge of nausea and lowered her face toward the dead man's.

The intruder's eyes snapped open like an owl's, Kate screamed, and he shoved her aside and vaulted to his feet, leaping toward Tom and the baby.

Tom turned instinctively, shielding Joshua from the stranger. The man landed on Tom's back and Joshua tumbled to the floor and rolled under the crib, screaming.

The man in black threw Tom against the wall and leaped for him, long fingers going for his throat. Tom met the attack with a stiff arm and upraised palm that flattened the intruder's nose like a pulped tomato. The man snarled—the first sound that Kate had heard from him—and threw Tom ten feet through the open screen door to the balcony. Then he pivoted, reminding Kate of a giant spider, and began scrabbling under the crib to get at Joshua.

Kate's first and strongest impulse had been to get to her child. But her brain had overridden her instinct, and she had left Joshua under the crib while she crawled across the carpet to the shotgun.

The intruder saw what she was doing. He gave up reaching for the screaming child and leaped to his feet and bounded across the room toward her.

Later, Kate did not remember pumping another shell into the chamber or lifting the weapon. Nor could she remember pulling the trigger.

But she would always remember the terrible blast, the sight of the man catapulted backward through the glass of the sliding door, and the terrible angle of his body sprawled across the balcony overlooking the ravine. Tom had just gotten to his knees and now he shielded himself from a hailstorm of shattered glass.

Kate staggered to her feet and stepped forward, staring through the smashed glass at the intruder's body. This blast had almost separated his left arm from his torso. She could see exposed ribs gleaming.

"Kat!" shouted Tom at the same instant the intruder jackknifed forward and seized her ankle.

She went down hard on her back, her head hitting the leg of the crib. The man pulled himself through the shattered door, using just his right arm.

Dazed, only half-conscious, forgetting her Hippocratic Oath and her lifelong pledge of non-violence, she raised the Remington, pumped the last shell in, and shot the man in the chest and face from point-blank range even as he reached past her for Joshua.

This time the blast knocked the man out the door, across the patio, and over the railing into the sixty-foot ravine below.

And then Kate remembered nothing except Joshua in her arms, still crying but unhurt, and Tom's arm around her, Tom's voice soothing her as he led her into the lighted living room and called the police.

Chapter Sixteen

KATE had been on the ER end of ambulance runs during her residency years ago, but it was as if she had never seen paramedics in action on site before. They arrived ten minutes before the police and seemed to take the blood- and glass-filled nursery for granted. One of the men went to check for signs of the intruder in the ravine while the remaining male and female paramedics set Tom's dislocated shoulder, pulled shards of glass from his back, and checked Kate and Joshua over and pronounced them unhurt. Kate and Tom both pulled on some clothes in preparation for the next wave of officialdom.

Three Boulder police cars and the sheriff's 4 × 4 arrived at the same time, blue and red lights flashing across the meadow and shimmering on the windows. The paramedics were trying to get Tom to go to the hospital, but he refused; the detectives interviewed Tom in one room, Kate in the other. She never let go of Joshua.

Powerful flashlights were probing the ravine when Tom and Kate pulled on their jackets, bundled Joshua in a heavy blanket, and stood at the edge of the patio to watch.

"It's at least eighty feet down there," said the sheriff. "And there's no way down to the stream except down this cliff."

"It's less than sixty feet," said Tom, standing at the edge

of the granite and sandstone bluff. The shrubs there were broken and torn. Kate could hear the stream trickling at the bottom of the ravine; it was a sound she had grown so used to that she normally ignored it.

"The body could have washed downstream," said the chief Boulder detective. He was young and bearded and had dressed hurriedly in sweatshirt and chinos under a corduroy jacket.

"The stream's pretty shallow this time of year," said Tom. "No more than six or eight inches of water in the deeper spots."

The detective shrugged. The sheriff's men were rigging a Perlon climbing rope around the large ponderosa pine at the edge of the patio.

"You're sure you didn't recognize the man?" asked the detective sergeant for the third time.

"No. I mean, I'm sure," said Kate. Joshua was sleeping in the folds of blanket, the pacifier still in his mouth.

"And you don't know how he got in?"

Kate looked around. "The sheriff said that the kitchen door had been jimmied. Is that correct, Sheriff?"

The sheriff nodded. "Pane cut out. Both inside locks opened. It looked fairly professional."

The detective made a note and looked over to where the sheriff's people and the paramedics were arguing about how to rig the ropes. Uniformed police officers walked along the edge of the ravine, shining flashlights down into the darkness.

The chief detective came out of the house holding a plastic baggie. Kate saw the gleam of steel in it. He held it up to the light. "Know what this is?" he asked.

Kate shook her head.

"Fancy little palm knife," he said, showing her how it was held, the steel knub against his palm, the double-edged blade protruding between the knuckles of two fingers. The detective turned to Tom. "He had this in his hand when he came at you?"

"Yeah. Excuse me a second, Lieutenant." Tom walked over to the sheriff's deputies and quietly showed them how the Perlon lines had to be rigged. Then he borrowed a web harness from a paramedic and clicked a carabinier in place as if to demonstrate how to prepare for a rappel.

"Hey!" shouted the deputy as Tom leaned back, one arm still in a sling, and gracefully rappelled over the edge of the cliff.

A paramedic tied on to his own line and followed him down the cliff. The uniformed officers swung their lights onto the duo as they bounced down rock and dropped gently into the shrubs and dwarf juniper at the base of the cliff. Tom looked up, waved with his good hand, and unclipped from the Perlon line. Deputies scurried to hook on and follow.

The sun came up before the search was called off. Kate had carried Joshua into the house and tucked him in her own bed; when she came back out, Tom was pulling himself easily up the rock face with one arm while the deputies and paramedics huffed and puffed to climb with both arms busy.

He stepped onto the patio, unclipped his carabinier, and shook his head.

"No body," gasped a deputy coming over the edge. "Lots of blood and broken branches, but no body."

The detective sergeant took out his notebook and stepped close to Kate. He looked tired and the brilliant morning light gleamed on gray stubble. "Ma'am, you're sure you hit this guy with both shotgun loads?"

"Three times," said Tom, putting his good arm around her. "Twice at ranges of less than four feet."

The detective shook his head and stepped back to the bluff. "Then it's just time until we find the body," he said. "Then maybe we'll figure out who he was and why he was trying to kidnap your baby."

Tom nodded and went into the house with Kate.

On Monday, Ken Mauberly called Kate into his office. She had been expecting the invitation.

Mauberly was the chief administrator for the Rocky Mountain Region CDC, but his office was the only one in the

NCAR/CDC complex without windows. He said that the view distracted him. Kate sometimes thought that this choice of an office said much about the character of the man: quiet, dedicated to work, self-effacing, competent, and fanatical only about his long-distance running.

He waved her to a seat and slouched in his own chair. His jacket was draped over the back of the chair, his tie was loosened, and his sleeves were rolled up. He leaned across the desk and folded his hands. "Kate, I heard about the problem you had Saturday night. It's terrible, just terrible to have your home invaded like that. Are you and the baby all right?"

Kate assured him that they were fine.

"And the police haven't caught the assailant?"

"No. They found some signs that he might have left the stream about half a mile below the house, but there's been nothing definite. They've put out some sort of bulletin based on the description Tom and I gave them."

"And your ex-husband is all right?"

Kate nodded. "His arm was injured slightly, but this morning he was pressing weights with it." She paused. "Tom is staying with us . . . with Julie and the baby and me . . . until they find the guy or we all get our courage back."

Mauberly tapped a pencil against his cheek. "Good, good. You know, it's funny, Kate. I've opposed capital punishment all of my adult life, but if I woke as you did to find someone in my child's bedroom . . . well, I wouldn't hesitate a second to end that person's life on the spot." Embarrassed, he set the pencil on the desk.

"Ken," said Kate, "I appreciate the sentiments, but you wanted to talk to me about something else, didn't you?"

The administrator leaned back in his chair and steepled his fingers. "Yes, Kate, I did. I haven't had a chance to tell you what a fine job you did on the Romanian tour . . . both while you were there and in the report you did afterward. Billington and Chen at the WHO tell me that it was pivotal in helping form policy toward the relief effort. Pivotal."

Kate smiled. "But what have I done for you recently?"

Mauberly returned the smile. "That's not quite how I'd put it, Kate. But it has been a couple of months since you've gone full time into another project. I'd hoped that you'd head up the Colorado Springs Hepatitis-B investigation . . . not that Bob Underhill isn't capable, don't misunderstand me, but—"

"But I've spent a lot of my time and the Center's resources in trying to cure my son," Kate said softly.

The administrator rubbed his fingers together. "That's totally understandable, Kate. What I'd hoped to do with you is discuss some alternatives. A friend of mine, Dick Clempton, is at Children's Hospital in Denver, and he's one of the best ADA men in—"

Kate unsnapped her briefcase, removed a thick file, and shoved it across the desk to her boss. Mauberly blinked.

"Read it, Ken," she said.

Without another word he pulled his glasses out of his shirt pocket and began reading. After the third page, he took his glasses off and stared at her. "This is hard fact?"

Kate nodded. "You see who signed the imaging and lab reports. Donna McPherson has repeated the tests twice. There's no doubt that the patient's body . . . Joshua's body . . . is somehow cannibalizing the necessary genetic components to reinvigorate its own immune system."

Mauberly glanced through the rest of the papers, skimming the more technical pages to read the conclusions. "My God," he said at last. "Have you conferred with anyone outside the Center?"

"I've gotten some ideas without revealing all of what you're looking at," said Kate. "Yamasta at the Georgetown University International Center for Interdisciplinary Studies of Immunology, Bennet at SUNY Buffalo, Paul Sampson at Trudeau . . . all good people."

"And?"

"And none of them have even a hypothesis how a SCID child can effect a spontaneous remission of such marked hypogammaglobulinemia with just blood transfusions as a catalyst.''

Mauberly rubbed his lower lip with the earpiece of his glasses. ''And do you? Have a hypothesis, I mean.''

Kate took a deep breath. She had not suggested such a thing to anyone yet. But now everything depended on sharing her thoughts with her boss: not just the incredible breakthroughs she thought might be possible, not just her job, but Joshua's life.

''Yes,'' she said, ''I have a theory.'' Unable to stay seated, Kate stood and leaned on the back of her chair. ''Ken, imagine a group of people—an extended family, say—living in a remote region of an isolated Eastern European country. Say that family has suffered from a severe but classic case of SCID . . . a form of the disease that exhibited all four strains: reticular dysgenesis, Swiss-type, ADA deficiency, and SCID with B lymphocytes.''

Mauberly nodded. ''I'd say that family would die out in a generation.''

''Yes,'' said Kate and leaned farther forward, ''unless there were a cellular or physiological mutation in that family—passed on only through recessive genes—which allowed it to cannibalize genetic material from donor blood so that their own immunodeficiency was overcome. Such a group could survive for centuries without being noticed by medical authorities. And given the rarity of the double recessive appearing, few offspring would be born with either SCID or the mutational compensation.''

''All right,'' said Mauberly, ''assuming there are a few people—a very few people—in the world with this accelerated immune response. And the child you adopted is one of them. *How* does it work?''

Kate went over the broad outlines of the data, never talking down to Mauberly as layman—he was too brilliant and too conversant in medical realities for that—but also never getting bogged down in either overly technical details or idle speculation.

''All right,'' she summarized, ''this indicates that—one,

Joshua's body has a way of adapting human blood as a repair mechanism for his own immunodeficiency; two, there is someplace—possibly that blood-rich shadow organ Alan isolated—where the blood is broken down; three, the constituent genetic material is disseminated throughout his body to catalyze the immune system."

"How?" said Mauberly. The administrator's eyes were very bright.

Kate spread her hands in front of her the way she did when guest-lecturing at a medical school. "Best guess is that the transmitter component of Joshua's disease is a retrovirus . . . something as persistent as HIV, only with life-giving rather than fatal consequences. From the data, we know the dissemination is very rapid, much more aggressive than HIV even in its most virulent stages."

"It would have to be," interrupted Mauberly, "if it were to have any survival value for the SCID-symptomized family or families in which the mutation appeared. A *slow* immunological reconstruction would be useless when the slightest head cold in the interim would be fatal."

"*Exactly*," said Kate, unable to hide her own excitement. "But if the mutated retrovirus can be isolated . . . cloned . . . then—" She was unable to go on, despite the importance of doing so.

Mauberly's gaze was elsewhere. His voice was shaky. "It's premature, Kate. You know what we're thinking is premature."

"Yes, but—"

He held up one hand. "But the payoff would be so dramatic . . . so *miraculous*." He closed Joshua's file and slid it back across the desk to her. "What do you need?"

Kate almost collapsed into her chair. "I need time to work on this project. We'll code-name it . . . oh, RS-91 or R^3."

Mauberly raised an eyebrow.

"RS for retrovirus search and for Romanian Solution," she said with the slightest smile. "R^3 for Romanian Recessive Retrovirus."

"You'll get the time," promised Mauberly. "And the budget. If I have to sell one of the Crays. What else?"

Kate had thought it all out. "Continued use of the imaging facilities, Pathology, and at least one Class-VI lab," she said. "And the best people to go with them."

"Why the Class-VI biolab?" asked Mauberly. The expensive and supersecure facilities were used only with the most dangerous and experimental toxins, viruses, and recombinant DNA experiments. "Oh," he said, seeing the answer almost immediately, "you'll be trying to isolate and clone the retrovirus." The thought sobered him. "All right," he said at last. "You can have Chandra."

Kate nodded in surprise and appreciation. Susan McKay Chandra was CDC's superstar, one of the two or three top viral and retroviral experts in the world. She normally worked out of Atlanta but had been a temporary researcher at Boulder CDC before. *Well*, thought Kate, *I did ask for the best*.

"We'll have to submit this to the Human Bio-Ethics Review Board," began Mauberly.

Kate stood up. "No! Please . . . I mean . . ." She calmed herself. "Ken, think . . . we're not experimenting on a human being."

Mauberly frowned. "But your son . . ."

"Has undergone a few advanced but very basic medical tests," said Kate. "And he will have to submit to a few more. Blood and urine tests. Another CT scan, more ultrasound, perhaps MR, and maybe isotopic scintigraphy if we find his bone marrow involved in this . . . although I'd rather avoid that because bone imaging can be uncomfortable . . . but we are not experimenting! Just carrying out standard diagnostic techniques for isolating the kind and severity of immunodeficiency that this patient has. The Review Board will tie us up for months . . . perhaps years."

"Yes, but—" said Mauberly.

"*If* we isolate the R^3 retrovirus and *if* we can clone it to adapt it to HIV or oncological research," pleaded Kate, "*then* we can approach the Board. We would have to. But then there would be no doubt as to the need for human experimentation."

Ken Mauberly nodded, rose, and came around the desk to her. Kate rose to meet him.

Amazingly, he kissed her on the cheek. "Go," he said. "As of ten A.M. today, you are officially detached for the RS-Project. Bertha will take care of the paperwork. And, Kate . . . if we can help you or the family with the aftereffects of Saturday's problem, well, just ask . . . we'll do it."

He walked her to the office door. Outside, Kate shook her head—not only at the magnitude of what had just happened, but at her realization that for a few minutes she had forgotten all about "Saturday's problem."

Kate hurried to her office to begin planning for her team and the project ahead. She worked feverishly, almost obsessively, although she did not admit, even to herself, that it was because each time she closed her eyes she saw the pale face and dark eyes of the intruder. If she allowed time to think of anything except work, she saw those black eyes fixed on the sleeping form of her son.

Kate and Tom met with the young police detective on what should have been Kate's lunch break on Tuesday. The detective's name was Lieutenant Bryce Peterson and now, in daylight, Kate noticed that not only did he wear a beard and sloppy clothes, but his long hair was pulled back in a ponytail—what Tom referred to as a "dork knob."

The meeting was not enlightening. The lieutenant's questions went over areas that both Kate and Tom had answered before and the detective had nothing new to tell them.

"You're sure that you didn't know the suspect?" said Lieutenant Peterson. "Even casually?"

Tom sighed and ran a hand through his thinning hair, a movement that Kate knew usually warned of an imminent loss of temper. "We don't know him, never met him, haven't seen him before, aren't related to him," said Tom, his blue eyes hard. "But we *could* pick him out of a lineup if you caught him. Are you any closer to catching him, Lieutenant?"

The detective tugged absently at his mustache. "You couldn't find a match in the computer. . . ."

Kate had been slightly surprised that she and Tom had watched images tick by on a VDT the evening before; she had expected to pore through mug shots just like the old TV shows. "No," she said. "None of the pictures looked like the man."

"But you're sure you could identify him if you did see him again?" asked the lieutenant. His voice was vaguely nasal, vaguely irritating.

"We *said* we could identify him," snapped Tom. "You tell us what the hell happened to him."

The lieutenant flipped through some paperwork as if the answer were there. Reading the upside-down papers, Kate could see that they were about some other case. "Obviously the thief was wounded, but not so severely he could not escape," said the lieutenant. "We have notices out to all area hospitals and clinics in case he seeks aid there."

"Wounded?" said Kate. "Lieutenant, this man was shot three times, at close range, by a shotgun."

"Twelve-gauge Remington loaded with number-six shot," Tom added dryly.

"By a shotgun," continued Kate, attempting and succeeding to keep her voice low and reasonable. "The first shot opened up his chest and did serious damage to his throat and jaw. The second shot almost took his left arm off and left ribs exposed. Lieutenant, I saw the damage. God knows what the third blast did to him . . . and the fall. You saw yourself that the cliff is almost vertical there."

The police detective nodded and stared at her blankly. His eyelids were heavy with that tired, hooded look that some men affected; Kate knew women who found that look sexy . . . she had always thought that it signified stupidity. "So?" said the lieutenant.

"So why are we talking wounded?" said Kate, her voice hard. "Why aren't we asking who carried his body away, and why?"

The lieutenant sighed as if fatigued by the questions of amateurs.

Tom set his hand on Kate's forearm before she said anything else in anger. "Why do you call him a thief?" he asked softly. "Why not kidnapper?"

The young cop looked up, eyes heavy. "There's no evidence that the suspect was attempting a kidnapping."

"He was in the *nursery!*" shouted Kate. "He was reaching for the *baby!*"

Lieutenant Peterson stared at her impassively.

"Look," said Tom, obviously trying to find some middle ground to keep the discussion from deteriorating further, "we understand that there are no prints because the guy was wearing gloves. His face isn't in your computer. But you have blood samples from the rocks and plants in the ravine . . . bits of clothing that tore on the way down . . . couldn't you use that? Or give it to the FBI?"

The lieutenant blinked slowly. "Why do you think the FBI would be involved in a local matter?"

Kate ground her teeth. "Doesn't the FBI usually get involved in kidnappings or attempted kidnappings?"

The lieutenant did not blink. "But, Doctor Neuman, we have no evidence that this was an attempted kidnapping. You live in a wealthy area. Your home has lots of expensive art, electronic equipment, silverware . . . it's an obvious target for—"

"Come on, Kat," said Tom, rising and taking her hand. "Your lunch hour's up, my patience is used up. Lieutenant, you let us know if there's any news at all, OK?"

Lieutenant Peterson gave them his best Don Johnson look.

In the car, driving her back up the hill to CDC, Tom opened the glove compartment and handed Kate a small wooden box. "Open it," he said.

She did, and said nothing, only looked at her ex-husband.

"Nine-millimeter Browning semiautomatic," Tom said. "I got it from Ned at the sports shop. We'll go out after work tomorrow and practice with it. From now on, it stays in the nightstand drawer."

Kate said nothing. She closed her eyes, saw the pale face and black eyes, and—for the hundredth time since early Sunday morning—tried not to start shaking.

Susan McKay Chandra arrived in Boulder on Thursday and was not happy. Kate had always thought the virus expert beautiful; Chandra had inherited her Indian father's small stature, mocha skin tones, and jet black hair, but her bright blue eyes and fiery temper were a gift from her Scottish-American mother. That temper was in the ascendant during the thirty-minute ride from Denver's Stapleton Airport to Boulder.

"Neuman, you have no idea how important the HIV work I'm doing in Atlanta is," she snapped at Kate, who had told the van driver she would pick up the virologist.

"Yes, I do," Kate said softly. "I monitor everything of yours that comes across the net and read the Bulletin abstracts even before they go to hard copy."

Chandra crossed her arms, not mollified by praise. "Then you must know that it's sheer idiocy to drag me out here on some half-assed project while every week my team does without me may cost thousands of lives."

Kate nodded slowly. "Look," she said. "Give me two hours. No . . . make that ninety minutes. If I can't convince you by noon, I'll buy you lunch at the Flagstaff House, get you a first-class ticket on the three P.M. Delta flight back to Atlanta, and drive you to the airport myself."

Chandra's blue eyes were not hostile, merely unrelenting. "Tough talk, Neuman. But I'll take you up on it. I'm afraid that nothing short of the Second Coming is going to convince me to stay away from my team."

As it turned out, it took a little less than an hour of going over the data in Kate's office. "Jesus H. Christ," Chandra all but whispered when they had reviewed the last file. "This child may be the biological equivalent of the Rosetta Stone."

Goosebumps rose along Kate's arms. "You'll stay then? At least until we get an idea how to isolate this retrovirus?"

"Will I stay?" laughed the other woman. "Just try to get rid of me, Neuman. How soon can we get into the Class-VI here?"

Kate glanced at her watch. "Will ten minutes be soon enough?"

Chandra stood a moment at the window, staring at the Flatirons. "Why don't we say ninety minutes. I think I'll buy you dinner at Flagstaff House. It may be a long time before either one of us takes time for a civilized meal again."

The letter from Lucian arrived four days later. Kate read it after coming home from work at nine-thirty P.M., almost too tired to check in on Joshua in his newly repainted nursery. Then she took a shower, said goodnight to Julie, went into the study where Tom was preparing his checklist for a Canyonlands trek, and sorted the mail. The sight of Lucian's letter made her heart skip in a strange and unexpected way. It had been sent via International Federal Express.

Dearest Kate and Little Joshua:

The summer progresses in Bucharest, the markets are much emptier than when you were here, the terrible heat is here, and so am I. There will be no residency in America; at least not this autumn. My uncle and his family cannot afford to make the loan to me, my father has much fame as a poet but no money (of course! he is a poet!), and no U.S. University has offered to sponsor me despite your eloquent (if true) letter of recommendation praising me as the most exciting discovery since Jonas Salk.

Ah, well, enough of my troubles. I will spend another fun-filled winter in beautiful Bucharest and then begin the application process again in the spring.

And how is my favorite hematologist and her new son? I trust this finds you both well. I would be concerned for Joshua's condition if I did not have unlimited faith in your medical abilities, Kate, as well as in the almost miraculous resources, medically speaking, in the U.S. of A.

By the way, did I ever tell you the joke about the time

our late, unlamented Supreme Leader and his wife went into a district hospital to have their hemorrhoids tended to by a non-Party physician?

I did? Odd, I don't remember telling that one.

Kate—something strange and a little disturbing happened last week.

You remember that I was earning money this summer as a teaching assistant in Dr. Popescu's advanced anatomy class? Well, it has been boring, but it allowed me to take out some of my frustrations by wielding a scalpel. Anyway, one of my less enjoyable tasks is to go early to the city morgue and sort through the unclaimed bodies there and choose the best cadavers for the new students. (This is where five years of training and my family's fortune has brought me.)

Last Friday I was going through the cold-storage lockers in the morgue, trying to make my selection from the usual assortment of deceased drug addicts and unclaimed accident victims and peasants who died from malnutrition, when I found a bizarre case. The corpse had been brought in a few weeks earlier, was still unclaimed, and had been marked for cremation the day after my visit. The official cause of death was "multiple lacerations due to accident," but it only took one look to know that this man had not died from any accident.

The corpse had been drained of blood. Not of most of its blood, but all blood. Kate, you know how difficult this would be in an accident. The body was that of a man in his mid or late fifties. There had been more than a dozen pre-mortem incisions made into his torso, legs, wrists, and neck. All cuts were clean—almost as if administered by scalpels—and all were near major arteries. There was one atypical wound, very messy, running from his left ankle, splintering the lower tibia and fibula, and then repeated on the right leg and ankle. Around the smaller wounds, there were strange secondary lividity patterns. Strange, that is, until I suddenly realized the method of death.

This man had been lifted upside down and impaled on

something much like a slaughterhouse hook which had been passed through the major bones of his lower legs. While he was hanging there, still alive from all evidence, one or several people had administered these expert slashes along major arteries. The amount of blood lost in a short time must have been amazing.

But even more amazing—and disturbing—was the cause of the indentations and lividity networks around these wounds. They were teethmarks. Not bites, but more like extreme hickeys where more than half a dozen mouths had simultaneously fastened around these wounds and held lips and tongues in place during the ingestion of this man's blood. How much blood did they teach us is in the human body, Kate? About six quarts, I think.

But there is more to this delightful Romanian tale. The man's face was battered and disfigured, but still recognizable. It was our missing Deputy Minister whom the papers had theorized had fled to the West with several thousand dollars in baksheeshed American money. It was your Mr. Stancu, Kate—the helpful bureaucrat with the dead novelist's name. The man who expedited your and Baby Joshua's visa in such unprecedented time.

Well, Mr. Stancu will be expediting nothing anymore. I told no one of this grisly bit of business. Mr. Stancu was cremated in the paupers' ovens the next day.

Why am I bothering you about this terrible thing on what I am sure is a beautiful, sunny Colorado day?

I'm not sure. But be careful, Kate. Watch over yourself and our tiny friend. This is a bad place, and sometimes there are things happening here which not even I can joke about.

With love from Bucharest,

And Lucian had drawn a cartoon of a large smiley face under a raincloud.

For several minutes Kate sat holding the letter and staring out the window at the darkness where the porch lights did not reach. Then she rose, walked past where Tom was bent over his gear spread out on the study floor, went down the hall to the bedroom, slid open the nightstand drawer, and took out the loaded Browning. She was still sitting there on the edge of the bed, holding the pistol, when Tom came in half an hour later.

Chapter Seventeen

THE summer of 1991 was as wet and rainy as anyone in Boulder could remember, but still, by late August, the foothills below CDC were brown, the meadow beyond Kate's house was dust-dry and browning, and lawns in town needed daily watering. Just as the local children were heading back to school on the week before Labor Day—a schedule which Kate, born and raised in Massachusetts, found appallingly premature—the stormy weather disappeared and the forecast changed to a regular schedule of hot, dry, summer-like days.

Kate hardly noticed. The world outside her office and the CDC labs seemed more and more unreal. Rising before sunrise, at work by seven A.M., rarely home before ten or eleven at night, it might as well have been midwinter for all the sunlight and fine weather she had appreciated.

She remembered a few non-research events of the month. Tom had lost his temper when she had shown him Lucian's letter, wondering just what that "ghoulish son of a bitch" was trying to do, scare her to death?

Tom had gone on his Canyonlands trek in August, but had called her whenever he could. After returning he spent a few days at the house but then moved his stuff to an apartment in Boulder, no more than ten minutes away. He still stopped by most evenings—at first to talk to Kate, and then, as her hours in the lab grew longer and longer, to check on Julie and Joshua before he drove home.

There had been a few calls and visits from Lieutenant Peterson or the older sergeant, each time to report no progress. After a while she instructed her secretary not to interrupt her when the police called unless there were something new to report. There never was.

Kate did remember the phone call she received at home near the end of the summer.

"Neuman? Is that you?"

It was almost midnight, she had just come in—dog tired but buzzing with excitement as usual—had checked on Josh, poured herself some iced tea, and was nuking a microwave dinner. The ring of the phone had startled her. The voice on the other end seemed vaguely familiar to her tired mind, but she could not quite place it.

"Neuman? I'm sorry to bother you this late, but your babysitter said that you wouldn't be home until after eleven."

"O'Rourke!" she said, suddenly identifying the soft Midwestern accent. "How are you? Are you calling from Bucharest?"

"No, from that other drab second-world city . . . Chicago. I've rotated back to the World for a while."

"Wonderful." Kate sat on a kitchen stool and set her iced tea on the counter. She was surprised at how happy she was to hear the priest's voice. "When did you get back from Romania?"

"Last week. I've been doing my dog and pony show at parishes around the country, trying to raise money for the ongoing relief program. It's not so easy now that Romania has been out of the news for so long. It's been a busy summer . . . newswise."

Kate realized how insane the entire year had been in terms of news. First the Gulf War and the national jubilation at its quick resolution—much of which she had missed during her Romanian stint—and now the upheaval in the Soviet Union. Two weeks earlier, the morning paper had heralded Gorbachev's removal from office because of illness. That night, when she had switched CNN on for the eleven-thirty headline news, word was that Gorbie was a prisoner and that the coup might be in trouble. The next time she took a break from lab work to check the news—Wednesday the nineteenth of August—Gorbachev was back in power, sort of, and the old U.S.S.R. was breaking up forever.

Kate now realized that she had never taken time to wonder how all of this distraction and disruption might be affecting the orphanage situation in Romania. "Yes," she said at last, "it has been busy, hasn't it?"

"How about you?" asked O'Rourke. "Have you been busy?"

Kate smiled at this. She had almost grown used to the eighteen-hour days. It reminded her of her residency, although her body had been much younger and more resilient in those days. "I've kept myself out of trouble," she said, wondering at why she used that phrase even as she heard herself say it.

"Good. And how is Joshua?"

Kate could hear the anxiety in the priest's voice and realized that it took some courage for him to ask. When she had left the country she had promised to write and keep him informed about the child's welfare, but except for one note in early June, she had not taken time to do so. She remembered how sick Josh had been when they had left the country and realized that the priest must half-expect to hear of the baby's death.

"Joshua's good," she said. "Almost all of the symptoms have been stabilized, although he still requires a transfusion about every three weeks." She paused. "We're doing some experiments on the cause of his problem."

"Good," O'Rourke said at last. It was obvious that he had hoped to hear more. "Well, there is a reason for this late-night call."

Kate glanced at the kitchen clock and realized that it must be almost one A.M. in Chicago.

"I'll be bringing my plea for funds to the Denver Council

of Churches next month—on September twenty-sixth, to be precise—and I wondered if you'd like to get together for coffee or something. I'll be in Denver all weekend.''

Kate felt her heart accelerate and frowned at the response. ''Sure,'' she said. ''I mean, I'm awfully busy right now and my guess is that I will be in September, too, but if you'd like to come out to Boulder some evening when you're here, maybe that Friday the twenty-seventh, perhaps you could come up to the house and see Josh.''

''That would be great.''

They talked schedules and directions for a moment. O'Rourke would have the use of a car, so there was no problem with his driving from Denver to Boulder. When that was finished, there was a pause for a second.

''Well,'' said the priest, ''I'll let you get some rest.''

''You too,'' said Kate. She could hear the fatigue in his voice. There was an awkward moment when neither took the opportunity to end the conversation.

''Neuman,'' he said at last, ''you were lucky to get the baby out when you did. You're aware that the government shut off new adoptions only a week or so after you left.''

''Yes.''

''Well . . . we were lucky.''

Kate tried to put a lightness in her tone. ''I didn't think that priests believed in luck, O'Rourke. Don't you believe that everything is . . . pardon the expression . . . ordained?''

She heard a sigh. ''Sometimes,'' he said, his voice very weary, ''I think that the only thing one can believe in and pray for is luck.'' She heard him shake the exhaustion out of his voice. ''Anyway, I look forward to seeing you and Joshua next month. I'll call when I get into Denver and double-check our plans.''

They had said good-bye with as much energy as they could muster. Then Kate had sat in the dark house and listened to the midnight silence.

The RS-Project continued on several fronts and each area of investigation thrilled and terrified Kate.

While she was in charge of the overall project, Chandra was the actual boss of the retrovirus search, Bob Underhill and Alan Stevens had taken over the analysis of Joshua's blood-absorbing "shadow organ," and Kate herself was trying to unlock the mechanism by which Josh's body liberated the donor RNA from blood and transcribed it to proviral DNA, ready to be distributed to cell nuclei throughout his body. Her second and more immediate goal was to devise a way for this same immune-repair mechanism to work without a massive transfusion of whole blood every three weeks.

Working with Chandra in the Class-VI lab was an education. The HIV specialist had taken less than forty-eight hours to get her "virus factory" up and running at RMR CDC. Kate had given her another three days of uninterrupted work before showing up for a briefing.

"You see," Chandra had said while showing Kate around the innermost biolab, the two of them in pressurized anticontamination suits and trailing oxygen-hose umbilici, "ten years ago we would have had to start from scratch in an attempt to isolate the J-virus."

"J-virus?" Kate had said through her intercom radio.

"Joshua virus," said Chandra. "Anyway, even five years ago we would have had to cover a lot of ground before we could find a starting place. But with the HIV research of the last few years, we can take some shortcuts."

Slightly distracted by the hiss of oxygen in the suit and the sight of technicians working with gloves and remote handlers through the clear plastic window behind them, Kate had concentrated on listening.

"You know that retroviruses are just RNA viruses that express their gene products after their RNA is transcribed to DNA by the reverse transcriptase enzyme, which has DNA polymerase and ribonuclease activities," said Chandra.

Kate did not mind being lectured on the obvious, because she knew it was just the way that Chandra framed her explanations to everyone. She nodded through the clumsy headpiece.

"So," continued Chandra, "the polymerase makes a single-stranded DNA copy of the viral RNA and then a second

DNA copy using the first template. Ribonuclease eliminates the original viral RNA. Then this new invader DNA migrates to the cell nucleus and gets integrated into the host's genome under the influence of the viral integrase enzyme and stays there as a provirus.''

Kate waited.

''Well, we assume that the J-virus behaves just like any other retrovirus,'' said Chandra, lifting a culture dish and setting it closer to a technician's gloved hand. ''Only we're guessing that it models itself after the HIV life cycle . . . or perhaps HIV mutated from the J-virus, we just don't know. At any rate, we're working on the assumption that J-virus follows the path of least resistance and binds gp 120 glycoprotein to CD4 receptors in T-helper lymphocytes, mononuclear phagocytes, and Langerhans cells. Now my research has shown that our old friend HIV never infects cells without CD4, but we don't know that about J. But CD4 is still the obvious place to start.''

Kate had understood immediately. The HIV provirus had infected cells and obstructed the immune response; the J-virus, according to Chandra's reasoning, broke down RNA the same way, transcribed it to DNA the same way, and invaded cell nuclei the same way, but *enhanced* rather than inhibited the cell's immune system. ''You're assuming the same vector for proviral integration,'' said Kate, ''but trying to find its footprints after transcription.''

''Of course,'' said Chandra. ''We can compare the cells after reverse transcriptase to the control cultures and find out just how the little fucker operates.'' She glanced at Kate. ''The J-virus, I mean.''

Kate ran her gloved hand over the counter and stopped it next to a cultured specimen of Joshua's blood. There were thirty-four similar cultures on this counter alone. Farther down the line were row upon row of HIV and SCID-cultured specimens sent from CDC Atlanta. ''Where do these come in?'' asked Kate, gesturing toward the infected cultures.

''Assuming that the J-virus doesn't differentiate between your son's SCID-infected cells and other SCID specimens—

and there's no reason it should, retroviruses don't discrimi-nate—then, theoretically, we can observe the action during the binding to CD4 cells in the precultured SCID templates.''

Kate looked at the other woman through their double layers of plastic. The experiments had been proceeding only a few days at this point, but she needed answers for her own work. "And have you witnessed what you expected to?" she asked, being careful to keep her voice steady.

"Shit," said Chandra. She had started to rub her nose before remembering that she was in a pressure suit. She wiggled to scratch the tip of her nose against her gloved hand through the suit's plastic window. "Sorry. Oh . . . yes, we've documented the J-binding to both the patient's SCID cells and the precultured specimens. It's close to the HIV model." Chandra was one of those researchers who almost seemed to lose interest in the previous step of a project once that step was accomplished. But Kate had deliberately allowed the woman several days of work without the interruption of briefings or memoranda; now she needed answers.

"When HIV binds to CD4," said Kate, looking at her adopted son's culture as if she might see some activity there, "the infection of T-lymphocytes creates some cytopathic ef-fects and obvious . . . footprints, I think you called them . . . such as formation of multinucleated synctia as the gp 120 on the surface of infected cells fuse with the CD4 of other CD4-bearing cells. That's at least part of the reason we see such a dramatic loss of helper T cells despite the fact that the HIV retrovirus is infecting just . . . oh, 1 in 10^5 CD4 cells in the blood."

Chandra looked at her as if she had forgotten that Kate was a research hematologist. "Yes?"

Kate kept sharpness out of her voice. "So do you see the same synctia formation?"

Chandra shook her head. "I helped pioneer the treatment of injecting HIV-positive victims with recombinant soluble CD4 protein to slow the infection at that point by inhibiting synctium formation. But it wouldn't work in the case of the J-virus."

Kate's heart sank. "Why not?"

"The J-viral integrase enzyme doesn't transfer the invading transcribed DNA on the 1 in 10^4 or 1 in 10^5 of the blood cells that we're used to here, Kate." Chandra's eyes through the reflective plastic looked very intelligent and very bright.

"What is the ratio?" asked Kate. If it were too small, the chances of cloning an artificial J-virus would go down markedly.

"From the first few hundred samples checked," said Chandra, her voice constrained, "we estimate 98.9 percent infection."

Kate felt as if someone had hit her in the stomach. She checked to make sure that the counter behind her was empty and sat on it. "Ninety-eight point nine?"

"That is conservative."

Kate shook her head. AIDS killed its host by infecting one out of every thousand or ten thousand white blood cells. The J-virus was so efficient that almost all of the cells in the host's body were reprogrammed within hours of infection.

"Cytotoxicity?" said Kate. Such a rapid and universal infection of cell nuclei must have terrible side effects.

Chandra shrugged. "Microbiologically . . . zip. Transfer and the transfection process require mucho energy, of course . . . but you've documented that with the baby's temperature rise during the process. The child is a chemical and genetic crucible after this blood absorption and reconstruction. But the deed is essentially done after a few hours, although our preliminary research suggests that it would take a week or so for complete genetic assimilation."

Kate gestured with a gloved hand toward the other cultures. "And the HIV specimens?"

Chandra blinked. "Because we're so familiar with HIV diagnosis through viral detection, I'm using that as a second control. We take the patient's blood—sorry, Joshua's—and co-culture it with the template SCID's and HIV, using a CD4 cell line or normal CD4 lymphocytes stimulated with phytohemagglutinin and IL-2. With the HIV virus we do an assay for reverse transcriptase on some of the cultures, the presence of p24 antigen on others. Then we cross-check that with the SCID and Joshua cultures that were done at the same time.''

"And the result?"

"Reverse transcriptase is quite visible in the J-virus cultures, although, as I said, without the cytotoxicity. The p24 antigen analysis doesn't work with the J-virus, which is a shame because with HIV patients the antigen can sometimes be detected directly in a blood sample via an enzyme-linked immunosorbent assay.''

Kate nodded. She had also hoped that this relatively simple avenue of diagnosis would be available for them.

As if to reassure Kate, Chandra hurried on. "We're still assuming that the J-virus creates a J-antibody, even though the results of the infection are immunoreconstructive rather than immunosuppressant. We should have that antibody for you today or tomorrow.''

Kate looked out at the dozen or so technicians working in the outer lab. Even though it was a shirtsleeve environment compared to the Class-VI inner lab, the technicians wore coats, surgical masks, cotton booties, and rubber gloves. Kate knew that the entire lab was pressurized, with the internal pressure lower than ambient pressure in the rest of the building. If the biolab leaked, it would leak inward. Even the apparently non-toxic J-virus was considered guilty until proven innocent.

"What techniques are you using to isolate the antibody?" asked Kate.

"The usual—enzyme immunoassay, Western blot, immunofluorescence, radioimmuno-precipitation assay.'' Chandra's voice revealed her eagerness to get back to work.

"Fine," Kate said crisply. "From now on I'd like daily reports sent up—you can have Calvin follow you around and type them up if you want," she added quickly to head off any protests. "But Bob's blood absorption work and my hemoglobin studies will be piggybacking on your breakthroughs, so we need daily updates. And I'd like half an hour of personal briefing every Monday and Saturday.''

Kate saw Chandra's eyes flare with anger—not at the thought of giving up her weekends, Kate was sure, since she worked weekends anyway, but at the idea of wasting time *explaining* her work. But the professional side conquered the researcher's momentary pique and she merely nodded. Kate was, after all, in a position to take away all of Chandra's toys and games if she wished.

By Friday, September 5, the J-virus antibody was isolated and tagged. By Wednesday the 11th, the J-retrovirus itself had been identified. Two days later Chandra began her attempts to clone the retrovirus. The same day, she revealed her hidden agenda for co-culturing the HIV specimens: Chandra was wasting no time in experimenting with the J-virus as a possible AIDS cure. Kate was not surprised; indeed, she would have been amazed if the dedicated HIV researcher had planned anything else. As long as it did not slow down the RS-Project, Kate had no objections.

Alan and Bob Underhill had completed a hypothetical schematic of the absorption organ by Thursday, September 19, and a full-team seminar was scheduled for Wednesday the 25th so that everyone could listen and comment. By this point, getting the entire team together was only slightly more difficult than assembling a dozen of the world's political leaders, given everyone's imperative to avoid interruptions.

Kate's work on both the DNA transfer mechanism and the blood-substitute problem was also going well. Almost too well, she thought. Not only did she see a way effectively to cure Joshua of the SCID aspect of his disease, but she was confident that her work would help Chandra in the HIV breakthrough.

Things were going too well. Not in any way superstitious, Kate still had twinges of anxiety that the balance of pain in the universe would reassert itself soon.

And then, late on Sunday the 22nd of September—just another workday as far as she was concerned—the calendar in her Wizard electronic organizer told her that the next day was the autumnal equinox, that Tuesday was Joshua's birthday—or at least the day they had chosen to celebrate his birthday—and that Father Michael O'Rourke would be visiting before the end of the week.

Kate knew that—even without compromising the details of the project—she would have wonderful things to tell him. What she did not know was that within the week her life would be changed forever.

Chapter Eighteen

KATE came home early on Tuesday to celebrate Joshua's eleven-month "birthday." These monthly celebrations had been Julie's idea: at a time when she was not sure that the baby would survive another week, much less another month, it seemed important to mark every milestone. Kate had chosen the twenty-fourth at random, although she did like the evenness of the number.

"The CBS Evening News" carried a story of miners running amok in Romania, commandeering trains to take them to Bucharest, where the rioting continued in some sort of unfocused protest against the government. Kate remembered that the current regime had used "miners"—many of whom were *Securitate* agents in miners' coveralls—to brutalize their own people the year before. She watched the video images of men smashing windows, tossing Molotov cocktails at buildings, using crowbars against doors, and she wondered what was really going on in that miserable country. She was glad that she and O'Rourke were out of there and hoped that Lucian and his family were lying low.

Joshua loved his cake. Not waiting for the slow spoonful offered by Kate or Julie, he tore into his piece of cake with his hands, soon smearing enough on his face to equal the amount still on his high-chair tray. Later, cleaning his face with a washcloth and then setting him down on the floor so he could play with his wooden-penguin toy, Kate looked at her adopted son with a clinical, if not critical, eye.

On the surface, Josh was the picture of health: chubby, rosy-cheeked, bright-eyed, and beginning to show real hair rather than just a nimbus of dark fuzz. But Kate knew that this was a manifestation of the last segment of what she thought of as his "healthy-manic" swing; in a week or less, the diarrhea and listlessness would return, followed by more serious lethargy and infection. Until the next transfusion.

Kate watched her baby lie on his back and wrestle with the wooden toy—two penguins on a wooden dolly, their rubbery flippers moving and beaks clacking as the wheels turned. Not a sophisticated toy in an age when Nintendo ruled, but one which fascinated Joshua for some reason.

Kate knew from her baby books and conversations with other mothers that an eleven-month-old should be sitting and standing by himself, perhaps even walking. Joshua was just mastering crawling. She knew that "normal" eleven-month-olds could pull on some of their own clothes, lift a spoon, say several words including "Mama," and understand the word "No." Joshua could not handle clothing or a spoon, did not speak other than the occasional gibberish and rarely had to be told "no." He was a hesitant child, physically and socially. While obviously comfortable and happy with Kate and Julie, it had taken him weeks before he would relax with Tom.

Joshua dropped the penguin toy, rolled over onto his stomach, and began half-creeping, half-crawling toward the dining room.

"He's been exploring more," said Julie, her mouth half-full of cake. "This morning he headed for the front door when I let him out of his crib."

Kate smiled. Neither she nor Julie thought that Joshua suffered from mental retardation as a result of his deprived infancy, merely delayed development. Kate had sought out opinions from at least three childhood development specialist friends, and each had different opinions on the long-term effects that five months in a Romanian orphanage or hospital would have on a child. Two of the specialists had seen Joshua, and both agreed that the boy seemed normal and healthy enough, merely small for his age and slow in development. So now, watching her son creep across the living room carpet and make noises rather similar to an airplane, Kate saw the behavior of a happy eight- or nine-month-old rather than the eleven-month-old whose ''birthday'' they were celebrating.

Later, tucking him in his bed in her own bedroom, Kate lifted Joshua one final time and patted his back, smelling the talcum-and-baby scent of him, feeling the fuzz of his hair against her cheek. His tiny hand curled against her face. His breathing showed that he was already asleep, drifting into whatever dreams eleven-month-olds dreamt.

Kate set him on his stomach, pulled the covers up, and went out to talk to Julie for a while before each woman went back to her own computer terminal and her own studies.

On Wednesday the three RS-Project teams came together in the windowless meeting room near the imaging lab. In addition to the team leaders and their top assistants, Director Mauberly and two other top CDC administrators were there.

Bob Underhill and Alan Stevens opened with their presentation on the absorption organ. When they were finished, the room was filled with a shocked silence.

Ken Mauberly broke the silence. ''What you're saying is that this child . . . Joshua . . . has a specially mutated adaptation of the stomach lining which can absorb blood for nutritional purposes.''

Underhill nodded. ''But that purpose is secondary, we think. The primary reason for this mutation's existence is to break down the blood into its constituent parts so that the retrovirus—what Chandra and Neuman are calling the J-virus—can most efficiently begin the distribution of the borrowed RNA for immunoreconstruction purposes.''

Mauberly chewed on his expensive fountain pen. ''But for this to work, the child would have to *ingest* blood.''

Alan Stevens shook his head. ''No. Blood is directed through the capillaries of the absorption organ no matter how it enters the body. We estimate that it actually would take several hours longer for it to begin working there via ingestion rather than transfusion, but of course we haven't experimented with this. . . ." He paused, looked at Kate, and then looked down at his notes. Stevens cleared his throat. "No one wishes to give the patient blood to ingest, although if we are to continue the analysis of the absorption organ, this would be necessary."

Mauberly was frowning. "I don't . . . I can't see the survival value in *drinking* blood. I mean, it makes one think of . . . well . . ."

Kate stood up. "Vampires?" she said. "Bela Lugosi?"

There was a ripple of nervous laughter.

"We've all made or heard those jokes since the project began," said Kate, smiling, defusing the tension, "and it's obvious given the fact of where Joshua was born. Transylvania. Vampire country. And there may be a reason for that." She nodded to Chandra.

The virologist stood up and used a remote control to turn out the lights and advance a slide on the projector. "These charts show a projected family or clan over twenty generations, since approximately fifteen hundred A.D. to the present, illustrating the spread of the J-virus mutation within that family. Given the trait's recessive-recessive nature plus the high mortality rate one would assume with the immunodeficiency disorder which goes with the trait, you see that even if we might consider it a relatively benign mutation, its spread would not be too considerable. . . ."

Everyone worked at decoding the long strands of hypothetical family growth, the J-virus mutation strands helpfully drawn in red. After thirty seconds it was Bob Underhill who whistled. "I thought that the mutation must be new or we would have seen it before, but this shows that it could be around for centuries without spreading too widely."

Chandra nodded and advanced the slide. "Assuming for the spread of the mutation through marriage and genetic dispersion, we would still be talking about a relatively small set of survivors from the initial breeding couple—three hundred to two thousand people, worldwide." Chandra looked at

Kate. "And these people would need a relatively constant supply of whole blood for transfusions to survive into adulthood, assuming the disease continues beyond infancy, and we have no reason to believe otherwise."

It was one of the CDC bigwigs, a doctor/administrator named Deborah Rawlings, who said, "But there were no transfusions in the fifteenth century . . . or anywhere until the last century. . . ." She paused.

Kate stood in the light from the projector. "Precisely. For this trait to be passed down at all, the survivors would have had to have actually ingested blood. Literally fed blood to their children, if the children possessed the J-virus recessive-recessive. Only in the last century would transfusions have saved the J-virus mutation individuals." She waited a minute for the full impact to settle on the specialists and administrators.

"Vampires," said Ken Mauberly. "The myth has its origins in reality."

Kate nodded. "Not fanged creatures of the night," she said, "but members of a family who did have to ingest human blood in order to survive their own faulty immune systems. The tendency would be for secrecy, solidarity, inbreeding . . . the recessive-recessive traits would have been more frequent as a result, much as with the hemophilia which plagued the royal houses of Europe."

An assistant virology researcher named Charlie Tate hesitantly raised his hand as if he were a high school student.

Kate paused. "Charlie?"

The young man adjusted his round glasses. "How in the hell . . . I mean, how did that first J-virus sufferer find out that blood would save him . . . or her . . . I mean, how did someone start drinking blood?"

"In the Middle Ages," said Kate, "there are records of noblewomen who *bathed* in blood because legend had it this would make their skin more beautiful. The Masai still drink lion's blood to absorb the animal's courage. Blood has—until recent decades—been the source of superstition and awe." She paused a second, looking at Chandra. "Now, with AIDS, it's regaining that terror and mystery." Kate sighed and rubbed her cheek. "We don't know how it began, Charlie," she said softly."But once it worked, the J-virus sufferers had no choice . . . find human blood or perish."

The silence stretched on for another thirty seconds before Kate went on."Part of my work has been to end that cycle," she said. "And it looks as if I have a solution." She advanced the slide, and an image of a pig's face filled the screen.

The doctors in the room giggled despite themselves.

Kate smiled. "Most of you know about the DNX break-through on human blood substitute this past June—"

Ken Mauberly held up his fountain pen. "Refresh our overworked administrative memories, please, Kate."

"DNX is a small biotech lab in Princeton, New Jersey," said Kate."In June of this year they announced that they had perfected a way of producing human hemoglobin in pigs via genetic engineering. They've given the research to the FDA and are applying for human trials even as we speak."

Mauberly tapped his pen against his lower lip. "How does this artificial hemoglobin help in the J-virus research?"

"It's not really artificial hemoglobin," answered Kate, "merely not created in the human body." She advanced the slide carousel again. "Here you see a simplified schematic of the process. By the way, I've been working with an old friend, Doctor Leonard Sutterman, who is chief hematology consultant for DNX, as well as with Doctor Robert Winslow, chief of the Army's blood research division at the Letterman Institute of Research in San Francisco, so we're duplicating research with permission here and being careful not to tread on DNX's pending patents.

"Anyway, here is the schematic. First, the researchers extract the two human genes we know are responsible for producing hemoglobin in the human body." Kate glanced at the administrators. "Hemoglobin, of course, is the oxygen-carrying component in the blood.

"All right—having extracted the genetic information, these genes are then copied and injected into day-old pig embryos taken from a donor pig. These embryos are then inserted into the womb of a second pig, where they grow to term and are born as normal, healthy piglets. The only difference is that these pigs have human DNA in them, directing them to produce human hemoglobin along with their own pig-variety blood.''

''Excuse me, Kate,'' interrupted Bob Underhill. ''What's the percentage on that?''

Kate started to answer and then paused. ''On which, Bob? The number of successful transgenic pigs or on the amount of human hemoglobin the successful ones produce?''

Underhill spread his hands. ''Either. Both.''

''About five pigs in a thousand successfully carry the transfers,'' said Kate. ''Of those, each averages about fifteen percent of their blood cells carrying human-type hemoglobin. But DNX is working on getting the ratio up closer to fifty percent of the cells.''

She waited a second, but there were no more immediate questions. Kate advanced the slide again. ''You see here that DNX's real breakthrough is not in the genetic engineering . . . that was straightforward enough . . . but in patenting a process to purify the swine blood so that useful human hemoglobin can be recovered. This is what so excites my friends Doctor Leonard Sutterman and Doctor Gerry Sandler with the blood division of the Red Cross.''

Kate advanced the slide to an empty frame and stood a minute in the brilliant light. ''Think of it, substitute human blood . . . only much more useful than whole blood or plasma.''

''How so?'' asked Deborah Rawlings.

''Whole red blood cells are made of perishable membranes,'' said Kate. ''Outside the body they have to be refrigerated, and even then spoil after a month or so. Also, each cell carries the body's immune codes, so blood has to be matched by type if it's not to be rejected. Pure hemoglobin avoids both these problems. As a chemical, it can be stored for months . . . recent experiments show that it can even be freeze-dried and stored indefinitely. The Army's Doctor Winslow estimates that about ten thousand of Vietnam's fifty thousand battlefield fatalities could have been saved if this oxygenated blood substitute had been available.''

"But plasma already has the shelf-life attributes you're talking about," said Rawlings, "and it doesn't require expensive genetic engineering.''

"Right," said Kate, "but it *does* require human donors. Plasma availability is restricted by the same factors that mean that whole blood is sometimes unavailable. The human hemoglobin acquired via the DNX process only requires pigs.''

"A lot of pigs," said Alan Stevens.

"DNX figures that four million donor pigs could provide risk-free blood for the entire U.S. population," Kate said softly. "And it would only take about two years to grow those donor pigs.''

Bob Underhill whistled again.

Mauberly raised his fountain pen like a baton. "Kate, I see where you're going with this for the RS-Project. Someone with the J-virus immunodeficiency disease could theoretically be injected with this genetically altered swine blood, but it seems to me that this wouldn't help at all.''

Kate nodded. "Right, Ken. The only genes cloned in the DNX process are those which govern the production of hemoglobin. This is my suggestion.'' She clicked her last slide on and gave everyone a minute to study it.

"You see," she said at last, aware that her voice was thickening with emotion for some reason, "what I've done is piggyback on Richard Mulligan, Tom Maniatis, and Frank Grosveld's work on transplanting human beta-globin genes via retrovirus for immunoreconstruction. Mulligan and the others have been concentrating on curing beta-thalassemics and adenosine deaminase deficiency, although they've also done some startling work with boosting tumor-infiltrating lymphocytes, TIL cells, with interleukin-2 hormone, putting the cells back in cancer patients, and watching the gene-boosted cells attack tumors.''

"But you're not after tumors," said Charlie Tate. The young man sounded like he was talking to himself.

"No," agreed Kate. "But I've used the same cloning and

retrovirus injection technique to isolate the regulatory genes which code for antigen-specific cellular and humoral responses.''

"SCID," Ken Mauberly said very softly. "The whole range of congenital immunodeficiency diseases."

"Yes," said Kate, irritated that her voice threatened to betray her by showing emotion. She cleared her throat. "Using the DNX-style genetically engineered human hemoglobin as a carrier template . . . taken from pigs, remember, not human beings . . I have been successful in cloning and attaching normal ADA genes to deal with the adenosine deaminase deficiency, as well as the necessary human DNA to deal with the other three types of Severe Combined Deficiency. The DNX blood substitute is an excellent carrier. As well as providing clean, well-oxygenated blood which does not have to be matched for the subject, the virally introduced DNA should cure all SCID symptoms."

There was a long moment of almost absolute silence.

Finally, Bob Underhill said, "Kate, that would allow the J-virus to continue rebuilding the child's immune system . . . without ever needing actual human blood again. Question . . . where did you get the DNA to clone for the ADA, B-lymphocyte, and other immunoreconstructive genes?"

She blinked. "My own blood," she said, her throat closing on her. She doused the projector lamp and took a minute to recover her composure before turning the lights back on. Some people in the room were rubbing their eyes as if the light hurt.

"Ken," Kate said, her voice steady again, "when can we begin human trials on Joshua?"

Mauberly tapped his pen. "We can begin applying to the FDA for permission almost immediately, Kate. But because of the DNX patent and the complicated nature of the process, my guess would be at least a year . . . perhaps longer."

Kate nodded and sat down. She would not tell them that the evening before, in the most flagrant violation of professional ethics she had ever imagined, she had injected her adopted son with the modified DNX hemoglobin. Joshua had slept well and been healthy and happy in the morning.

Mauberly took the floor. "We're all excited by these developments," he said. "I'll notify CDC Atlanta immediately, and we'll begin to discuss possible involvement by the World Health Organization and other agencies."

Kate could imagine the scramble of researchers through Romania and Eastern Europe, hunting for other J-virus individuals.

"Doctor Chandra," said Mauberly, "would you like to brief us at this time on the results of the J-virus research on our hunt for an HIV cure?"

"No," said Chandra.

Mauberly nodded and cleared his throat. "All right," he said, "but soon, perhaps?"

"Soon," agreed Chandra.

Ken Mauberly tucked his pen back in his shirt pocket and clapped his hands together. "Well, all right then. I imagine everyone wants to get back to work. I only want to say—"

The room emptied of researchers before he could finish.

Tom came into her office at about six P.M. For a second Kate could not believe it was Tom—he never had come up to her CDC office—and then her heart began to pound wildly. "Joshua?" she said. "What's wrong?"

Her ex-husband raised an eyebrow. "Nothing's wrong. Relax. I just came from there . . . Josh and Julie are playing in the mud near the patio. They're both fine."

Kate exited the program she had been working on. "Then what?"

"I thought it was a good night to take you to dinner," he said.

Kate took her reading glasses off and rubbed her eyes. "Thanks, Tom. I really appreciate the offer. But I've got another couple of hours of work to do before—"

"I have reservations at Sebanton's," he said softly, still holding the door open.

Kate turned the computer off, hung her white coat on the rack near the door, and pulled on the blazer she had worn for the presentation that morning. "I'll have to go home," she said. "Wash up. Feed Joshua."

"Joshua's been fed. Julie loves the idea of putting the kiddo to bed tonight. Leave your Cherokee in the parking lot, I'll give you a ride to work in the morning. Now, use your executive lav," he said. "Reservations are for six-thirty."

Boulder, Colorado, was a town with too many restaurants, most of them indifferent, a few very good, and one or two excellent. Sebanton's was none of the above because it was not in Boulder. The French restaurant was on the main street of Longmont, an unassuming cow town twelve miles down the Diagonal Highway. Even finding the little restaurant was a chore since it was tucked away between ugly storefronts that had once been a small town's drugstore or department store or hardware store, and were now flea markets and taxidermy shops. But Sebanton's, while hard to find and not aesthetically pleasing from the outside, was simply the finest French restaurant in Colorado . . . possibly in the Rocky Mountain region. Kate did not consider herself a gourmet, but she had never turned down an invitation to Sebanton's.

Two hours later the view out the restaurant window was softened by darkness, and the small interior was illuminated only by candlelight. Kate returned to the table and smiled at the coffee and cheesecake that had materialized while she was on the phone.

"Julie and Josh OK?" asked Tom.

"Both fine," said Kate. "She put Josh down about eight. She says he had a great day creeping around the patio and that he seems to feel fine." She leaned forward and said, "All right, Tommy. What's the occasion?"

He sat back and lifted his coffee cup with both hands. "Does there have to be an occasion?"

"No," said Kate, "but I can tell that there is. Your face always gets a little extra red when you're building up to something. Tonight you could guide Santa's sleigh."

Tom set his coffee down, coughed, folded his hands, unfolded them, and leaned back to cross his arms. "Well, there is something. I mean . . . I've been thinking about you up there on the hill by yourself . . . nobody but Julie around, and she'll be leaving in December."

Kate softly bit her lip. "It's all right, Tom. I'll find someone. Besides, things are going to slow down in the lab so I'll have more time to spend with—"

Tom shook his head and leaned closer. "No, I don't mean that, Kat. Bad start. What I mean is . . . how would you feel about me moving back in for a while? Not permanently, but just for a few weeks or months. Just to see if it feels right. . . ." He stopped. His face was redder than the Victorian wallpaper in the restaurant.

Kate took a deep breath. She knew that she and Tom were not destined for a new beginning. She loved him . . . she had always loved him in one way or another . . . but she was also certain that their marriage had been wrong, out of synch, a union that had done little except mess up a wonderful friendship. She was certain of that.

Or am I? thought Kate. *He's changed. He's different around Joshua. Hell, I've changed.* She looked down at her coffee, watching the cream in it swirl and feeling a similar swirl of emotions.

"Hey," said Tom, "you don't have to answer now. It's probably a dumb idea. I wasn't talking about reconciliation, just about . . ." He faltered.

Kate put her hand on his, noticing how small and white hers seemed next to his tanned and massive paw. "Tom," she said, "I don't think it's a good idea . . . but I'm not sure anymore. I'm just not sure."

He grinned at her—that boyish, unselfconscious grin that had made her dizzy the first time they met. "Look, Kat," he said, "let's just table it for a while. Or better yet, let's talk about it over a drink. Do you still have that brandy that the Harrisons sent from England last Christmas?"

She nodded. "But it's a workday tomorrow . . ."

"And whatshisname, your priest buddy is coming," finished Tom with a smile. "Right. We'll just have one snifter full. Maybe two. Then I'll carefully drive myself down the hill to my efficient little efficiency. Good enough?''

"Good enough," said Kate, feeling the effects of the wine she had already drunk as she stood up. She steadied herself with a casual grip of the table. "I'm drunk," she said.

Tom touched her back. "You're exhausted, Kat. You've been putting in eighty-hour weeks since you got back from Romania. I would have dragged you out of there tonight even if I hadn't had anything to propose."

She set her hand against his cheek. "You're sweet," she said.

"Yup," said Tom, "that's probably why you divorced me." They walked together to his Land Rover.

Kate had given Tom an access card for the development's security gate and he used it now rather than disturb Julie, who almost certainly was still working on her dissertation. It was only nine P.M., but it was very dark out and the few stars showing through the clouds seemed to gleam with a cold brilliance.

"We missed the Autumn Equinox Celebration this week," Kate said softly as the Land Rover bounced and jostled down the rutted road. The Equinox Celebration had been one of Tom's made-up holidays, each of which had started as a joke and become something of a real tradition during their years together.

"Not too late to celebrate it," Tom said. "We just don't try to balance any eggs on end . . . wait a minute."

He had stopped the Land Rover just as they came around the last bend before the house, and Kate immediately noticed what he had seen: all the lights were out on the house—not just interior lights, but porch light, garage security light, patio light, everything.

"Shit," whispered Tom.

Kate's heart seemed to skip a beat. "We've had a couple of outages this summer . . ."

Tom inched the Land Rover forward. "Did you notice if the Bedridges' was lit up?"

Kate turned in her seat to look across the meadow toward their nearest neighbor a quarter of a mile away. "I don't think so. But that doesn't mean much . . . they're in Europe."

The Land Rover's headlights illuminated the dark garage, breezeway, and a bit of the patio as they turned into the slightly inclined driveway. Tom doused the lights and sat there a minute. "The security gate was working," he said. "I forget, does it have some sort of backup generator?"

"I don't know," said Kate. *Julie should have heard us,* she was thinking. *She should have come to the door.* There was no hint of candlelight inside the front or second-story windows on this side of the house. *Julie works in the study next to my room—Joshua's room—until I get home. We wouldn't see the candlelight from here if she stayed with Joshua.*

"Stay here," Tom said at last.

"The hell with that," said Kate, opening her car door.

Tom muttered something but tugged the keys out. They were three feet from the front door when Julie's terrified voice said, "Stay away! I have a gun!"

"Julie!" cried Kate. "It's us. What's wrong? Open the door!"

The door opened onto blackness and a flashlight beam flicked on, first in Kate's face, then in Tom's. "Quick . . . get in!" Julie said.

Tom slammed and locked the door behind him. Julie was holding Joshua against her while juggling the flashlight in her left hand and the Browning automatic in her right. Tom took the weapon from her as the young woman whispered excitedly, "About twenty minutes ago . . . I was working at the computer . . . all the lights went out . . . I was looking in the dining room for the flashlight and candles when I saw shadows out on the patio . . . heard men whispering. . . ."

"How many men?" Tom asked, his voice very soft. Kate had taken the baby, Julie had flicked off the flashlight, and now the three adults huddled together in the darkened hallway.

Julie was just a silhouette as she shook her head. "I dunno

. . . three or four at least. For a minute I thought maybe it was guys from the power company come to fix the electricity . . . *and then they started rattling the patio door*." Her voice was ragged. Kate touched her shoulder as Julie paused to take a few deep breaths."Anyway, I ran in, got Josh and the pistol, and came back out just as the guys were breaking the glass on the patio door. I yelled at them that I had a gun and then they weren't there anymore. I ran around the house making sure all the windows were closed and . . . it's dead, Tom, I tried it right away."

He had moved to the hall phone. Now he listened a second, nodded, and set it back.

"Anyway," said Julie, "it was just a minute or two later that I heard the truck and saw the lights out front. It didn't sound like the Cherokee and . . . oh, Jesus, I'm glad to see you guys."

Holding the pistol at his side and taking the flashlight from Julie, Tom moved from room to room, the two women behind him. He would flash the light for a second, then flick it off. Kate saw the shattered glass on the patio sliding door, but the door was still locked. They moved past the kitchen to the study, beyond the study to the master bedroom.

"Here," said Tom and handed Kate the Browning. He went into the bedroom closet a minute and came out with the shotgun and the box of shells. Dumping shells into the pocket of his tweed sportscoat, he pumped the shotgun once. "Come on," he said. "We're getting out of here."

There were shrubs and boulders along both sides of the driveway and Kate was sure each of them was moving as she watched Tom spring the ten paces to the Land Rover. She saw that the hood was up slightly the same instant that she heard Tom say, "Goddamn it." He slid behind the wheel anyway but the starter did not even crank. Nor did the lights come on.

He jogged back to them at the doorway, the shotgun at port arms.

"Wait," said Kate. "Listen." There was a sound from beyond the kitchen; something had broken or dropped downstairs, on the lower level where Julie's room and the other guest suite were.

"Miata," whispered Tom and led the way down the hall and into the dark kitchen, toward the breezeway to the garage.

The refrigerator clanked on and Kate jumped a foot and swung the Browning toward it before she recognized the sound. Joshua stirred and began to cry softly. "Shhh," whispered Kate. "Shhh, baby, it's all right." They moved down the breezeway in the dim light through the windows along each side, Tom first, then Kate, Julie clinging tightly to Kate's shirt. There was another sound from the house behind them.

Tom kicked open the garage door and extended the shotgun with the flashlight directly above it. Both swung in fast arcs, the flashlight beam illuminated storage shelves, the closed garage door, the open side door, the Miata with its hood up and wires visibly ripped free.

They moved back into the breezeway and crouched there. Tom doused the light.

"Hey," whispered Julie, her teeth chattering audibly, "it was only a two-seater anyway." She grasped Kate's hand where it held the baby. "Just kidding."

"Quiet," whispered Tom. His voice was soft but steady.

They huddled there near the garage door, below the level of the breezeway windows, staring down the fifteen feet of tiled floor toward the door to the kitchen. They had left the door open a crack. Kate tried to listen but could hear nothing above Joshua's soft whimpering in her ear. She rocked and patted the baby, still feeling Julie's hand on her arm.

There was a movement of black against black, Tom switched on the flashlight, and his shotgun roared an instant before Julie screamed and the baby began wailing.

The white face and long fingers had disappeared from the kitchen doorway a second before Tom's shotgun blast ripped off part of the doorframe. Kate was sure that the face had ducked out of sight in that second. She was also sure that it was the same face she had seen in the baby's room two months earlier.

Tom flicked off the flashlight, but not before she had caught the look of shock as his gaze met Kate's. He had also recognized the man.

There was a scrape and sliding from inside the garage.

Trying to hush both the baby and the pounding of her own heart, Kate slid against the wall and slowly raised her eyes to the breezeway window. Two dark forms moved with incredible quickness outside on the small patch of yard between the breezeway and the cliff. Tom had also glimpsed them.

"Fuck this," he whispered to them. "We need to get outside where we can get into the meadow . . . head for the road."

Kate nodded. Anything was better than this claustrophobic corridor where anyone could come at them from any direction. In the dim light from the windows, she looked down at the pistol in her hand. *Could I really shoot someone?* Another part of her mind answered almost immediately, *You've already shot someone. And if he comes after you or Joshua, you will shoot him again.* She blinked at the clarity of the thought which cut through the swirling mists of conflicting duties, her Hippocratic imperative, and heart-pounding fears like a searchlight through fog: *You will do what you have to do.* Kate looked at the pistol and noticed with almost clinical detachment that her hand was not shaking.

"Come on," whispered Tom. He pulled them to their feet. "We're going out."

The breezeway had a door that opened onto the walk leading from the garage to the front door, but before Tom could open it everything happened at once.

A shape launched itself through the kitchen door again. Tom whirled, lowered the shotgun to hip height, and fired.

The window behind them exploded into shards as two men in black clothing hurtled through the glass. Kate raised her pistol even as she tried to shelter Joshua from the spray of glass.

Someone came through the breezeway door. Tom pumped the shotgun and turned toward the man.

Julie screamed as dark arms and white hands came out of

the garage and seized her by the hair, pulling her into the darkness.

The shotgun roared again. A man screamed something in a foreign language. Kate stumbled backward into the corner, still sheltering Joshua from the melee of dark forms, crunching glass, and a sudden lick of flames visible from the open kitchen door. She leaned into the garage and extended the Browning, trying to separate the dark form of the intruder there from the struggling shadow that had to be Julie.

"Julie!" screamed Kate. "Drop!"

The smaller shadow fell away. A man's white face was just visible as it turned toward the breezeway. Kate fired three times, feeling the automatic buck higher in her hand each time. Joshua let out a piercing wail in her ear and she hugged him tighter as she said, "Julie?"

The shotgun blasted again behind her and she was suddenly slammed into the breezeway corner as several forms collided with her. Tom's face loomed for an instant, she saw that at least three black-clad men were wrestling with him and that the shotgun had been wrenched from his hands, and before she could open her mouth to speak or scream or cry, he said, "Run, Kat," and then the struggling forms swirled away through the open door.

At least three other dark shapes were pulling themselves to their feet in the breezeway, their forms silhouetted by the soft glow of flames from the kitchen. Something moved in the garage but Kate could not tell if it was Julie or not. One of the men in black reached for her pistol.

Kate fired three times, the dark shape fell away and was replaced by another hurtling form. She raised the Browning directly into a white face, made sure it was not Tom, and fired twice more. The face snapped backwards and out of sight as if it had been slapped by an invisible hand.

Two other men rose from the floor. Neither was Tom. A man's hand slid around the doorframe from the garage. Kate lifted the pistol and fired, heard the hammer click uselessly. A heavy hand fell on her ankle.

"Tom!" she gasped and then, without thinking, curled both arms around Joshua and threw herself through the shattered window. Dark shapes scrambled behind her.

Kate hit hard in the flower garden and felt the wind go out of her. The baby had breath enough to cry. Then she was up and running, loping across the yard, trying to get behind the garage and beyond, into the aspen trees near the access road.

Two men in black stepped out and blocked her way.

Kate skidded to a stop in loose loam and reversed herself, running back toward the balcony and doors to the lower level.

Three men in black stood between her and the house or the breezeway. The windows of what had been the nursery were painted orange with flame from inside the house. There was no sign of Tom or Julie.

"Oh, God, please," whispered Kate, backing toward the cliff edge. Joshua was crying softly. She set her free hand on the back of his head.

The five forms advanced until they formed a semicircle, forcing her back until her heels were on the exposed granite at the edge of the cliff. In the sudden silence, Kate could hear the crackling of flames and the soft sound of the creek sixty feet below her.

"Tom!" she screamed. There was no answer.

One of the men stepped forward. Kate recognized the pale, cruel face of the intruder. He shook his head almost sadly and reached for Joshua.

Kate whirled and prepared to jump, her only plan to shield Joshua from the fall with her own body and hope that they hit branches. She took a step into space . . .

. . . and was pulled back, a gloved hand wrapped in her hair. Kate screamed and clawed with her free hand.

Someone jerked the baby from her grasp.

Kate let out a sound more moan than cry and twisted around to face her attacker. She kicked, clawed, gouged, and tried to bite.

The man in black held her at arm's length for a second, his face totally impassive. Then he slapped her once, very hard, took a firmer grip on her hair, spun her around, lifted her, and threw her far out over the edge of the cliff.

Kate felt an insane moment of exhilaration as she spun out over treetops illuminated by flame—*I can grab a limb!*—but the limb was too far, her fall was too fast, and she felt a surge of panic as she tumbled headfirst through branches that tore at her clothes, ripped at her shoulders.

And then she felt a great pain in her arm and side as she hit something much harder than a branch.

And then she felt nothing at all.

Dreams of Blood and Iron

My enemies have always underestimated me. And they have always paid the price.

The light coming through the small windows of my bedroom has an autumnal edge to it now as it moves across the rough white walls, across the broad boards of the floor, and onto the tumbled quilt covering my bed. My prison.

I have been dying here for years, for an eternity. The others whisper to each other, thinking that I cannot hear the urgency in their voices. I know that there is some problem with the Investiture Ceremony. They are afraid to tell me about the problem; afraid that it will upset me and hurry my final dissolution. They are afraid that I will die before the Investiture takes place.

I think not. The habit of life, however painful, is too difficult to break after all these centuries. I can no longer walk, can hardly lift my arm, but this accursed body continues to attempt to repair itself, even though I have not partaken of the Sacrament since my arrival home more than a year and a half ago now.

I may soon ask about these whispers and urgent comings and goings. It may be that my enemies are stirring again. And my enemies have always underestimated me.

I began my reign in August of 1456, staging the anointment ceremony in the cathedral at Tîrgovişte, the city where my

174

*father had ruled. I devised my own title: "Prince Vlad, Son
of Vlad the Great, Sovereign and Ruler of Ungro-Wallachia
and of the Duchies of Amlas and Făgăraş." After my escape
from the Sultan and in recognition of the alliances I had
formed with Transylvania's boyar noblemen, John Hunyadi
thought it wise to orchestrate the return of a Dracula to the
Dracul throne.*

*At first my voice was soft, conciliatory. In a letter I wrote
to the mayor and councilmen of Braşov a month after my
ascension to the throne of Wallachia, I used my best court
Latin to address them as* honesti viri, fratres, amici et vicini
nostri sinceri—*or as "honest men, brothers, friends, and
sincere neighbors." Within two years, most of those fat bur-
ghers would be writhing on the stakes upon which I had
impaled them.*

*I remember with a joy that not even such oceans of time
have been able to dim, that Easter Sunday of 1457. I had
invited the boyars—those noble couples who felt that I ruled
at their pleasure—to a great feast in Tîrgovişte. After the
Easter Mass, the visitors repaired to the banquet hall and
open courtyards where long tables of the finest food had been
set aside for these gentlemen and their families. I allowed
them to finish their feast. Then I appeared, on horseback, in
the company of a hundred of my most loyal soldiers. It was
a beautiful spring day, warmer than most. The sky was a
deep and terrible blue. I remember that the boyars cheered
me, their ladies waving lace handkerchiefs in their admira-
tion, their children lifted to shoulders the better to see their
benefactor. I doffed my plumed cap in response to their
cheers. It was the signal my soldiers were awaiting.*

*The oldest boyars and their wives I ordered impaled on the
stakes I had raised outside the city walls while the unsus-
pecting fools attended mass. I was not the inventor of impalement as a punishment—my own father had used it
occasionally—but after this day, I was known as Vlad
Ţepeş—"Vlad the Impaler." I did not dislike the title.*

*With the older boyars and their wives still writhing on the
stakes, I began marching the able-bodied in the crowd toward*

my castle on the Argeş River, some fifty miles away. The weakest did not survive the three-day march without provisions, but, then, I had no use for the weakest. The survivors— the strongest—I used to rebuild Castle Dracula.

The castle was old and abandoned, even then, its towers tumbled down and its great hall fallen in. I had found it and sheltered there during my flight from the Sultan and Hunyadi and resolved then and there to rebuild it as Castle Dracula, my eyrie and final retreat.

The location was perfect—high on a remote ridge above the Argeş River, which cut its deep canyon from Wallachia through the Făgăraş Mountains into the south of Transylvania. There was a single road along the Argeş—narrow, dangerous in the best of seasons, and easily defensible once the castle was rebuilt. No enemy, neither Turk nor Christian, could approach me in Castle Dracula without advance warning.

But first it had to be rebuilt.

I had had a kiln built along the river's banks, and the bricks from that kiln were passed uphill from man to man (or woman to woman) in my human chain of boyar slaves. The local villagers were amazed to see such slaves, dressed as they still were in the rags of their boyar Easter finery.

From horseback, I directed the reconstruction of this ancient Serbian ruin. The five towers were rebuilt, two dominating the highest point on the ridge, the three others lower on the northern slope. The thick walls were made doubly thick with brick and stone so as to repulse even the heaviest Turkish cannonade. The battlements were high, eighty feet and more, and they grew out of the stone of the cliff itself so they appeared to be a sheer thousand-foot wall. The central courtyards and donjons conformed themselves to the space between the great towers, as well as to the rough topography of the ridgetop that was less than one hundred feet wide at its widest. A great earthen ramp was extended out from the southern cliff face, and from that ramp a wooden bridge allowed the only access to the keep. The center of that bridge was always raised, and was designed so that it could not only be lowered to allow entry but could, with the severing of two great cables, be dropped into the chasm below.

In the center of Castle Dracula, I had the few surviving boyar slaves deepen the well so that it fell through solid stone more than a thousand feet to an underground tributary of the Argeş. The subterranean river had carved its own caverns in the mountain, and I directed the construction of an escape passage from that well to the caves that opened onto the Argeş a thousand feet below. Even today, I am told, the caves along the river there are referred to by the villagers as pivniţă, or "cellar." With its escape routes and deep donjons, its caverns and sunken torture pits, Castle Dracula indeed had its "cellar."

A few of the boyars survived the four-month reconstruction of my new home. I had them impaled in rows on the cliffs overlooking the village.

In the summer of 1457, I crossed the Carpathians at the pass at Bran. Hunyadi was locked in mortal combat with the Turks at Belgrade, but I had other scores to settle. On the plains near Tîrgovişte, I attacked the retreating army of Vladislav II, my father's assassin. In single combat I bested him. When he asked for mercy, I ran the point of my short sword up under his jaw, through his brain, and out through the top of his skull. I displayed that skull of the rest of that summer on the top of the highest wall of Tîrgovişte. Songs were sung of it. I drank the Sacrament from Vladislav's headless corpse.

My enemies were legion. I knew from the outset that I must command respect and fear from everyone if I were to survive.

That winter the Genoese ambassadors to my court doffed their hats but left on the skullcaps they wore underneath. When I politely inquired as to why they remained covered in my presence, one of the ambassadors answered: "This is our custom. We are not obliged to take our skullcaps off under any circumstances, even in an audience with the Sultan or the Holy Roman Emperor himself."

I remember nodding judiciously. "In all fairness, I wish

to recognize your customs," I said at last. The ambassadors smiled and bowed, their skullcaps still on. "And to strengthen them," I added.

I called in my guards, chose the longest nails I could find, and had them driven in a circle through the caps and into the skulls of the screaming ambassadors. I drove the first nail into each one, saying as though in a litany, "Witness, this is the manner in which Vlad Dracula will strengthen your customs."

The woman was brought before me for defying my court edict that each maiden of the kingdom would preserve her virginity until given permission by her Royal Prince to lose it. The stake was five feet long and I had it heated over the fire until it was red hot. As my dinner guests, including ambassadors from six nearby nations, watched, I had the red-hot stake driven through the woman's vagina, up through her entrails, and continued driving it until it emerged through her screaming mouth.

I fortified the island of Şnagov north of the village of Bucharest, enlarging and adding to the ancient monastery there. In the central hall, I had laid a tiled floor with alternating squares of black and red. To amuse myself, I would have a group of courtiers scurry around the floor while the court orchestra played a brief tune and the soldiers held their spears inward around the perimeter, assuring that none would escape. The courtiers would each have to choose a tile.

At the end of the tune I would throw a heavy lever and several of the waxed tiles would drop open, the trapdoors sending the screaming courtiers thirty feet to sharpened stakes in the pit below. Almost five hundred years later, in 1932, an archaeologist friend sent me a photograph from the excavations on Şnagov Island: remnants of the stakes were still visible; the skulls were still stacked in neat rows.

* * *

It was three winters after the rebuilding of Castle Dracula that one of my mistresses announced that she was pregnant, thus hoping to gain precedence over my other concubines. Assuming that she was lying, I asked her if she would mind being examined. When she demurred, I had her brought to the main hall while the court was assembled.

She protested her love, her sorrow for her error, but I ordered my bodyguards to proceed. They sliced her womb open from vulva to breastbone and peeled back the walls of muscle and flesh while she writhed, still alive.

"Witness this!" I cried to the white faces staring up at me. My words echoed in the stone hall. "Let the whole world see where Vlad Dracula has been!"

Chapter Nineteen

KATE became aware of the pain before she was aware of anything else; she did not know who she was, where she was, or why the world seemed composed of separate stilettos of pure pain, but she knew that she hurt.

She swam up from a great depth, remembering the water above her face at the bottom of . . . *of what?* . . . of the fall that seemed to comprise all that she remembered of her previous life. She remembered lifting her face through that ceiling of water. She remembered beginning the climb, dragging her injured left arm behind her, blinking water and something heavier out of her eyes as she climbed upward through the mud and nettles and crumbling shale and aspen and thorny piñon . . .

I remember the flames. I remember the taste of ashes. I remember the other bodies in the light from the ambulances and fire engines . . .

Kate gasped awake, blinking wildly. White ceiling. White bed. The functional sag of an i.v. bag. White walls and gray medical monitors.

Father O'Rourke leaned closer and touched her uninjured arm just above the plastic hospital bracelet there. "It's all right," he whispered.

Kate tried to speak, found her tongue too dry, her lips too swollen. She shook her head violently from side to side.

The priest's bearded face was lined with worry, his eyes visibly assaulted by sadness. "It's all right, Kate," he whispered again.

She shook her head again and licked her lips. It was like speaking with cotton balls in her mouth, but she managed to make sounds. She had to explain something to O'Rourke before the tides of drugs and pain pulled her down under the ceiling of consciousness again. "No," she croaked at long last.

O'Rourke squeezed her good hand with both of his.

"No," she said again, trying to turn and hearing the i.v. rattle on its stand. She shook her head and felt the bandages thick and heavy on her forehead. "It's not all right. Not at all."

O'Rourke squeezed her hand, but he nodded. He understood.

Kate quit struggling and let the currents drag her under.

The young police detective—Lieutenant Peterson, Kate remembered through the shifting curtain of pain and drugs—came in the morning. The older, sad-looking sergeant stood by the door while the lieutenant sat in the empty visitor's chair.

"Mrs. Neuman?" said the detective. He was moving a breath mint from one cheek to the other and the click of the candy against his teeth made Kate remember the sound her left arm made as she climbed the night before. No, *two nights before*, she reminded herself, using all of her energy to concentrate. *It is Saturday. It was Thursday night that your life ended. It is Saturday now.*

"Mrs. Neuman? You awake?"

Kate nodded.

"Can you talk? Can you understand me?"

She nodded again.

The lieutenant licked his lips and glanced at the sergeant, whose gaze remained unfocused or turned inward. "Well, Mrs. Neuman, I've got a few questions," said the lieutenant, flipping open a small notebook.

"Doctor," said Kate.

The lieutenant raised his eyebrows. "You want I should call the doctor? You feeling bad?"

"Doctor," repeated Kate, gritting her teeth against the pain in her jaw and neck when she spoke. "*Doctor* Neuman."

The police lieutenant rolled his eyes slightly and clicked his ballpoint pen. "Okay—Doctor Neuman . . . you wanna tell me what happened Thursday night?"

"Tell *me*," gritted Kate.

The lieutenant stared.

She took a breath. It had been hours since her last shot and everything hurt beyond reason. "Tell *me* what happened," she said. "Tom dead? Julie dead? Baby dead?"

The young lieutenant pursed his lips. "Now, Mrs. Neuman . . . what we have to concentrate on right now is getting some details so we can do our job. Then you concentrate on getting better. Your friend, Father Whatshisname, he'll be back pretty soon—"

Kate used her good hand to grasp the lieutenant's wrist with a strength that obviously shocked him. "Tom dead?" she rasped. "Julie dead? Baby dead?"

Lieutenant Peterson had to use his other hand to free his wrist. He sighed and said, "Now look, Mrs.—*Doctor* Neuman. My job is to get as much—"

"Yes," said the sergeant. The older man's gaze had shifted to Kate. "Yes, Doctor Neuman. Your ex-husband is dead. So is Ms. Strickland. And I'm afraid your adopted child also died in the fire."

Kate closed her eyes. *The other bodies on the gurneys as they loaded me aboard the ambulance in the glow of flames . . . carbon-black skin, blackened lips pulled back, teeth gleaming . . . the small body in the clear plastic bag made for small bodies . . . I didn't dream it.*

She opened her eyes in time to catch the glare the lieutenant was giving the older detective. Peterson looked back at her, obviously irritated. "I'm sorry, Doctor Neuman. You have our condolences." He clicked his pen again. "Now, can you tell us what you remember from Thursday night?"

Fighting to stay afloat on the waves of pain from her arm and skull, fighting the currents that threatened again to pull her down into the dark, welcome depths, Kate formed each word with care while she told him everything she remembered.

She opened her eyes and it was night. Rectangles of reflected white light on the walls and the glow of a night-light on the panel behind her were the only illumination. O'Rourke lowered the book he had been reading in the dim light and scooted his chair closer. He was wearing the sweatshirt he had worn in Bucharest. "Hi," he whispered.

Kate floated in and out. She concentrated on staying in.

"It's the smack on your head," O'Rourke said softly. "The doctor explained about the effects of the concussion, but I don't think you were really awake when he was explaining."

Kate formed the words carefully in her mind before allowing her lips to have them. "Not . . . dead," she said.

O'Rourke bit his lip, then nodded. "No, you're not dead," he said.

She shook her head angrily. "Baby . . ." she said. For some reason, the "J" in Joshua hurt her jaw and head to say. She said it anyway. "Joshua . . . not dead."

O'Rourke squeezed her hand.

Kate did not squeeze back. "Not dead," she said again, whispering in case any of the men in black were beyond the curtain or outside the door. "Joshua . . ." The pain made her head swim, made the undertow stronger. "Joshua is not dead."

O'Rourke listened.

"Have to help," she whispered. "Promise."

"I promise," said the priest.

Ken Mauberly came on Sunday morning when Kate was alone. Despite the pain, she could concentrate and speak. But the pain was still very bad.

She knew it would soon be worse as soon as she saw the administrator's face.

Despite the condolences, Mauberly was all optimism and quiet cheeriness. "Thank God you were spared, Kate," he said, adjusting his glasses and fiddling with the flowers he had brought. He set them in a vase and fluffed at them. "Thank God you were spared."

Kate set her hand on the mass of bandages that was her right temple. It seemed to steady things a bit when she spoke. "Ken," she said, surprised to note that her voice belonged to her again, "what is it?"

He froze with his hands still on the flowers.

"What is it, Ken? It's something else. Tell me. Please."

Mauberly sagged. He pulled a chair over and collapsed into it. There were tears behind his glasses when he spoke. "Kate, someone broke into the lab on the same night that . . . on the same night. They started fires in the biolab section, smashed seals, burned papers, trashed the computers, stole the floppy disks . . ."

Kate waited. He would never cry over vandalism.

"Chandra . . ." he began.

"They killed her," said Kate. It was not a question.

Mauberly nodded and removed his glasses. "The FBI . . . oh, God, Kate, I'm sorry. The doctor and the staff psychologist said it was way too early to tell you and—"

"Who else?" demanded Kate. Her hand was on his forearm.

Mauberly took a breath. "Charlie Tate. He and Susan were working late when the intruders got in past security."

"J-virus cultures?" asked Kate, wincing at the extra pain the "J" caused her. "Joshua's blood samples?"

"Destroyed," said Mauberly. "The FBI thinks that they were flushed down the disposal sink before the fire began."

"Cloned copies?" said Kate. Her eyes were closed and she could see Susan McKay Chandra bent over an electron microscope eyepiece, Charlie Tate saying something with a laugh behind her. "Did they get the cloned copies in the Class-VI lab?"

"They're all gone," said Mauberly. "No one thought of sending cultures out of the building at this stage. If I'd only

. . ." His voice caught on a high note of anguish. He touched Kate's good arm with his soft fingers. "Kate, I'm sorry. You've been through hell and this is only making it worse. Concentrate on getting better. The FBI will find these people . . . whoever did this, the FBI will find them . . ."

"No," whispered Kate.

"What was that?" Mauberly scooted closer with a screech of chairlegs on tile. "What, Kate?"

But she had closed her eyes and pretended to be gone.

The FBI had come and gone, the two doctors and half a dozen friends and another half-dozen co-workers had arrived and been shooed out by the red-haired nurse, and only Father O'Rourke was there when the last bands of late-September light painted the east wall orange. Kate opened her eyes and looked out the window past the silhouette of the priest. He seemed lost in thought as he leaned on the radiator at the window. The sunset was sending low bands of light directly down Sunshine Canyon into the west wing of the hospital. It was not quite seven P.M. and the hospital had a Sunday-evening quiet to it.

"O'Rourke?"

The priest turned away from the window and came to the chair by her bedside.

"Will you do something for me?" she whispered.

"Yes."

"Help me find the people who killed Tom and Julie . . ." *Blackened corpses, flesh scaled like the ashes of a log. Their bodies smaller, shrunken by flame. Brittle arms raised in a boxer's stance. The gleam of teeth in a lipless smile.*

"Yes," said O'Rourke.

"More," whispered Kate, grasping his large hand with her good right hand and the cast of her left hand. "Help me find Joshua."

She felt his hesitation.

"No," she said, her voice rising above a whisper but still in control, not hysterical. "The burned baby corpse wasn't Josh's . . . too *big*. Believe me. Will you help me find him?"

The priest hesitated only another few seconds before squeezing her hand again. "Yes," he said. And then, after a minute when the sunlight faded from the east wall and the view outside the window grew suddenly darker, "Yes, I'll help."

Kate fell asleep holding his hand.

Chapter Twenty

KATE left the hospital on Monday, September 30, although her head still ached abominably, her left arm was in a temporary cast, and the doctors wanted her to stay at least another twenty-four hours. She did not feel that she had another twenty-four hours to spend in bed.

Because the part of the house that had not burned had been damaged by smoke and water, and because she would not have returned to that house under any circumstances, Kate took a room at the Harvest House hotel, not far from CDC. O'Rourke and other friends had retrieved some of her clothes from the undamaged bedroom of the house and Kate's secretary, Arleen, had bought some new things for her. Kate wore the new things.

Julie Strickland's remains, after an autopsy and positive identification through dental records, had been flown home for burial in Milwaukee. Kate had talked to Julie's parents by telephone on Monday evening and had lain in the darkness of the hotel room for an hour afterward, wanting to cry, *needing* to cry, but unable to cry.

Tom's body was cremated on Tuesday, October 1. He'd once told friends that he wanted his ashes tossed to the winds along the Continental Divide in the center of the state, and after the packed memorial ceremony at a Boulder mortuary, a caravan of almost forty vehicles, most of them four-wheel drive, left for Buena Vista to carry out his wishes. Kate was not feeling well enough to go along. Father O'Rourke drove her back to the hotel. The FBI continued to file through the hotel lobby to question her over and over about details. As though believing her story about men in black, probably Romanians trying to kidnap the Romanian orphan for reasons unknown, they promised her that all U.S. passport control stations had been alerted. They could not tell her for *whom* they had been alerted.

Kate talked to Ken Mauberly on Tuesday night and learned that Chandra's body had been returned to her husband and family in Atlanta. He also told her the details of virology-researcher Charlie Tate's funeral in Denver.

"It turns out that Charlie was a passionate amateur astronomer," said Mauberly, his voice soft over the phone line. "I went to his memorial service Sunday evening in the planetarium down at the Denver Historical Museum. The whole service—short eulogies by friends, a brief talk by his Unitarian minister—was held in the star chamber with only the constellations overhead for illumination. When the eulogies were finished, a star suddenly brightened in the sky. Charlie's widow—you remember Donna, don't you, Kate?—well, Donna stood up and explained that the light from that star was forty-two light-years from Earth and had begun its journey in the year that Charlie had been born in 1949 . . . perhaps even the day of his birth . . . only to arrive this week. Anyway, the star grew brighter and brighter until the dome was this bright, milky color . . . sort of like just before sunrise . . . and we all filed out under this magnificent light. And the headstone that they're having carved . . . well, the epitaph is very touching." Mauberly paused.

"What does it say, Ken?" asked Kate.

Mauberly cleared his throat. "Charlie wrote his own epitaph years ago. It reads—'I have loved the stars far too fondly ever to fear the night.' " There was silence a moment. "Kate, are you still there?"

"Yes," she said. "I'm still here. Ken, I'll talk to you tomorrow."

* * *

Kate had requested a second and more thorough autopsy be done on the body of the infant found in the burned house, and at first the county coroner had balked. The child's corpse had been recovered in the collapsed section of the house only when the flames there had burned themselves almost out—Kate discovered that she had spent almost an hour and a half crawling up the steep slope with her broken arm and concussion, being found only as the bodies were being discovered—and there was little left of the infant's corpse to analyze: no teeth for dental records, no dental records in any case, and no way to determine the cause of death because of the severity of the burns to the small body and the massive internal damage done by collapsing walls and masonry. After an initial inspection, the cause of death had been established as Death from Burns and Other Injuries Related to the Fire and the coroner had got on with the other autopsies relating to the case.

"Do it over and do it more carefully," Kate had said to the startled coroner. "Or I will. We need a blood sample, a full X-ray series, magnetic resonance images of the internal organs, and actual samples of the stomach lining and upper intestinal tract. It's crucial to both the FBI's investigation and the CDC's search for a possible plague virus . . . if you drop the ball the second time, both organizations will be on your neck. Do it again and do it carefully."

The coroner had been irritated but had complied. On Wednesday, October 2, Kate brought the thick report out to Alan Stevens at the CDC imaging lab. Everyone there was pleased to see her, but she had no time for pleasantries. She barely glanced at the sealed-off Class-VI biolabs where Chandra and Tate had died, and had not even sat down in her own office after confirming that the floppy disks, files, and project reports were indeed gone. She met Alan in a basement conference room that had just been repainted but still smelled of smoke.

"Kate, I'm so terribly sorry . . ." began the red-haired technician.

"Thank you, Alan." She slid the report across to him. "This was done by the county coroner. Do we need to do it over?"

Alan bit his lip as he flipped through the stapled pages. "No," he said at last, "the conclusions are sloppily written up, but the data looks solid enough."

"And could that child be Joshua?"

The technician settled his glasses higher on his snub nose. "This baby is the right gender, the right age, approximately the right size, and there's no reason for another child to have been in the house . . ."

"Could it be Joshua, Alan? Look at the section under 'blood samples.' "

He nodded. "Kate, it's not unusual in fires and massive trauma cases like this that there is little blood left in the body."

"Yes, I know," Kate said as patiently as she could. She did not mention her emergency room residency or her training with one of the country's finest pathologists before choosing hematology. "But *all* of the blood missing or boiled away, Alan?"

"It's unusual, I admit," said the technician. "But not unheard of."

"All right," said Kate. She handed him the extra folder with the X ray and MRI hard copy. "Is this Joshua?"

Alan spent almost thirty minutes studying the stills and comparing them to hard copy and stored computer visuals in the imaging control room. When he was finished, they returned to the conference room. "Well?" said Kate.

Her young friend's face was almost forlorn. "I can't find the stomach-wall abnormality for certain, Kate . . . but you can see the extent of the internal damage from whatever fell on the child. A support beam perhaps. But the actual tissue samples support the identification. I mean, the cellular pathology is similar."

"Similar," said Kate, standing. "But not necessarily the same as Joshua's?"

Alan took his glasses off and squinted at her. His face looked very vulnerable and very sad. "Not necessarily . . .

there's no way to be sure with this postmortem data . . . *you* must know that. But the chances of an infant of similar size, with such an unusual cell pathology, being found in the same house . . .''

Kate walked to the door. "It just means that they sacrificed one of their own," she said.

Alan frowned at her. "One of *whose* own?"

"Nothing," said Kate and opened the door.

Alan rose with the files. "Don't you want these?"

Kate shook her head and left.

The infant was buried in a lovely cemetery near Lyons, a small foothills community where Kate and Tom had sometimes walked. When she had requested a headstone, the salesman had gone into the back room for a minute and brought out a photocopy of an elaborate stone with an infant's cherubic face, a lamb, and a curling flower.

Kate shook her head. "A plain stone. No ornamentation whatsoever."

The salesman nodded enthusiastically. "And the deceased's name to be inscribed . . . ah, yes . . . Joshua Neuman," he said and cleared his throat. "I . . . ah . . . have read the newspaper accounts of the tragedy, Doctor Neuman. My deepest sympathies."

"No," said Kate, and the flatness in her tone made the man glance up over his bifocals. "No name," she said. "Just inscribe the stone—Unknown Romanian Infant."

On Friday, October 4, Kate withdrew a total of $15,830 from her savings account, another $2,200 from her checking account, put most of the cash in folders with other loose papers that went into her carry-on bag, stuffed the rest of the bills in her purse, took the shuttle limousine to Stapleton International Airport, and boarded a United flight to New York with tickets in her purse for a connecting PanAm flight to Vienna.

The plane had moved away from the gate when a man dressed all in black dropped into the empty seat next to her.

"You're late," said Kate. "I thought you'd changed your mind."

"No," said O'Rourke. "I promised, didn't I?"

Kate chewed on her lip. Her headache, although much improved over the migraine-intensity a few days earlier, still roared through her skull like a rasping wind. She found it hard to concentrate, but did so anyway. "Did your senator friend get through to the man at the embassy in Bucharest?"

O'Rourke nodded. The bearded priest looked tired.

"And is the embassy guy going to contact Lucian?"

"Yes," said O'Rourke. "It will be done. They chose someone who is . . . ah . . . not unused to delicate assignments."

"CIA," said Kate. She rubbed her forehead with her good hand. "I keep thinking that I've forgotten something."

O'Rourke seemed to be studying her face. "The travel arrangements you requested have been made. Lucian will know where and when to meet us. My friends at Matthias Church in Budapest have made the contacts with the Gypsies. Everything we discussed is in place."

Kate continued to rub her forehead without being aware of doing so. "Still . . . it feels like I've forgotten something."

O'Rourke leaned closer. "Perhaps you've forgotten you need time to mourn."

Kate pulled back suddenly, turned away as if looking out the window during the takeoff, and then turned her gaze back on the priest. "No . . . I feel it . . . I mean, Tom and Julie's and Chandra's deaths are in me like a pain more real than this concussion or this arm . . . but I can't take time to feel it all yet. Not yet."

O'Rourke's gray eyes studied her. "And Joshua?"

Kate's lips grew tight. "Joshua is alive."

The priest nodded almost imperceptibly. "But if we can't find him?"

Kate's thin smile held no warmth, no humor, only resolve. "We'll find him. I swear on the graves of the friends I just

buried and the eyes of the God you believe in that we'll find
Joshua. And bring him home.''

Kate turned away to watch out the window as the plains of
Colorado fell behind as they flew east, but for the longest
time she could feel O'Rourke's gaze on her.

Chapter Twenty-one

KATE had never been to Vienna before, but her jumbled, jet-lagged impressions of it were pleasant: beautiful old architecture co-existing with the most modern refinements, parks, gardens, and palaces set along the circular ring roads of the old city, easy affluence, efficiency, cleanliness, and an obvious care for aesthetics that had not faltered in centuries. She thought that she might like to return to Vienna someday when she was sane.

She and O'Rourke had arrived shortly after sunrise and taken a cab to the Hôtel de France on Schottentör, near Rooseveltplatz, and a cathedral that O'Rourke said was called the Votivkirche.

"You've been to Vienna before," said Kate, trying to focus through the headache and jet lag.

"Even cities as prosperous as Vienna have orphanages," said O'Rourke. "Here, I'll check us in."

Their rooms were on the fifth floor, in a modern edition of the hotel carved out of a two-century-old building behind the main structure. Kate blinked at the gray carpet, gray walls, teak furniture, and twenty-first-century appointments.

O'Rourke dismissed the bellboy in German and turned to leave for his own room when Kate called to him from the door.

"Mike . . . I mean, Father . . . wait a minute."

He paused in the narrow hall. Behind him, greenhouse-style windows looked down on slate roofs and old courtyards.

"O'Rourke," said Kate, trying to return from the dark place her sad weariness kept taking her, "I forgot to reimburse you for your ticket and for . . . all this." She gestured lamely at the hallway.

The priest shook his head. "I've got a loan from a well-to-do childhood buddy." He grinned for the first time in the week he had stayed with her, showing white teeth against his dark beard. "Dale's a writer and never does anything with his ill-earned profits anyway. He was happy to give me a loan."

"No, I'll reimburse you for . . . everything," she said, hearing the exhaustion in her own voice. She frowned at him. "You never told me while we were discussing all this . . . where does your diocese or bishop or whoever your boss is . . . where do they think you are?"

O'Rourke's grin remained. "On vacation," he said. "Six years overdue. Everyone from His Excellency to the WHO administrator I work with to my housekeeper in Evanston think that it's a great idea that I'm finally taking some time off."

Kate leaned tiredly against the doorframe. "And what would it do to your reputation if they learned that you're traveling across Europe with a woman?"

O'Rourke tossed his room keys in the air and caught them with a jingle. He traveled with a single leather carry-on garment bag and he slung the strap over his shoulder with the practiced ease of an inveterate traveler. "It would improve my reputation immensely if some of my old seminary buddies and instructors could see me now," he said. "They always thought I was too serious. Now you get some sleep and we'll get together for a late lunch or early dinner whenever you waken. All right, Neuman?"

"All right, O'Rourke." She watched him stroll whistling down the hall and noticed his slight limp before she closed and locked her door.

* * *

They had an appointment with the Gypsies in Budapest on Sunday evening, and O'Rourke had booked them aboard the Vienna-Bucharest hydrofoil leaving at eight A.M that Sunday morning, October 6.

"It's the last day the hydrofoil runs," he said as they walked in Rathaus Park the next day. "Winter's coming on."

Kate nodded but did not really believe it. The day was warm, in the mid-sixties at least, and the blaze of fall foliage in the gardens and along the Ringstrasse merely added to the crisp perfection of the weather. Kate's mood called for rain and cold.

"We have the day," the priest said softly, as if reluctant to invade her thoughts. "Any ideas how to spend it? You should be resting, of course."

"No," Kate said firmly. The idea of lying in her hotel bed made her want to scream with impatience.

"Well, the Kunsthistorisches Museum has a wonderful collection of art," he said. "And this is a big year for Mozart."

"Didn't you tell me that the Kunsthistorisches had a portrait of the real Dracula?" asked Kate. She had been reading everything she could on historical Transylvanian rulers since she had first diagnosed Joshua's illness three months earlier.

"Yeah . . . I think so," said the priest. "Come on, we can catch the Number 1 tram."

The small sign under the portrait read VLAD IV, TZEPESCH: WOIEODE DER WALACHEI, GEST. 1477, DEUTSCH 16. JH. A smaller sign under the painting said, in German and English: *On Loan from the Ambras Museum, Innsbruck*. Kate stared at the face in the life-size portrait.

As a doctor, she saw the large, slightly protruding eyes as possibly hyperthyroidal, the prognathous jaw and extruded underlip of a type sometimes associated with mental retardation or certain types of pituitary and bone disorders. *Platyspondylist?* she wondered. *The kind of characteristic abnormality found with thymic dysplasia and other Severe Combined Immune-Deficiency symptoms?*

"Cruel eyes, aren't they?" said O'Rourke. The priest stood with his hands locked behind his back, rocking slightly on his heels.

Kate was almost startled by the question. "I wasn't thinking about whether they were cruel," she said. She tried looking at the portrait without medical prejudice. "No," she said at last, "I'm not struck by the cruelty in that gaze . . . arrogance, to be sure. But he was a prince."

"Voivode of Wallachia," agreed O'Rourke. "That's the really frightening thing about Vlad the Impaler's monstrosities—they were more or less par for the course in those days. That's the way princes remained princes." He turned and watched Kate's absorbed gaze. "You really think Bela Lugosi here has something to do with the strain of Joshua's disease?"

Kate pretended to smile. "Dumb, huh? But you heard the clinical description of the immunoreconstructive process the disease feeds on. Drinking blood. An enhanced lifespan. Amazing recuperative powers . . . almost autotomizing."

"What's autotom—whatever?"

"Autotomizing is the way some reptiles like salamanders can actually shed their tails in an emergency and regrow them," said Kate. Her head hurt less when she thought about things medical. The black tide of sorrow receded then as well. "We don't know much about regenerative powers in salamanders . . . only that it occurs on a cellular level and that it requires an immense amount of energy."

O'Rourke nodded toward the portrait. "And you think maybe Vlad had some salamander in his royal lineage?"

Kate rubbed her forehead. "It's crazy. I know it's crazy." She closed her eyes a moment. The museum echoed with footsteps, coughs, conversations in German that sounded as harsh as the coughs, and an occasional laugh which sounded as insane as she felt.

"Let's sit down," said the priest. He took her arm and led her to an area on the second-floor rotunda where cake and coffee could be purchased. He chose a table away from the traffic flow.

Kate was fuzzy for a moment, becoming aware of things again as O'Rourke urged her to take another sip of strong Viennese coffee. She didn't remember his ordering it.

"You really believe that the Dracula legends might have something to do with Joshua's . . . abduction?" His voice was just above a whisper.

Kate sighed. "I know it doesn't make sense . . . but if the disease were contained in a family . . . requiring a rare double recessive to manifest itself . . . and the sufferers needed human blood to survive—" She stopped herself and looked down the hallway toward the room where the painting hung.

"A small, royal family," continued O'Rourke, "requiring secrecy due to the nature of their disease and their crimes, having the money and power necessary to eliminate enemies and retain their secrecy . . . even to sending kidnappers and murderers to America to retrieve a baby from that family . . . a baby adopted by mistake."

Kate looked down. "I know. It's . . . nuts."

O'Rourke sipped his espresso. "Yes," he said. "Unless you belong to a church that has had secret correspondence for centuries about just such an evil and reclusive family. A family which originated somewhere in Eastern Europe half a millennium ago."

Kate's head snapped up. Her heart was already pounding and she felt the rise in blood pressure as a sharper pain in her aching skull. She ignored it. "Do you mean—"

O'Rourke set down the cup and held up a single finger. "Still not enough to base a theory on," he said. "*Unless* . . . unless you tie it to the strange coincidence of having met someone who looks very much like the late, unlamented Vlad Ţepeş."

Kate could only stare.

O'Rourke reached into his coat pocket and took out a small envelope of color photographs. There were six of them. The background was obviously Eastern Europe . . . a dark factory town . . . a medieval city street, Dacias parked along the curb. Kate knew intuitively that the photographs had been taken in Romania. But it was the man in the foreground who held her attention.

He was very old. That was immediately apparent from his posture, the curve of spine, the sense of a shrinking body lost in oversized clothes. His face was just visible above the lapels of an expensive topcoat, beneath the short brim of a homburg. But although sharpened and abraded by age and injury, it was a familiar face: no mustache here, but the broad underlip, the extended jaw, eyes sunken in the skull but still vaguely hyperthyroidal.

"Who?" whispered Kate.

O'Rourke slipped the photographs back in his coat pocket. "A gentleman I originally traveled to Romania with almost two years ago . . . a gentleman whose name you've probably heard."

Two men began arguing loudly in German just behind O'Rourke's chair. A man and a woman, Americans from the looks of their casual clothes, stood three feet away watching Kate and the priest, obviously waiting impatiently for the table.

O'Rourke stood up and extended his hand to her. "Come on. I know a quieter place."

Kate had seen pictures of the big wheel before; everyone had. But it was somehow more charming when encountered in reality. She and O'Rourke were the only passengers in an enclosed car that could have easily held twenty people. The car behind them, although empty this evening, was actually filled with dining tables set with linen and china. Slowly, the wheel rotated their car two hundred feet to its highest point and then stopped as other people loaded far below.

"Neat Ferris wheel," said Kate.

"*Riesenrad*," said the priest, leaning on a railing and looking out the opened window at the fall foliage burning in last glow of autumn twilight. "It means giant wheel." As he said that, the glow on the clouds faded and the sky began to pale and then darken. The car moved slightly around, swept down past the loading point, and then climbed above the treetops again.

Lights were coming on all over Vienna. Cathedral towers were suddenly illuminated. Kate could see the modernistic towers of UNO City off toward the Danube; Susan McKay Chandra had once described to Kate the excitement of attending a conference there at the headquarters of the United Nations Commission for Infectious Diseases.

Kate winced, closed her eyes a second, and then looked at O'Rourke. "All right, tell me about this man."

"Vernor Deacon Trent. You've heard the name?"

"Sure. He's the Howard Hughes-style reclusive billionaire who made his fortune in . . . what? . . . appliances? Hotels? He has that big art museum named after him near Big Sur." Kate hesitated. "Didn't he die last year?"

O'Rourke shook his head. The car swooped low and the sounds of the few rides still operating came more clearly through the open window. Their car rose again. "Mr. Trent bankrolled the mission that brought me and a bunch of other guys—a WHO bigwig, the late Leonard Paxley from Princeton, other heavy hitters—into Romania right after the revolution. I mean *right* after. Ceauşescu wasn't cold yet. Anyway, I went back to the States in February of last year, 1990, to try to round up some Church-sponsored aid for the orphanages over here, and before I left Chicago in May of that year, I'd read that Mr. Trent had suffered a stroke and was in seclusion somewhere in California. But he was still in Romania the last time I saw him."

"That's right," said Kate. "*Time* had a thing about the corporate battle over control of his empire. He was incapacitated but not dead." She shivered at the suddenly cool breeze.

O'Rourke pulled the window almost shut. "As far as I know, he still hasn't died. But I was struck at the time we first came to Bucharest how much Mr. Vernor Deacon Trent looks like that old portrait of Vlad Ţepeş."

"A family resemblance," said Kate.

The priest nodded.

"But the painting we saw today was a copy . . . done a century after Vlad Ţepeş lived. It may be inaccurate."

O'Rourke nodded again.

Kate looked at the lights of the old city. Screams came up from the loop-the-loop roller coaster below. "But if it *is* a family resemblance, then it may have some connection with . . . something." She heard how lame that last word sounded, even to herself, and she closed her eyes.

"There are about twenty-four million people in Romania," O'Rourke said softly. "It has an area of . . . what? . . . somewhere around a hundred thousand square miles. We have to start somewhere, even if all of our theories are half-assed."

Kate opened her eyes. "Do you have to say a Hail Mary or something when you swear, O'Rourke? I mean, do you do penance?"

He rubbed his cheek but did not smile. "I give myself a dispensation . . . since I can't give myself absolution." He glanced at his watch. "It's after six, Neuman. We'd better find a place to eat and get to bed early tonight. The hydrofoil is scheduled to leave at eight and the Austrians are nothing if not prompt."

Chapter Twenty-two

T HE hydrofoil was sleek and enclosed, the forward compartment holding half a dozen rows of no more than five seats per row on each side of the aisle, the curving Perspex windows giving a panoramic view of both banks of the Danube as the engines fired to life and moved the boat out carefully from the dock. The old city fell away quickly and within moments the only signs of habitation were the elevated fishing and hunting shacks along either side of the river; then these also fell behind and only forest lined the shores.

Kate looked at her Donau-Dampfschiffahrts-Gesellschaft schedule, saw that it would take about five hours to travel down the Danube to Budapest, and said to O'Rourke, "Maybe we should have flown directly."

The priest turned in his seat. He was dressed in jeans, a denim shirt, and a well-broken-in leather bomber jacket. "Directly to Bucharest?"

Kate shook her head. "I still don't think they would let me in the country. But we could have flown directly to Budapest."

"Yes, but the Gypsies wouldn't meet with us before tonight." He turned back to watch the south shore as the hydrofoil accelerated to thirty-five knots and rose on its forward fins. The ride was perfectly smooth. "At least this way we get to see the sights."

The warm sunlight fell across their row of seats and Kate half-dozed as the hydrofoil carried them northeast around the curve of the Danube near Bratislava, then southeast until a young woman announced over the intercom that the shore to their right now belonged to Hungary, with Czechoslovakia still on the left. The forest along the river seemed more advanced into autumn here, with many of the trees bare. As they turned south, the sky began to cloud up and the warm band of sunlight across Kate first dimmed and then disappeared. Warm air began to blow out of the ship's ventilators to make up for the sudden chill outside.

O'Rourke had thought to have the hotel pack a lunch for them, and they opened the sealed containers and munched on salad and roast beef as the Danube hooked south into Hungary proper. Just as they had finished their lunch, O'Rourke said, "This area is known as the Danube Bend. It's been important since Roman times . . . the Romans actually had summer homes along here. It was the border of the Empire for centuries."

Kate glanced at the forested riverbanks and could easily imagine the northeast shore being the edge of the known world. The cold wind spiraled leaves onto the gray and choppy surface of the Danube.

"There," said O'Rourke, pointing to their right. "That's Visegrad. The Hungarian kings built that citadel in the thirteenth or fourteenth century. King Matthias occupied it during the height of the fifteenth-century Renaissance."

Kate barely glanced to her right. She saw the ancient fortification on the hill and a broad wall running down to an even older-looking tower near the riverbank.

"That's where our friend Vlad Dracula was imprisoned from 1462 to 1474," said the priest. "King Matthias had him under house arrest for most of the last years of his life."

Kate swiveled in her seat to watch the old wall and tower fall behind on the right. She continued staring even after the fortifications were out of sight. Finally she turned back to her companion. "So you don't think I'm completely crazy to be interested in the Dracula family? Tell me the truth, O'Rourke.''

"I don't think you're completely crazy," he said. "Not completely."

Kate simulated a smile. "Tell me something," she said. "Sure."

"Why do you know so much about so many things? Were you always this smart?"

The priest laughed—an easy, sincere sound that Kate realized she loved to hear—and scratched his short beard. "Ahh, Kate . . . if you only knew." He looked out the window a moment. "I grew up in a small town in central Illinois," he said at last. "And several of my childhood friends were really smart."

"If these small-town buddies include Senator Harlen and that writer, they must've been," said Kate.

O'Rourke smiled. "I could tell you a few things about Harlen, but yeah, you're right, our little group had some pretty smart kids in it. I had a friend named Duane who . . . well, that's another story. Anyway, I was the dummy of the group."

Kate made a face.

"No, seriously," said the priest. "I realize now that I had a learning disability—probably a mild case of dyslexia—but the result was that I flunked fourth grade, was left behind all my buddies, and felt like a moron for years. Teachers treated me that way, too." He folded his arms, his gaze turned inward at some private memory. He smiled. "Well, my family didn't have enough money to get me into college, but after 'Nam— after the Veterans' Hospital I should say—I was able to use the G.I. Bill to go to Bradley University, and then to seminary. I guess I've been reading ever since, sort of to make up for those early years."

"And why the seminary?" Kate asked softly. "Why the priesthood?"

There was a long silence. "It's hard to explain," O'Rourke said at last. "To this day I don't know if I believe in God."

Kate blinked in surprise.

"But I know that evil exists," continued the pries. learned that early on. And it seemed to me that someone . . . some group . . . should do its best to stop that evil." He grinned again. "I guess a lot us Irish think that way. That's why we become cops or priests or gangsters."

"Gangsters?" said Kate.

He shrugged. "If you can't beat them, join them."

A woman's voice announced over the intercom that they were approaching Budapest. Kate watched as the farms and villas began appearing, to be superseded by larger buildings and then the city itself. The hydrofoil throttled back and came off its forward planes; they began to bounce along in the wakes of barges and other river traffic.

Budapest had perhaps the most beautiful riverfront Kate had ever seen. O'Rourke pointed out the six graceful bridges spanning the Danube, the wooded expanse of Margitsziget— Margaret Island—splitting the river, and then the glory of the city itself—old Buda rising high on the west bank, younger, sprawling Pest stretching away to the east. O'Rourke had pointed out the beautiful parliament building on the Pest side and was describing Castle Hill on the Buda side when exhaustion and dismay suddenly washed over Kate like a great wave. She closed her eyes a second, overwhelmed by sorrow, a sense of futility, and the sure knowledge that she had been displaced forever in space and time.

O'Rourke quit talking at once and gently touched her forearm. The hydrofoil's engine rumbled as they slowed and backed toward a pier on the Pest side of the river.

"When do we meet the Gypsy representative?" asked Kate, her eyes still closed.

"Seven tonight," said O'Rourke. He still touched her arm.

Kate sighed, forced the tide of hopelessness back far enough that she could breathe again, and looked at the priest. "I wish it were sooner," she said. "I want to get going. I want to get there."

O'Rourke nodded and said nothing else while the hydrofoil rumbled and bumped its way to the end of this leg of their voyage.

* * *

O'Rourke had booked rooms for them in a Novotel in the Buda side of the city, and Kate marveled at the island of Western efficiency in this former Communist country. Budapest made Kate think of Bucharest, Romania, in twenty-five years—perhaps—if capitalism continued to make inroads there. Never very interested in economic theory, Kate nonetheless had a sudden insight, however naive, that capitalism, or at least the individual initiative component of it, was like some of the life forms that found a foothold in even the most marginal of ecological niches until eventually—*voilà!*—a proliferation of life. In this case, she knew, the proliferation would grow and multiply until the balance of old and new, public and commercial, aesthetically pleasing and standardized mediocre would be lost and all the tiresome, leveling byproducts of capitalism would make Budapest look like all the other cities of the world.

But for now Budapest seemed a pleasant balance of respect for antiquity and interest in the Almighty Dollar—or Forint, whichever the case might be. CNN and Hertz and all the usual pioneer buds of capitalism were present, but even a glimpse of the city in the cab had shown Kate a rich mix of the old and the new. O'Rourke mentioned that all of the bridges and the palace on Castle Hill had been blown up by the Germans or destroyed in fighting during World War II, and that the Hungarians had rebuilt everything lovingly.

In her room, staring out the window at a stretch of autobahn that could have been any American Interstate, Kate rubbed her head and realized that all of this apparent interest in travel trivia was just a way to distract herself from the dark tide that continued to lap at her emotions. That, and a way to avoid the anxiety at the coming entry into Romania.

She was surprised to realize that she *was* afraid of what lay ahead—afraid of the Transylvanian darkness which she'd glimpsed from the hospitals and orphanages of that cold nation—and in that sudden, sharp realization of fear, she had the briefest glimmer of hope that there was a path she could follow to a place where there were some emotions other than sorrow and shock and hopelessness and grim resolve to recover what could not be recovered.

There was a knock at the door.

"Ready?" said O'Rourke. His bomber jacket was cracked and faded with use, and for the first time Kate noticed that the web of laugh lines around the priest's eyes contained small scars. "I figure we can get a light dinner here at the hotel and then go straight to the rendezvous."

Kate took a deep breath, gathered up her coat, and slung her purse over her shoulder. "Ready," she said.

They did not talk during the brief cab ride to Clark Adam Ter, the traffic circle at the west end of the Chain Bridge and just below the walls of Castle Hill. O'Rourke said nothing as they rode the funicular railway up the steep hillside to the ramparts of the Royal Palace itself.

"Let's sightsee," he said softly as they stepped out of the cog railway. He took her arm and led her past glowing streetlamps toward a huge equestrian statue farther south along the terrace.

Kate knew from going over city maps that the Matthias church was in the opposite direction, and she had no urge whatsoever to sightsee, but she could tell from the tone of O'Rourke's voice and the tension in his hand on her arm that something was wrong. She followed without protest.

"This is Prince Eugene of Savoy," he said as they circled the giant statue of a seventeenth-century figure on horseback. The view beyond the balustrade was magnificent: it was not quite six-thirty in the evening, but the city of Pest was ablaze with lights and traffic, brightly lit boats moved slowly up and down the Danube, and the Chain Bridge was outlined with countless bulbs that made the river glow.

"That man near the steps is following us," whispered O'Rourke as they moved into the lee of the statue. Kate turned slowly. Only a few other couples had braved the chill evening breeze. The man O'Rourke had indicated was standing near the steps to the terrace near the cog railway; Kate caught a glimpse of a long, black leather jacket; glasses and beard beneath a Tyrolean hat. The man was studiously looking out over the railing at the view.

Kate pretended to consult her city map. "You're sure?" she said softly.

The priest rubbed his beard. "I think so. I saw him catch a cab behind us at the Novotel. He rushed to get in the car next to ours on the funicular."

Kate walked to the broad railing and leaned on it. The autumn wind brought the scent of the river and dying leaves and auto exhaust up to her. "Are there any others?"

O'Rourke shrugged. "I don't know. I'm a priest, not a spy." He inclined his head toward an elderly couple walking a dachshund near the palace. "They may be following us, too . . . I dunno."

Kate smiled. "The dog too?"

A tug pushing a long barge up the river saluted the city with three long hoots. Traffic whirled around Clark Adam Ter below with a cacophony of horns, then swept across the Chain Bridge, tail lights blending with the red neon on the buildings across the river.

Kate's smile faded. "What do we do?"

O'Rourke leaned on the railing with her and rubbed his hands. "Go on, I guess. Do you have any idea who might be following you?"

Kate chewed a loose piece of skin on her lip. Her head ached less this evening, but her left arm itched under the short cast. She was so tired that concentrating was like driving a car on dark ice—a slow and skittish process. "Romanian *Securitate*?" she whispered. "The Gypsies? American FBI? Some Hungarian thug waiting to mug us? Why don't we go ask him?"

O'Rourke shrugged, smiled, and led her back toward the upper terrace. The man in black leather moved away from them slightly and continued to be absorbed by the view of Pest and the river.

They continued strolling, arm-in-arm—*just another tourist couple*, Kate thought giddily—past the funicular station, across a wide space labeled *Disz ter* by the street sign, and down a street that O'Rourke said was named *Tarnok utca*. Small shops lined the cobblestoned way; most were closed on this Sunday evening, but a few showed yellow light through ornate panes. The gas streetlamps cast a soft glow.

"Here," said O'Rourke, leading her to the right. Kate glanced over her shoulder, but if the man in black leather was following, he was concealed by shadows. Carriages were lined along the small square here and the sound of horses chewing on their bits and shifting their hooves seemed very clear in the chill air. Kate looked up at the neo-Gothic tower of the small cathedral as O'Rourke led her to a side door.

"Technically this place is named Buda St. Mary's Church," he said, holding the massive door for her, "but everyone calls it the Matthias Church. Old King Matthias is more popular in legend than he probably ever was in real life. Shhh . . ."

Kate stepped into the nave of the cathedral as the organ music suddenly rose from silence to near-crescendo. She paused and her breathing stopped for a second as the opening chords of Bach's "Tocatta and Fugue in D-minor" filled the incense-rich darkness.

The interior of the old Matthias Church was illuminated only by a rack of votive candles to the right of the door and one large, red-glowing candle on the altar. Kate had an impression of great age: soot-streaked stone—although the soot may have been only shadows—on the massive columns, a neo-Gothic stained glass window over the altar, its colors illuminated only by the blood-red candlelight, dark tapestries hanging vertically above the aisles, a massive pulpit to the left of the altar, and no more than ten or twelve people sitting silently in the shadowed pews as the music soared and echoed.

O'Rourke led the way across the open area in the rear of the church, down several stone steps, and stopped at the last row of pews in the shadows to the left and behind the seating area in the nave. Kate merely sat down; O'Rourke genuflected with practiced ease, crossed himself, and then sat next to her.

Bach's organ music continued to vibrate in the warm, incense-laden air. After a moment, the priest leaned closer to her. "Do you know why Bach wrote 'Tocatta and Fugue'?"

Kate shook her head. She assumed it was for the greater glory of God.

"It was a piece to test the pipes in new organs," whispered O'Rourke.

Kate could see his smile in the dim, red light.

"Or old organs for that matter," he went on. "If a bird had built a nest in one of the pipes, Bach knew that this piece would blast it out."

At that second the music rose to the point that Kate could feel the vibrations in her teeth and bones. When it ended, she could only sit for a moment in the dimness, trying to catch her breath. The few others who had been there, all older people, rose, genuflected, and left by the side door. Kate watched over her shoulder as a white-bearded priest in a long, black cassock locked the door with the sliding of a heavy bolt.

O'Rourke touched her arm and they walked back to the rear of the nave. The white-bearded priest opened his arms, he and O'Rourke embraced, and Kate blinked at the two—the modern priest still in his bomber jacket and jeans, the older priest in a cassock that came to his shoe-tops, a heavy crucifix dangling around his neck.

"Father Janos," said O'Rourke, "this is my dear friend Doctor Kate Neuman. Doctor Neuman, my old friend Father Janos Petofi."

"Father," said Kate.

Father Janos Petofi looked a bit like Santa Claus to Kate, with his trimmed white beard, pink cheeks, and bright eyes, but there was little of Santa Claus in the way the older man took her hand and bent over to kiss it. "Charmed to meet you, Mademoiselle." His accent sounded more French than Hungarian.

Kate smiled, both at the kiss and the honorific that gave her the status of a young unmarried woman.

Father Janos clapped O'Rourke on the back. "Michael, our . . . ah . . . Romany friend is waiting."

They followed Father Janos to the rear of the cathedral, through a heavy curtain that passed for a door, and up a winding stone staircase.

"Your playing was magnificent, as always," O'Rourke said to the other priest.

Father Janos smiled back over his shoulder. His cassock made rustling sounds on the stone steps. "Ah . . . rehearsal for tomorrow's concert for the tourists. The tourists love Bach. More than we organists, I think."

They emerged onto a choir loft thirty feet above the darkened vault of the church. A large man sat at the end of one pew. Kate glimpsed a sharp face and heavy mustache under a wool cap pulled low and a sheepskin coat buttoned high.

"I will stay if you need me," offered Father Janos.

O'Rourke touched his friend on the shoulder. "No need, Janos. I will talk to you later."

The older priest nodded, bowed toward Kate, and disappeared down the stairway.

Kate followed O'Rourke to the pew where the swarthy man waited. Even with her eyes adapted to the candlelight in the church, it was very dark up here.

"*Dobroy*, Doctor New—*man*?" said the man to O'Rourke in a voice as sharp-edged as his face. His teeth gleamed strangely. He looked at Kate. "Oh . . . *rerk*?"

"I'm Doctor Neuman," said Kate. The echo of Bach's music still vibrated in her bones through layers of fatigue. She had to concentrate on reality. "You are Nikolo Cioaba?"

The Gypsy smiled and Kate realized that all of the man's visible teeth were capped in gold. "*Voivoda* Cioaba," he said roughly.

Kate glanced at O'Rourke. *Voivoda*. The same word that had been under the Vienna portrait of Vlad Ţepeş.

"*Beszel Romany*?" asked Voivoda Cioaba. "*Magyarul*?"

"*Nem*," replied O'Rourke. "*Sajnalom. Kerem . . . beszel angolul*?"

The gold teeth flashed. "Yesss . . . yesss, I speak the English . . . *Dobroy*. Velcome." Voivoda Cioaba's dialect made Kate think of an old Bela Lugosi movie. She rubbed her cheek to wake up.

"Voivoda Cioaba," said Kate, "Father Janos has explained to you what we want?"

The Gypsy frowned at her for a moment and then the gold teeth glimmered. "Vant? *Igen*! Yes . . . you vant to go Romania. You come from . . . *Egyesult Allamokba* . . . United States . . . and you go to Romania. *Nem*?"

"Yes," said Kate. "Tomorrow."

Voivoda Cioaba frowned deeply. "Tomarav?"

"*Hetfo*," said O'Rourke. "Tomorrow. Monday night."

"Ahhh . . . *hetfo* . . . yesss, ve cross tomarav night . . . Monday. It isss . . . iss all . . . how do you say? . . . arranged." The Gypsy swirled fingers in front of his face. "*Sajnalom* . . . my son, Balan . . . he speak the English very good, but he . . . business. Yesss?"

Kate nodded. "And have we agreed on how much?"

Voivoda Cioaba squinted at her. "*Kerem*?"

"*Mennyibe kerul*?" said O'Rourke. He rubbed his thumb and fingers together. "*Penz*."

The Gypsy threw his hands apart as if brushing away something in the air. He held up one finger and pointed at Kate. "*Ezer* . . . you." He pointed at O'Rourke. "*Ezer* . . . you."

"One thousand each," said O'Rourke.

"U.S. American dollars cash," said Voivoda Cioaba, enunciating carefully.

Kate nodded. It was what Father Janos had communicated to O'Rourke earlier.

"Now," added the Gypsy. His teeth flashed.

Kate shook her head slowly. "Two hundred for each of us now," she said. "The rest when we meet our friend in Romania."

Voivoda Cioaba's eyes flashed.

"*Ketszaz ejszakat* . . . ah . . . tonight," said O'Rourke. "*Nyolcszaz on erkezes*. Okay?"

Kate extended the envelope with the four hundred dollars

in it, Voivoda Cioaba lifted it with nimble fingers and slid it out of sight under the sheepskin jacket without glancing within, and there came the flash of gold. "Okay." His hand came out with a map and he spread it on the pew.

Kate and O'Rourke leaned closer. The Gypsy's blunt finger stabbed at Budapest and began following a rail line southeast across the country. Voivoda Cioaba's voice had the hypnotic lilt of litany as he recited the names of stops along the way. Kate closed her eyes and accepted the litany in the incense-smelling darkness of the cathedral.

"Budapest . . . Újszász . . . Szolnök . . . Gyoma-endröd Békéscsaba . . . Lökösháza . . ."

Kate felt the vibration through her leg as the Gypsy's finger stabbed heavily at the map. "Lökösháza."

Chapter Twenty-three

KATE knew the Orient Express from the Agatha Christie book and from countless movies: plush cars, elegant dining, luxurious fittings everywhere, and stylish but mysterious passengers.

This was the Orient Express, but not *that* Orient Express.

She and O'Rourke had arrived early for the seven P.M. departure from Budapest's Keleti Railway Station. The place had been bustling and echoing, a huge, outdoor, iron-and-glass open shed that reminded Kate of etchings of train stations from the previous century. She knew the terminal at the opposite end of this trip—Bucharest's Gara de Nord Station—because she and other World Health Organization workers had gone there in May to document the hundreds of homeless children who lived in the station itself, sleeping in broken lockers and begging from hurrying passengers.

She and O'Rourke had prepaid Ibusz, the Hungarian state tourism agency, for two first-class apartments on this Orient Express, but when they checked in there was only one apartment available for them, and "first class" meant a narrow, unheated cubicle with two bunks, a filthy sink with printed warnings that the water—if available—was dangerous and undrinkable, and only enough room for O'Rourke to sit on the low sink while Kate slumped on the bunk, their knees almost meeting. Neither complained.

The train started with a jolt, leaving the station on time. Both watched in silence as they sped out of Budapest, past the rows of Stalinist apartments on the outskirts, then through sparsely lighted cinderblock suburbs, and then into the darkness of the countryside as the train barreled south and east. Wind whistled through the loosely fitted windows and both Kate and O'Rourke huddled in overcoats.

"I forgot to bring food," said the priest. "I'm sorry."

Kate raised her eyebrows. "There's no dining car?" Despite the squalor of the "first-class apartment," she still had an image of elegant dining amid linen and porcelain vases holding fresh flowers.

"Come," said the priest.

She followed him into the narrow corridor. There were only eight apartments in this "first-class" car and all the doors were shut. The train rocked and bounced as they careened around curves at twice the speed of an American train. The sensation was that the car was going to leave the narrow-gauge rails at every turn.

O'Rourke slid back the heavy, scarred door at the end of the compartment; rows of heavy twine had been tied across the entrance. "The other end is the same," said the priest.

"But why . . ." Claustrophobia surged in Kate like nausea.

O'Rourke shrugged. "I've taken this train from Bucharest west, and it's the same coming the other way. Maybe they don't want the other travelers mixing with first class. Maybe it's some security precaution. But we're sealed in . . . we can get *off* the train when it stops, but we can't go from car to car. But it doesn't matter, because there's no dining car."

Kate felt like crying.

O'Rourke rapped on the first door. A heavyset matron with a permanent frown answered.

"*Egy uveg Sor, kerem,*" said the priest. Kate heard the first word as "edge." O'Rourke looked over his shoulder at Kate. "I think we need a beer."

The frowning woman shook her head. "*Nem Sor . . . Coca-Cola . . . husz Forint.*"

O'Rourke made a face and handed across a fifty-forint bill. "*Kettö Coca-Colas,*" he said and held up two fingers. "Change? Ah . . . *Fel tudya ezt váltani?*"

"*Nem,*" said the frowning woman and handed across two small Coke bottles. She slid her door shut.

Back in the compartment, Kate used the Swiss Army Knife that Tom had given her to open the bottles. They sipped Coke, shivered, and watched black trees whip by the windows.

"The train gets into Bucharest about ten in the morning," said O'Rourke. "Are you sure you don't want to stay on it?"

Kate bit her lip. "It seems nuts to get off in the middle of the night, doesn't it? Do you think I'm nuts?"

The priest drank the last of his soft drink and then paused another thirty seconds. "No," he said at last. "I think the border crossing might well be the end of the trip. Lucian warned us."

Kate looked out at darkness as the train lurched around another bend at high speed. "It's paranoid, isn't it?"

O'Rourke nodded. "Yes . . . but even paranoids have enemies."

Kate glanced up.

"Joke," said the priest. "Let's follow the plan."

Kate set her bottle down and shivered. She could not imagine traveling in this nightmare train during the dead of winter. The only illumination was from a single, sickly 10-watt bulb set into the ceiling. "What's to keep the Gypsies from robbing and killing us?" she said.

"Nothing," said O'Rourke. "Except for the fact that Janos has done business with them before and would tell the authorities if we just disappeared. I think we'll be all right."

The headlight on the train illuminated trees passing in a strobe effect. Suddenly a pasture opened up into blackness and the sudden absence of trees made Kate dizzy. "Tell me about the Gypsies, O'Rourke."

The priest rubbed his hands and blew into them for warmth. "Ancient history or recent?"

"Whichever."

"European Gypsies or our Romanian variety?"

"Romanian."

"They don't have an easy time of it," said O'Rourke. "They were slaves until eighteen fifty-one."

"Slaves? I thought European countries outlawed slavery long before that."

"They did. Except for Romania. Except for Gypsies. They haven't fared much better during modern times. Hitler tried to solve the 'Gypsy Question' by murdering them in concentration camps all over Europe. Over thirty-five thousand were executed in Romania during the war just for the crime of being Gypsies."

Kate frowned. "I didn't think that the Germans occupied Romania during the war."

"They didn't."

"Oh," she said. "Go on."

"Well, about a quarter of a million Gypsies identified themselves as Gypsies during the last Romanian census. But the majority don't want the government to know their background because of official persecution, so there are at least a million in the country."

"What kind of persecution?"

"Officially," said the priest, "Romania under Ceauşescu didn't recognize Gypsies as a separate ethnic strain—only as a subclass of Romanian. The official policy was 'integration'—which meant that Gypsy encampments were destroyed, visas were denied, Gypsy workers were given second-class citizenship and third-class jobs, Gypsy ghettos were created in the cities or Gypsy villages in the country were denied tax money for improvement, and Gypsy people were treated with contempt and viewed with stereotypes reserved for blacks in America seventy years ago."

"And today?" said Kate. "After the revolution?"

O'Rourke shrugged. "Laws and attitudes are about the same. You saw yourself that a majority of the 'orphaned babies' that the Americans were adopting were Gypsy children."

"Yes," said Kate. "Children sold by their parents."

"Yeah. Children are the one commodity that Gypsy families have in abundance."

Kate looked out at the darkness. "Didn't Vlad Ţepeş have some sort of special relationship with the Gypsies?"

O'Rourke grinned. "That was a while ago, but yes . . . I've read that, too. Old Vlad Dracula had Gypsy bodyguards, an all-Gypsy army at one point, and frequently used them for special assignments. When the boyars and other officials rose up against Dracula, his only allies were the Gypsies. It seems that they hated authority even then."

"But Vlad the Impaler *was* authority."

"For a few years," said O'Rourke. "Remember, he spent more time fleeing for his life before and after his princely days than he did ruling. The one thing Dracula never failed to give his Gypsy followers was the one thing they have always responded to—gold."

Kate made a face and tugged her purse closer. "Let's hope that two thousand American dollars is the kind of gold they still obey."

Father Michael O'Rourke nodded and they sat in silence as the train rocked and clattered and roared toward the Romanian border.

Lökösháza was a border town, but O'Rourke said the actual Customs inspections were in Curtizi, a Romanian town a few miles down the track. He said that it was evocative of the bad old days—suspicious passport control officers banging on your compartment door at midnight or sunrise, depending upon which direction the train was headed, guards with Sam Browne belts, automatic weapons, dogs sniffing under the train, and other guards tossing mattresses and clothes around the compartment as they searched.

She and O'Rourke did not wait for Customs. Most of the remaining Hungarian passengers were disembarking in Lökösháza and she and O'Rourke joined them, hustling down the platform with the crowd, moving away from the streetlights when they got beyond the station. It was a small station and a small town, and two blocks from the railway they were nearing the edge of the village. It was very dark. A cold wind blew in from the fields beyond the empty highway. Dogs in the neighborhood were barking and howling.

"That's the cafe Cioaba described," said O'Rourke, nodding toward a closed and shuttered building. The large sign in the window read ZÁRVA, which O'Rourke translated as "closed"; a smaller sign said AUTÓBUSZ MEGÁLLÓ, but Kate did not really believe that any buses would be along that night.

They moved into the shadows of an abandoned cinderblock building across the street from the cafe and stood there, shifting from foot to foot to keep warm. "It feels more like December than early October," whispered Kate after ten or twelve minutes had passed.

O'Rourke leaned closer. Kate could smell the soap and shaving-cream scent of his cheek above the neatly trimmed beard. "You haven't sampled a Hungarian or Romanian winter," he whispered. "Trust me, this is a mild October in Eastern Europe."

They heard the train start up and move out of the station with much venting of steam and clashing of cars. A minute later a police car moved slowly down the highway, but Kate and O'Rourke were far back in the shadows and the vehicle did not pause.

"I think maybe Voivoda Cioaba decided that four hundred was enough," Kate whispered a moment later. Her hands were shaking with cold and frustration. "What do we do if—"

O'Rourke touched her gloved hand. The van was old and battered, one headlight askew so that it illuminated fields instead of the highway, and it pulled into the closed cafe's parking lot and blinked its lights twice.

"Onward," whispered O'Rourke.

Voivoda Nikolo Cioaba drove them only ten or so kilometers from Lökösháza before leaving the paved highway and bouncing down a rutted lane, past a huddle of Gypsy caravan wagons that Kate recognized from storybooks, and then down to the edge of a gulley where the rough track ended.

"Come," he said, his gold teeth gleaming in the glow from a flashlight he held. "We walk now."

Kate stumbled and almost fell twice during the steep descent—she had the insane image of walking all the way into Romania through 'this boulder-strewn darkness—but then they reached the bottom of the gulley, Voivoda Cioaba turned off the flashlight, and before her eyes could adapt, a dozen shielded headlights were turned on. Kate blinked. Six almost-new Land Rovers were parked under camouflage netting hung from wooden poles. Twenty or more men—most dressed like Cioaba in heavy sheepskin coats and tall hats—sat in the vehicles or lounged against them. All eyes were on Kate and O'Rourke. One of the men came forward: a tall, thin man with no beard or mustache; he wore a heavy wool blazer with a ragged sweater beneath it.

"My . . . *chavo* . . . son," said Voivoda Cioaba. "Balan."

"Pleased to meet you," said Balan with a vaguely British accent. "Sorry I wasn't able to accompany my father to the meeting last night." He extended his hand.

Kate thought that there was something salesman-like in the handshake. Voivoda Cioaba showed his gold grin and nodded, as if proud of his son's language ability.

"Please," said Balan, holding open the door of the lead Land Rover. "It is not a long voyage, but it is a slow one. And we must be many kilometers from the border by sunrise." He took their bags from them and tossed the luggage in the rear of the vehicle as Kate and O'Rourke clambered into the backseat.

The other men had gotten in their Land Rovers with a great banging of doors. Engines roared. Kate watched as women in long robes appeared from the rocks and pulled down the poles and camouflage netting with practiced speed. Balan sat behind the wheel, his father in the leather passenger seat, as their vehicle led the way down the gulley and then out onto a flatter stretch of river valley. There was no road. Kate glanced over her shoulder but the other Land Rovers' head-lights were almost completely covered with black tape, allowing only a thin crescent of light to escape.

The rest room on the Orient Express had been miserable—one of the filthiest lavatories Kate had ever seen in her trav-els—but after a mile or two of kidney-jarring, spine-prodding travel, she was very glad that she had used it before reaching Lökösháza. It would be embarrassing to have this caravan stop while she ran behind some boulder.

Kate was half asleep, the rhythmic bouncing and jarring almost hypnotic now, when Balan said, "If I may be so bold to ask . . . why do you choose to enter the People's Paradise in such a manner?"

Kate tried to think of something clever and failed. She tried to think of something merely misleading, but her mind had moved beyond fatigue to some region where thought flowed like cold molasses.

"We're not sure we'd be welcomed properly via the usual routes," said O'Rourke. Kate could feel his leg against hers in the cramped rear bench. There were boxes piled on the floor and seat next to him.

"Ahhh," said Balan, as if that explained everything. "We know that feeling."

O'Rourke rubbed his cheek. "Have things gotten better for the *Rom* since the revolution in Romania?"

Balan glanced at his father and both men looked over their shoulders at the priest. "You know our name for ourselves?" said Balan.

"I've read Miklosich's research," said O'Rourke. His voice sounded ragged with fatigue. "And I've been to India, where the Romany language probably originated."

Balan chuckled. "My sister's name is Kali—an ancient Gypsy name. The man who wishes to purchase her for a wife is named Angar, also an honorable Gypsy name. India . . . yesss."

"What do you usually smuggle?" asked Kate. She realized too late that it was not a diplomatic question, but she was too tired to care.

Balan chuckled again. "We smuggle whatever will bring us the best price in Timişoara, Sibiu, and Bucharest. In the past we have smuggled gold, Bibles, condoms, cameras, guns, Scotch whiskey . . . right now we are carrying X-rated videotapes from Germany. They are very popular in Bucharest, these tapes."

Kate glanced at the boxes next to O'Rourke and under their bags in the back.

Voivoda Cioaba said something in rapid-fire Magyar.

"Father said that we have frequently smuggled people *out* of Romania," added Balan. "This is the first time we have smuggled anyone *in*."

They were crossing rolling pastureland. The dim lights illuminated only the slightest trace of ruts between rocks and eroded gullies.

"And this route is secure?" said O'Rourke. "From the border guards, I mean."

Balan laughed softly. "It is secure only as far as the baksheesh we pay makes it secure."

They bounced along in silence for what seemed like hours. It began to rain, first as an icy drizzle and then hard enough that Balan turned on the single wiper blade in front of him. Kate snapped awake as the Land Rover suddenly bounced to a stop.

"Silence," said Balan. He and Voivoda Cioaba stepped out and closed the doors without slamming them.

Kate craned but could barely make out the other vehicles pulled in behind low shrubs. A river was nearby: she could not see it in the dark, but could hear the water running. She cranked down her window and the cold air lifted a little of the fog of fatigue that hung over her.

"Listen," whispered O'Rourke.

She heard it then, some sort of massive diesel engine. Sixty feet above them, an armored vehicle suddenly came into sight along a highway or railway bridge. A searchlight joggled on its forward carapace, but it did not sweep left or right. Kate had not even known the bridge was there in the rain and darkness.

"Armored personnel carrier," whispered the priest. "Russian-built."

Another vehicle, some sort of jeep, followed, its headlights illuminating the gray flank of the armored car ahead of it. Kate could see the rain as silver stripes in the headlight beams. One of the men in the open door of the jeep was smoking; she could see the orange glow.

They must see us, she thought.

The two vehicles rumbled on, the sound of the diesel audible for a minute or more.

Voivoda Cioaba and Balan got back in the Land Rover. Without speaking, the young man engaged the four-wheel-drive and they bounced down into the river itself. The water rose only to the hubs. They rocked and teetered along on unseen rocks, passing under the bridge. Kate could see barbed wire running down to the water to their right and left and then the fence was behind them in the darkness and then they were roaring up a grade so steep that the Land Rover spun wheels, slid, and almost rolled before Balan found traction and brought them over the lip of the bank.

"Romania," Balan said softly. "Our Motherland." He leaned out his open window and spat.

Kate did sleep for what might have been hours, awakening only when the Land Rover stopped again. For a terrible second she did not know where she was or who she was, but then the sadness and memory rolled over like a black wave. *Tom. Julie. Chandra. Joshua.*

O'Rourke steadied her with a strong hand on her knee.

"Get out," said Balan. There was something new and sharp-edged in his voice.

"Are we there?" asked Kate but stopped when she saw the automatic pistol in the Gypsy's hand.

The sky was growing lighter as Balan led O'Rourke and her away from the Land Rovers. A dozen of the other men stood there in a circle, their dark forms made huge by the large sheepskin jackets and caps.

Voivoda Cioaba was speaking rapidly to his son in a mixture of Magyar, Romanian, and Romany, but Kate followed none of it. If O'Rourke understood it, he did not look happy at what he heard. Balan snapped something back in sharp Romanian and the older man grew still.

Balan lifted the pistol and pointed it at the priest. "Your money," he said.

O'Rourke nodded to Kate and she handed over the envelope with the other sixteen hundred dollars in it.

Balan counted it quickly and then tossed it to his father. "*All* your money. Quickly."

Kate was thinking about all the cash in the lining of her carry-on bag. More than twelve thousand dollars in American bills. She was reaching for the bag when O'Rourke said, "You don't want to do this."

Balan smiled and the gleam of his real teeth was more eerie than his father's gold grin. "Oh, but we do," said the thin Gypsy. He said something in Magyar and the men in the circle laughed.

O'Rourke stopped Kate from opening the bag with a touch of his hand on her wrist. "This woman is hunting for her child," he said.

Balan stared, impassive. "She was careless to mislay him."

O'Rourke took a step closer to the Gypsy. "Her child was stolen."

Balan shrugged. "We are the *Rom*. Many of our children are stolen. We have stolen many children ourselves. It is no concern of ours."

"Her child was stolen by the *strigoi*," said O'Rourke. "The *priculici . . . vrkolak*."

There was a subtle stirring in the circle of men, as if a colder wind had blown down the river valley.

Balan racked the slide of the automatic pistol. The sound was very loud to Kate. "If the *strigoi* have her child," the Gypsy said softly, "her child is dead."

O'Rourke took another step closer to the man. "Her child *is strigoi*," he said.

"*Devel*," whispered Voivoda Cioaba and raised two fingers toward Kate.

"When we meet our friends in Chişineu-Criş, we will pay you an extra thousand dollars because of the danger you have faced tonight," said O'Rourke.

Balan sneered. "We leave your bodies here and we have all of your money."

O'Rourke nodded slowly. "And you will have shown that the *Rom* are without honor." He waited half a minute before going on. The only sound was the unseen river gurgling behind them. "And you will have given the *strigoi* and the *Nomenclature* bureaucrats who serve them a victory. If you let us go, we will steal the child from the *strigoi*."

Balan looked at Kate, looked at the priest, and then said something to his father. Voivoda Cioaba replied in firm Magyar.

Balan tucked the automatic pistol out of sight in his rumpled blazer. "One thousand American dollars cash," he said.

As if they had just stopped so that everyone could stretch their legs, the men returned to their vehicles. Kate found that her hands were shaking as she and O'Rourke followed Balan and his father back to the car. "What is a *strigoi*?" she whispered.

"Later."

O'Rourke's lips were moving as the Land Rover began rolling toward the weak sunrise and Kate realized that he was praying.

The village of Chişineu-Criş lay on Romania's E 671 Highway north of Arad, but the Land Rovers did not go beyond the edge of the city.

Lucian's blue Dacia was waiting at the boarded-up church on the west side of town, just where he said he would be. There was enough light to see the young man's grin as he saw Kate.

O'Rourke paid the Gypsies while Kate was engulfed in Lucian's hug. Then he shook the priest's hand vigorously and hugged Kate again.

"Hey, cool, you really did it. You got in with the Gypsy smugglers. *Outstanding*."

Kate leaned against the Dacia and watched the Land Rovers bounce back into the wooded countryside. She caught a final glimpse of Voivoda Cioaba's gold grin. Then she looked at Lucian. The young medical student's haircut was more severe, almost punk, and he was wearing an Oakland Raiders baseball jacket.

"Did you have a good trip?" asked Lucian.

Kate crawled into the backseat of the Dacia as Lucian dropped into the driver's seat and O'Rourke tossed the luggage in the rear.

"I'm going to sleep until we get to Bucharest," she said, laying her head on the cracked vinyl of the seat. "You drive."

Chapter Twenty-four

K ATE was on the Orient Express again, but she could not remember how she got there or why. The compartment was even smaller than the one they had ridden in from Budapest to Lökösháza, and this one did not even have a window. She and O'Rourke were squeezed together even more tightly than before, their legs all but interlocked as he sat across from her on the low shelf. The bunk she sat on was larger, however, and it was made up with the gold duvet cover and oversized pillows that she and Tom had bought in Santa Fe years ago. And the compartment was warmer than before, much warmer.

She and O'Rourke said nothing as the motion of the train rocked them back and forth and from side to side. With each motion, their legs touched more fully—first their knees, then the inside of their knees, and finally their thighs—not rubbing against one another of their own volition, but making contact passively, inexorably, insistently, through the gentle rocking of the train.

Kate was very warm. She was wearing not the wool trousers she had actually traveled in, but a light tan skirt she had treasured in high school. The skirt had ridden up as their legs rubbed. She realized that each time she rocked forward her knee lightly brushed Father O'Rourke's groin, and each time the rhythm of the train rocked him forward, his denim-clad leg brushed gently up her inner thigh until his knee almost touched her there as well. His eyes were closed although she knew that he was not asleep.

"It's warm," she said and took off the blouse her mother had made for her when she entered junior high at a private Boston academy.

There was a rap at the carved wooden door and the conductor came in to collect their tickets. Kate was not embarrassed that she was wearing only a bra and that her skirt was hiked up to her hips—after all, it was *their* cramped and overheated compartment—but she was a bit surprised to notice that the conductor was Voivoda Cioaba. The Gypsy punched their tickets, winked at her, and showed his gold teeth. Kate heard the lock click shut when he left.

Father O'Rourke had not opened his eyes while the Gypsy conductor was in the room, and Kate was sure that the priest was praying. Then Mike O'Rourke did open his eyes and she was sure that he had not been praying.

There was no upper bunk, merely the queen-sized lower berth. Kate sank back into the pillows as O'Rourke stood, leaned forward, and laid his body half atop hers. His eyes were very gray and very intense. She wondered what her own eyes were revealing as O'Rourke rolled her skirt the final few inches to her waist and deftly slid her underpants down her thighs, past her knees, off her ankles. She did not remember him undressing, but now realized that he was wearing only Jockey shorts.

Kate set her fingers in O'Rourke's hair and pulled his face closer to hers. "Are priests allowed to kiss?" she whispered, suddenly fearful that she would get him in trouble with his bishop, who was riding in the next compartment.

"It's all right," he whispered back, his breath sweet on her cheek. "It's Friday."

Kate loved feeling his mouth on hers. She let her tongue slide between his teeth at the same instant she felt him grow hard against her thigh. Still kissing him, she lowered both hands to his sides, slid fingers beneath the elastic of his shorts, and tugged out and down with a movement so smooth that it was as if both had rehearsed it for years.

She did not have to guide him. There was the slightest second of hesitation and then the slow, warm moment of his entering and her encircling him. Kate ran her hand down his muscled back and spread her palm on the warm crease of his buttocks, pulling him closer even when he could come no closer.

The train continued to rock them so that neither had to move, merely surrender to the gentle swinging of their bed in the car on the clacking rails as the rocking grew quicker, the moist warmth more insistent, the gentle friction more urgent.

Kate had just opened her mouth to whisper Mike O'Rourke's name when the door slid open with a crack of the broken lock and Voivoda Cioaba stepped in with his golden grin. Behind him were four of the night men dressed in black hoods.

Someone was shaking her by the arm.

Kate awoke slowly, each sense responding sluggishly, sense impressions arriving separately like tourists with watches tuned to different time zones. For a moment she was awake and technically aware but also totally disoriented, her mind stranded in that egoless void which the mind allows for only scant seconds upon awakening from the deepest of sleeps.

Lucian was bending over her, his youthful face illuminated by the small oil lamp he carried.

"It's time to go to the Arab Student Union," he whispered. Then he set the lamp down and left her small room.

Kate sat up, feeling tiredness pull at her even as the physical echoes of her dream grew fainter and fled. She could not quite remember . . . something about Tom? Or had it been O'Rourke or Lucian? The cold air in the dark room made her shiver.

Memory pressed on her like a cold and unwelcome suitor. *Tom. Julie. Joshua!* She felt the pain of her left arm and the air was suddenly rank with the smell of smoke and ashes. Sorrow threatened to push her into the cold darkness that surrounded her. The memories of the past few weeks were not discrete images, but a single, inseparable mass with a terrible weight which she kept at bay only by concentrating on the next thing that had to be done.

The Arab Student Union.

As full consciousness returned, Kate remembered that it was not her first night in Bucharest, despite the strangeness of the basement room she was sleeping in, but her third. It was raining. Pellets of sleet pounded against the small window set high on the wall. She remembered now that it had been raining for each of the three days and nights she had been back in Bucharest.

She looked down and realized that she had fallen asleep that afternoon in her corduroy pants and dark sweater. There was a small frameless piece of mirrored glass propped on the battered dresser near the door and Kate used it to pull a brush through her hair until she finally gave up. She slung a purse over her shoulder and went to join Lucian in the other room.

The medical student had found Kate and O'Rourke a basement apartment on a narrow street in an old section west of Cişmigiu Gardens. The apartment consisted of Kate's tiny bedroom and the rough-walled "sitting room" where O'Rourke slept on a couch during the few hours he was there. The toilet upstairs was "private" in the sense that no one lived on the ground floor or first floor because of "renovations," although Kate had seen no workers or signs of recent work on the gutted rooms up there. The massive metal radiators in the basement were as cold and dead as steel sculptures; the only heat came from a small coal-burning fireplace in Kate's bedroom. Lucian had brought a heavy sack of coal along with a warning that the burning of it was still illegal, and Kate tried to restrict her need for warmth to one lump in the morning while getting dressed and to a tiny fire in the evening.

It was very cold.

Kate was still shivering as Lucian led her out to the Dacia. "Where's O'Rourke?" she asked. The priest had left shortly after breakfast that morning without saying where he was going.

Lucian shrugged. "Probably still hunting for Popescu."

Kate nodded. The inaction during the past three days had driven her close to madness. She had not been sure what they would find upon returning to Bucharest—a clue perhaps, some sign of Joshua's forced return—but in the absence of any immediate clue she had done little but huddle in the basement rooms while O'Rourke made forays into the city. It made sense on the face of it; neither of them had visas, the assumption was that the authorities were on the lookout for her, and they could not go to the American Embassy, UNICEF, the WHO, or any other familiar organizations for help.

But O'Rourke could use the few local Catholic churches and the Bucharest headquarters for the single Franciscan order in Romania to make contacts. And their first goal had been to find Mr. Popescu, the administrator of the hospital where Kate had worked and discovered Joshua. There was no compelling reason to believe that the greasy little administrator was part of the plot to kidnap her adopted child, but finding Popescu was a place to start.

But O'Rourke had not found him—queries from priest friends at the hospital had resulted only in the information that Popescu was on leave—and the frustration after three days was driving Kate out of hiding, if not actually to the brink of insanity.

The Dacia started after much fiddling with the choke and they bounced out onto the bricks of Bulevardul Schitu Magureanu along the west side of Cişmigiu Gardens. Despite the fact that it was only the second week in October, most of the trees bordering the street were bare of leaves. The icy rain pelted against the windshield and only the wiper on the driver's side worked, squeegeeing back and forth with a screech of a single, long fingernail against a blackboard.

"Tell me again about the Arab Student Union," said Kate.

Lucian glanced at her. His face was mottled with shadow-streaks from the occasional streetlight shining through the rain-splattered windshield. There were few functional street-lights in Bucharest this autumn, but the Dacia had come onto the wide Bulevardul Gheorghe Gheorghiu-Dej and there was some light here. The avenue was all but empty.

"The Arabs attend the university on full scholarship," said Lucian, "but almost none of them go to classes. They spend their years here changing money and being brokers in the black market. The Arab Student Union is the center for much of this."

Kate tried to peer out at the street, but the windshield in front of her was a shifting mass of icy rain. She glanced at the dark canal on her right as they turned onto the even broader avenue of Splaiul Independenței. The incredible mass of the unfinished presidential palace was just visible across rubbled fields and behind tall fences. There were one or two lights on in the huge structure, but these only served to accentuate the hopeless and inhuman scale of the place. Kate shivered. "And the guy we're seeing might know something about Joshua?"

Lucian shrugged. "My contacts say that Amaddi keeps tabs on the *Nomenclature*. He certainly serves their needs when they deal with the black market. It may be worth our time talking to him . . ." Lucian glanced at her. "It's foolish for you to come along though, Kate. I can—"

"I want to talk to him," said Kate. Her tone left no room for debate.

Lucian shrugged again. He pointed out the University Medical School as they drove past it and they turned north again, past a row of dilapidated dormitories, then down a long alley lined with dark and decaying Stalinist apartment blocks. Ragged curtains blew from shattered windows, and there were holes in the masonry large enough for a person to step through. The rain had let up a bit and Kate could see large rats fleeing from the beam of the headlights. The entrance to the building they stopped in front of had a torn steel mesh dangling from the doorway.

"These are empty, aren't they?" asked Kate.

Lucian shook his head. "No, these are the Arab dormitories."

Kate cranked down her window and could make out a feeble glow of what might be lantern light behind some of the tattered curtains.

Lucian pointed toward a lower building with no windows, its walls and single doorway spray-painted with graffiti. "That's the Student Union. Amaddi said that he would meet us there."

There were no lights in the foyer or outside corridor. Lucian flicked on a lighter and Kate could make out chipped and filthy tile and an inner hallway almost filled with cardboard boxes and crates. Following Lucian as he squeezed past the crates, she realized that the boxes were marked PANASONIC and NIKE and SONY and LEVI's. At the end of the corridor was a closed metal door. Lucian rapped twice, waited a second, and then rapped once. The door squeaked open and Lucian clicked the lighter shut and stepped aside to let Kate go first.

The room was large, at least twenty meters square, and the perimeter was stacked with more cartons and boxes. Dining tables and plastic chairs lay tossed in a heap to one side, and only a single table with a lantern on it was set out near the far end of the room. The dark and bearded man who had opened the door for them gestured toward the table and stepped back into the shadows.

Three men sat at the table; two were obviously enforcer-types—leather coats, necks broader than their skulls, flat stares—but the third was a small man with a poor excuse for a beard and acne scars visible even at a distance. He beckoned Kate and Lucian to the table.

"Sit," he said in English and waved them toward two folding chairs.

Kate remained standing.

"This is Amaddi," said Lucian. "He and I have . . . done business before."

The little man grinned, showing very white teeth. "A Sony

diskman . . . an Onkyo stereo receiver . . . five pairs of 501 Levi's . . . four pairs of Nike shoes, including the new Nike Air crosstrainers . . . a subscription to *Playboy* magazine. Yes, we have done business.''

Lucian made a face. "You have a good memory.''

The young Arab's gaze moved to Kate. "You are American.''

It was not a question and Kate did not try to answer.

"What would you like to buy, Madame? Money, perhaps? I can give you a rate of two hundred fifty *lei* to the dollar. Compare that to the official rate of sixty-five *lei* to one dollar American.''

Kate shook her head. "I want to buy information.''

Amaddi raised an eyebrow. "Good information is always a scarce commodity.''

Kate shifted her purse. "I'm willing to pay for this particular commodity. Lucian says that you serve the *Nomenclature*.''

Amaddi's eyebrow had remained arched. Now he smiled slightly. "In this country, Madame, everyone serves the *Nomenclature*.''

Kate took a step closer to the table. "I have reason to believe that members of the *Nomenclature* have kidnapped my adopted child and brought him from America to Bucharest. Or at least to Romania. I want to find him.''

For a long moment Amaddi did not blink. Finally he said, "And why . . . in this land of too many unwanted children . . . why would anyone, *Nomenclature* or peasant . . . steal another child?''

Kate held the young man's gaze. The light made it seem as if his irises were completely black. "I'm not sure why. My son . . . Joshua . . . was born in Romania a year ago. Although he was an orphan, someone wanted him back. Someone important. Someone with the money and power to send their agents to America. If you have heard about a child brought back here, I will pay for the information.''

Amaddi steepled his fingers. The two men seated beside

him stared impassively. The room was very quiet and smelled of cooking spices and strong after-shave lotion.

"I know of no such child," Amaddi said slowly. "But I have a client who is very high in the . . . how shall we say it? The unofficial *Nomenclature*. If anyone had knowledge of such an improbable event, my client would be that person."

Kate waited. She was marginally aware of Lucian trying to catch her eye, but she kept her gaze locked with the young Arab student's. He spoke first.

"My client is a very powerful man," he said softly. "Giving you his name would entail much risk on my part."

Kate waited another thirty seconds before saying, "How much?"

"Ten thousand," Amaddi said, his face impassive. "Ten thousand American dollars."

Kate shook her head almost sadly. "This information is not the commodity I need. It guarantees me nothing. This man may know nothing about my child."

Amaddi shrugged.

"I would pay five hundred American dollars for his name," said Kate. "To show my willingness to do business with an honest man such as yourself. Then, if other information became available to you . . . information of some real value . . . we would discuss such serious amounts."

Amaddi took out a matchbook, opened the cover, and cleaned between his side teeth. His gaze darted toward his companions for an instant. "Perhaps I have understated the importance of this person," he said. "Few others . . . if any . . . know that he is a member of the *Nomenclature*. Yet he is so highly placed that no action of the *Nomenclature* occurs without this person's approval."

Kate took a breath. "Is this man then a member of the *strigoi* as well as the *Nomenclature* The *priculici*?" She struggled to keep her voice level. "The *vrkolak*?"

Amaddi blinked and lowered the matchbook. He snapped something in Romanian at Lucian. Kate heard the word *strigoi*. Lucian shook his head and said nothing.

"What do you know of the *Voivoda Strigoi*?" Amaddi demanded of her.

In truth, Kate knew nothing. When she had asked O'Rourke the meaning of the Romanian and Slavic words he had used when bargaining with the Gypsies for their money and lives, the priest had answered, "*Strigoi* translates roughly as warlocks, although it also implies evil spirits, vile ghosts or vampires. *Priculici* and *vrkolak* are Romanian and Slavonic for vampires." When Kate had pressed O'Rourke on why the naming of these words had impressed the Gypsies, the priest had said only, "The *Rom* are superstitious folk. Despite rumors that they have served the *strigoi* for centuries, they fear these mythical rulers of Transylvania. You heard Voivoda Cioaba say *Devel* when I suggested that Joshua was of the *strigoi*."

"And he gave me the sign to ward off the evil eye," Kate had said. "And then he let us go." O'Rourke had only nodded.

Amaddi stood up and smashed his palm flat on the table, shaking Kate out of her reverie. "I asked, what do you know of the *Voivoda Strigoi*, woman?"

Kate resisted the urge to flinch in the face of the young Arab's intensity. "I think they have stolen my child," she said, her voice steady. "And I will have him back."

Amaddi glared at her a long minute and then laughed, the sound echoing off cement walls. "Very well," he said. "In the face of such courage, you will have the person's name for five hundred American dollars. And we shall do further business in the future . . . if you live." He laughed again.

Kate counted out the five hundred dollars and held it until Amaddi took a Cross fountain pen from his pocket and wrote a name and address on a slip of paper. Lucian looked at the name, glanced at Kate, and nodded. Kate released the money.

Amaddi walked them to the door. "Tell your American friend the old Romanian proverb," he said to Lucian. "*Copilul cu mai multe moase ramana cu buricul ne taiat*."

Lucian nodded and led the way down the dark corridor.

In the Dacia, with the rain falling heavily again, Kate let out a breath. "You recognized the name he wrote?"

"Yeah," said Lucian, his usual smile absent. "He's well known in Bucharest. My father knew him."

"And you think he might actually be a member of this secret *Nomenclature*?"

Lucian started to shrug but visibly stopped himself. "I don't know, Kate. I just don't know. But it gives us a place to start."

She nodded. "And what was the proverb that Amaddi threw at me?"

Lucian started the car and rubbed his cheek. "*Copilul cu mai multe moase romana cu buricul ne taiat* . . . it's sort of like, what is it? 'Too many cooks spoil the soup'? Only this one translates as, 'A child with too many midwives remains with his navel-string uncut.' "

"Ha-ha," said Kate.

They drove back through the empty streets in silence.

O'Rourke was waiting in the cold and shadowed basement room when they entered. He looked red-eyed and unshaven, although still dressed in his black priest suit and Roman collar. He sat sprawled in the sprung armchair and only stared at Lucian as the two bustled around to light the coal fire in the other room and put a pan of soup on the hot plate.

"Did you find Popescu?" asked Kate.

"No. I was in Tîrgovişte all day."

"Tîrgovişte?" Then Kate remembered that the city about fifty miles northwest of Bucharest had been the site of the orphanage from which Joshua had been transferred. "Did you find anything?"

"Yes," said O'Rourke. His voice was thick with fatigue. "The officials at the orphanage still don't have any information about Joshua's parents. He was found in the alley near the orphanage."

"Too bad," said Lucian, tasting the soup with a wooden spoon. He made a face. "I hope you two like your swill on the bland side."

"But I did bribe a custodian there to give me a description of the two men who arranged Joshua's transfer from Tîrgo-vişte to Bucharest," said the priest. "The custodian could describe the two men because they came in person to make the transfer."

"And?" said Kate. She pulled the slip of paper from her coat pocket. If the gods were kind, Lucian would be able to tell if the man named there matched this description.

"One was middle-aged, short, overweight, officious, with slicked-back hair and a penchant for Camel cigarettes."

"Popescu!" said Kate.

"Yes," said O'Rourke. "The man with Popescu was young, also Romanian, but with a flawless American accent. The custodian said that he heard the younger man joke in English with the orphanage administrator. He said that this younger man wore expensive Western jeans . . . Levi's . . . and the kind of American running shoe with the curving wave on the side. Nikes. He and Popescu drove Joshua away in a blue Dacia."

Kate turned and stared at Lucian.

The young man set the wooden spoon back in the soup. "Hey," he said. "Hey. There are a million blue Dacias in this country."

O'Rourke stood up. "My custodian eavesdropped on part of the conversation while they were getting Joshua ready to travel," he said softly. "The young Romanian with the flaw-less American English said that he was a medical student. The joke in English was that if he couldn't find a rich American to buy the baby, he would sell the child to the vivisectionists at the University Medical School."

Lucian backed away from the hot plate, toward the door. Kate blocked his way.

"The custodian said that Popescu called the younger man by name when they were counting the money to bribe the orphanage administrator," said O'Rourke. "He called him Lucian."

Dreams of Blood and Iron

MY life now consists almost totally of whispers and dreams. The dreams are of days and enemies long dead; the whispers in the hall and on the stairs and in my very room, as if I were here only as a corpse, are of the recovery of the child for the Investiture Ceremony. The whispers are smug now. They speak of their cleverness in recovering the baby. They do not talk of how the child was lost or which enemies abducted him. They can not imagine or do not seem to remember what terrifying wrath would have descended on them, what terrible tolls of punishment would have been extracted, were I the Vlad of old confronted with such knowledge of my underlings' incompetence.

It does not matter. I am not the Vlad of old. The slow erosion and certain tempering of decades and centuries have seen to that.

But my dreams are memories untouched for several of those centuries, and in my dreams I am seeing myself for the first time. I listen to the whispers as the final details of the Ceremony are planned, as my Family argues amongst itself as to whether their Father can be present in his dying and detached state. But even as I eavesdrop on these whispers, it is the dreams that compel my attention.

* * *

*Frederick the III's poet laureate, Michael Beheim, has
written of my encounter in 1461 with three barefoot Benedic-
tine monks: Brother Hans the Porter, Brother Michael, and
Brother Jacob. Beheim heard the story from the third monk,
Brother Jacob, and their distorted version has been written,
quoted, and retold for five centuries. Poet Beheim's impartial-
ity might be discerned from his original title for the poem as
he sang it to the Holy Roman Emperor in 1463*: Story of a
Bloodthirsty Madman Called Dracula of Wallachia.

*Few have ever bothered to challenge Brother Jacob's ac-
count through poet Beheim's pen. None have ever heard the
entire account. Until now.*

*The circumstances were thus: In those days the bishop
of Ljubljana, Sigismund of Lamberg, seized on the popular
assumption that the monks in the Slovenian abbey of Gorrion
in the city of Gornijgard had adopted the outlawed reforms
of Saint Bernard, and used that excuse to drive the monks
from the monastery in order to make the property his own.
Three of those monks—Brother Hans the Porter, Brother
Michael, and Brother Jacob—fled across the Danube north
to a Franciscan monastery in my capital city of Tîrgovişte.*

*Even though I was later forced to convert to Catholicism
for political reasons, I hated that vile religion then, and I
care nothing more for it now. The Church was merely a rival
power in those days—and a ruthless one—despite its attempts
to cloak its grasping, clutching machinations in the guise of
piety. I doubt that it has changed. And the Franciscans were
the worst. Their monastery in Tîrgovişte was a thorn in my
side which I tolerated because the act of plucking it out
would cause more political pain than the relief the extraction
merited. The common people loved their fawning, praying,
fasting Franciscans even as the monks bled the people dry
with their alms and tithings and ceaseless whining for more
money. The Church in Wallachia then—especially that
damned Franciscan monastery which, unaccountably, despite my best efforts of the day, still stands in Tîrgovişte
today—was a parasite growing bloated and sated on blood*

*money which would have served my kingdom better had it
come to me.*

The Franciscans could not stand the Benedictines in those
days, and I suspect that they sheltered the three fleeing Bene-
dictine monks merely to further irritate me. And it did.

I encountered Brother Jacob, Brother Michael, and
Brother Hans the Porter a mile or so from their monastery
as I returned to my palace from a hunt. Their less-than-
deferential manner irritated me and I commanded the one
called Michael—the tallest of the three—to appear at an
audience in my palace that very afternoon.

Beheim relates that I frightened the monk with a harsh
interrogation, but in truth the skinny friar and I had a pleasant
chat over warm ale. I was soft-spoken and courteous, revealing nothing of my inherent distaste for his corrupt religion.
My questions were mere polite theological probings. Brother
Michael warmed to his proselytizing as the ale warmed his
guts, although I could see the alarmed squint of his ferretlike
little eyes as my questions grew personal.

"So the burdens of this life are merely an unpleasant pre-
lude to the promise of the next life?" I asked softly.

"Oh, yes, My Lord," the skinny monk hurried to agree.
"Our Saviour has affirmed this."

"Then," I continued, pouring more ale for the man,
"someone who serves to shorten that burdensome period by
hurrying the suffering mortal to his reward before he can
accumulate more sins might be seen as being a benefactor?"

Brother Michael could not hide a slight frown as he lowered
his lips to his ale. But the slurping sound he made might have
been taken as affirmation. I chose to interpret it so.

"Then," I went on, "some poor servant of the Lord such
as myself who has sent many hundreds of souls—some say
thousands—on to their reward before sin could further
blacken their chances—would you say that I am a savior of
those souls?"

Brother Michael moistened his already moist lips. Perhaps
he had heard of my sometimes mischievous sense of humor.

Or perhaps the ale was beginning to affect him. Whatever the reason, he could not quite muster a smile, although he tried. "One might suggest that possibility, Sire," he said at last. "I am only a poor monk, unused to the rigors of logic or the demands of apologetics."

I opened my hands and smiled. "As you say, if we accept that premise," I said cordially, "then it stands to reason that someone such as myself who has helped thousands of souls shrug off their earthly burdens, why, that someone would have to be considered a saint for all of the souls he has saved before sin could damn their chances. Wouldn't you agree, Brother Michael?"

The skinny friar licked his wet lips again and looked even more like a ferret who has just discovered that a cage has been lowered over him while he was distracted. "A . . . uh . . . a saint, My Lord? Certainly it might be posited, but . . . ah . . . well, My Lord, sainthood is a difficult and delicate proposition to . . . ah . . . prove, and . . . uh . . ."

I decided to take pity on the panicked man. "Tell me this then," I said, my voice sharpening a bit. "Could someone such as I, even if not guaranteed sainthood, find salvation through Jesus Christ?"

Brother Michael almost burbled in his relief at being asked this question. "Oh, yes, Sire! Salvation is yours just as it is every man's. Our Lord and Saviour has extended his mercy through His death on the cross, and that mercy cannot be denied if the petitioner is truly penitent and wishes to change his . . . that is, Sire, if the penitent sinner wishes to walk in the grace of Our Lord's teachings and commandments."

I nodded. "And your fellow monks, of course, would express the same opinions on my chances for salvation?"

Again the ferret squint. Finally he managed to say, "All of my fellow brothers know the teachings of Jesus and the power of God's mercy, Sire."

I smiled—sincerely this time—and ordered the skinny friar to stay put while we called for his companions.

The evening shadows were long across the stone floor when I put the questions to Brother Hans the Porter, a smaller,

*stouter man whose tonsure looked like it had been adminis-
tered by a gardener's shears.*

"Sir Monk," I said, "you know who I am?"

"Of course," said the little man while his two companions
looked on with some anxiety. It was obvious that this was the
fanatic of the group. His eyes were unafraid and tinged with
the flames of righteousness. There was no deference in his
voice, none in his posture. I chose to ignore the absence of
courtesy in his not using the traditional "Sire" or "My Lord"
in addressing me.

"You know my reputation?" I said.

"Yes."

"You know that it is true?"

The small monk shrugged. "If you say it is so."

"It is true," I said softly. From the corner of my eye I
could see Brother Michael blanch. Brother Jacob, who indeed looked like a Jew, was very pale and very impassive.
"It is true," I continued in the same conversational tones,
"that I have tortured and murdered thousands of people,
most of them guilty of no overt act against me or my regime.
Many of my victims have been women—many of them pregnant women—and many were young children. I have tortured, beheaded, and impaled many such so-called innocent
women and children. Do you know why this is so, Brother
Hans the Porter?"

"No." The portly little monk stood with his hands clasped
loosely in front of him, his legs apart as if standing easily to
hear some peasant's confession. There seemed only slight
interest in his face.

"It is so because just as Jesus was a good shepherd, I am
a good gardener," I said. "When one must cut the weeds out
of one's garden, one must not only pull the weeds at the
surface. A good gardener is compelled to dig deep to eradi-
cate the roots which grow far underground and which
threaten to spawn new weeds in seasons yet to come. Is this
not so, Brother Hans the Porter?"

The monk looked at me for a long moment. Despite his
portly appearance, his face was strong in bone and muscle.

"I am not a gardener," he said at last. *"I am a servant of Our Lord Jesus."*

I sighed. *"Then answer me this, servant of Your Lord Jesus,"* I said, trying to keep the asperity out of my voice. *"Given that all that is said about me is true, that thousands of innocent women and children have died at my hand or my command, I command you to tell me my fate after death."*

Brother Hans the Porter did not hesitate. His voice was calm. *"You will go to Hell,"* he said. *"If Hell will have you. Were I Satan, I think I could not stomach your presence, even though the screams of the tormented damned souls are said to be like music to Satan's ears. But you would understand Satan's preferences much better than I."*

It was difficult for me to hide a smile. I envisioned the talk at my court and other courts when I sent these three friars away with their donkeys laden with wealth for their abbeys. I admire courage in my enemies.

"So you think I am not a saint?" I said softly.

Then Brother Hans the Porter made a mistake. *"I think you are mad,"* he said in his deep, soft, somewhat sad voice. *"And I take pity on the fact that madness has led you to eternal damnation."*

At this comment my good humor fled. I called my guards and had them hold Brother Hans the Porter while I took an iron stake and impaled the man. Forgoing the relative mercy of impaling him between his fat buttocks, I drove short spikes through his ears and eyes and a longer one down his throat. He was still writhing when I drove a large metal nail through his feet and had him hoisted by a cable to hang head down like a piece of market poultry. I called in my court to witness this.

Then, while Brother Michael and Brother Jacob stood pale and staring, I called for Brother Hans the Porter's donkey and had the animal impaled on a great iron stake there in the court. The operation was loud and not as simple as it sounds.

When it was finished, I turned to Brother Jacob. *"You have heard your companions' opinions on the chances of my salvation,"* I said. *"Now, what is your opinion on this matter?"*

Brother Jacob threw himself facefirst onto the stone floor in an attitude of total supplication. Brother Michael joined him there a second later.

"Please, My Lord," quaked Brother Jacob, his hands extended and clasped so tightly that they were as white as virgin vellum. *"Mercy, My Lord! I beg mercy, in the name of God!"*

I strode over the floor until my boots touched each man's cheek. *"In whose name?"* I roared. Not all of the anger was feigned; I was still irked at Brother Hans the Porter's final remarks before his confidence had turned to anguished screams.

Brother Michael had the quicker wit. *"In your name, My Lord! We ask mercy in the Blessed Name of Vlad Dracula! In Your Name we beseech You!"*

I could hear the reverence in both voices as their pleas found a focus. I lifted my boot onto Brother Jacob's neck. *"And to whom will you pray henceforth when you wish either mercy or divine intervention?"*

"To Our Lord Dracula!" gasped Brother Jacob.

I shifted balance and set my boot on Brother Michael's neck. *"And who is the only power in the universe who has the power to answer or deny your prayers?"*

"My Lord Dracula!" managed Brother Michael, the air going out of him like bad wind out of an old wine bladder as I trod more heavily on his spine.

There was a moment where there was no sound in the crowded court except for the dripping of blood from Brother Hans and his donkey. Then I lifted my boot off Brother Michael's neck and walked slowly away, finally dropping languorously onto my throne. *"You will leave my city and my country tonight,"* I said. *"You may take your animals and as much food for the voyage as you wish. If my soldiers find you within Wallachia's or Transylvania's borders when the sun rises three mornings from now, you will pray to your new*

God—that is to say, to me—that you could have died as easily as Brother Hans the Porter or his braying ass. Now go! And spread the word of Vlad Dracula's infinite mercy.''

They went, but based upon the lies Brother Jacob later dictated to the all-too-eager-to-slander poet Michael Beheim, they had not learned their lesson adequately.

But those at court that day had. As had the Franciscan friars who stayed behind in their monastery in Tîrgovişte. They were sullen in there behind their cloistered walls, but they were increasingly quiet from that day forward.

And the carefully honed legend of Vlad Dracula grew sharper, and extended its reach to the hearts of my enemies.

Chapter Twenty-five

WHEN O'Rourke was finished talking, the three of them stood in silent tableau there in the hissing lamplight, Lucian frozen halfway between the hot plate and the door, O'Rourke standing in shadow by the sprung sofa, and Kate standing closest to the lantern. Her gaze had been moving back and forth between the haggard-looking priest and the younger man, but now she stared only at Lucian. Her thought was, *If he runs we will have to chase him down. O'Rourke looks exhausted. I will have to do it myself.*

Lucian did not run.

O'Rourke rubbed his stubbled cheek. There was no victory in his eyes, only sadness.

If Lucian is one of them, thought Kate, *then they know where we are. The men in black. The men who killed Tom and Julie and Chandra. The men who stole Joshua. . . .* She felt her heartbeat accelerate, was vaguely conscious of her fists knotting as if of their own accord.

Lucian stepped back to the hot plate, lifted the wooden spoon, and slowly stirred the now-bubbling soup.

Kate wanted to strangle him at that moment. "Is it true?" she asked. "Lucian, was it you?"

If he had shrugged, she would have lifted the wooden chair behind her and brought it down on his head at that moment.

He did not shrug. "Yes," he said. "It was me." He looked at her a second and then lifted the spoon and tasted the soup.

"Put the spoon down," said Kate. She found herself wondering if she could dodge in time if Lucian threw the pan of boiling soup at her.

Lucian set the spoon down and took a step toward her.

O'Rourke stepped between them just as Kate raised both fists. Lucian raised both hands, palms outward.

"Let me explain," he said softly. His Romanian accent seemed stronger. "Kate, I would never do anything to hurt Joshua . . ."

She felt her composure slip then and remembered pulling the trigger when the man in black had seemed to threaten her baby three months earlier . . . an eternity earlier. She wished that she had a gun now.

"No, I mean it," said Lucian, reaching past O'Rourke to touch her arm.

She pulled her arm away. Lucian held up his hands again. "Kate, it was my job to get the baby out of the country safely, never to hurt him."

It seemed as if Michael O'Rourke had not blinked during the entire exchange. Now he stepped aside, unplugged the hot plate, and carefully set the pan of soup aside on a tile ledge, out of Lucian's reach. "You said you can explain." He crossed his arms. "Explain."

Lucian tried to smile. "I expect you'll have some explaining to do yourself, priest. After all, it's hardly coincidence that you—"

"*Lucian!*" snapped Kate. "We're talking about *you*."

The young man nodded and raised his hands again as if urging calm. "All right . . . where to begin?"

"It was your job to get the baby out of the country," said O'Rourke. "What do you mean your job? Who gave you that job? Who are you working for?"

Kate glanced at the door, half expecting *Securitate* forces to break in. There were no sounds except for the hiss of the lantern and the pounding of her heart.

"I'm not working for anyone," said Lucian. "I'm working

with a group that's been fighting for freedom for years . . . centuries.''

Kate made a rude sound. "You're a partisan. Freedom fighter. Sure. And you fight the tyrants by kidnapping babies."

Lucian looked at her. His eyes were very bright. "By kidnapping babies *from* tyrants."

"Explain," said Father Michael O'Rourke.

Lucian sighed and dropped into the couch. "Can we all sit?"

"You sit," said Kate, folding her arms to keep her hands from shaking. "Sit and talk."

"OK," said Lucian. He took another breath. "I'm a member of a group that resisted Ceauşescu when he was in power. Before that, my father and mother fought Antonescu and the Nazis."

"By kidnapping babies," interrupted Kate. She could not keep her voice from shaking.

Lucian looked at her. "Only when they belong to the *Voivoda Strigoi*."

O'Rourke shifted his weight as if his artificial leg were paining him. His face looked very strong in the lantern light. "Explain."

Lucian twitched a smile. "*You* know about the *strigoi*," he said, "You Franciscans have been fighting them for centuries."

"Lucian," said Kate, stepping between the men, "why did you take Joshua from the orphanage in Tîrgovişte? Were you working for Popescu's people?"

The young man laughed, more easily this time. "Kate, *nobody* works for Popescu. That medical pimp worked for anyone who paid him. We paid him."

"Who is 'we'?" snapped Kate.

"The Order. The group my family has belonged to for centuries. Our struggle has been not just for the political survival of our country, but for the survival of its soul. Behind the Ceauşescus, behind the previous Communist regimes, behind Ion Antonescu, behind them all . . . have been the *strigoi*. The evil ones who walk like people but who are not. The Dark Advisors. The ones with power who drain our nation's future away as surely as they have drained the life-blood of its people.''

"Vampires," said Kate. Her attention was so focused on Lucian at that moment that the periphery of her vision seemed to fade.

The young man did shrug this time. "That is the Western name. Most of the myth is yours . . . the sharp teeth, the opera cape . . . Bela Lugosi and Christopher Lee. Your *nosferatu* and vampires are stories to frighten children. Our *strigoi* are all too real.''

Kate found herself blinking rapidly. "Why should we believe you?''

"You don't have to believe me, Kate. You were the one person who could discover the truth of the *strigoi* on your own. Go ahead . . . tell me what you and your fellow researchers found at America's famous CDC. Tell me!" He did not wait for her reply. "You found a child's immune system which can repair itself, reverse the effects of even Severe Combined Immune Deficiency . . . if it has blood.''

Kate tried to swallow but her throat was too constricted.

"Did you isolate the blood-absorption mechanism in the stomach lining?" asked Lucian. "I have. In the corpses of their dead and the bodies of their living . . . like Joshua. Were you able to track the immunoreconstruction process in T-cells and B-cells as the retrovirus revitalized the purine pathway? Do I really have to convince you that there are human beings here who rebuild their bodies using the DNA properties from other people's blood? Or that they have amazing recuperative powers? Or that they could—theoretically— live for centuries?''

Kate licked her lips. "Why did you and Popescu take Joshua from the Tîrgovişte orphanage? Why did you lead me to him and pull strings to have me adopt him?''

Lucian sighed. His voice was tired. "You know the answer to that, Kate. You've seen our medical equipment in this country. We know that the *strigoi* disease is similar to the HIV virus. We know that the *strigoi* retrovirus has amazing properties. But serious gene-therapy analysis is beyond this country's abilities. My God, Kate, you've seen our toilets . . . do you really think that we can construct and operate an effective Class-VI lab?''

''Who is 'we'?'' repeated O'Rourke. ''What is the 'Order'?''

Lucian looked at the priest towering over him. ''The Order of the Dragon.''

Kate heard the sudden intake of her own breath. ''I've read about that. Vlad the Impaler belonged to that—''

''He *defiled* it,'' snapped Lucian, his voice angry for the first time that night. ''Vlad Dracul and his bastard son pissed on everything the Order stood for . . . *stands* for.''

''And what does it stand for?'' asked O'Rourke.

Lucian jumped to his feet so quickly that Kate thought he was attacking O'Rourke and her. Instead, the young man ripped the buttons off his shirt and exposed his chest.

The amulet there glinted gold: a dragon, talons extended, body curling in a circle, the circle of scales superimposed on a double cross. The amulet was very old, the words inscribed on the cross almost rubbed away. ''Go ahead,'' Lucian said to O'Rourke. ''You can read Latin.''

'' '*Oh, how merciful is God!*' '' read O'Rourke, leaning closer. ''And '*Just and Faithful*.' '' He stepped back. ''Just and Faithful to whom?''

''To the Christ defiled by Vlad Dracul and his spawn,'' said Lucian. He closed the front of his shirt, sealing it with the only remaining button. ''To the people whom the Order was created to defend.''

''To defend by stealing babies,'' said Kate, her voice dripping with sarcasm.

Lucian wheeled on her. ''Yes! If the baby is the next Prince of the *Voivoda Strigoi*.''

Kate began laughing. She backed up until she felt the wooden chair behind her legs and dropped onto it, still laughing. She stopped just as the laughter began sounding like sobs. "You kidnapped Dracula's baby so that I could adopt him . . ."

"Yes." Lucian smoothed his hair back with both hands. His hands were shaking slightly. He nodded toward O'Rourke. "Ask him, Kate. He knows more than he has told you."

She looked at the priest.

"The Franciscans here have heard rumors of the *strigoi* for centuries," said O'Rourke. "And of the Order of the Dragon."

"How do we know you're not one of the *strigoi*?" said Kate, never looking away from the young medical student.

Lucian paused. "Did you see John Carpenter's remake of Howard Hawks' *The Thing*?"

"No."

"Shit," said Lucian. "I mean, that doesn't matter. Anyway . . . they find out who's human in the movie by testing the other guys' blood. I'd be willing to give some if you two would."

O'Rourke arched an eyebrow. "You're serious, aren't you?"

"You're goddamn right I'm serious, priest. I can vouch for Kate, but between thee and me, I'm not too sure about thee."

"What would a test prove?" said Kate. "If you don't show signs of having the retrovirus, you could still be working for the . . . *strigoi*."

Lucian nodded. "Sure. But you'd know I wasn't one of them."

Kate sighed and rubbed her face. "I think I may be going crazy." She squinted up at Lucian. "What was all that with Amaddi tonight . . . some sort of elaborate scam?"

"No," said Lucian. "My father and other members of the Order have known about Amaddi's contacts with the *strigoi* *Nomenclature* for some time. But none of us have been able to approach him."

"But you did business with him."

"To gain his confidence."

"So the name he gave us is real?" asked Kate. "The man is really *strigoi?*"

Lucian shrugged. "During the past few months, both the *strigoi* and the few surviving members of the Order have gone into hiding. If this person is *strigoi*, it explains several things."

"I'm not saying that I believe any of this," said Kate. "But if it's true . . . and you say your parents are members of the Order of the Dragon . . . can they help us find this man?" Kate had only met Lucian's parents once, but it had been a gracious afternoon of special wine and home-cooked treats in a lovely old apartment in east Bucharest. Lucian's father, a writer and intellectual, had impressed her as someone of great wisdom and influence.

"The *strigoi* murdered my parents in August," said Lucian. His voice was soft. "Most of the members of the Order here in Bucharest were tracked down and killed. Most simply disappeared. My parents' bodies were left hanging in the apartment where my sister or I would find them. A warning. The *strigoi* are very sure of themselves these days."

Kate fought down the urge to hug Lucian or touch his cheek. *He may be lying.* Every instinct she trusted said that he wasn't.

"You talked about the hospital administrator . . . Popescu . . . in the past tense," said O'Rourke.

Lucian nodded. "Dead. The police found his body, drained of blood, in the same week that Mr. Stancu—your Ministry man—ended up on the slab at the medical school."

"Why would they kill Mr. Popescu?" asked Kate. She heard the answer in her own mind a second before Lucian spoke again.

"They tracked the child . . . Joshua . . . from the orphanage to Popescu's hospital. I'm certain that the weasel told them everything he knew about you . . . and me . . . before they cut his throat."

"And you've been in hiding since then?" said O'Rourke.

"I've been in hiding since the day Kate left," said Lucian.

"I urged my parents and friends to flee, but they were stubborn . . . brave." Lucian turned away, but not before Kate saw his eyes fill with tears.

Maybe strigoi are good actors, she thought. She was exhausted. The lingering smell of the hot soup in the room made her a bit dizzy.

"Look," said Lucian, spreading his large hands on his knees as he sat on the sofa arm. "I can't show you any other credentials than this . . ." He tapped his chest. ". . . proving that I belong to the Order, or that the Order exists. But use common sense. Why would I have helped smuggle Joshua to the hospital and then helped you adopt him if I were *strigoi?*"

"We don't even know if your *strigoi* exist," said Kate.

Lucian nodded. "All right. But I think I can give you a demonstration that may prove it."

Kate and O'Rourke waited.

"First we go to the medical school tonight and do a blood test on me to prove that I am *not strigoi*," said Lucian. "The equipment is primitive, but a simple interactive test should show whether my blood exhibits the *strigoi* retrovirus reaction."

"J-virus," Kate said softly.

"What?"

"J-virus." She looked up. "We named it after Joshua at CDC."

"OK," said Lucian. "We do a simple J-virus test, and then we stake out . . . if you'll pardon the expression . . . the house of the man Amaddi named. We follow him wherever he goes."

"What?" said O'Rourke.

"Because if he's *strigoi*," said Lucian, "he'll lead us to the others. My father was certain that Joshua had been the child chosen for the Investiture Ceremony . . . and it must be almost time for that to begin."

"What is—" began Kate.

"I'll explain when we drive over to the medical school labs," said Lucian. He lifted the soup onto the burner and plugged the hot plate in again.

"What are you doing?" asked O'Rourke.

"If we're going vampire hunting, I want something in my stomach," said Lucian. He did not smile as he began stirring the soup.

The University Medical School was dark except for the south wing, where a guard sat dozing. Lucian led them through leaf-scattered gardens to a basement door. He fumbled with a heavy ring of keys and unlocked a portal that Kate thought would have looked more at home on a Gothic castle than as part of a medical school.

The basement corridor was narrow, crammed with battered chairs and cobwebbed desks, and it smelled of rat droppings. Lucian had brought a penlight. At one point he unlocked a side door which swung open with a creak.

Who's waiting for us? thought Kate. She tried to catch O'Rourke's eyes but the priest seemed lost in thought.

The room appeared to be a storage room for even more ancient medical texts—Kate could smell the mildew and see the rat droppings here—except that a blanketed cot, a reading lamp, and a countertop hot plate had been added. Kate noticed recent American paperbacks stacked alongside medical texts.

"You've been living here?" asked O'Rourke.

Lucian nodded. "The *strigoi* ransacked my apartment, terrorized homes of friends of mine, and . . . I told you about my parents. But they only made a cursory check of the medical school." He smiled. "If I were to return to classes . . . well, a dozen of my 'friends' and instructors would inform on me . . . but this wing of the building is empty at night." He shut off the light and led them farther down the corridor, then up two darkened flights of stairs.

In the lab, Kate said, "I don't understand. Are the *strigoi* in charge of the police and border guards? Are the police part of this?"

Lucian paused in arranging his microscope and equipment. "No," he said. "But in this country . . . and others, I am told . . . everyone works for the *strigoi* at one time or another. They control those who control."

Kate was finding it hard to believe that this area was the working section of a medical school laboratory: there was a clutter of pre–World War II–type optic microscopes, cracked beakers, dusty test tubes, chipped tile counters, and battered wooden stools. The place looked like someone's nightmare image of an American ghetto high school's science lab years after it had been deserted. Only Lucian had said that this was *the* laboratory area for the medical school.

"So Ceauşescu was a *strigoi*?" asked O'Rourke.

Lucian shook his head. "Ceauşescu . . . both of the Ceauşescus . . . were instruments of the *strigoi*. They took orders from the leader of the *Voivode Strigoi* family."

"The Dark Advisor," said O'Rourke.

Lucian glanced up sharply. "Where did you hear that term?"

"So there was a Dark Advisor?"

"Oh, yes," said Lucian. He moved an antique autoclave onto the counter and plugged it in. "Kate, would you find some lancets?"

Kate glanced around, hunting for sterile-pacs, but Lucian said, "No, there in the sink."

A chipped enamel bedpan held several steel lancets. She shook her head and handed the pan to Lucian. He set the pan in the autoclave and it began to hum.

"This test isn't important," she said. "It proves nothing."

"I think it does," said Lucian. He pulled down blackout shades on the windows and turned on a light over the microscope bench. "Besides, I have something else to show you." Lucian crouched in front of a small refrigerator and removed a small vial. "Standard whole blood," he said. He used an eyedropper to prepare three slides with the whole blood. Then he removed the lancets from the autoclave and brought alcohol and swabs out from under the counter. "Who's first?"

"What are we supposed to see here?" said O'Rourke. "Little vampire platelets leaping on our blood cells?"

Lucian turned to Kate. "Do you want to explain?"

"When Chandra . . . when the experts at our CDC had isolated the J-virus," she said, "it became easy in retrospect to notice the effect on whole-blood and immunodeficient precultured samples. The J-virus . . . it's really a retrovirus . . . binds gp120 glycoprotein to CD4 receptors in T-helper lymphocytes—''

"Whoa, whoa," said O'Rourke. "You mean you can just look at blood samples in a microscope and tell if they're *strigoi*?"

Kate paused and looked at Lucian. "It's not quite that simple. We can't just look in the eyepiece, but . . . yes, you can tell a difference when the J-retrovirus interacts with alien blood cells."

Lucian set the first slide in place. "Did you discover the amazing ratio of infected cells?" He was talking to Kate.

"We placed it at almost ninety-nine percent," she said.

"What does that mean?" asked O'Rourke.

Kate explained. "The HIV retrovirus goes after about one CD4 cell in a hundred thousand. That's a lot when you realize how many billions of cells we have. But the J-virus . . . well, it's greedy. It tries to infect all of the alien blood cells it encounters."

O'Rourke took a step away from the counter. His face looked very pale above his dark suit and Roman collar. "But it can't be that contagious . . . we'd all be vampires . . . *strigoi* . . . if it worked like that."

Kate made herself smile. "No, it's not contagious at all, as far as we can tell. It's generated in the host's body by a complex recessive-recessive gene trait that we don't understand. It's also co-dependent upon the SCID-type immune deficiency disease that comes as part of the package."

"Which means?" said O'Rourke.

Lucian answered without lifting his face from the microscope. "Which means that you have to be dying of a rare blood disease in order to gain virtual immortality from the same disease. It's not catching." He looked up. "Although we might all wish that it were. Who goes first?"

Kate made a "you first" gesture.

"Awesome, dude," said Lucian in his mock mutant turtle dialect. He lifted a lancet, pricked his finger, squeezed enough blood free so that he could transfer a smear to the prepared slide, and handed the lancet pan to Kate. "You want to do the honors with our Father here?"

Kate swabbed O'Rourke's middle finger, drew blood, prepared his slide, and did the same for herself. "I still say that this proves nothing," she said.

Lucian spent several minutes treating the samples while Kate watched. "Well, at least it proves that we can't *see* any little vampire platelets in my sample," he said at last, standing back from the microscope. Kate bent over and peered through.

O'Rourke waved away his turn. "I could never see anything but my own eyelashes," he said. "What's all the stuff you're doing to it?"

Kate's sample went onto the slide tray next. "Preparing it for an assay to check reverse transcriptase," said Kate.

O'Rourke sounded disappointed. "So we couldn't see little vampire platelets even if we tried?"

"Sorry, dude," said Lucian and brought out a centrifuge that Kate thought looked as if it had been designed in the Middle Ages. "But the assay shouldn't take too long." He held up a clean vial. "Now I want to take one more sample."

Kate had the impulse to glance over her shoulder. She wondered what she would do if someone were standing in the shadows there. "From whom?" she said.

"Exactly," said Lucian. He doused the light and led them by penlight down the corridor, back into the basement, and then down another flight of stairs into an even deeper basement.

Kate smelled it first. "The morgue," she whispered to O'Rourke.

Lucian stopped at the last set of swinging doors. "It's OK. This is the old morgue. The students and teachers use the newer, smaller one in the west wing. But this is where the cadavers are stored before the students get them. And sometimes the city uses it as an overflow depot for unclaimed bodies."

"Mr. Stancu from the Ministry?" said Kate.

"Yeah, this is where I saw him. But my letter to you wasn't totally candid, Kate. I'd been tipped by a friend in the Order that Stancu had been murdered. Just like Popescu."

"Can we meet this friend of yours?" said O'Rourke.

"No."

"Why not?"

"He was murdered the same week they killed my parents," said Lucian. "They cut his head off." He opened the doors and the three of them went into the chilly darkness. Bare steel tables with ceramic basins and pedestals loomed in the darkness. They were not clean.

"You know," said O'Rourke, his voice flat, "that we only have your word that your parents were killed."

"Mm-hmm," agreed Lucian. He handed the penlight to Kate. "Thank you," he said as she held it steady. He opened a door and slid the long tray out. Lucian lifted the sheet.

"Kate, do you recognize?" said Lucian, his voice very tight.

"Yes." The last time she had seen Lucian's father, the man had been complimenting her in French, laughing, and pouring more wine for everyone at the table. Now it looked as if his throat had been cut in two places. His skin was very white.

Lucian closed the drawer and opened the one next to it. "And this?"

Kate looked at the middle-aged woman who had blushed with pleasure at Kate's invitation for the Forsea family to visit her in Colorado when Lucian brought them over after finishing medical school. Mrs. Forsea had done her hair especially for their afternoon meeting. Kate could still see a curl of the graying hair. The throat wounds were almost identical to her husband's.

"Yes," said Kate, grasping O'Rourke's hand and squeezing without meaning to. *What if they were actors? Not really Lucian's parents? The whole thing a complex plot?* Kate knew better.

Lucian slid the drawer shut.

"Is this what you wanted to show us?" said O'Rourke.

"No." He fumbled with the ring of keys and unlocked a heavy steel door set in the far wall. It was colder and darker in the next room, but Kate could see glowing dials and diodes illuminating a low, metal cylinder that looked like one of the steel watering tanks she had seen on ranches in Colorado. The surface of the tank was bubbling and broiling.

Two steps closer and Kate stopped, her hands flying to her face.

"Jesus!" breathed O'Rourke. He raised one hand as if to cross himself.

"Come," whispered Lucian. "We'll take the final sample." He led them forward.

The steel tank was about three feet deep and seven feet long and it was filled with blood. At first Kate could not believe it was blood despite the color revealed in the dim light and the obvious viscosity, but Lucian had watched her reaction and said, "Yes, it is whole blood. I stole it from District One Hospital and other places. Much of it comes from the American relief agencies."

Kate thought of the dying children who had needed whole blood transfusions while she was working in Bucharest the previous May, but before she could snap something at Lucian she saw what floated in the tank just beneath the rolling surface.

"Oh, my God." She had whispered. Now, despite her horror, she leaned closer to peer into the tank, squinting in the red and green glow from the dozen or so medical instruments that clustered at one end of the trough, insulated leads and cables flowing into the bath of slowly bubbling human blood.

It was . . . or had been . . . a man, naked now, eyes and mouth wide open as the face floated just beneath the surface. Different parts of his body gleamed in the oily light as unseen currents in the blood moved him to the surface and then let him submerge again. He had been slashed almost to pieces with what looked—to Kate's eye, trained to trauma wounds—to have been a large, bladed weapon.

"A sharpened shovel," said Lucian, as if reading her mind.

Kate licked her lips. "Who did it?" She knew what Lucian would answer.

"I did it." His gaze seemed normal, neither angry nor penitent. "I found him alone, knocked him on the back of the head with a long-handled shovel . . . I think you call it a spade . . . and then chopped him up as you see."

O'Rourke crouched next to the tank. Kate could see droplets of blood spattering the back of the priest's hand as he clutched the steel rim. "Who is he?"

Lucian raised his eyebrows. "Didn't you guess? This is one of the men who murdered my parents." He moved to the oscilloscope on the metal cart next to the tank and changed the display by throwing a switch.

Kate stared at the corpse in the tank. The man's left ear was missing and that side of his face had been sliced open from the cheekbone to chin; the neck was almost severed—she could see the spinal cord as the body bobbed slightly—and there were massive gouges on his upper shoulder, arm, and chest. Kate could see exposed ligaments and ribs. The body had been opened up at the waist and the interior organs were clearly visible. . . .

The body opened like a medical student's cadaver.

Kate looked at Lucian. Then she noticed for the first time what the electronic monitors behind him were monitoring.

She backed away from the tank with an involuntary intake of breath. "It's alive," she whispered.

O'Rourke glanced up, startled, and then wiped his hands on the side of the tank. "How could this poor—"

"It's alive," Kate whispered again. She walked to the instruments, ignoring Lucian. Blood pressure was flat, heart rate was so low that it registered little except the occasional spasm of a random surge as the cardiac muscle moved blood through its chambers and back into the medium of blood that surrounded it, and the EEG was like nothing she had ever seen: alpha and theta spikes so irregular and far apart that they might as well have been messages from some distant star.

But not flatline. Not brain dead.

The thing in the tank was in some state more removed from reality than sleep, but more alert than a coma victim. And it was definitely alive.

Kate looked at Lucian again: still the friendly, open expression and the soft smile. The smile of a murderer. No, the smile of a sadist perhaps.

"They slaughtered my parents," he said. "They hung my mother and father by their heels, slit their throats as if they were swine, and drank from their open wounds." He looked back at the corpse in the tank. "This thing should have died a century ago."

Kate moved back to the tank, rolled up her sleeves, and reached in with both hands, her fingers sliding through lesions and broken ribs to touch the man's heart. After half a moment there was the slightest movement, as of a swallow stirring slightly in the palm of one's hand. A second later, there was an almost indiscernible movement of the man's whitened eyes.

"How can this be?" asked Kate, but she knew . . . had known since she herself had pulled the trigger of Tom's shotgun and then seen the same man again on the night of the fire.

Lucian gestured at the instruments. "That's what I'm trying to find out. It's why I can't leave the medical school." He waved at the body in the tank. "The legends say that the *nosferatu* come back from the dead, but the fact is that they can die. . . ."

"How?" said O'Rourke. "If this man is still alive after this . . . savagery, how would you kill one?"

Lucian smiled. "Decapitation. Immolation. Evisceration. Multiple amputation. Even simple defenestration . . . if they fell far enough onto something hard enough." The smile wavered. "Or just deny them blood after their injuries, and they'll die. Not easily, but eventually."

Kate frowned. "What do you mean, 'not easily'?"

"The retrovirus feeds on foreign blood cells in order to

rebuild its own immune system . . . or entire physical systems," said Lucian. "You've seen it on the micro level at your CDC lab." He opened his palm toward the tank. "Now you see it on the macro level. But . . ." He walked to a multiple-IV feed above the tank and unclipped the drip. "Deny it fresh blood, host blood, and the virus will feed on itself."

Kate looked at the man in the tank. "Feeding on its own cells? Cannibalizing its own blood cells even though the retrovirus has already transcribed the DNA there?"

"Not just the blood cells," said Lucian. "The J-virus attacks whatever host cells it can reach, first along the arterial system, then the major organs, then brain cells."

Kate folded her arms and shook her head. "It doesn't make sense. It has no survival value for the person at all. It . . ." She stopped, realizing.

Lucian nodded. "At that point the retrovirus is trying to save only the retrovirus. Cannibalism allows a few weeks' grace time, even while the body is decaying around it. Perhaps months. Perhaps . . . in a body that has been transcripted for centuries . . . years."

Kate shuddered.

O'Rourke walked to the instruments, then back to the tank. His limp was visible. "If I understand what you two are saying, then a *strigoi* could linger in a type of physical Hell for months or more after clinical death. But surely he couldn't be conscious!"

Lucian pointed to the EEG. Where Kate had palpated the man's heart, the brain waves had shown a definite series of spikes.

O'Rourke closed his eyes.

"Are you torturing this man?" asked Kate.

"No. I'm documenting the reconstruction." He opened a drawer in one of the carts and handed Kate a stack of Polaroid photographs. They looked like standard autopsy photos—she could see the steel examination table under the white flesh of the corpse—but the man's body was much more mutilated than it looked now in the tank. There were deep wounds in the photographs where only livid scars were visible on the actual torso.

"Sixteen days ago," said Lucian. "And I'm almost sure from the data that the reconstructive process is accelerating. Another two weeks and he'll be whole and hearty again." He chuckled. "And probably a little bit pissed at me."

Kate shook her head again. "The simple question of body mass . . ."

"Every gram of body fat is converted, absorbed and reabsorbed and gene-directed to fill in as building material where needed," said Lucian. He shrugged. "Oh, you wouldn't get the whole man back if I cut off his legs or removed his pelvis . . . mass redistribution has its limits . . . but anything short of that and . . . *voilà!*" He bowed toward the tank.

"And they need fresh blood," said Kate. She glared at the medical student. "Is this Joshua's fate?"

"No. The child has received transfusions, but as of the time he left Romania, he had not partaken of the Sacrament."

"Sacrament?" said O'Rourke.

"The actual drinking of human blood," said Lucian.

"That's sacrilege," said O'Rourke.

"Yes."

"The shadow organ," muttered Kate, Then, louder, "When they drink the blood directly, the J-virus carries out the DNA transcription and immunoreconstruction more efficiently?"

"Oh, yes," said Lucian.

"And it has other effects? On the brain? The personality?"

Lucian shrugged. "I'm no expert on the effects of psychological and physical addiction, but—"

"But the *strigoi* . . . change . . . after they've actually drunk human blood?" said Kate.

"We think so."

Kate leaned against an oscilloscope. Random spikes pulsed green echoes onto her skin. "Then I've lost him," she whispered. "They've turned him into something else." She stared at a dark corner of the large room.

Lucian moved closer, lifted a hand toward her shoulder, then dropped it. "No, I don't think so, Kate."

Her head snapped up.

"I think they're saving Joshua for the Investiture Ceremony," he said. "That will be the first time he partakes of the Sacrament."

Father Michael O'Rourke made a sarcastic noise. "You're suddenly quite the expert on matters *strigoi*."

"No more than you . . . *priest*," Lucian snapped back. "You Franciscans and Benedictines and Jesuits, you watch and watch and watch . . . for centuries you watch . . . while these animals bleed my people dry and lead our nation into ruin."

O'Rourke stared without blinking. Lucian turned away and busied himself with the IV, resuming the drip.

"You can't just leave it . . . him . . . here," said Kate, gesturing toward the tank.

Lucian licked his lips. "There are others who will benefit from the data even if I die. Even if all of us die." He whirled at them and clenched his fists. "And do not worry. There are few of us in the Order of the Dragon who have survived, but even if I die someone will come here and cremate this . . . this *dracul*. There is no way that I will allow it to live and prey upon us again. No way at all."

The medical student removed a large syringe from the drawer, extracted blood directly from the body's neck, resumed the IV drip, locked both the inner door and the morgue, and led them upstairs to the lab. He finished the assay in ten minutes and showed Kate the results: three normal samples and one teeming with the J-retrovirus attacking introduced blood cells.

Lucian led them out of the lab, out into the rainy night again. Kate breathed deeply in the parking lot, allowing the soft rain to wash away the stink of formaldehyde and blood from her clothes.

"What now?" asked Kate. She felt exhausted and emotionally brittle. Nothing was clear.

Lucian turned on the single wiper blade, its squeak timing

the night like a metronome. "One of us should stake out this man's house." He held up Amaddi's slip of paper.

"Let me see that," said O'Rourke. He looked at the slip of paper in the dim light, blinked, and then laughed until he collapsed against the hard cushions of the backseat.

"What?" said Kate.

O'Rourke handed back the slip of paper and rubbed his eyes. "Lucian, does this man work for the ONT?"

Lucian frowned. "For the Office of National Tourism? No, of course not. He's a very rich contractor who dabbled in the black market for heavy equipment . . . his state-supported company erected the presidential palace and many of the huge, empty buildings Ceaușescu ordered built in this section of the city. Why?"

O'Rourke looked as if he was going to laugh again. He rubbed his cheek instead. "The name . . . Radu Fortuna. Is he a short man? Swarthy? A thick mustache and a gap between his front teeth?"

"Yes," said Lucian, puzzled. "And one of us should be watching his house around the clock." He glanced at his watch. "It is almost eleven P.M. I will take the first shift."

O'Rourke shook his head. "Let's all go," he said. "We'll watch the house while we watch each other."

Lucian shrugged and then pulled the Dacia out into the empty, rain-glistened streets.

Chapter Twenty-six

MR. Radu Fortuna's home was hidden behind high walls in the *Nomenclature* section of east Bucharest. Large homes like this in the center of the city had long since been converted into embassies or offices for state ministries, but here in the oldest and finest section of the city, Ceauşescu and his political heirs had rewarded themselves and the chosen of their *Nomenclature* with fine homes unchanged since the pre-war reign of King Carol.

"Shit," muttered Lucian as he drove by the walled estate. "I should have realized from the address."

"What's the matter?" said Kate.

Lucian turned and went around the block. The streets here were wide and empty. "During Ceauşescu's days, no one but the Leader and his *Nomenclature* cronies were allowed to drive here. This entire eight-block section was off-limits."

O'Rourke leaned forward. "You mean you could get arrested just by driving here?"

"Yeah." Lucian dimmed his headlights and came around the block again. "You could *disappear* just for driving here."

"Did that change when Ceauşescu died?" asked Kate.

"Yeah. Sort of." Lucian stopped and backed into an alley that was all but hidden by low trees, most still heavy with their sodden leaves, and bushes that had not been trimmed in decades. Branches scraped against the side of the Dacia until only the windshield looked out at the walls and gate and entrance drive of Radu Fortuna's mansion. "The *poliţie* and *Securitate* still patrol here, though. It wouldn't be a great idea to get stopped, since I'm certainly on their detention list and you don't have any papers at all." He backed the Dacia deeper until they were peering through scattered branches at the street.

The rain stopped after a while, but the dripping from the branches onto the roof and hood of the car was almost as loud. The interior of the Dacia grew cold. Windows fogged and Lucian had to use a handkerchief to wipe the windshield clean. Sometime around midnight a police car cruised slowly down the street. It did not stop or throw a searchlight in their direction.

When it was gone, Lucian reached under the seat and brought out a large Thermos of tea. "Sorry there's just one cup," he said, handing the lid to Kate. "You and I will have to share the flask, Father O'Rourke."

Kate huddled over the hot cup, trying to stop shaking. Since O'Rourke's revelations about Lucian a few hours ago, the center of things seemed to have fled. She did not know who or what to believe now. Lucian seemed to be saying that O'Rourke was also part of some plot involving the *strigoi*.

She did not have the energy to question either of them. *Joshua!* she thought. With her eyes shut tightly, she could see his face, smell the soft baby scent of him, feel the silky touch of his thin hair against her cheek.

She opened her eyes. "Lucian, tell us an Our Leader joke."

The medical student handed the Thermos to O'Rourke. "Did you hear about the time that Brigitte Bardot visited our workers' paradise?"

Kate shook her head. It was very cold. She could see floodlights in the compound across the street glinting on coiled razor wire atop the wall. It had started to rain again.

"Our Leader had a private audience with Bardot and was smitten at first sight," said Lucian. "You've seen photos of the late Mrs. Ceauşescu. You can understand why. Anyway, he begins babbling in an attempt to impress the French actress.

'I am in charge here,' he says. 'Anything Mademoiselle wishes is my command.' 'All right,' says Bardot, 'open the borders.' Well, for a moment Ceauşescu is . . . how do you say it? . . . nonplussed. But then he regains his composure and leers his monster's smile at her. 'Ahhh,' he says in a conspirator's whisper, 'I know what you want.' He winks at her. 'You want to be alone with me.' ''

Lucian took the Thermos back from O'Rourke and sipped tea.

The priest cleared his throat in the backseat. Kate wondered if his leg hurt him on cold, wet nights like this. She had never heard O'Rourke complain, even when the limp was very visible.

"I was in Czechoslovakia when Chernobyl happened years ago," said O'Rourke. "Were there jokes here about that?"

Lucian shrugged. "Sure. We joke about everything that scares the shit out of us or makes us want to cry. Don't you?"

Kate nodded. "Like the definition of NASA after the Challenger disaster in that same year of '86," she said. "Oops . . . Need Another Seven Astronauts."

No one laughed. They were not talking to amuse one another.

"In Czechoslovakia," said O'Rourke, "the gag was that the new national anthem for the U.S.S.R. after Chernobyl was *Pec nám spadla, pec nám spadla* . . . 'Our oven has collapsed, our oven has collapsed.' '' After a moment of silence, the priest said, "It's a folk song."

"Here, after Chernobyl," said Lucian, "we asked each other what the three shortest things in the world were."

"What were they?" said Kate, finishing the last of her tea.

"The Romanian constitution, the menu in a Polish restaurant, and the lifespan of a Chernobyl fireman."

They sat in the darkness without speaking for several minutes. Rain beat a tattoo on the roof.

"What do you think will happen to Gorbachev and the U.S.S.R.?" O'Rourke asked Lucian.

The medical student chuckled softly. "They are both extinct, but neither knows it yet. When Gorbachev came back from the attempted *coup* in August and announced that he still had faith in the Marxist system, he was announcing his own obsolescence.''

''And the nation?'' said Kate.

Lucian shook his head. ''There is no nation there, only an empire that can no longer cow its subjugated parts into submission. The Soviet Union is already on the scrap heap of history, just as socialist Romania is. Neither organism has had the decency to realize that it is dead . . . a *nosferatu*.'' He tapped fingers on the plastic steering wheel. ''But Russia has Yeltsin and he is an ambitious man . . . a *very* ambitious man. I see a glint in his eye that reminds me of our former leader here. Yeltsin will use Russian sovereignty to break up the U.S.S.R. by next spring.''

''So soon?'' said Kate.

''Sooner perhaps. I would not be surprised if the C.C.C.P. is officially buried by the new year.''

''But what if Gorbachev—'' began O'Rourke.

Lucian held his hand up for silence, then leaned forward and cleaned the windshield of condensation.

The electric gates of Radu Fortuna's compound were opening. Kate sunk lower in her seat, knowing as she did so that it was silly to try to hide.

A black Mercedes slipped through the gates, turned left onto the street, and accelerated away. The headlights had passed over their Dacia without pausing.

''Is that him?'' whispered Kate.

Lucian shrugged, started the Dacia after three grinding attempts, and pulled out just as the Mercedes turned out of sight. The Dacia rattled and squeaked as Lucian accelerated down the street at forty or fifty miles per hour, his headlights still off. They slid onto Strada Galati and saw the taillights of the Mercedes three blocks ahead. Lucian hunched over the wheel and floored the accelerator. The Dacia complained more loudly but roared and rattled down the empty street.

''Follow that car,'' whispered Kate.

* * *

They kept the Mercedes in sight while driving north on Strada Galati, found a bit of midnight traffic—mostly trucks—to blend with going west on Bulevardul Ilie Pintilie, but almost lost the Mercedes when it disappeared around the traffic circle at Piaţa Victoriei. Lucian guessed correctly that the sedan had turned north onto Şoseaua Kiseleff, and after a moment of sickening tension the Mercedes was visible again splashing through an intersection two blocks ahead. Lucian whipped the Dacia up to almost ninety kph until the Mercedes was less than a block ahead, then he slowed to keep pace. It helped that the few other cars and trucks on the main boulevard were also ignoring all posted speed limits.

They stayed right again onto the Bucharest-Ploieşti Road and passed out of the tree-lined sections of the city, past huge buildings and monuments dark and silent in the night, then they were in the countryside, with fields falling away on either side. The Mercedes passed the turnoff to Otopeni Airport without slowing, but Lucian brought the Dacia down to sixty kilometers per hour as they all caught sight of the usual military and police vehicles along the road to the international airport. Beyond Otopeni, he accelerated again, keeping only one truck between the Mercedes and Dacia.

"We don't even know if this is Radu Fortuna," said O'Rourke from the backseat.

"Why did you know his name?" asked Kate. "Why did you laugh?"

The priest explained about his first trip to Romania two years earlier with the billionaire Vernor Deacon Trent's "assessment team."

Lucian almost drove off the road. "Vernor Deacon Trent was here?" His voice was shaky.

"He may still be here," said O'Rourke. "His foundation and corporation announced his illness weeks after the rest of us returned. To this day, no one knows where he is or in what condition. He's sort of the Howard Hughes of the nineties."

Lucian shook his head. The single windshield wiper

whipped back and forth in front of him. "Vernor Deacon Trent is no Howard Hughes," he said tightly. "And how does Comrade Radu Fortuna figure in with Mr. Trent?"

O'Rourke explained about the opinionated ONT guide during that bizarre tour.

Lucian smiled with humor. "I suspect that Trent and Fortuna were having some fun with you."

Kate looked away from the rainswept windshield and dark fields. "You're saying that Vernor Deacon Trent may be *strigoi*?"

Lucian was silent for a long interval. "The Order has believed that Trent may have been one of the original Family members," he said finally. "Perhaps the legendary Father."

"Father?" said Kate, but at that moment the Mercedes ahead of them turned off the highway onto a secondary road.

"Shit," said Lucian. He had followed the truck past the road and now he had to slow, find a place wide enough to turn around, and make a U-turn. The Mercedes was the dimmest of taillight glows by the time the Dacia was bouncing down the narrow, potholed lane after it. They passed village homes and low, "systematized" apartments on their left, all dark.

Kate glanced at the odometer again. They had come about thirty-five kilometers from Bucharest.

"I think I know where they're going," said Lucian.

Kate saw the sign as they entered the second small village: Şnagov.

"I've read about this place," she said.

The Mercedes turned right at a fork in the road in the center of the village and sped up again. Lucian doused the headlights and followed as best he could. The bumpy road was almost invisible in the dark and rain.

"We'll lose them," said O'Rourke as the taillights disappeared around a bend.

Lucian shook his head. A mile or so farther on and they could see the Mercedes' brakelights flare and then the headlights became visible to their left as the black sedan turned down an even narrower lane. Lucian let the Dacia slowly approach the turnoff.

"Hurry!" said Kate as the Mercedes dwindled down the long lane.

"Can't," said Lucian. "It's a private road. See the checkpoint?"

Kate saw it then as the Mercedes stopped—a gate with several vehicles parked near it. Flashlights flared briefly as someone checked the identities of the Mercedes driver and occupants. Kate could make out the lights of a huge home a quarter of a mile or so beyond the checkpoint.

"Goddamn it," breathed Kate. "Is there another way to that house?"

Lucian drummed his fingers on the wheel. "I don't think the house is the destination," he said as if musing to himself. Headlights suddenly became visible far behind them. "Damn. Hang on." With the headlights still off, he flogged the Dacia down the highway, squealing around turns and bouncing over sudden dips. The last lights fell away behind them and a forest closed in on either side.

"I want to go back," said Kate, her heart pounding with frustration and anger. "If there's a chance that Joshua is at that house, I want to go back even if I have to cross the fields on foot."

Lucian did not slow. "That compound was on the lake," he said. "I know another way."

There was no other traffic as they drove another mile or two alongside a railroad track, the road deteriorating the farther they got from the village, until finally, just as the lane crossed the tracks, Lucian turned left onto an even narrower road. Gravel and puddles made noise beneath the wheels. He turned on the parking lights as the Dacia crept forward under a dripping arch of bare branches.

"Sort of a national forest area," he said, frowning as he concentrated on missing potholes the size of small lakes. Finally he cursed and turned on the headlights.

They passed under a sagging wooden arch with faded letters, and the lane dwindled to little more than a wide path through the thick forest. Just as Kate was ready to ask if Lucian knew where he was, the lane opened up onto an asphalt surface again and they drove past a dark and silent stucco building on their left.

"Restaurant and guesthouse," said Lucian, not even glancing toward it. "It's been shut since Ceauşescu died." Several smaller lanes led to their right and left, but Lucian kept the Dacia on the widest of them. Kate could see overturned picnic tables and weed-cluttered grassy areas now. The area looked like an American state park that had been abandoned for decades.

Suddenly Lucian slowed, stopped, backed the Dacia, and turned left down an asphalt lane no wider than a footpath. The lane ended a hundred yards downhill, and gravel hissed under the wheels. Kate could see a faint gleam of water between the trees ahead.

Lucian parked the car. "We need to hurry." He reached into the glove compartment and pulled out a flashlight and something heavier. Kate blinked when she realized that the second object was a pistol of some sort—a semiautomatic from the shape of it. Lucian tucked the pistol away in his jacket and tried the flashlight. The beam was strong. "Let's go," he said.

They went another hundred feet downhill through wet grass and suddenly there was a low wire fence in front of them. There was a gate to their left, but it was locked. Lucian clambered over the gate and Kate followed. O'Rourke's artificial leg obviously gave him some problem, but he made no noise as he used his upper-body strength to pull himself up and over. The three crouched on what appeared to be a small, grassy peninsula with a dock, a shack, and heaps of what Kate realized were rowboats stacked upside down. The rain had stopped but the forest dripped behind them. Cuckoos and bullfrogs were making noise from the swampy inlet to their left.

Lucian leaned close to whisper. "I don't think they still keep a guard in the shack, but let's be as quiet as we can." He motioned to O'Rourke and the two men lifted the top rowboat, righted it, and carried it to the gravel loading area near the dock. Lucian gestured for silence again and disappeared in the shadows near the shack, returning with two heavy oars.

Kate clambered aboard first and settled into the bow while Lucian locked the oars in and O'Rourke pushed them off and lifted himself into the stern. They floated past the dock and Lucian rowed almost silently until they were far out past the dock and the darkened shack.

Kate's eyes had adjusted to the dark now and she realized that they were in a wide lagoon. A large, dark building— obviously the restaurant/guesthouse they had driven by— terminated one end of the lagoon a few hundred yards to their left, and Kate could see weed-littered steps coming down to the water there. Ahead of them, a dark line of trees was the source of more swamp sounds. Kate realized how loud the cacophony was now, and Lucian's stronger strokes with the oars were muted by the bullfrog and cuckoo noises from three sides.

Lucian aimed the rowboat between two tree-lined points, out into what Kate realized was the actual lake. It seemed very wide in the darkness, the opposite shore—if it *was* the opposite shore—the smallest of treelines across the horizon.

They had passed out of the entrance to the lagoon—only a hundred and fifty feet or so across there—and into the choppy waves, strong currents, and cold winds of the main lake when Kate looked down, lifted wet feet, and said, "We're shipping water."

"*La naiba!*" said Lucian. "Sorry. Can you two bail?"

"With what?" said O'Rourke. "All we have is our hands." The priest leaned over the side a minute. "It doesn't look too deep here. I think I see weeds or something in the water."

Kate heard Lucian chuckle. "The lagoon was a few meters deep," he said. "Out here it's a bit deeper. Lake Şnagov is said to be the deepest lake in all of Europe. As far as I know, they've never plumbed its depths."

There was silence for a minute except for frog and cuckoo sounds. O'Rourke said, "Shall we make for the shore?"

"No," said Kate. "We'll bail with our hands if we have to."

Lucian rowed. The lagoon entrance receded and then was lost to sight as they pulled to their left, deeper into the dark expanse of lake. Kate could see the bright lights of a large building a mile or two across the water. "Is that the place where Radu Fortuna's Mercedes was headed?" she whispered to Lucian.

The young man grunted. "We're not headed there, though," he whispered. "We're going to the island." He nodded toward a dark hump which Kate only now realized was not part of the north shore. It was still half a mile or more away.

"But if Fortuna is at the house on shore—" she began, then stopped as sounds of a large boat's engine coughing to life crossed the water to them. She turned around and watched from the bow as a ship's running lights came on below the brightly lit estate. Suddenly there were more lights and three small speedboats roared away from the distant dock and pounded out into the lake.

"Shit," whispered Lucian and shipped his oars. The three of them crouched expectantly and watched as the speedboats growled their way toward them. Searchlights stabbed out and across the water.

"Down!" whispered Lucian, and they all crouched in three inches of water, only the tops of their heads above the gunwales.

The speedboats crossed and crisscrossed the half mile of water between the estate and the opposite side of the island, then swept around to the other side, their searchlights probing both the shore and the expanse of lake beyond. One of the boats roared out toward the lagoon they had just rowed from, its searchlight on and the smacking of its hull sharp and clear across the dark water. The boat swerved and seemed headed straight toward them.

Kate crouched and found that she was whispering to herself, citing a litany to the darkness, the clouds above, and the low profile of their rowboat. The speedboat roared closer.

"If they shoot, go into the water," whispered Lucian. He racked the slide on the automatic pistol.

Kate wondered if O'Rourke could swim well with his artificial leg. Well, she was a good swimmer—three times a week she swam laps at the Boulder Rec Center—and if need be, she'd drag both men back to shore. *Joshua*, she thought, adding his name to her whispered litany.

The speedboat arced to its right and passed them sixty yards to their left. The waves were higher now as a wind came up, and their little rowboat could not have been more than the briefest of silhouettes against an equally dark shoreline. Kate, O'Rourke, and Lucian crouched in the lapping water as the speedboat roared into the lagoon, stabbed searchlights along the shore there—visible as a glow through autumn-bare trees—and then pounded its way back out and around the perimeter of the lake, occasionally checking out something along the shore with its light. Once there was the rattle of small-arms fire, sharp and metallic and clear across the water, and then the boat completed its circuit and roared back toward the island.

The large boat—some sort of cruiser forty or fifty feet long by the looks of it—was chugging its way toward the island now, all three speedboats as escort. Kate moved back to the bow of the rowboat, feeling the water lapping above her ankles. She was soaked and cold. Above them, the clouds made gaps through which she could see the stars. A cold wind blew at them from the north.

Lucian began rowing again. When he paused to gasp for breath, O'Rourke said, "Let me take a turn," and moved to the center seat. Kate was shivering now, wishing that she had volunteered first, but she wanted to stay in the bow and watch the island.

The large boat had tied up at a dock on the left point of the island while two of the speedboats also put in. The third one continued to orbit. Kate heard shouts and then saw flashlights gleam on the dock. They were doused and suddenly torches flared to life. Dark figures beneath the line of torches were clearly visible as they filed from the dock up under the trees onto the island proper.

"We need to time this right," said Lucian, stopping O'Rourke's rowing and pointing to a place several hundred meters east of the dock. "We can put in there, but we have to make a dash for it when the patrol boat is on the far side of the island." He removed his watch and stared at the radium dial as the boat continued its counterclockwise patrol.

"Three minutes ten seconds," said Lucian as the speedboat growled its way around the southwest point again. "Are you fresh enough to row that fast?" he asked O'Rourke.

The priest nodded. When the speedboat disappeared around the east point again, he put his back into it. The rowboat's progress seemed slow, the current pushing them west stronger than ever. Kate could hear O'Rourke's grunts and wheezing breath.

"Two minutes," whispered Lucian, studying his watch.

Kate could just hear the speedboat's engine on the other side of the small island, could see dark shapes on the dock. *What if they see us? What if the boat speeds up?* O'Rourke rowed steadily, the clumsy oars biting deep. The island seemed no closer than it had before.

"One minute," whispered Lucian.

Kate could hear the speedboat now, purring its way around the northwest corner of the island. They were closer—the island seemed taller, the dark trees distinct, but O'Rourke seemed to be putting most of his energy into not letting the current sweep them west into the dock. The oars sounded very loud as they bit at the water. If the patrol boat came around now, they would be directly in its path.

"Thirty seconds," hissed Lucian.

O'Rourke put his head down and pulled. The heavy rowboat—all the heavier with its passengers and increasing load of water—plowed through rough waves. The current here was very strong. There was enough starlight now for Kate to see the sweat on the priest's neck.

"Fifteen seconds," said Lucian.

They were ten meters from shore.

"There," whispered Lucian, pointing to what may have been an inlet under the trees.

The patrol boat roared around the point a hundred and fifty meters to their left. Its searchlight was on, probing toward the shore. When it passed the dock, Kate caught a glimpse of men with automatic weapons squinting into the searchlight. The beam swept off the shore, ahead of the boat, straight toward them.

Chapter Twenty-seven

O' ROURKE grunted as they glided under branches that grasped at Kate like bony hands. Then the bow was scraping rock with a noise that Kate was sure could be heard all the way across the island. Lucian ducked forward, O'Rourke tried to mute his gasps, and Kate grabbed on to roots and kept them from sliding back out into the current as the speedboat pounded its way past not ten yards from them.

Her heartbeat drowned even O'Rourke's panting until the patrol boat passed around the east point again. There was a soggy rope in the space under the bow. Water lapped halfway up Kate's calves.

Lucian went over the side, scrambled up the bank, tied the bowline around a stump, and motioned them up. Kate could hear O'Rourke sliding on dead leaves behind her as he grabbed for roots and rocks.

Fifteen feet up the bank and they were in a line of trees bounding a wide, grassy area. There was a *snick* near Kate's ear and she could just make out a knife in Lucian's hand as he gouged bark from an evergreen tree. *Marking where the boat is*, she thought. She was glad that someone was thinking.

They huddled at the edge of the treeline. "The chapel," whispered Lucian, and Kate squinted west. Three spires rose above bare limbs. A line of torches flickered as more dark shapes followed an unseen path from the dock to the half-hidden church. Kate could hear voices now—male voices chanting something which was not quite Gregorian. The wind rose around them, rustling pine branches and setting Kate to shivering.

Lucian leaned closer. Kate thought she could see the pistol in his hand again. "It's the beginning of the Investiture Ceremony," came his whisper. "I should have known it would be at the chapel at Şnagov Monastery."

The chanting seemed louder now.

"It's the chapel where Vlad Dracula's headless body was buried in fourteen seventy-six," whispered Lucian. "They excavated his tomb in nineteen thirty-two, but the grave was empty. Empty except for chewed animal bones." Lucian turned and moved toward the chapel and torches in a silent, crouching run.

Kate hesitated only a second, touching O'Rourke's shoulder to make sure the priest was there, and then she followed.

The chapel was lit by torchlight, with more torches lining the walkway from the dock. A second large boat had arrived and a steady stream of dark-robed figures filed from the tiny pier to the church. Lucian led the way along the edge of a grassy area the size of a football field. Once he paused for breath and whispered to Kate and O'Rourke, "This was all inner courtyard and fortifications in Vlad Ţepeş' day." Kate felt bricks or stones underfoot, set flush with the sod.

They almost walked into the guard. Lucian was leading the way under dripping trees, Kate had one hand on the back of his shirt and her other hand on O'Rourke's shoulder in the darkness, when suddenly a match flared twenty feet in front of them. Kate had the briefest of glimpses of a man's face in the match glow—a face under a black ski-mask hood. *Tom. Julie.*

Lucian froze in place while Kate and O'Rourke stopped in midstep. Kate breathed through her mouth and watched the ember glow of the cigarette. After a long minute her heartbeat slowed; evidently the shuffle of feet and low chanting from the line of cowled figures on the other side of the chapel had masked any noise.

"This way," whispered Lucian and led them to the right, past an ancient well with its steep-roofed shelter, between what felt like rosebushes, and into a row of low trees. Kate could see another sentry near the corner of the chapel fifteen yards away. Torchlight made little impression on his black hood, black sweater, and the matte-black of the automatic weapon cradled in his arm.

They continued right, away from the chapel, crossed a low wire fence, and then Lucian led them to their left through an orchard. Dark buildings—two peasant-style farmhouses and a low brick barn—loomed to their right. "The current monastery," whispered Lucian. "They will not show a light or come out when the *strigoi* are here."

They circled the chapel, keeping the torches in sight, moving around to the southwest end of the island. "Stay here while I look around." Lucian moved away through the thick brush.

Kate heard O'Rourke shift his bad leg as they crouched there; she just caught the small intake of pained breath. She touched the priest's shoulder. Lucian suddenly was a presence next to her. "We can get closer on this side." His whisper was the softest breath in the silence. Kate realized that the chanting had ceased.

Torches illuminated the open doors of Şnogov Chapel. The crosses carved there similar to the double-cruciform of Lucian's Order of the Dragon pendant. Near the chapel was a whitewashed cottage and, ten yards closer to where the three of them hid in a vineyard, an ancient square tower. Lucian slid out of the vineyard and moved across the open space to the tower. Kate heard the soft rasp of a knife on hinges, and the old door became a black portal. Lucian gestured them closer.

Kate hugged her knees. "I don't know if I can do this," she whispered to the priest. The idea of crossing the open space so near the *strigoi* guards terrified her.

O'Rourke leaned so close she could feel the scratch of his

beard against her cheek. "We'll go together," he whispered and took her hand.

They moved in a crouch, trying to set their feet only on grass. When they reached the open door, Kate hesitated two beats before stepping into the darkness. O'Rourke closed the door behind them. Lucian was crouched on the lowest step of a steep stairway. "There's a window," he whispered, his voice almost inaudible. "But there are guards just below it." They moved up the stairs slowly, testing for any creaks. The steps were centuries old but massive and sound; there were no creaks.

The tower window was only ten feet above the ground and it looked out over rows of what appeared to be more rose-bushes and another low vineyard. Half a dozen black-garbed sentries stood in the rose garden and along the trellised vines nearer the path, their presence made visible in silhouette against the torchlit chapel. More torches were visible through the open doors, the male voices audible.

"What are they saying?" whispered Kate.

Lucian shook his head. "It's not Romanian."

O'Rourke leaned closer to the half-open window. Birds rustled above them in the raftered recesses of the tower. "It's Latin," he whispered.

Kate recognized the cadence of the Latin syllables but could not make out words. She strained to see through the chapel doors, strained to see the form of an infant in the arms of one of the black forms, but there were only the vague shapes, the occasional Latin syllable, and the frustration at not being able to see better. She clutched Lucian's jacket and pulled him closer until she could whisper directly in his ear. "Did you remember binoculars along with your pistol and knife?"

The young man shook his head.

Suddenly, with the abruptness of a church service ending, the chanting and moaning of ritual voices ceased, there was a moment of silence within the chapel and a general stirring among the guards, and then the cloaked figures came out onto the paved area between the church and the whitewashed cottage. Hoods came off, cloaks were removed, cigarettes were lighted, voices were raised in a more conversational tone, and the effect was startling in its resemblance to the scene outside any American church after a Sunday morning service. Men stood in clumps of three or five—Kate heard no women's voices, so she assumed they were all men—smoking and talking softly.

Kate leaned so far out in trying to see and hear that O'Rourke had to pull her back before one of the guards in the rose garden below looked up. The voices were maddeningly indistinct, but she had made out German, Italian, and English amongst the murmur of Romanian. "Can you understand—" she hissed at Lucian.

He shushed her and listened. It was hard to tell the actual size of the gathering since the dark forms looked much alike as they moved in and out of torchlight, but Kate guessed that there had been almost a hundred people in the chapel or waiting outside along the walkway to the dock.

"There . . . that's Radu Fortuna!" whispered Lucian and pointed at one of the men just emerging from the chapel door.

"Yes," whispered O'Rourke.

Kate strained to see, but the torchlight was tricky, the men were moving, and she saw only distant faces in shadow before Lucian pulled her back. "Did you hear?" she whispered again. "Did you understand?"

"Shhh." Lucian's finger touched her mouth. Guards were shouting to guards in Romanian. A deep voice barked commands from near the chapel doors.

They saw me, was Kate's panicked thought. A second later, *They've found the boat. We'll never get off the island.*

Flashlights stabbed on and one of the guards in the garden below switched on a hand-held spotlight much brighter than the flashlight beams. Kate, Lucian, and O'Rourke all flinched back from the window, but in a moment it was apparent that the beams were aimed elsewhere. Kate edged up to the window and looked just as one of the men fired a short burst from his automatic weapon.

She flinched away again but not before seeing a large

brown dog running between the trees in the orchard near the monastery huts. They all heard the howl and barking.

More shouts in Romanian. Some laughter. One by one the flashlight beams switched off.

It took half an hour for the men to file back to their boats and board, for the torches to be extinguished—the guards snuffed and retrieved the last ones along the walkway—and then there came the sound of the patrol boats roaring away to escort the ferries. The chapel was dark.

Kate sat on the narrow landing with the two men for the better part of an hour before anyone spoke or moved. She imagined the black-garbed guards still lying in ambush in the dark. Finally the resumption of insect sounds, the throb of frogs from the lake's edge, and the sight of the brown dog sniffing along the chapel stones unchallenged gave them courage to tiptoe downstairs, open the heavy door, and retrace their tracks back through the orchard and east. The stars had come out and Kate caught a glimpse of the knife in Lucian's hand.

''For the dog if he barks,'' whispered the medical student, but the dog did not approach them as they scurried around the edge of the old courtyards.

The boat was where they had left it. The two men waded in and tipped the boat to let the half foot of water out. Kate was last aboard, untying the line and slipping down rocks onto the bow. Lucian pushed off with one of the oars and edged out slowly from under the tree.

The broad lake appeared empty. The great estate on the southwest shore was dark. They did not speak as Lucian rowed them across the lake and into the lagoon. They were silent as the three of them carried the rowboat back to its heap of rowboats, flipped it, and set it softly on the pile of rowboats. There was still no light or sound from the shack in the boatyard.

The Dacia looked undisturbed, but Lucian had them wait in the darkness of the trees as he slipped out, approached the car warily, and checked its interior. The two joined him and the old vehicle started without protest.

Lucian left the abandoned park area with the car lights out, picking his way along by starlight, finally turning the headlights on as they left the sleeping village of Şnagov.

"I didn't see Joshua," Kate said, her voice sounding strange and strained even to herself. "I didn't see any children."

"No," said O'Rourke. The priest had slid into the front passenger seat; Kate rode in back.

"Did you hear any of what they said?" she asked Lucian.

He drove in silence for another minute. "I think I heard someone say something about it being the first night . . . good for the first night, I think."

"First night of what?" Kate pressed her cheek against the cold window on her right to help her stay awake.

"The Investiture Ceremony," said Lucian. "I should have known Şnagov Monastery would have been the site of the first night's ceremony."

"Because it's important to the *strigoi?*" said O'Rourke.

Lucian chewed his lip. His face was very pale in the dim light from the instrument lights. "It was one of Vlad Ţepeş' fortresses. Legend had it that he was buried there."

"You said that the grave was empty," said Kate.

"Yes. But they found a headless corpse in another tomb in the chapel, set near the doorway rather than next to the altar where one would expect royalty to have been buried." He slowed the car at the intersection to the main highway and turned left, toward Bucharest. "Archaeologists think that it may have been a little joke the monks pulled . . . moving his corpse."

O'Rourke scratched his beard. "Or a deliberate act. They may have considered his burial so close to the altar a sacrilege."

Lucian nodded. "If it *was* Vlad Dracula. The Order maintains that the Prince had one of his servants decapitated and buried in royal robes . . . even wearing one of the rings of the Dragon . . . in order to throw off his enemies."

Kate was close to losing her temper. "It doesn't really matter who was buried there five centuries ago, does it? What matters is what they were doing there tonight . . . and what it has to do with Joshua."

They passed Otopeni Airport and saw the reflected lights of Bucharest ahead. It was clouding up again. Only trucks were on the highway. "*If* it is the Investiture Ceremony," said Lucian as if thinking aloud, "and *if* Joshua is the chosen one, then there will be several more nights of *strigoi* ceremony before he receives the Sacrament of human blood." He rubbed his cheek. "Or so go the legends."

Kate's voice was hard. "And do your legends tell you *where* the ceremonies are held? Şnagov again?"

"No," said Lucian. "But I don't think there'll be anything else at the monastery. Perhaps places important to the *strigoi* Family . . . important to the legend of Vlad Ţepeş. I don't know."

Kate lay back on the dusty cushions. "This is nuts." She pounded her fists against the door. "My baby has been kidnapped and I'm out playing Indiana Jones."

Lucian made a noise. "It wasn't as interesting as Indiana Jones," he said. "I couldn't see anything clearly. If there was a human sacrifice, I missed it." He realized what he had said and bit his lip.

No one stopped them as they took back streets to their abandoned tenement and basement apartment. Lucian parked in an alley a block from the building and they let themselves in with more exhaustion than precaution. No one was waiting in the cold darkness.

"What next?" asked O'Rourke. "Do we stake out Radu Fortuna's place again in the daylight?" He glanced at his watch. "It's almost daylight now."

Lucian seemed to sag onto the cushions of the couch. "I don't know. I can't think."

"Stay here tonight," said Kate. "I think we should stay together. There are two mattresses on the little bed in there. We'll drag one out for you."

Lucian could only nod.

"Let's sleep," she said. "We're all stupid with fatigue. We'll talk about things later." She realized that she needed solitude as much as sleep, that the idea of being alone—even in the freezing, dank basement room—was an almost physical necessity for her now.

They dragged out Lucian's mattress, there was a small domestic moment of finding an extra blanket, and then Kate was alone, the door locked. She slipped out of her grimy clothes, pulled flannel pajamas from her one bag, and crawled under the covers. She was shaking, more from the aftereffects of the long night than from the cold, but sleep settled on her like vertigo.

Suddenly she slammed awake and ran to the door, unlocking it with clumsy fingers. Lucian's flashlight beam caught her in the eyes and she waved it away, seeing the two men's startled faces even as she began to explain.

"I've been thinking all along that I'm going after Joshua as much for medical reasons as for personal ones. Do you understand? We had extracted and cloned the retrovirus at CDC . . . I told you that . . . Chandra was beginning to understand the mechanism, I think, but more importantly, her team was doing trials on the virus's effect on cultured samples . . . cancer, HIV . . ."

"Neuman," said O'Rourke, "can we talk about this later?"

"No!" said Kate. "Listen. It's important . . . I mean, the retrovirus has incredible immunological and oncological implications. But I've been fixated on finding *Joshua* . . . in retrieving the sample of *Joshua's* blood . . ."

Lucian was nodding. "I see. But you realize that any of the *strigoi* would do. Those men we saw tonight . . ."

"No!" Kate lowered her voice. "The body . . . the *thing* you have in the vat at the medical school. His blood has the pure J-virus. I was so stupid . . . so obsessed with Joshua."

Lucian was staring, rubbing his eyes. "I had no idea you could apply the *strigoi* virus for immunoreconstruction." He stood up, naked, and began struggling into his jeans.

Kate set her hands on his shoulders and pushed him back onto the mattress, noting idly that his body was muscled in the way she liked men's bodies, a swimmer's or runner's physique. "Later today," she said, "we'll get redundant samples, assay them to make sure that there's no contamination, and then get them to CDC Boulder. I'll include instructions so Ken Mauberly will know exactly what to do with the new team."

"How . . ." began the priest.

"Your job will be to get the sample and my note to the U.S. Embassy," she said. "One of your Franciscan priest buddies in mufti, perhaps. I'm sure the *strigoi* are watching for us to appear at the embassy."

"Yes," said Lucian. "That is certain."

"But all we have to do is get the sample *in*," continued Kate. She pointed at O'Rourke. "You invoke Senator Harlen's name in a note, or do whatever political magic you can, and the sample will be in a diplomatic pouch headed Stateside by tonight."

The priest rubbed his beard. "It might work."

"It will work," said Kate. She was so tired that she sagged against the doorframe. "I didn't need Joshua's blood after all."

"But that doesn't make any difference in your going after him, does it, Kate?" said O'Rourke.

She blinked at him. "No. No difference at all."

O'Rourke pulled his blanket up. "Then we might as well get a couple of hours' sleep before we cure AIDS and cancer. It promises to be another long day."

Chapter Twenty-eight

IT was all on fire.

Lucian stopped the Dacia half a block from the medical school and he and Kate watched as the ancient fire trucks drove up over the curb or blocked the street while firemen ran hose to a single hydrant and shouted at each other through the fence surrounding the university. Smoke climbed in thick columns through the brisk morning air. Kate could see flames in the shattered medical school windows, the orange glow mirroring the reflected sunrise in the office-building windows on the west side of the street.

"Stay here," said Lucian and walked toward the barricade of fire trucks and official vehicles. Despite the early hour, a small crowd had gathered.

Kate stepped out of the Dacia and leaned dejectedly against the car door. She had wakened after only two hours' sleep to find Lucian still asleep in the outer room and O'Rourke gone. There had been no note. She and Lucian had shared a cold breakfast, waited another twenty minutes for the priest, and then left a note saying only *Gone to get the sample*. Kate had thrown her single large carry-on bag in the back of the Dacia, leaving only her toothbrush at the basement apartment.

Another fire truck roared by as Lucian walked back to the car. "The fire started in the basement," he said. "The morgue and medical labs are gone." He settled behind the wheel, and

Kate dropped into the passenger seat. The column of smoke was thicker now.

"Could it have been an accident?" she asked.

Lucian tapped the wheel. "We have to assume it's not. The *strigoi* must have traced me to the school and found their man. I doubt if they went to the trouble of removing him before they set the fire."

Kate shuddered at the thought of the thing in the tank writhing while flames filled the basement. "What do we do?" she said.

Lucian started the Dacia and drove back to the area of narrow streets west of Cişmigiu Gardens. He had pulled to a stop opposite their building when Kate said, "Keep moving!"

Lucian put the Dacia in gear and drove slowly down the street. "What?" he said without turning his head.

"The shade was down in my basement window when we left," she said. "It's up now."

"Perhaps Father O'Rourke—" began Lucian and then said, "Shit." He was looking at the rearview mirror. "There's a car following us. It was parked in the alley near the corner."

Kate resisted the urge to look back.

"It's a black Mercedes," whispered Lucian. "The *Securitate* like to use them."

"They can't be very inconspicuous tailing people in a Mercedes," said Kate, keeping her voice light. Her heart was pounding and she felt a little sick.

"The *Securitate* don't need to be inconspicuous," said Lucian. He had turned right onto Strada Ştirbei Vodă and now had to wait as a streetcar lumbered out of a narrow sidestreet and took on passengers. Traffic coming the other way on the narrow brick street kept him from passing. "Damn," he whispered. "There's another one."

Now Kate did turn and look. There were two Mercedes sedans behind the horse and wagon immediately behind them. The streetcar finally moved on and Lucian kept the Dacia close behind it, waiting for an opportunity to pass.

"I think there's one ahead of us," he said, his voice absolutely flat. "Yes, a black Mercedes in front of the trolley. Four men in it, just like the cars behind us."

Kate tried to quell a rising panic in her breast. "Isn't it good that it's *Securitate?*" she said. "Not *strigoi?*"

Lucian chewed his lip. "These *Securitate* probably *are strigoi*. Or they work for them." He glanced at sidestreets but did not turn. The wagon had turned off behind them and the Mercedes were close enough now that Kate could see the cigarettes of the men in the front seat.

"How did they find us?" whispered Kate. She was clutching her travel bag, thinking of the vials of serum in it. To have come so far for nothing.

Lucian's voice was hard with tension. "Your priest maybe? Perhaps he ratted on us when we were close to sending the blood sample to the embassy. Maybe he's been *Securitate* all along."

"No," said Kate, but her mind whirled with dark possibilities. *Where are you, O'Rourke?* "Can we get away?" she said.

Lucian had chewed his lip until it was bloody. "They've probably got the city sealed," he said, glancing in his mirror. Suddenly the streetcar rumbled into a sidestreet and their Dacia was part of a convoy of black sedans. There were now two in front as well as the two immediately behind them.

"They'll stop us in a minute," said Lucian. "Somewhere they can shoot if they have to . . . not that they wouldn't shoot in a crowd." He quit chewing his lip and stared at nothing for a moment. "A crowd," he whispered. "There was an anti-government rally this morning." He grinned almost demonically. "Hang on, Kate."

They were just coming up to Calea Victoriei when Lucian spun the wheel hard right and accelerated into the wide Piaţa Gheorghi-Dej opposite the bullet-riddled Art Museum and the Hall of the Palace of the Socialist Republic of Romania. Striped barricades blocked off the major part of the plaza, but Lucian accelerated again and smashed through the wooden barriers. Kate looked behind them in time to see all four

Mercedes swing right, bounce across curbs, and come rushing after them. Pedestrians on Calea Victoriei leaped aside.

Kate turned to see the rally ahead of them—perhaps three hundred people with as many police surrounding them. Trucks full of miners in overalls glowered at both police and protesters. Various flags and posters flew above the peaceful congregation, but the assemblage parted with shouts and screams as Lucian drove straight into the fringes of the crowd, steering wildly to avoid hitting people. Police whistles shrilled as Lucian drove the Dacia in a half-circle, wheeling deeper into the confused mass of protesters and gray-coated police.

"Out!" he shouted, opening his own door while the car was still moving. He had grabbed a heavy textbook from the seat and now dropped it onto the accelerator before rolling out the door.

Kate clutched her purse and bag and jumped out the passenger side, hitting the bricks hard and losing her footing. She rolled and tumbled into the backs of people's legs and at least one man and a woman went down with her. More people screamed as the Dacia cut its slow path through the crowd and the Mercedes screeched to a halt just beyond the fringes of the mob.

Getting shakily to her feet, Kate threw the strap of her duffel bag over her shoulder, checked to make sure she had her purse, and looked down at herself. Her coat was dusty and one knee was bleeding beneath her black polyester pants, but her clothes were not torn. Lucian had bought her local clothes upon arrival so that she could go out without attracting undue attention. *Lucian*.

She moved with the crowd now, craning to see him, but the crowd was ebbing back and forth like a single, panicked organism. The Dacia had gone up over the curb and rolled to a stop near the bullet-scarred Athenée Place Hotel, and the Mercedes were moving through the plaza now like black sharks cruising among swimmers. But the source of the screams was behind her, and Kate wheeled to see the gray-

overalled miners leaping down from their trucks and wading
into the protesters with clubs and metal pipes. Kate saw flags
dip and fall as the people dropped them and fled, then watched
as a woman carrying a small child was clubbed by two miners.
She could not see Lucian anywhere.

Police were blowing whistles, soldiers had appeared from
nowhere and were leaping from trucks, but they ignored the
miners and the miners ignored them as the brutality and panic
spread across the plaza. Kate ran wildly with two women in
black and a professional-looking man with gray hair. Two
young men with long hair joined them in their mad dash for
the shelter of Calea Victoriei and the hotels there, but shots
suddenly rang out and one of the young men fell as if tripped
by a wire. Kate paused, started back for him, thinking of the
few medical supplies in her bag, but then glanced back at the
rushing police and miners crossing the plaza toward her and
looked at the bloody mass that had been the back of the
college student's head. She turned and ran with the screaming
crowd again.

There were more police cars coming down Calea Victoriei,
their sirens dopplering up and down the scale, lights flashing.
Kate turned down Ştirbei Vodă and ran back the way she and
Lucian had driven. Some of the people along the street here
were pressing toward the plaza, but others were fleeing as
they saw the miners out of control. Kate glanced back and
saw one of the big men in gray overalls charging down the
street toward an older woman trying to move quickly just
behind Kate. The woman still clutched a placard to her chest
that read FREEDOM in both English and Romanian.

Kate knew that the "miners" were often *Securitate* agents
whom the new government used to terrorize the opposition
just as Ceauşescu had; and many of the miners were actually
miners, brutal thugs who still toed the Communist and neo-
Fascist party lines and were brought into the city as shock
troops. They obviously enjoyed their work.

The miner rushing behind Kate grasped the older woman
by the collar, threw her up against an iron fence, and began
beating her with a thick wooden dowel. The woman

screamed. Kate paused, knew that it was insanity to intervene, and then crouched between two parked cars to fumble in her big bag. Frightened pedestrians rushed past on the sidewalk and street, but no one stopped to help the woman being beaten. She had slumped against the fence now, but the miner had set his legs wide and was methodically clubbing her to the pavement.

Kate removed two disposable syringes of Demerol from her medkit, tossed away the wrappings, walked straight to the miner and plunged both needles into the back of the man's broad neck. She stepped back as the miner cursed, staggered back from the bleeding woman, and turned a shocked and infuriated face in Kate's direction. He spat and shouted something at her, raising the club.

Kate was wearing thick-soled peasant shoes that Lucian had bought her. They were as heavy as combat boots. Kate balanced on her left leg and kicked the miner in the balls with the same full follow-through that Tom had taught her in their touch football games in Boulder. She imagined a kick that would have to clear the crossbar from thirty yards out and put that much energy into it.

The big miner made no noise at all as he went down and curled up on the pavement. He did not get up. There were more screams and police whistles from up the street toward the plaza. More miners were chasing down fleeing protesters, and one of the black Mercedes was trying to force its way through stalled traffic on Ştirbei Vodă.

Kate knelt by the bleeding woman and helped lift her to her feet. It looked as if the woman's nose was broken, and there were teeth missing between pulped lips. Suddenly a man crossed the street and put his arm around the woman, speaking to her in encouraging tones. He was obviously a spouse or relative. *Where were you when we needed you?* Kate thought at the man and then left them, retrieving her bag and heading down the street in a fast walk.

When she glanced behind her, she saw the Mercedes only half a block away, police flashers behind it. Suddenly to her left there was an opening in the iron fence and she pushed in through curious onlookers, went down stone steps, and realized where she was.

Cişmigiu Gardens. The same entrance O'Rourke had brought her to that May day so many eternities ago.

Kate moved deeper into the gardens, taking the narrow sidewalks and less-traveled lanes. From the streets beyond there came the sound of sirens, receding screams, and at least one more shot. Kate realized that her leg was bleeding more seriously than she had thought; she found a stone bench set behind a hedge and away from the walks and used the last of her Kleenex to clean the wound as well as possible. Her skin was gashed from her knee to just above her ankle. Kate used a cotton handkerchief and a Tampax from her duffel bag as an improvised field dressing.

The bleeding contained for the moment, she sat there, aching and disoriented. A cold wind came up and sent leaves spiraling down around her. The flowerbeds were unkempt, the flowers lifeless after heavy frosts. Heavy footfalls echoed from the main sidewalk just beyond a thick hedge.

Kate began to weep then, unable to hold the burning down in her throat any longer. She lowered her face into her hands and just wept.

Kate did not know how long she sat there crying—it might have been a few minutes or half an hour—but she was suddenly aware that it was raining. Hurried footsteps sounded again on the unseen sidewalk as searchers or park-goers ran for cover. Kate simply sat there and lifted her face to the cold rain. Leaves dropped around her like wet paper as the rain turned to sleet. She lowered her face and let the icy pellets pound her head and shoulders.

Kate realized that she was laughing softly. As the sudden, icy rain let up, she raised her face again to the gray sky and said softly, "Do your worst, you bitch." Misfortune had always been a female entity to Kate. But then so had the idea of God.

The sleet stopped at the same time as Kate's laughter. She shivered—her cheap coat was soaked through—but ignored the cold as she focused the problem-solving part of her mind on the situation. The tears had helped—emptying her, calming her—and she approached the situation as if it were a difficult piece of hematological diagnosis.

She was an illegal alien in a hostile country where almost unimaginable resources were arrayed against her and the chances of finding Joshua had dwindled almost to zero. Even if she found the child, she had been able to put together no plan except to run with him for the border or the American Embassy. Meanwhile she was separated from both of her friends in the country, an American priest and a Romanian medical student, and sure of neither as a true friend. *What if O'Rourke did tip the Securitate and the strigoi? What if Lucian were the strigoi equivalent of a double agent, setting her up to be used and then discarded?*

Kate shook her head. She did not have enough data to assess either man's loyalty, although O'Rourke's disappearance just before the fire that destroyed their J-virus source seemed incriminating. It was all a moot point unless she could join forces with one or both of them again.

Do I really want to see them again?

Yes, she realized. Not just because she was cold, wet, scared, and unable to speak Romanian, but because she had complex feelings for each of them.

Deal with that later. What's the next step?

It seemed that if the *strigoi* were actually on their tail to the point of staking out the apartment and burning the medical school lab, then there was no way that she could follow Radu Fortuna again. Security would be heightened. Whatever part of the *strigoi* Investiture Ceremony that was going on tonight would go on without her.

Where to find Lucian or O'Rourke?

All of the places she could think of to re-establish contact with Lucian would also be obvious to the *strigoi:* the medical school, District Hospital One, his or his parents' old apartments. Kate shook her head.

O'Rourke. We never talked about a meeting place other than the basement apartment, but where . . . not the Francis-

*can center here in Bucharest. O'Rourke said that it is watched
by the government as a matter of course. He always calls his
contacts there and arranges a meeting through some kind of
code. Where, then?*

Kate sat in silence for another twenty seconds, then rose
and walked briskly toward the far end of the park, avoiding
groups of people, shielding her face when she passed others
hurrying for cover.

O'Rourke was sitting on the park bench near the lagoon
where they had sat and talked in May. He was alone, his
heavy wool coat collar turned up, but he glanced up when
she stopped near the children's playground and his smile was
visible from thirty feet away.

"I was up before dawn and off to meet the head of the
Franciscan monastery in Bucharest," said O'Rourke. "I said
I'd meet you at the medical school at nine. Didn't you see
my note?"

"No," said Kate. "There was no note." They were crossing the bridge over the narrow channel between park lagoons.

"I left one," said O'Rourke. "Maybe Lucian picked it up
and didn't tell you about it."

"Why would he do that?"

The priest made a gesture with his hands. "I don't know.
But then, there's a lot we don't know about Lucian, isn't
there?"

And about you, thought Kate, but said nothing.

"Anyway, I made the arrangement with Father Stoicescu
to deliver the J-virus sample to the American Embassy later
this morning. But when I got to the medical school, there
were the police and firemen. . . . I called Stoicescu and canceled the meeting, then went back to the apartment, but the
police were there. I could see men going into the building and
there were expensive automobiles up and down the street."

"The *Securitate* drive Mercedes," said Kate and explained
about the insanity of the last hours.

O'Rourke shook his head. "I couldn't think of what to do

except come to the park and hope you would think of it as a rendezvous point.''

"I almost didn't," said Kate. They had reached one of the west entrances to the park. Kate hesitated and pulled back into the trees. "It's not safe out there."

The priest glanced toward the street. "I know. If the *Securitate* know where we were staying, then the *strigoi* must know that we're in the country . . . and why."

"How?" said Kate. Her hands folded into fists.

O'Rourke shrugged. "Possibly Lucian. Maybe the Gypsies talked. Maybe some other loose end . . ."

"Your phone calls to the Franciscans?" said Kate.

"I doubt that. We speak in Latin, never use real names, and arrange the meetings through an old code we developed when I was working with the orphanages here." He scratched his beard. "But it's always possible . . ."

"And really doesn't matter now," said Kate. "I just don't see what we can do next. If Lucian was captured—"

"Did you see him captured?"

"No, but—"

"If he was arrested by the police or *Securitate*, there's nothing we can do," said O'Rourke. "And if he escaped . . . which is likely . . . then he has an infinitely better chance than we do in Bucharest. It's his city. And there's his alleged Order of the Dragon."

"Don't make fun of it," said Kate.

"I'm not." Footsteps were approaching behind a hedge and O'Rourke pulled Kate farther back among the dripping trees. Two men in workers' clothes walked past quickly without glancing beyond the hedge. "I'm not making fun of it, but I don't think it's a very efficient organization. It couldn't even tell Lucian where the next night of the Investiture Ceremony is going to be held."

Kate held back her anger. "Well, we didn't do any better."

"I did," said O'Rourke. "Come on." He took Kate's arm and led her out through the gate and along the street to a parked motorcycle covered with a plastic tarp. The motorcycle had a sidecar and looked ancient to Kate, like something out of an old World War II movie. O'Rourke tugged off the plastic, folded it, and tucked it under the low seat of the sidecar. ''Get in.''

Kate had never ridden in a sidecar . . . had only ridden on a motorcycle a few times with Tom . . . and found that it was a trick to fold oneself into the small space. The windscreen was chipped and discolored with age, the leather seat cracked and taped in a hundred places. When she had finally folded her legs well enough to fit in the egg-shaped pod, O'Rourke handed her a blanket and pair of goggles. ''Put these on.''

Kate adjusted the goggles, imagining how she looked with her soaked peasant coat and scarf and these absurd things. Even the goggles were semi-opaque with age. ''Where did you get all this?'' she asked.

The priest was adjusting his own goggles and a leather flying helmet that made Kate want to giggle. ''Father Stoicescu had offered this the other day,'' he said. ''One of the visiting fathers had purchased this while he was here and left it in a garage near the university. I didn't see a need for it until today.'' He turned a key, fiddled with a fuel valve on the side of the ancient machine, and leaped up to come down on a pedal. Nothing happened.

''Are you sure you know how to drive this thing?'' Kate felt exposed and ridiculous sitting along the curb in the sidecar. She expected the *Securitate* Mercedes to arrive any second.

''I used to have one before I went to 'Nam,'' muttered O'Rourke, fiddling with another lever on the side. He stood again, rose, dropped his weight on the pedal. Again nothing. ''Shit on a stick,'' grumbled the priest.

Kate raised an eyebrow but decided to say nothing.

O'Rourke tried again and was rewarded with a few pops from the cylinder, a backfire, and silence. ''Damn cheap gas,'' he said and fiddled with something above the engine.

''Did you say that you knew where the ceremony was tonight?'' Kate said softly. It had begun to rain again and there were no pedestrians or traffic at the moment, but she still felt the urge to whisper.

O'Rourke paused in his fiddling to lean over and pull a map out of an elastic compartment on the inside of the sidecar. "Look," he said.

Kate noticed it was a Kummerly + Frey roadmap, scale 1:1000000, and then she unfolded it, realized that half of it was of Bulgaria, folded it to have central Romania revealed, and saw the red pencil around several cities. "Braşov, Tîrgovişte, Sighişoara, and Sibiu," she said. "They're all circled. Which one is it . . . and why?"

O'Rourke tried the pedal again and the machine roared to life. He revved the throttle a few times until it was running smoothly, then throttled back and leaned her way. His finger stabbed down on Tîrgovişte, a city about fifty miles northwest of Bucharest. "These are all cities of special importance to the *strigoi* Family," he said. "I think they'll be the sites for the next four nights of the ceremony."

"How do you know?"

O'Rourke glanced over his shoulder and pulled out into the street with a roar and a cloud of exhaust fumes. Kate hung on to the edge of the sidecar with her free hand. She found the sensation of riding in the low pod singularly unpleasant. "How do you know?" she repeated in a shout.

"Let me explain later," he yelled back. He turned into traffic on Bulevardul Gheorghe Gheorghiu-Dej, then turned north again on Bulevardul Nicolae Bălcescu through the center of town.

"Just tell me how you know that Tîrgovişte is the place for tonight's ceremony," demanded Kate, leaning closer to him as they paused for a red light just past the Intercontinental Hotel.

O'Rourke rubbed his cheek. Kate thought that he looked very little like a priest with his beard, helmet, and goggles. "Father Stoicescu mentioned the Tîrgovişte monastery I visited two days ago," he said. The light changed and they moved ahead with the thin traffic. It was still drizzling. "There's no phone contact with them."

"So?" Kate did not have to shout as long as they were moving this slowly.

"They were arrested," he said. "*Securitate* just rounded them up. After all these centuries of being tolerated by the authorities, the monastery was suddenly cleaned out. One of the monks was out shopping for groceries in the marketplace, returned just in time to see his fellow monks loaded aboard police vans, and managed to get into Bucharest to inform the Franciscan headquarters here."

"I don't understand," shouted Kate. They had passed the Triumphal Arch in the north part of town and were headed past Herăstrău Park on Şoseaua Kiseleff. To their right she could see only bare chestnut trees and brown grass. There were no black Mercedes behind them.

"The Franciscans know of the *strigoi*," O'Rourke shouted back. "The Tîrgovişte monastery has monitored the *strigoi* Family for centuries. If the *Securitate* is rounding up the priests . . . even for a short detention . . . it may be because there's something happening in Tîrgovişte tonight that they don't want us to know about."

Kate said nothing but felt little confidence in this analysis. "What about Lucian?" she shouted over the engine roar. She noticed that they had changed from the Kiseleff Road to one labeled "Chitilei."

O'Rourke leaned her way without taking his eyes off the road and traffic ahead. "If he's free and if his Order of the Dragon is real . . . or even if it's not . . . the best bet on our meeting up is being at the next site for the ceremony."

Kate used her hand to rub her goggles free of a film of muddy water. She could imagine what her face looked like. Again, the logic left something to be desired, but she had no better suggestion. They had just passed the last row of Stalinist apartments and the ring roads at the edge of the city when the motorcycle engine pitch dropped and O'Rourke began to brake. Kate saw the cars backed up ahead a moment after she saw the signs pointing straight ahead to PITEŞTI and TÎRGOVIŞTE.

"Accident?" she said. Police flashers were visible a block ahead.

O'Rourke stood on the pedals. "Shit," he whispered to himself. Then, "Sorry."

"What is it?"

"A roadblock. Police seem to be inspecting papers."

Kate looked behind her and saw the traffic backing up there as well. Three cars back there was a black Mercedes with four dark figures in it.

Chapter Twenty-nine

THE police ahead, not content to wait until the traffic reached their roadblock, were moving down the line of cars, peering in windows and demanding papers. O'Rourke revved the motorcycle and began turning around on the narrow stretch of road.

Kate tugged at his sleeve.

"I see the Mercedes," he said, the loose strap of his flying helmet flapping. "We'll just have to risk it."

Kate used both hands to clutch the rim of the sidecar, lowered her head so that little more than her scarf and goggles were visible, and peered to her left as they roared back the way they had come.

The four men in the Mercedes did not glance up as they passed. Looking back, Kate could see the Mercedes sweep out of line and drive on the left side of the road to the barricades. The police saluted and let it through. Other cars and a few motorcycles were turning back from the roadblock.

O'Rourke pulled over when they were in the fringe of the city again, parking near some workers' apartments. Kate studied the grim Stalinist buildings, each with its complement of empty shops on the ground floor, while the priest studied the map. She shifted her legs in the tight pod and turned back to him. "What next?"

"Maybe take the main road to Piteşti," he said. "Take E

70 to this village . . . Peteşti, south of Găeşti . . . and then follow 72 north to Tîrgovişte.''

"What if they have E 70 blocked?" asked Kate.

O'Rourke tucked the map back in its elastic slot. "We'll deal with that when it happens.''

E 70 was blocked. The line ran back almost two miles. The priest understood enough Romanian to decipher the grumbles of truckdrivers walking back to their rigs: the police were examining papers at the point the street left the city and became a four-lane highway to Piteşti.

O'Rourke turned the motorcycle around and drove back into the city. It was already early afternoon and Kate's stomach was growling. She had eaten no real breakfast and she could remember only a few spoonfuls of soup the night before.

There were bread shops along this main street of Bulevardul Pacii, but they were empty and had been since seven A.M. Aggressive streetcars, ignoring other traffic, made O'Rourke swerve across uneven brick and cracked asphalt, and Kate thought that the sidecar was going to flip over more than once. She saw a truckers' restaurant open near the railroad tracks and pointed it out to the priest. Once in the parking lot, with the motorcycle engine quieted, O'Rourke took off his flying helmet and rubbed a sweaty forehead.

"Do we dare go in?" asked Kate.

"If you're as hungry as I am, you'll dare," said O'Rourke. They left their goggles and his helmet in the sidecar and went inside.

The space was cavernous, cold, and filled with smoke from a hundred cigarettes. Waiters hurried from table to table, carrying large bottles of beer. Each trucker had half a dozen empty beer bottles in front of him and seemed intent upon ordering half a dozen more.

"Why so many at once?" whispered Kate as they found a table near the kitchen.

O'Rourke smiled. Kate noticed for the first time that he had removed his Roman collar and was wearing just a dark shirt and pants under the heavy wool coat. "They're afraid the place will run out of beer," he said. "And they will before dinnertime." He tried to wave down a waiter but the men in dark vests and grimy white shirts ignored him. Finally the priest stood and planted himself in front of one of the hurrying men.

"*Daţi-ne supă, vă rog*," said O'Rourke. Kate's stomach rumbled at the thought of a large bowl of soup.

The waiter shook his head. "*Nu . . .*" He snapped off an angry string of syllables, obviously expecting O'Rourke to move aside. He did not.

"*Mititei? Brînză? Cîrnaţi?*" asked the priest.

As nervous as Kate was, her mouth watered at the thought of sausage and cheese.

"*Nu!*" The waiter glared at them. "*American?*"

Kate stood and took a twenty-dollar bill from her purse. "*Ne puteţi servi mai repede, vă rog, ne grăbim!*"

The waiter reached for the bill. Kate folded it back between her fingers. "When we get the food," she said. "*Mititei. Brînză. Salam. Pastrama.*"

The waiter glared again but disappeared into the kitchen. O'Rourke and Kate stood until he returned. Truck drivers stared at them.

"Nothing like being inconspicuous," whispered the priest.

Kate sighed. "Would you rather we starved?"

The waiter returned with a less surly manner and a greasy white bag. Kate looked in, saw the wrapped sausages, stuffed eggs, and slices of salami. He reached for the twenty dollars again but Kate held up one finger. "*Băutură?*" she said. "Something to drink?"

The waiter looked pained.

"*Nişte apă*," said Kate. "*Apă minerală.*"

The waiter nodded tiredly and looked at O'Rourke. "Beer," said the priest.

The waiter returned a minute later with two large bottles of mineral water and three bottles of beer. He obviously wanted the transaction to be over. O'Rourke took the bottles;

the waiter took the twenty-dollar bill. The truckers resumed their conversations.

Outside, it was drizzling again. Kate stuffed the food and bottles under the cowl of the sidecar. O'Rourke was out on the street and headed east in a minute. "I don't know what to do except head back into town," he shouted.

Kate was watching the trolley and train tracks that ran parallel to the road here. There were graveled ruts running alongside them. "The tracks run west here!" she shouted and pointed.

O'Rourke understood immediately. He wheeled the motorcycle in front of an oncoming streetcar, bounced across a curb, pounded across a littered field, and swerved onto the graveled track. In a minute they were echoing between the backs of Stalinist apartment buildings. The priest tried to avoid the broken bottles and jagged bits of metal along the track.

Near the edge of town, the graveled path turned to mud and then died out altogether. "Hang on!" shouted O'Rourke and jerked the motorcycle up onto a crossing, then down onto the railroad ties. Kate's sidecar hung over the rail.

They bounced along for three or four miles, Kate sure every inch of the way that her fillings were going to vibrate out. She could not imagine how O'Rourke could see; her own vision was a vibrating triple image dulled by the goggles and drizzle. "What if a train comes?" she shouted as they passed the last of the outlying peasant homes. Only a few old men in their gardens had looked up.

"We die!" O'Rourke shouted back.

Five miles out of the city and at least three miles beyond the roadblock, they stopped at a junction with a muddy dirt road that led north and south. Ahead of them, around a thick copse of trees, a train's whistle seemed very loud.

"Guess we get off here," said O'Rourke and swung north on the road. The track was muddy and Kate had to get out and push twice before they reached a junction with Highway E 70, running northwest like an abandoned and unpatched

Interstate. It seemed like a century since O'Rourke had driven her to Piteşti along this road to see the baby-buying in action last May.

There were no police cars on the westbound lane. They saw no black Mercedes when they switched to a narrow and bumpy Highway 72 beyond the large village of Găeşti. The sign said TÎRGOVIŞTE 30 KM.

No longer speaking above the engine roar, Kate's head throbbing from the beating along the railroad tracks, they drove north toward the mountains and the gathering dark.

They stopped to eat along the Dimboviţa River, less than ten kilometers from Tîrgovişte. Highway 72 was narrow, winding, and unencumbered by villages larger than a few modest homes tucked next to the road. O'Rourke parked the motorcycle deep under the trees, near the slow-moving river. The cheese was sharp, the sausage old, and the *ouă umpluţi*— the stuffed eggs—stuffed with something neither of them recognized. The meal was one of the most delicious Kate could ever remember, and she drank straight from the mineral water bottle to wash it down. The rain had stopped, and although the sun showed no sign of coming out, it seemed warmer than it had been in days. Kate found bits of her clothing that were actually dry.

"Your Romanian seems to have worked back at the restaurant," said O'Rourke. He seemed to be savoring the beer.

Kate licked her fingers. "Basic survival tactics last spring. Not all my meals were at the hospital restaurant." She paused before attacking her last bit of stuffed egg. "I hope those truckers were at the end of their haul rather than the beginning."

O'Rourke nodded. "The beer, you mean? Yes. Well, driving sober is a rarity in this country." He glanced at his own almost-empty bottle. "I guess I'll stop with one."

Kate took off her scarf. "You said 'shit' twice today and now you're swilling beer. Hardly the behavior of a proper priest."

Instead of laughing, O'Rourke looked out at the river. His

eyes were a lustrous gray and in that second Kate caught a glimpse of the handsome boy in the tired and bearded face of the man. "It's been a long time," he said, "since I was a proper priest."

Kate hesitated, embarrassed.

"If the Romanian trip hadn't come up two years ago, putting me in touch with the orphan problem here," he went on, "I would have resigned then." He took another drink.

"That sounds funny," Kate said. "The word 'resigned,' I mean. One doesn't think of priests resigning."

O'Rourke nodded slightly, but kept his eyes on the river.

"Why would you leave the priesthood?" Kate said very softly. There was no traffic on the road and the river made little noise.

O'Rourke spread his fingers and Kate realized how large and strong his hands looked. "The usual reason," he said. "Inability to suspend one's disbelief." He lifted a stick and drew geometric shapes in the soft loam.

"But you said once that you believed—" began Kate.

"In evil," finished the priest. "But that hardly qualifies me to be a priest. To administer sacraments. To act as a sort of half-assed intermediary between people who believe much more than I and God . . . if there is a God." He tossed the stick into the river and both of them watched it whirl out of sight in the steady current.

Kate licked her lips. "O'Rourke . . . why are you here? Why did you come with me?"

He looked at her then and his gray eyes seemed very clear and very honest. "You asked me to," he said.

Tîrgovişte was a town of about fifty thousand people set in the valley of another river, the Ialomiţa, and beyond it Kate could see the foothills of the Carpathians rising into cloud. At first glance, Tîrgovişte was as polluted and industrial as the oil town Piteşti, but then they rumbled through the busy outskirts and found themselves in the old center of the pre-medieval city.

"That's the old palace," said O'Rourke, taking his right

hand off the throttle to point at ruins beyond a six-foot wall. "It was founded by Mircea the Old back in the late thirteen hundreds, but Vlad the Impaler burned it down in a battle with the Turks in 1462. Just before he lost power, I think."

Kate wiped mud from her goggles.

"That's the Chindia Tower," said O'Rourke, pointing to a circular stone tower visible above the compound wall. "Old Vlad built it as a watchtower and as an observation post to watch the tortures he held in the courtyard below. The new building just outside the wall there is the museum." O'Rourke pulled the motorcycle into a side street, but signs on the door proclaimed the museum closed. "Too bad," said the priest. "I know the assistant curator there. He's an officious little prick . . . quite loyal to Ceauşescu . . . but he knows an awful lot about Tîrgovişte's history."

Kate shifted her weight in the sidecar. Her feet were almost asleep. "Two shits and a little prick," she said. "Your debits are adding up, Father."

"And have been for years, sister." He gunned the throttle and moved slowly down the sidestreet. "My guess was that this is where they'd hold tonight's part of the ceremony, but I don't see any preparations." All of the gates to the palace historical compound had been chained and padlocked with signs saying CLOSED in English and French.

"It's not dark yet," said Kate. "Vampires don't come out until it's dark." She closed her eyes. She felt very sleepy and very discouraged. But when she closed her eyes she saw a perfect image of Joshua laughing at one of his monthly birthday parties, his small hands clenching and unclenching in delight, his dark eyes luminous in candlelight. . . . Kate snapped her eyes open. "Now what?" she said.

O'Rourke stopped the motorcycle. "I think we need to find a place to hide the bike and ourselves," he said. "And then we wait until the vampires come out."

"And if they don't?" said Kate. "If this isn't the site?"

"Then we're well and royally screwed."

Kate patted his arm. "Two shits, a little prick, and now a

royally screwed," she said. "You'd better get to confession soon, O'Rourke."

The priest pulled off his leather helmet and vigorously rubbed his scalp. His hair stood in matted clumps. He was grinning through his beard. "I agree," he said. "And since all of the priests in Tîrgovişte have been rounded up by the *Securitate*, you may just have to hear my confession."

Kate made a face. The motorcycle moved on through quiet sidestreets.

The barn was all by itself in an empty field less than half a mile from the palace grounds. It obviously had not been used in years except to store the remains of a tractor with iron wheels and no engine, although the hay in the loft was relatively new. There was no farmhouse around. Across half a mile of field, the towers of a petrochemical plant were visible through a renewed drizzle.

"Systematization," said O'Rourke, looking both ways before pushing the motorcycle off the narrow lane and down the path to the barn. "Ceauşescu probably bulldozed the farmhouse."

"The hay is recent," said Kate.

O'Rourke nodded to two scrawny cows far across the field, their ribs visible even at that distance. "With all the chemical dumping, their milk probably glows a nice toxic green," he said.

"Nice thought," said Kate, following him into the barn and pulling the sagging doors as closed as they would go. She was shivering visibly now. Her head felt warm and she was dizzy.

O'Rourke set his hand against her forehead. "My God, Neuman . . . you're burning up."

She clutched her bag closer. "I've got antibiotics, aspirin . . ."

"What you need is to get warm," he said, clambering up a rotted wooden ladder to the loft. "It's OK," he called down.

The straw was not actually fresh, but it was relatively clean.

O'Rourke made a nest in it and set the sidecar blanket down. "Take off the raincoat and your outer layers," he said. He was pulling his own sodden coat off.

Kate hesitated only a second. Then she shucked off her wet coat and scarf, found her cheap sweater and polyester pants soaked through, and tugged them off. Even her underwear was damp, but she left on her bra and white cotton pants. Her legs and arms were a mass of goosebumps and she knew that her nipples were visible through her unstructured bra. Kate dropped into the straw and pulled half of the blanket up and around her. The wool was scratchy and smelled of gasoline. "I have a change of clothes in the bag," she said through chattering teeth.

"You wouldn't have some for me in there would you?" asked O'Rourke. He was much wetter than she had been. He squeezed his black shirt and water ran out. The skin of his chest and upper arms was very white and Kate could see his fingers shaking with the cold. His black trousers were visibly soaked, but he hesitated a moment after unbuttoning them. "Close your eyes," he said.

"Don't be silly," snapped Kate, clenching jaw muscles to keep her teeth from chattering. "I'm a doctor, remember? Do you want a lecture on hypothermia?"

"No," said O'Rourke and unzipped his pants. He put both their sets of clothes on a wooden railing where the weak sunlight could reach them through the single filthy window in the loft.

He doesn't wear underwear! was Kate's single thought. Only then did she notice the plastic of the prosthesis beginning just below his left knee and realized that his request might have come from something other than simple modesty.

Kate's eyes left the prosthetic leg and looked at the man. Father Michael O'Rourke was not as lean as Lucian, muscles not quite as well defined, but when he turned to spread the clothes on the railing, Kate found herself admiring his small rear end in a way that was far from medical. When he turned around, she followed the line of dark hair from where it covered his chest down to the thick patch of pubic hair. His penis and scrotum were contracted from the cold.

Kate turned away and fumbled in her bag for clothes.

"Don't get the other clothes wet," said O'Rourke, slipping onto the blanket and pulling up the loose end. He was facing her, their knees not quite touching, and there was just enough extra blanket to cover him. "Get warm first, then put them on."

In other circumstances, with any other man, she would have known that was a line. Now, with Michael O'Rourke, she wasn't sure. "Just a sweater," she said, pulling out a navy cotton sweater and tugging it on while undoing the clasp of her wet bra and slipping it off as subtly as she could before putting her arms through the arms of the sweater. She was not unaware that the motion made her breasts seem larger. "The rest is mostly jeans and skirts that would look out of place here," she whispered, tugging the blanket tight again. "I'll have to wear the damn polyester stuff Lucian bought me if we're going back out on the street." She pulled a dry pair of underpants from the bag and slipped them under the corner of the blanket. *How to do this without being so obvious?* She gave up being subtle, hunkered down in the blanket, slipped off the wet panties, and pulled on the dry ones.

O'Rourke clasped his bare arms outside the blanket, and Kate realized that he was also trying to keep from shivering. He was not succeeding. She wondered if any of the shivers were from nervousness. They were huddled in their little depression in the straw like two Indians crouched face-to-face.

"Come here," whispered Kate and lay back in the straw, pulling the blanket so that O'Rourke was obliged to come with it. There was an awkward moment of rearranging the blanket and then they were lying next to each other, not quite touching but sharing warmth under the wool. Kate tried to think of a joke to break the tension palpable between them, then decided not to. O'Rourke was looking at her with those clear gray eyes, and she was not quite sure if there was a question there or not.

"Turn around," she whispered.

With each of them in a fetal position, there was just enough blanket to cover them securely. Without hesitating, Kate slipped against him spoon fashion, feeling her breasts compress under the cotton sweater, feeling the backs of his thighs still moist with rain against the front of hers. Her hands touched his cold shoulders, slipped down his arms. She could feel the muscles tense and quivering with cold and realized that O'Rourke had been soaked and freezing during most of the long drive to Tîrgovişte. She snuggled closer and slid her bandaged left arm around his body, her hand flat against his chest.

"I don't think . . ." began O'Rourke.

"Shhh," whispered Kate, molding his legs and hips to hers. "It's all right. We'll just get warm and rest a bit until it gets dark." She felt his chest expand as if he were going to say something else, but he stayed silent. A moment later she felt him relax.

Kate felt her own excitement, felt the warmth and moisture between her thighs and the slight sense of heaviness in her breasts that always signified arousal in her, but she also felt a great sense of calm descend on her for the first time since the fire. She set her face close to the back of his neck, feeling the soft tickling where his uncut hair curled slightly there and breathing in the clean male scent of him. He had stopped shivering.

Kate was very aware of her nipples separated from his skin by only the light cotton, was conscious of the warmth of the cheeks of his behind against her thighs, and sensed the curve of his back solid against the cusp of her belly, but she let the urgency such proximity produced just slide away for now, become a pleasant background sensation, as she relaxed into the warmth of the moment.

And slept.

It was dark when she woke and for a second there was a surge of panic that they had overslept and missed the Ceremony, but then Kate saw the dim remnants of twilight through the dusty panes and knew that the sun had just set. They had hours left until midnight.

O'Rourke was asleep—Kate had not even the briefest confusion about where she was or whom she was with—but he had turned in his sleep so that they lay facing each other. Kate's bandaged left arm was still encircling him, but O'Rourke had huddled closer under the small blanket, his hands clasped together in front of him so that they lay in the warm valley between her breasts. There was no chance that he was feigning sleep; O'Rourke was snoring ever so softly, his mouth open slightly in that vulnerable unselfconsciousness Kate had seen so often when she checked on Joshua in the night.

Kate studied O'Rourke's face in the bit of light available: his lips were full and soft, his eyelashes long—she could imagine how cute he had been as a boy—and there were traces of red and premature gray in his brown beard. His relaxed face made her realize how much subtle strain there usually was in his otherwise open and friendly countenance, as if Mike O'Rourke carried a heavy weight which he relinquished only in sleep.

Kate glanced down but could not see the artificial leg in the gap where the small blanket had parted above them. She did see the long curve of his naked thigh where his leg lay next to hers.

Without thinking about it, because thinking would change her mind, Kate leaned closer, kissed O'Rourke's cheek, and—when his eyes opened and lips closed in surprise— kissed him softly but firmly on the mouth. He did not pull away. Kate pulled back a second to let her eyes focus on his, saw something more important than surprise there, and brought her face closer to kiss him again. This time her lips parted only seconds before his did. She used her bandaged left arm to pull him tighter against her, feeling his hands, still folded, between her breasts and the slow but steady rise of his penis against her thigh.

They gasped for breath and then kissed again, and this time something infinitely more complex than their mutual urgency and excitement was communicated in the kiss—it was a slow and simultaneous opening of sensation, a resonance as real as the pounding of their hearts.

Kate pulled back, her senses literally swimming in a vertigo of feeling. "I'm sorry, I—"

"Hush," whispered O'Rourke, lifting his hands to the back of her head, fingers sliding into and under her hair, pulling her close again for another kiss.

Kate thought that the moist perfection of that kiss would never end. When it did, her voice was shaky. "I mean, it's all right if we do. I mean, I have an IUD . . . but, really, I understand if you—"

"Hush," he whispered again and lifted her sweater over her head. Her nipples responded to the cold air at the same instant her eyes were covered, then she could see again and he was pulling the blanket back in place. "Shhh," he said, touching her lips with one finger while his other hand found her underpants and tugged them down and off.

"If you don't want to, it's all—" she began, voice thick.

"Shut up," whispered O'Rourke. "Please." He kissed her again, then slipped his left arm behind her, fingers strong on her back, and rolled half on top of her, his left arm taking the weight.

"Please," she echoed and said no more as she lifted her face and kissed him, one hand splayed on the back of his head, the other sliding down his back to the base of his spine. There were scar ridges there—most small, but at least one long and ridged. She felt the briefest touch of the prosthesis as he lifted and then lowered himself between her legs, but then she was aware only of the warmth of the rest of his body, of his kisses, and of his erection warm and insistent against the curve of her belly.

Kate moaned and moved her right hand down, under his thighs, cupped him, slid up him, and guided him to her. She was very wet as she raised her knees and cradled him.

O'Rourke was in no hurry. He kissed her deeply, raised his face to look at her with what seemed infinite tenderness, then kissed her again so slowly and so passionately that Kate thought she might have lost consciousness for a second or two. Her hips moved and he entered her then, with no clumsiness, no rough male desperation, but with the same moist, slow firmness that she felt in his kiss.

Kate stopped breathing for an instant as he paused and seemed ready to withdraw, but he returned with infinite slowness. Then he was moving deep within her, still slowly, so slowly that she could feel the perfect contact as he moved across the most sensitive interior part of her and then almost withdrew and moved again.

The next few minutes were like memories of a future in which their lovemaking had grown better and better, more intimate with each act of love. Nothing seemed forced or awkward. They moved together for several urgent moments, Kate's senses lifted to a point of excitement where she could hardly breathe, and then O'Rourke shifted his weight slightly and his right hand was between them, part of the moisture and contact, and each time he drew back a bit—the slow movement then making Kate feel as if she were folding around him and in on herself—his moist fingers stroked her gently downward, she felt the sensation of being rubbed against both his fingers and the shaft of his penis, and then his hand would rise slowly against her even as he slid deeper. In moments Kate found herself excited beyond anything she had experienced before, her hips moving more rapidly, demandingly, then slowing as the cadence of their movement slowed, their tempo increasing again in a perfect unison of lubricated friction.

Kate was no novice at making love—she had been passionate with Tom and with a few lovers in the years before and after Tom—but nothing had prepared her for the intimacy and excitement she felt now. Just when it felt like neither she nor O'Rourke could last another instant, that each would have to shudder to orgasm in the same movement, then their rhythm would change as if choreographed through long experience and they would begin rising through another circle of sensation.

They rolled together now, the blanket falling away unheeded, ending with Kate on top and O'Rourke's broad hand on her chest so that his fingers touched both breasts. He was looking at her, his face lost in that sensuous zone between pain and pleasure. She saw that he had bitten his lip and she lowered her face to kiss away the drop of blood there. He tried to slow her movements now with his hand firm on her hip, but Kate sensed that there could be no more slowing, no more waiting. Throwing her face back, she set both hands on his chest and moved with a rocking, downward shifting motion that brought them to the edge and beyond. For a throbbing second, Kate did not know whose impending orgasm she was feeling more strongly, hers or O'Rourke's.

Then O'Rourke's eyes closed, Kate's closed a second later, she came with a flood of warmth that echoed through her in widening ripples, and an instant after that she felt O'Rourke pulsing inside her as he groaned.

A moment later Kate lay full length on him while O'Rourke hugged her close and pulled the blanket above them. He remained in her, still hard, holding her with strong hands as she half-dozed with her cheek against his chest. It grew full dark. The cold was a palpable thing in the barn now. Somewhere far across the field, a goat bleated.

"Does this ruin everything?" Kate whispered at last, coming out of a half-dream.

"It doesn't ruin anything," whispered O'Rourke. His hands rubbed her back.

"But your vows . . ."

"I'd already decided to leave the priesthood, Kate. My trip to Chicago was to resign in person." He turned his face to one side and freed his hand long enough to brush away a bit of straw that clung to his beard. He returned the hand to her back. "I've honored the vow of celibacy for eighteen years without believing in the reason for it."

"Eighteen years," whispered Kate. She touched his chest with her fingertips. When she lifted her face from his chest to whisper something, he kissed her.

"Did you feel . . ." she began.

"As if we had been lovers for years?" he finished. "As if

we were remembering times we had made love in the past? Yes, I did. Do.''

Kate shook her head. She did not believe in the supernatural, had never believed in miracles . . . but this physical telepathy made her shiver. O'Rourke pulled the blanket tighter and kissed her ear. "We'd better get dressed and find out if the ceremony is happening tonight,'' he whispered.

It rushed in then: the alien place, the cold, the dark, the nightmare of Joshua in the hands of cruel strangers. "Hold me just another minute,'' she whispered back, lowering her cheek to his chest again.

He held her.

Chapter Thirty

T HE *strigoi* security forces began arriving sometime after ten-thirty, their dark vans, Mercedes, and military vehicles rumbling down the empty sidestreets of Tîrgovişte and taking up positions around the museum and old palace grounds. There had already been guards at the three gates, as well as razor wire atop the walls. Now the black-garbed figures with automatic weapons guarded the approaches, commandeered rooftops across nearby streets, and lit the torches within the compound around the Chindia Tower. There were few homes around the palace grounds—most of the buildings there were small businesses or related to the factories which surrounded the old section—but those few homes and shops were dark and empty: the people of Tîrgovişte, as if forewarned, had cleared the area before nightfall.

Kate and O'Rourke watched through the shattered wall on the third floor of a half-razed building half a block from the compound. They had seen the guards, checked the walls, and retreated before the rest of the security forces had arrived. Kate had been in favor of trying to get over the wall while there was still time, but O'Rourke had led her to a covered cistern behind the abandoned building. "This is a forgotten way into the compound. This dry cistern opens into a sewer that was part of the original complex. We can enter this way . . . one of the young priests crawled the entire way in as a lark. But it will be better if we try after dark.''

"How do you know this way in?" Kate had whispered.

He had told her then: His earlier trip to Tîrgovişte had been as much to reconnoiter the palace compound and meet with the Franciscan monks here as to check on the orphanage. The monks had shown him the area, produced old maps and architectural drawings done during the restoration of the palace compound fifty years earlier, and led him to this cistern.

Kate had pulled away from him then. "You knew the ceremony was going to be here," she said. "You knew all about this stuff.''

O'Rourke shook his head. "Not all about it. We guessed that this would be the site for the second night of the Investiture Ceremony. The palace grounds were closed to the public yesterday and there's been tight security.''

"Who's *we*?" asked Kate.

"The other Franciscans. I swear, Kate, I never heard of any of this until I came to Romania two years ago.''

"Why didn't you tell me?''

O'Rourke started to speak, then stopped. He touched her cheek. "I'm sorry. I should have. When you left the country with Joshua, I thought it was over with.''

Kate had balled her fists. "But you knew the danger! You knew they'd come after me!''

"No!" He took a step toward her and then stopped when she backed away. "No, I didn't know the child had anything to do with the *strigoi*. You have to believe me on that, Kate.''

She stared at him. "You said that Lucian knew. He and the Order of the Dragon or whatever it's called.''

O'Rourke shook his head. "Some of the monks who were arrested here today belong to the Order of the Dragon. It's a real organization . . . secret all these centuries . . . but I had no idea Lucian had any contact with it. I'm still not convinced. It's one of the reasons I called Father Stroicescu early this morning.''

"And what did he say?''

O'Rourke opened his hands. "He's not in the Order. The priest that was a member was picked up here in Tîrgovişte. I don't know if Lucian is lying."

"Why should he be? He's helped me, hasn't he?"

O'Rourke said nothing.

"All right," Kate had said. "I'll trust you for now." She closed her eyes. Her body could still feel the sensation of him inside her. *My God, what have I done?* "Let's get into the compound."

"Later," O'Rourke said, and she could see him shiver. Their clothes were not quite dry and the night wind was cold. "When the VIPs begin arriving."

The VIPs began arriving an hour before midnight. The line of Mercedes glided between the barricades and guards and disappeared inside the main gate. Kate could see torchlight reflected on the top third of Chindia Tower visible above the compound walls. "It's time," she whispered.

O'Rourke nodded tersely and led her down the shattered stairway to the cistern in the dark courtyard. Even in the dim light she could see how pale he was.

"What's wrong?" she asked.

O'Rourke bit his lip. "Tunnel," he said.

Kate produced the single flashlight she had packed in her bag. "We have this."

"It's not the darkness," he said and clenched his jaws. Kate saw that his teeth were chattering and that there was a film of sweat on his forehead and upper lip.

"You're ill," whispered Kate.

"No." O'Rourke turned away from the cistern and leaned against a wall. "The tunnel . . ." He clenched his teeth.

Kate understood. "You said that during the war . . . Vietnam . . . you were a tunnel rat. It's where—"

O'Rourke wiped the sweat from his face. "I was checking out a tunnel complex that the platoon had found near a village." His voice quavered, then steadied. "Tunnels branching from tunnels. Bazella and his boys had dropped in concussion and fragmentation grenades, but there were so many turns, so many ups and downs . . . Anyway, it'd been an NVA headquarters . . . infirmary, barracks, the whole bit. But the NVA—the North Vietnamese regulars—had cleared out. Except for one rotting corpse wedged in the tunnel a few meters from its exit point on the riverbank. I figured I could squeeze by . . ." O'Rourke stopped and stared at nothing.

"The body was booby-trapped," whispered Kate. Her fingers held the memory of the scars on his back and upper legs.

O'Rourke nodded. "They'd hollowed out the guy's stomach and rigged him with C-4 and a simple trip wire to the detonator. When I touched his leg, he blew mine off." He tried to laugh but the sound was sad and hollow.

Kate moved closer and set her face against his neck.

"It's not full-blown claustrophobia," he whispered. "I mean, you've seen me on planes and trains. As long as I can see a way *out* . . ." He broke off. "I'm sorry."

"No," whispered Kate. "It's good. I think it's better that you wait here. It makes more sense. If I get in trouble, someone has to be out here to go for help."

This time O'Rourke did laugh. "Go for help to whom? Where? We're all there is, Kate."

She managed a smile. "I know, but I keep waiting for the cavalry to come over the hill."

"Give me a minute," said O'Rourke. He took several deep breaths, swung his arms around a few times, and leaned out over the dry cistern. It was only eight or nine feet to the bottom and there were gaps and footholds in the loose stone. "Hold the light steady . . . good, there . . . that's where Father Danielescu said the entrance was."

Kate saw only stone and desiccated creepers.

"Hold it steady until I find a way into the old sewer line," said O'Rourke. "Then hand down the light and join me." He swung out over the wall and felt his way to the bottom. Once a stone tumbled to the littered floor of the cistern, but O'Rourke stepped down easily. Kate held the light on the wall while he felt the stones, removed a penknife, and pried at one until it came loose. The others came out more easily.

"Light," he said, standing and holding his hands high.

Kate dropped the flashlight to him. He held the beam on footholds while she descended. They crouched and peered into the hole.

"Ugghh," said Kate, clenching her fists. Rats' eyes had gleamed back and now she could hear the screeching of the things as they fled the light. The flashlight beam gleamed on their oily black backs. The sewer line—if that is what it was—was only three feet across, and it narrowed only a few yards in where the rats' eyes had burned back at them.

"How can we go into that?" whispered Kate.

O'Rourke leaned close. "The good news is that I bet there's not a single North Vietnamese in there. I'll go first." He found a sturdy stick on the floor of the cistern and held it in his right hand, the flashlight in his left. His body blocked the light when he forced his shoulders through the entrance.

Kate closed her eyes and thought of Joshua.

"It's wide enough," came O'Rourke's taut whisper. "Father Danielescu said that it went all the way through, and I think he's right. Come on, I'll hold the light."

Kate tried to estimate the distance they would have to crawl. A football-field's length? Two-thirds that distance? It was endless. The ancient tunnel could collapse and no one would ever know they were there. The rats would eat their eyes. This was insane.

"Coming," she whispered and crawled into the hole.

Except for the terror of the fire and the death of Tom and Julie, the hundred yards of tunnel was the most terrible and horrifying experience of Kate's life. She could hear O'Rourke's panting, could see the tremor of incipient panic in his body silhouetted against the flashlight glow ahead, but the rest was sharp rock and mud and the scurry of rats and darkness made all the worse by the heightening sense of claustrophobia as the narrow passage grew narrower, each tight section tighter. Occasionally O'Rourke would stop and she would grasp his leg or, if the tunnel was wide enough there, force a hand forward to hold his hand, but they spoke little and their panting took on a more desperate rhythm the deeper they crawled into the darkness.

"What about bad air?" she whispered after they forced a particularly narrow point where the old rock-lined sewer had collapsed. They had squeezed between mud and roots, and Kate could not imagine making it backward through that bottleneck. The thought took her breath away and left her panting in short, sharp gasps.

"Rats live here," gasped O'Rourke. Kate could hear them scurrying ahead of him and down side passages that were no wider across than her thighs. "If they can breathe, I guess we can."

"Was your priest friend sure that this was passable?"

O'Rourke paused in his crawling. "Well, I didn't actually speak to that young priest . . ."

"But you know that he *did* make it all the way into the compound?" demanded Kate. Her chest felt constricted, as if someone were pulling a metal band tight there.

"Yes!" said O'Rourke and began crawling forward again, muttering something Kate did not catch.

"What was that?"

"I said that the priest crawled in here when he was a boy," said O'Rourke, pushing fallen rocks out of the way. The flashlight created a corona around his beard and hair.

"When he was a *boy!*" Kate grabbed O'Rourke's boot. "How *small* a boy, goddamn it?"

The priest paused to gasp for breath again. "I don't know. Not too small, I think. I hope." He began moving forward again, his shoulders scraping rock on both sides.

A few minutes later Kate was pushing a root out of her way, wondering at the strange, bifurcated shape of the thing, when she rested on her elbows and said, "O'Rourke . . . Mike . . . shine the light back here, would you?"

She was holding a human forearm, the space between the radius and ulna packed solid with dirt. She dropped it quickly, wiggling to one side to crawl past it.

"This is good," whispered O'Rourke. "We must be in the cemetery within the compound. Right behind the church."

Kate nodded and brushed her hair out of her eyes. She had handled cadavers as a medical student, had helped with autopsies as a doctor, and held no undue fear of the dead. She just preferred to know ahead of time when she was going to handle a corpse.

It was at this moment that the flashlight went out. Kate froze and felt O'Rourke's body freeze into immobility for several seconds. "Shit," he whispered and banged the flashlight with the heel of his hand. Not even a glimmer. Kate grasped O'Rourke's right ankle while he fiddled with the batteries and tapped the flashlight again. Nothing. She could feel the tension coursing in him like an electric current; his skin became clammy and his muscles grew as rigid as marble. It was as if both legs were now prostheses.

"O'Rourke," she whispered. "Mike?"

Silence. She felt him shift positions, lying on his back now, and from the slight rustlings and shifts in his body, she could imagine his hands lifted, his fingers tapping against the rough roof of the tunnel as if it were a coffin. His breathing was shallow and far too rapid.

"Mike?" she whispered again, reaching higher to touch his arm. She could feel the vibration building deep within him, like the first tremors of tectonic plates slipping after years of mounting pressure.

"O'Rourke," she snapped. "Talk to me."

He made a noise that was somewhere between a clearing of his throat and a gasp.

"Talk to me," she whispered again, her voice less sharp. "It's all right. We can get there without the light. We just keep crawling, right?" She squeezed his arm. It was like touching a granite statue that was vibrating slightly.

He made another noise, then whispered something unintelligible. "What?" Kate was stroking the back of his clenched fist.

His voice was tense, taut with control. "Too many tunnels under the compound. Only this one opens into the church."

Kate squeezed his hand. "So? We stay in this one. No problem."

He was shaking as if from fever. "No. We could crawl right under the grate and into one of the other sewers."

"Won't we see light?" whispered Kate. She could hear rats scrabbling behind her. Without the flashlight to keep them away, they could crawl over her legs . . . her face.

"I . . . don't . . . know . . ." His whisper trailed off and the shaking grew worse.

Kate squeezed his leg above the knee. "Mike, was tonight the first time you've made love since you became a priest?"

"What?" The syllable was exhaled.

Kate forced her voice to be conversational, almost whimsical. "I just wondered if this was something priests do regularly . . . violate their vows, I mean. You must have plenty of opportunities, what with all the lonely young wives in a parish. Or the lonely young volunteers and Peace Corps girls in Third World countries."

"God . . . *damn* . . . it," breathed O'Rourke. He jerked his leg away from her touch. She could hear his arm rise as if he were clenching his fist. "No," he said, his voice growing firmer, "it's not a habit of mine. I haven't been with anyone since . . . since before I got blown apart in 'Nam. I wasn't a good priest, Kate . . . but I was an earnest one."

"I know that," she whispered, her voice soft. She found his hand, pulled it down, scrunched forward in the darkness, and kissed it.

His breathing was rapid but more regular now. She could feel the tremors passing out of his body like slow aftershocks. Kate rubbed her cheek against his open palm.

"I'm sorry," he whispered. "I see what you were doing. Thank you."

Kate kissed his fingers. "Mike, we're almost there. Let's keep moving." Something brushed her legs and she heard a rat scurry back down the tunnel. She hoped it was only a rat. The raw earth here smelled of decay.

O'Rourke tried the flashlight again, gave up on it, tucked it in his belt, rolled over on his stomach, and kept inching forward. Kate followed, keeping her head up and eyes open for any slight gleam of light despite the grit that kept falling into her hair and eyes.

They saw it sometime later—it may only have been minutes, but neither of their watchfaces was luminous, and their sense of time was out of kilter. The gleam would have been so faint as to be invisible in a normally dark room, but to their eyes, adapted to absolute darkness, it was like a beacon. They clawed the last ten yards and stared up at the grate in the roof of the tunnel. The sewer was wider here, and Kate could almost crawl abreast of O'Rourke. They lay on their backs and reached up to the outlined metal grid.

"An iron grille," whispered O'Rourke. "They must have put it here since Father Chirica crawled in this way years ago. Probably to keep the rats out." He threaded fingers through the heavy grille and pulled. Kate could hear his teeth gnash and could smell the sweat from him. The grille did not budge.

O'Rourke pulled his hands away with a groan. Kate felt the panic threatening to carry her away then, pure fear rising like nausea in her throat. She honestly did not believe that they could make the trip backward through the long tunnel. "Is there another entrance?" she whispered.

"No. Only the one opening into the cellar of this church. It was part of Vlad Ţepeş' palace once . . . there were underground cells and passages . . ." O'Rourke snarled and attacked the grille again with his hands. Flakes of rust fell like snow but the metal did not budge.

"Here," whispered Kate and grabbed at the grille. "Let's push instead of pull." They set the heels of their hands against the grille and pushed until their arms were numb. They lay there panting, with scrabbling coming closer in the tunnel.

"It must be set in cement," whispered O'Rourke, feeling around the edge of it. "And it would be barely wide enough for our shoulders. Mine at least."

Kate tried to slow her panting. "It doesn't matter," she said. "We're going out through it." She raised her face to the grille. The room above was dank, smelling of wet stone, but the air was infinitely sweeter up there. "The metal's old and rusted," she whispered. "The bars aren't very thick."

"Iron doesn't have to be thick." O'Rourke's voice was flat. She could see the palest glow where his face was.

"Iron rusts like a sumbitch," hissed Kate. "Come on, set your legs up . . . like this . . . with your knees against it. Yeah, wedge your body like mine so all your weight's on your back. Okay, on the count of three, we push until it breaks or we do."

O'Rourke grunted his way into position. "Just a second," he whispered. There was an almost inaudible muttering.

"What?" said Kate. Her back was already hurting.

"Praying," said O'Rourke. "All right, I'm ready. One . . . two . . . *three*." Kate strained and arched until she felt muscles tearing, and even when she could strain no more she continued straining. She felt rust falling into her eyes and mouth, felt the rough rocks of the tunnel floor cutting through her coat and blouse into her back, felt her neck twist as if a hot wire were being pulled through the nerves . . . and still she strained. Next to her, Mike O'Rourke was straining even harder.

The grille did not break, it ripped out of the encircling stone and cheap cement like a cork coming out of a champagne bottle. Kate went up and out first, lying on the cool stones and breathing in cool air for a full fifteen seconds before lowering her arm to help O'Rourke up. He had to take off his jacket and rip his shirt, but he squeezed through the irregular hole into blackness.

They hugged there on the floor of the crypt of the chapel, their exaltation slowly changing to anxiety as they waited for black-clad guards to come in to check on the terrible noise of their entry. Although distant sounds of the Investiture Ceremony were audible to them, no footsteps or alarms sounded.

After a moment they rose, held each other steady, and went up stairs and through an unlocked door into the chapel proper. Torchlight bled colors through a few stained glass windows. Kate looked at O'Rourke, saw his streaked and lacerated face, his torn and smeared clothes, and had to smile. She must look even worse. The chapel was small and almost circular, empty in the way only archaeological sites can be empty, but there was a door with a single clear pane which looked out on Chindia Tower less than fifty yards away. The grass lanes and palace ruins between them and the tower were filled with torches, human figures, the same black guards they had seen at Şnagov Island, and even a parked helicopter and two long Mercedes limousines.

Kate saw none of this. She had eyes only for the clump of red-cowled figures walking slowly past the chapel toward the base of the tower. One of them carried a bundle which might have been mistaken for a package wrapped in red silk. But Kate made no mistake; she had seen the flash of pink cheek and dark eyes by torchlight as the men carried the bundle past the chapel, past chanting clumps of other cowled figures.

O'Rourke held her back, restrained her from ripping open the door and running into the crowded torchlight.

"It's my baby," gasped Kate, finally falling back against the priest but never removing her eyes from the door of the tower where the men and bundle had disappeared. "It's Joshua."

Dreams of Blood and Iron

I am beginning to believe that I cannot die. It has been almost two years since I have partaken of the Sacrament, but still Death does not come. I could refuse food or water, but such an act would be pure folly: my body would cannibalize itself over a period of months rather than die willingly. Even I, who have known more pain in my single lifetime than most generations of families have known cumulatively, even I could not face that torture.

So I lie here in the day, listening to the voices of my Family, much as I lay here during my early childhood. At night I rise and move around my room, stalk the corridors of this old house, and peer from the windows I peered from as a toddler. My muscles have not . . . will not . . . atrophy completely.

I am beginning to believe that God's great punishment to me is this denial of death. Centuries ago, when I was young, the possibility of eternal damnation woke me with a cold sweat in the weak, dark hours of the morning. Now the thought of eternal punishment is the simple fact of being condemned to live forever.

But in the day I doze. And while I lie there, not truly awake and not fully asleep, neither dead nor moving among the living, I dream my memories.

* * *

My enemies fell upon me.

Joined by my treacherous brother Radu, Sultan Mehmed II and his legions of azabs, janissaries, Rumelian sipahis, and slant-eyed Anatolians crossed the Danube and sought to dethrone me. Mehmed's army was much stronger than my own. I did not confuse honor with idiocy. Upon my order, our forces withdrew to the north and left desolation in our wake.

The cities, towns, and villages of my kingdom were put to the torch. Granaries were emptied or destroyed. Livestock which could not be driven north with the army was butchered where it stood. Upon my order, wells were poisoned and dams were built to create marshes where Mehmed's cannon must pass.

Those are the historical facts of that retreat—what modern strategists would call a "strategic withdrawal"—but it conveys nothing of the reality. I lie here with evening painting the dark wood of the beams above me a dull blood color and I remember the roads swollen with weeping refugees from our own cities and villages, oxen carts and plow horses and entire clans on foot, carrying their meager belongings, while behind us the flames lighted the horizon while the skies darkened with the smoke of our self-immolation. I lay here this winter just past and eavesdropped on the Family housekeepers talking on the stairs and landing—my hearing is still that good when I wish it to be—and they whisper to each other about Saddam Hussein's war with the Americans and about the oil fires he lit in his wrath blackening the desert skies. They mutter about the fighting in Yugoslavia to the west and shake their kerchiefed heads about how terrible modern war is. Saddam Hussein is a child compared to Hitler and Hitler was an infant compared to me. I once followed Hitler's retreating army into his heartland and was amazed at the artifacts and infrastructure he left intact. Saddam set fire to the desert; in my day, I took some of the lushest land in Europe and turned it into a desert.

This age knows nothing of war.

We retreated into the heart of my kingdom, because all

Transylvanians then learned at their mother's breast that the salvation of our people and nation would always be the deepest folds in the highest mountains, the darkest forest in the most remote regions where wolves howl and the black bear roams.

I have read Stoker. I read his silly novel when it was first published in 1897 and saw the first stage production in London. Thirty-three years later I watched that bumbling Hungarian ham his way through one of the most inept motion pictures I have ever had the misfortune to attend. Yes, I have read and seen Stoker's abominable, awkwardly written melodrama, that compendium of confusions which did nothing but blacken and trivialize the noble name of Dracula. It is garbage and nonsense, of course, but I confess there is one brief, almost certainly accidental passage of poetry amidst all the puerile scrawlings.

Stoker's idiot, opera-cloaked vampire pauses when he hears a wolf howling in the forest. "Listen to them," he stage-whispers. "The children of the night. What beautiful music they make."

In this accidental bit of poetry, something of the Transylvanian and Romanian soul is revealed. It is the wolf's howl—solitary, terrifying, echoing in empty places—which is the music of the Romanian soul. In the forest darkness we find our salvation and rebirth. In the mountain fastness we set our backs to the stone and turn to face our enemies. It has always been so. It will always be so. I have bred and led a race of children of the night.

In that summer of 1462, thousands of my soldiers and many more thousands of my boyars and peasants fled north from the Sultan's hired hordes. It was the hottest summer in living memory. Where we passed, nothing remained. My spies reported that Mehmed's janissaries grumbled that there was nothing to loot in the charred cinders of our cities, nothing to eat in the ashes of our farms. I ordered pits to be dug along the only possible line of advance, sharpened stakes to be planted, and then had them covered over with care. I remember pausing with our rear guard one June evening and listening to the screams of the Sultan's camels as they tumbled into our pits. It was sweet music.

I led raids against the mass of Turkish swine, using paths and passes known only to a few of my people, surprising them from the rear, cutting out their stragglers and wagon trains of sick and wounded the way a wolf pack cuts out and pulls down the weakest of the herd, then impaling them where the others would find the bodies.

I sent my agents among the desolate leper colonies and into the plague-ridden shadows of my still-standing cities, bringing Turkish clothes for the sick and dying to wear as we sent them into the Sultan's camps to mingle with the janissaries and Anatolians and sipahis and azabs, to drink from their cups and to eat from their common bowls. I ordered living victims of syphilis, the Black Death, tuberculosis, and the pox to join the Turks, and I rewarded them generously when they returned with the turbans of the men they infected unto death.

But they came on, my enemies, dying of thirst and hunger and illness, afraid to sleep in their own camps at night, terrified of the forest dark and the wolf's howl, but they came on. We left a single path of forage and unpoisoned springs for them to follow, a trail as clear as a line of gunpowder leading to a powder keg.

They turned west to Bucharest and found that town empty of life and sustenance; they swept north to Şnagov, where hundreds of my boyars and troops waited on my fortified island there. Mehmed and Radu could not reduce Şnagov. The lake was too deep for men in armor to cross without fear of drowning. My walls were too high to scale once the lake was crossed. My instruments of war rained down too terrible a punishment on them.

Mehmed followed me north again, leaving Şnagov in his rear and condemning more of his men to night harassment and morning impalement.

Then, on the night of June 17 in the Year of Our Lord 1462, I attacked Mehmed's army not with a raiding force but with 13,000 of my bravest boyars and their handpicked *troops. We scattered the guards, split the garrison, skewered those who tried to stand, and drove through the mass of their camp like a hot sword through soft flesh. We had brought torches and flares soaked in gunpowder, and these we lighted to find the Sultan's red tent. I fully planned to kill the dog myself and drink his blood before the sun rose again.*

We gained the red tent and slaughtered all those inside, but it was the wrong red tent. It gave me little solace to know that we had beheaded Mehmed's two viziers, Isaac and Mahmud. By the time I regrouped my men, the Sultan's cavalry was pouring in from three sides. Even then, I could have carried home the attack, for Mehmed had lost nerve and fled the camp, his unmounted men were fleeing and milling in demoralized confusion, but one of my commanders, a boyar named Gales, failed to attack from the west with the second wave as I had ordered. Because of Gales' cowardice, Mehmed escaped, and my force had to fight its way out of the tightening ring of Ottoman cavalry.

It was there, in the camp of Mehmed, that I took two arrows through the chest. I snapped them off and held them up by the light of torches and flares, rallying my men. The secret healing force which had set me apart from mere men since birth was stronger in me then. And I had partaken of the Sacrament an hour before leading the raid. I heard the cry "Lord Dracula cannot die!" and then my surviving boyars came to my side, we formed a wedge of shields and blades, and we fought our way out of that madness.

The Sultan returned to his army. Some say that he had to be dragged back to the camp by his generals and my brother Radu. I did not drink his warm blood that night.

In my anger, I ordered the coward, Commander Gales, to my command tent an hour before dawn. My guards disarmed him, stripped him, shackled his arms behind his back, and hung him from the iron gimbal ring which I always had brought on our campaigns. Then, still covered with the soot and blood of battle, my chest in great pain, I went to work. My only tools were an awl, a corkscrew gimlet, and my father's razor of the finest-honed steel in all of Europe. They were enough. I drank from his living body until the sun rose, then slept, arose, gave orders for the march back to Tîrgovişte, and returned to dine and drink from him until sunset that day. It has been written that the Turks forty leagues away heard the coward's screams that day.

In Tîrgovişte, we prepared for a year or more of siege. The city was closed, the newly rebuilt walls and towers manned, the cannons primed, cattle and chickens driven into the fort, and underground streams were diverted into the city through the secret sewers I had ordered built. Sultan Mehmed's rabble and the hungry Radu came on.

They stopped twenty-seven leagues from our walls. Mehmed and his men had passed through a hundred forests to reach the foothills of the Carpathians and the doors of Tîrgovişte, but on this morning they encountered a new forest, a forest they paused at before passing through.

In my previous winter of campaigning against the Turks I had killed thousands of my foes. I was eager to keep a precise count of the Ottoman dead, so I had ordered my boyar commanders to cut off the heads of the fallen and carry them home for easy counting. By February, the troops were grumbling: too many heads, too many heavy, leaking bags. At the end of the campaign I had the heads counted, took careful inventory, and then sliced the noses and ears off to send to my friend and sometimes ally, King Matthias Corvinus of Hungary. He never responded to my letter and gift, but I know that he must have been impressed.

Of course we took thousands of Turkish prisoners during the campaign. By the week in June when Mehmed approached the walls of my capital, our cells and stockades held more than twenty-three thousand prisoners.

Now, as Mehmed's huge but exhausted and starved army angrily started their morning march a mere twenty-seven leagues from almost certain victory at Tîrgovişte, they stopped at the forest I had ordered raised. A forest of some twenty-three thousand impaled Turks, some still writhing in the morning light. Taller stakes held the bodies of the Sultan's favorite commanders, friends he had assumed he could ran-

som, friends such as Hamza Pasha and the legendary Greek, Thomas Catavolinos.

The Sultan's own toady and chronicler Laonicus Chalcondyles has written of this morning: "So overwhelmed by disbelief in what he saw, the Emperor said that he could not take the land away from a man who does such marvelous things and can exploit his rule and his subjects in this way and that surely a man who had accomplished this is worthy of greater things."

So said Chalcondyles. But Chalcondyles certainly lied through his rotting teeth. Were we to have been there that morning, and I was, watching from horseback from less than half a league away, we would have seen a demoralized army turning and shoving their way from the stench of death rising from my new forest. And we would have seen their shaken Sultan near to pissing his ballooned, silk pants. And we would have seen him ordering his men into camp within sight of my forest, as if they could not leave or tear their eyes away, and before dark that night they had dug a trench deeper than the Danube around their cowering army and had lit a thousand fires to hold me at bay. I think that I could have walked into their camp and said "Boo!" that night and watched the army flee in terror.

Sultan Mehmed and his band turned away from Tîrgovişte the next morning and began their long march back to Brăila, their fleet, and their accursed homeland. My spies reported then that his army marched into Adrianople at night so that the populace would not see their shame, and that by the time the Sultan returned to Constantinople his once-proud legions of Anatolians, Rumelians, azabs, and janissaries were so much dragged-out dog meat. But the Sultan ordered great rejoicing throughout the land for his brilliant victory over Dracula.

So much for Islamic victories, I think, while I listen to the visiting Family and to busy chambermaids talking of war in desert places.

Chapter Thirty-one

KATE would have rushed out into the torchlit palace grounds after Joshua if O'Rourke had not restrained her. There were at least a hundred cowled *strigoi* visible in the courtyards between her and Chindia Tower, where the baby had been carried, but Kate would have attempted to cross that space if O'Rourke had not at first held her back and then just held her.

"We can't do anything now," he whispered. There were guards within ten yards of the chapel door. "We'll watch where they take him."

Kate had grasped his torn shirt in her two fists. "Can we follow them?"

O'Rourke was silent and she knew the answer herself: it would take too long to crawl back out through the tunnel, they would not know which Mercedes the child had arrived in, and the guards would be checking for anyone following their *strigoi* masters. Kate pounded her fist against O'Rourke's chest. "This is so . . . *maddening*." She took deep breaths to avoid tears, then watched the tower, hoping for some sign of her son.

Chindia Watchtower was an eighty- or ninety-foot stone tower, four-sided at the bottom but soon becoming a cylinder with crenellated battlements at the top. Illuminated by torch-light, the tower looked to Kate like a rook that had escaped its chessboard. There were two arched windows on the side she could see, each window taller than a man, and a single stone and iron balcony outside the first window about forty feet up. She noticed a crack running from the broad base to just below the battlements, with clumsy iron rods holding stone and brick together like giant staples.

O'Rourke noticed her gaze. "That's from the earthquake a few years ago," he whispered. "The tower's been closed to tourists ever since. Ceauşescu authorized the funds to fix it, but it was never done."

Kate nodded absently. She knew that O'Rourke was trying to distract her from thinking about the terrible danger that Joshua was in. *What if they make him drink human blood tonight?* Perhaps they already had. She had not seen the baby at Şnagov, but there was much she had not seen there.

Slowly the crowds of red-cowled figures moved away from the chapel and the palace ruins and gathered at the base of Chindia Tower. There was music, as if a band were playing, and then Kate saw the portable tape unit, amplifiers, and speakers not far from the grounded helicopter and parked limousines. The music was vague, soulless—some Eastern European state anthem, perhaps—but then the tempo changed, chords rose in triumph, and Kate realized that the speakers were blaring the theme from *Rocky*. She shook her head. If this was all a nightmare, it had just gone from the surreal to the ridiculous.

Red-cowled figures stepped through the door onto the platform above the crowd. A great cheer went up from the men below. Then Kate gasped as she saw one of the men—was it Radu Fortuna? She could not tell for sure—hold a silk-wrapped bundle out over the railing as if offering it to the crowd below. The bundle stirred, and Kate gripped O'Rourke's arm, sure that Joshua was going to be dropped.

The figures on the balcony seemed to listen to the cheering for a minute and then they stepped back through the arched doorway. Kate thought of some mad parody of a pope's appearance. The music ended and the crowd below mingled, broke into clumps, and moved away from the tower. Kate saw cigarettes being lit and cowls being taken off. None of the faces looked familiar, although none were close enough to see too clearly. The feeling in the courtyard was like some Rotary meeting after business was finished.

But no one left yet.

It was twenty or thirty minutes later when the group of men came out of the tower. Kate strained but could not make out the baby for a minute. *Did they leave him in there? Is someone or something in there with him?* Her heart pounded. Then she saw the fifth man in the procession carrying something awkwardly, and could make out the red bundle in the red-clad arms.

Those in the courtyards made way, allowing a corridor through the crowd, and Kate's view was blocked again. She had never felt so futile and frustrated.

Now the guards in black were making a cordon around the red-and-white-striped helicopter. A starter coughed, the rotors began to turn slowly, and the mob moved back instinctively, making a wider circle around the machine. Kate saw the doors close on several of the VIPs in red and then the engine sound filled the palace grounds, rotors blurred, the helicopter shuddered, seemed to lean forward on its skids, and then rose, dipped to the left, and climbed quickly above the bare trees to the north, navigation lights flashing. The crowd watched the lights until they disappeared in cloud, and then the men began filing back to their limousines, chauffeurs holding doors open and guards slouching at attention.

"Was that some sort of government helicopter?" whispered Kate. She wondered if it was headed back to Bucharest. It had been flying northwest, away from the capital, when it disappeared in the low clouds.

"It's a Jet Ranger, American made," whispered O'Rourke. "I don't know what kind of choppers the government uses, but I doubt if they'd be American. My guess is that it's privately owned."

Kate nodded. She was not surprised that O'Rourke could identify the machine: males seemed so proud of their ability to give the proper name to the proper piece of machinery.

Especially aircraft and war machines. Kate wished she had a dollar for every time she would be watching some silly war movie with Tom on cable and he would say something like—"Look at that! It's supposed to be an old Sherman tank but they're using an M-60." Or "Do they really expect us to think that F-5 is a MiG-29?" It was all nonsense to Kate. She thought that boys learned all of that trivia because they loved to build models and never really grew out of the pride of naming exotic machinery.

Still, wanting to keep talking while the courtyards emptied and the last guards moved farther from their chapel, her chest aching from the sense of loss and futility, Kate whispered idly, "How do you know it was a whatchamacallit . . . a Jet Ranger?"

O'Rourke surprised her. "I've flown one."

She glanced at him in the dim light. His hair and beard were caked with rock dust and rust. She imagined her own hair. "*Flown* one?"

He turned and grinned, bobbing his head in a boyish way. "When I was in Vietnam, I was the only grunt I knew who actually enjoyed riding in slicks."

"Slicks?" Kate ran her fingers through her hair, brushing out things she did not want to think about.

"Helicopters. Hueys." O'Rourke looked back at the cars driving out through the guarded main gate. "Anyway, I knew a warrant officer there who flew slicks into the A Shau Valley and still enjoyed the flying. He gave me a few checkout rides there, and later, after I'd gotten the new leg, it turned out that he was opening a flying service in California near where I was spending time in a VA hospital." O'Rourke rubbed his beard as if embarrassed by telling such a long story. "Anyway, he gave me lessons."

"Did you get a license?" asked Kate. She was watching the exodus, wondering how they might find out where the next night's ceremony was. The town, the lovemaking, the tunnel, the torches, and the music were all unreal. *Joshua was real.* She forced herself to focus.

"No," he said, testing the door. It was locked but only

with a padlock and rusty hasp on the outside that could be kicked open. "I didn't think there was a big market for one-legged chopper pilots, so I went into the seminary instead." Suddenly he pulled her low and dragged her back into the smaller room, keeping her head low. "Shhh!" he whispered.

A minute later the padlock was tried and opened, flashlight beams swept the main chapel area, and then Kate heard the sound of the door being shut and locked again. They waited five minutes before either spoke again.

"Final check, I'd guess," whispered O'Rourke. They crept back to the door. The courtyard was empty and dark. The main and secondary gates closed. Chindia Tower was only a dark silhouette against low clouds lit by fires and lights from the chemical plants to the northeast.

They waited another twenty minutes, Kate rubbing her face to fight off the numbness of exhaustion, and then O'Rourke kicked the door open, the hasp tearing out of rotten wood.

"The museum people may be upset at what we're doing to their chapel," whispered Kate. It was a weak joke, but she felt weak at the relief of knowing they didn't have to go back out through the tunnel.

They moved slowly, keeping low behind tumbled stone walls and bloomless rosebushes, but there were no guards inside the palace grounds and no traffic on the streets beyond. It was as if they dreamt the entire ceremony.

The walls were still topped by razor wire and broken glass, but O'Rourke found a low pedestrian gate in the back of the compound that was climbable. Kate tore her slacks again as she went over the top.

The streets of Tîrgovişte were still silent and empty after the evening's invasion of *strigoi* VIPs, but Kate and O'Rourke kept to the shadows and alleys. Even the city's dogs were not barking tonight.

The motorcycle was still in the barn. While O'Rourke fiddled with the balky machine, Kate climbed the ladder to retrieve her travel bag and the blanket from the loft. The reflected lights from the petrochemical plant came through the dusty window and illuminated the nest in the straw where she and O'Rourke had made love only hours before. *Did that really happen?* Kate sighed tiredly, folded the blanket, and went back down the ladder.

O'Rourke had the doors open and was pushing the clumsy machine outside.

"I'd give a thousand dollars for a bath tonight," she said, still brushing muck from her hair and clothes. "Five hundred just for an indoor toilet."

"Get your checkbook out," said O'Rourke and gunned the engine to life.

The Franciscan monastery was in a section of Tîrgovişte so old that the streets were not wide enough for more than one Dacia-sized car at a time. There were no Dacias or any other type of automobiles on the streets. The motorcycle exhaust sounded obscenely loud to Kate as it echoed back off the ancient stone-and-wood buildings. The motorcycle's weak headlight revealed that every house here seemed to have some personal touch which belied the poverty and socialist drabness that had been imposed from above for so long; bits of brightly covered trim, splendidly arched windows on an ancient home little more than a hovel, intricate stonework on the bottom third of an old house, skillfully executed iron-work on a gate connected to a sagging fence, even the glimpse of elaborate linen curtains in a window of what could have passed for a farm shed in the States.

The monastery was a long, low one-story building set back from the street in a section where empty lots alternated with dark and frequently windowless buildings. O'Rourke cruised past once, turned around, inspected the building on another pass, and then turned down an alley and went slowly past the rear of the structure. It was dark and had an abandoned feel to it. There was a padlock on the gate, but the fence was low enough to climb. Kate caught a glimpse of elaborate gardens and trellises in the dark backyard.

"Wait here a minute," O'Rourke said softly, parking the motorcycle in a copse of trees near where the alley met a larger street. "If the *strigoi* are hunting for us, they may have left someone behind."

Kate touched his arm, feeling the electricity of the renewed contact despite her fatigue and depression. "It's not worth risking," she whispered.

O'Rourke grinned. "A bath," he said. "Indoor plumbing. Maybe fresh clothes."

Kate started climbing out of the sidecar. "I'm going with you."

O'Rourke shook his head. "Compromise. Get on the bike. If I come out in a hurry, gun the thing and pick me up on the run. Do you know how to start it and drive it?"

Kate frowned but nodded. She'd watched him enough during the trip to know that she could get it moving. For some reason she thought of her Miata back home, destroyed in the fire. She had loved that machine . . . loved the sense of freedom and exhilaration it imparted when she drove it hard on winding mountain roads, the clean Colorado sunlight on her face, the wind in her hair . . .

"Kate?" said O'Rourke, squeezing her shoulder. "You with me?"

"Yeah." She rubbed her cheeks and eyes with the heels of her hands. Exhaustion lay on her like a physical weight.

O'Rourke slipped down the alley, his black clothes making him almost invisible, and Kate sat there dully, listening to the cold wind stir brittle leaves. There were no insect sounds, no birds, and no sound of traffic from the main road a hundred feet farther down the alley. She tried to remember the sense of excitement and humanity she had sensed in her walks through Bucharest in May, the young couples kissing in dark doorways, the laughter, the grandparents watching their children in the park at Cişmigiu Gardens. It was all from another world.

"It's empty," said O'Rourke from behind her and she jumped three inches. She'd been half-dozing again.

They left the motorcycle in among the trees, climbed the low fence, and entered the monastery through a side window that was unlocked.

"There's been a Franciscan presence in Tîrgovişte since the thirteenth century," O'Rourke said softly as he lit a candle.

"The light . . ." began Kate.

"We'll stay in the inner rooms and halls. The shutters are closed. I don't think the police will be back. The nine residents here were brought to Bucharest for questioning and probably will be released there tomorrow . . . today really . . . now that the *strigoi* have had their little ceremony."

Kate followed him down the corridor, glancing in rooms as she passed them. The candle stretched their shadows along rough walls to the ten-foot ceiling. Kate had never been in a monastery and was not quite sure what to expect: Gothic trappings, perhaps . . . dungeon-like cells, wooden bowls and utensils, perhaps a few well-used cat-o'-nine-tails for self-flagellation.

Get a grip, Kate, she thought. She wanted to go to sleep again.

The house was larger and cleaner than most homes she had seen in Romania, less cluttered, but it might have been the residence of a large farm family. The rooms were simple, but contained comfortable-looking beds and dressers. Only the simple crucifixes on the walls of each bedroom suggested a monastery. The kitchen was more modern than most Romanian kitchens: no wooden bowls here, but lots of plastic plates and tumblers that reminded Kate of summer camp. The dining room had a battered and unadorned but undeniably elegant twenty-foot table that would have sold for several thousand dollars in an American antiques store. One of the rooms on the other side of the dining room had been turned into a modest chapel with a small altar and individual kneelers for twenty or so people. Kate's impression, even by candlelight, was of simplicity, cleanliness, and community.

"Have you spent time here?" whispered Kate. It was hard not to whisper in the silence.

"Occasionally. It was a good jumping-off place when I was working with children in the mountain cities. Father Danielescu and the others here are good people." O'Rourke opened another door.

"Ahhhh," said Kate. The bath was large and deep and had tiled ledges on three sides. It was immaculately clean. Kate ran her hand along the tile and enamel of the tub itself, then frowned. "Where are the taps? How do you get water in this thing?"

O'Rourke set the candle on the ledge and walked over to the corner, where there was a counter with a farmhouse-style pump over a huge galvanized tin tub sitting above what appeared to be a small propane stove with a single burner. "It takes a while," said O'Rourke, "but it's the hottest water in Tîrgovişte." He began pumping.

For fifteen minutes they were busy filling, heating, carrying and dumping, but eventually the tub was filled. They paused then. Kate showed more embarrassment than O'Rourke. *Is he still a priest? Am I ruining something important? Was that just an aberration in the loft? A sin to be confessed?*

To hell with it, she thought and began unbuttoning her filthy blouse.

"I'll go check the doors and shutters," said O'Rourke, pausing in the doorway. "You go ahead and take your time, I'll bathe next."

Kate stood in her underwear and stared him in the eye. "Don't be silly. That would be a waste of time and hot water. Besides, I'll have my eyes closed when you get in. The tub's big enough. We won't even know the other is there." She removed her bra and white cotton pants.

O'Rourke nodded and went down the dark hall.

Kate felt like crying when she lowered herself into the steaming water. It seemed there was no heating in the monastery other than fireplaces in the central rooms, the air temperature in the house equaled the late-autumn chill outside, and the bath literally steamed, raising a delicious fog that rolled over the edge of the tub, slid along the tiled ledges, and crept along the floor.

The water was hot. A lump of soap shaped like a small meteorite sat on the ledge; she lathered herself and let the soap create bubbles as she lay neck deep in the hot water, laid her head back, and closed her eyes.

She heard O'Rourke come in, squinted at him as he set down towels and a pile of folded clothes, and then closed her eyes while he stepped out of his own clothes and into the tub. He sat on the ledge for a minute, she heard the soft sound of plastic on the floor, and she realized he was taking off his prosthesis. Kate opened her eyes and looked at him.

"Now you've really seen me naked," he said with no sign of embarrassment. He raised his good leg and his shortened left leg and gingerly settled in the steaming bath. "There is a heaven," he whispered.

The water rose higher around Kate's chin, and she felt his thigh brush hers. There was room in this antediluvian hot tub for the two of them to sit side by side in opposite directions without crowding.

"I feel like we should be doing something," whispered Kate. "Going after Joshua." O'Rourke handed her a sponge and she squeezed water onto her face. "Something."

"We don't know where they went," he said softly.

Kate nodded, letting her arms and hands float. The heat made her breasts ache and reminded her of all the bruises she'd received and muscles she'd strained in the long nightmare crawl through the palace tunnel. "You had cities circled. Places you thought the ceremony might be held. Lucian thought that there would be four nights of ceremony. Did your priest friends know where the next two nights will be held?"

"No." O'Rourke lathered his arms and shoulders. "There are dozens of cities and sites that were important to the historical Vlad Ţepeş and that might be part of any ritual centered on him. Braşov, Sibiu, Rîmnîu Vîlcea, Rîşnov Citadel, Bran, Timişoara, Sighişoara, even Bucharest itself."

"But you had several circled on the map," said Kate. She had to sit up and sponge her chest and neck or fall asleep.

"My guess was Sighişoara, Braşov, Sibiu, and the so-called Castle Dracula," he said. "They're extremely important places in the actual history of Vlad Ţepeş. But I don't know which places . . . or which night."

Kate brushed soap out of her eyes. "There *is* a Castle

Dracula? I thought the Romanian Office of National Tourism just invented that.''

"They take tourists to phony sites . . . like Bran Castle that had nothing to do with Vlad Ţepeş," said O'Rourke. "Or they drive the few Dracula tourists way up to Borgo Pass and other places that Bram Stoker wrote about but that have no historical significance. But there is a Castle Dracula . . . or at least the ruins of it . . . on the Argeş River, less than a hundred miles from here." He described it then, the heap of rocks high on a crag overlooking the remote Argeş Valley.

"You've been there?" said Kate.

"No. The road is impassable much of the year, and the passable parts have been closed off most of this year. There's a hydroelectric plant up there beyond the castle in the Făgăraş Mountains above the city of Curtea de Argeş and the military is very vigilant about guarding that area. Also, Ceauşescu had the site closed because there was some serious restoration going on at the ruins. They probably abandoned the project when Ceauşescu died."

Kate suddenly felt very awake. "Unless the restoration was a *strigoi* project."

O'Rourke sat up so quickly that water sloshed. "For the ceremony . . ."

"Yes. But which night? And can we get there?"

"We can get close," said O'Rourke. He reached to the towels on the ledge, dried his hands, and unfolded the map he had carried in from the motorcycle. "Either by heading south and by picking up Highway Seven to Piteşti, then up Seven-C to Curtea de Argeş . . . or the very long way northeast to Braşov, then way north to Sighişoara, then southwest to Sibiu and all the way down the Olt River Valley to Highway Seventy-three C. That would be . . . I don't know . . . two hundred fifty to three hundred miles on some iffy roads."

Kate shook her head. "Why would we go that way?"

O'Rourke set the map down and began soaping his beard thoughtfully. "The Jet Ranger left flying to the northwest. If that was its actual route, it might be headed toward any of a million places, but . . ." He paused to dip his face in the water and came up spluttering. "Sighişoara is that way. About a hundred and fifty miles from here."

Kate remembered the reading she had done about Vlad Ţepeş. "He was born there." She frowned. "If Lucian's right and there are four nights to the Investiture Ceremony and the ceremony celebrates Vlad Ţepeş' career, wouldn't they have started at Sighişoara?"

O'Rourke lifted his hands above the soapy water. "What if they were working backward in time? Şnagov is where Vlad was supposed to have been buried. Tîrgovişte is where he ruled . . ."

"And Sighişoara is where he was born," finished Kate. "Fine, but what about the fourth and final night? Your Castle Dracula doesn't seem to fit the itinerary."

"Unless it was where the next Prince is to be initiated," whispered O'Rourke. His eyes were focused on something distant.

Kate slumped back in the cooling water. "We're guessing. We don't know didley. I wish Lucian were here."

O'Rourke raised an eyebrow.

"Not this minute," said Kate, flustered. "But he seemed to know . . ."

"If he was telling the truth." O'Rourke shifted his shortened leg. "Turn around and slide back this way."

Kate hesitated a second.

"I'll scrub your back and shampoo your hair," he said, holding up a small vial of shampoo. "It's not scented and perfumed American shampoo, but it's probably better for your hair than whatever we picked up crawling through the palace graveyard."

Kate turned around and sat in the middle of the tub while O'Rourke first lathered her back and then massaged her scalp with strong fingers. The shampooing went on and on, and if she believed in magic she would have asked for three wishes just to keep the sensation going on forever. *And never face tomorrow.*

"Turn around," she said, sliding forward and turning. "I'll do you."

After the shampoos, after the ritual lathering and rinsing of their bodies, they kissed and even held each other, nude in the still steaming water, but there was no surge of passion, and not just because each was bruised and exhausted. It was as if they were friends as well as lovers, two friends who had known each other forever. *I'm tired*, thought Kate. *I'm sentimentalizing this.*

No, you're not, said another part of her mind.

"Wherever the site is for tomorrow night's ceremony," said O'Rourke, breaking the spell, "we can't do much tonight. The mountain roads are dangerous at night and police often stop private vehicles. We'd be better off blending in with traffic in the daytime. We'll flip a coin in the morning to see which way we go."

"It will be hard getting out of here," said Kate. The candle was burning low. The air was very cold.

"Once more unto the breach, dear . . . holy shit it's cold!" said O'Rourke, who had pulled himself up onto the tiled ledge and swung sideways. His body steamed in the cold air. He began toweling himself rapidly.

Kate stepped out and did the same. It was like going from a sauna to the freezing outdoors. She huddled under the thin blanket. "Tell me we're going to sleep here together for a few hours," she said, teeth chattering. "Together."

"The beds are very much single," said O'Rourke. He balanced on one leg while he attached the prosthesis.

Kate frowned. "You don't sleep with that on, do you? I mean, other than in haylofts."

O'Rourke finished attaching it and stood. Kate noticed that the modern prosthetic looked very lifelike. "No," he said, "but some consider it undignified to hop to one's bed."

"Single bed?" said Kate, shaking now as her body cooled.

"Good blankets," said O'Rourke. He smiled gently. "And I took the liberty of carrying one single bed in and setting it next to the other in the nearest bedroom."

Kate lifted her bag and a stack of clean clothes with one arm and slipped the other around the priest. *Ex-priest*, she thought. *Or soon to be ex-priest*. "Not to be unromantic about this," she said, "but let's get under those good blankets before we freeze our asses off."

O'Rourke carried the dying candle with him as they found their way to the room.

Chapter Thirty-two

THE day was like a return to early autumn; the blue skies emphasized each remaining leaf in the forests along Highway 71 to Braşov. Kate thought that "highway" was a generous term for the narrow strip of patched and potted asphalt that ran north and east from Tîrgovişte, wound its tortured way through passes in the Carpathian Mountains, and then dropped dramatically again before connecting with Highway 1 south of Braşov.

Rejuvenated by last night's bath, several hours' sleep, and the clean new clothes that O'Rourke had found—at least one of the monks at Tîrovişte Monastery had been small enough that Kate could wear his dark sweater over her last clean, black skirt and look moderately presentable—she was tempted to take off her scarf, tilt her head back, and enjoy the sunlight as she bounced along in the sidecar.

It was not possible. The sense of urgency to find Joshua was too great, the terror at making the wrong decision too deep.

They had not flipped a coin to decide the direction. After looking at the map in the morning light, both of them had lifted their heads and said, "Sighişoara." On Kate's part it was nothing but intuition. *Something about traveling in Transylvania makes one superstitious,* she thought.

"If we're wrong about where the ceremony is tonight, we have a final crack at tomorrow night," said O'Rourke.

"Yes," said Kate, "*if* Lucian was telling the truth. Our information is shaky, based on hearsay, and generally half-assed. If this plan was a medical diagnosis, I'd sue the physician for malpractice."

There were few cars this morning but traffic was heavy: heavy semis belching pollution behind them in blue and brown clouds, tractors that looked like they came out of a Henry Ford turn-of-the-century museum, their iron wheels chewing up more of the well-chewed asphalt road, rubber-wheeled horse carts, wooden-wheeled horse carts, painted-wheel pony carts, the occasional Gypsy wagon, herds of sheep standing stupidly in the road looking lost while their herders lagged behind with the same expression, cattle being flicked along by children no more than eight or nine years old who did not even look up at the heavy trucks as they roared past or at the motorcycle as it weaved to avoid hitting cows, bicycles wobbling their way to what appeared to be nowhere in particular, the occasional German car breezing past at 180 kph with a blast of its arrogant German horn, the driver not even glancing at the motorcycle and its occupants, a few Dacias limping along or sitting broken down in the middle of the road, army vehicles evidently trying to race the German cars as they roared and smoked their way down the center of the highway, and pedestrians.

There were many pedestrians: Gypsies with their swarthy skins and loose clothes, old men with white-stubbled cheeks and soft hats that had lost all form, flocks of schoolgirls near the two tiny villages and one small town they had passed through—Pucioasa, Fieni, and Matoeini—the girls' much-mended but stiffly starched blue skirts and white blouses seeming very bright in the sunlight, the unschooled children tending cattle, both boys and bovine wearing expressions of infinite boredom, old peasant women waddling down the side of the road—there was no shoulder to the highway, only a three-foot ditch filled with foul-smelling water most of the way—and older peasant women being led by tiny children much as the cows were being led, and the occasional *ofiter de politie* standing outside his village police headquarters.

The police did not even look up as the motorcycle rumbled through Fieni, a thoroughly soot-soaked industrial town. O'Rourke was careful to obey the speed limits.

"We'll need gas in Braşov!" he shouted.

Kate nodded and kept her eyes on the weaving bicycle just visible beyond the horse cart that had pulled out in front of them.

This was no time to close her eyes and enjoy the sunlight.

Once past the mountain village of Moroeni the traffic mysteriously dwindled to nothing, the winding road was empty, the air grew cooler, and few of the trees had retained their leaves. Kate asked if she could drive the motorcycle for a while.

"You've done it before?"

"Tom used to let me drive his Yamaha 360," Kate said confidently. *Once. A little distance. Slowly.* She was good with machines though, and had been watching O'Rourke closely.

O'Rourke pulled onto the gravel shoulder where the road began its switchback, parked, and stepped off. He left the engine idling. "Watch the clutch," he said. "It's a mess. No second gear to speak of." He limped around to the sidecar while Kate stood stretching.

He's hurting, she thought. *Driving that thing with the clutch pedal and everything has been an ordeal.* She mounted the bank, waited while O'Rourke settled in, grinned at him, and started off with a little too much throttle.

The ancient motorcycle and sidecar tried to do a wheelie, O'Rourke let out a single, very strange sound, Kate compensated a bit too fast by squeezing the brake handle hard enough to send O'Rourke's head into the plastic wind visor and almost toss her off the saddle, she decided to go straight to third gear, missed it a couple of times, got them going again vigorously in first gear, looked up just in time to avoid driving off the cliff edge, took most of the width of the asphalt to recover, then got the machine on the right side, going the right speed, with the right smoothness. Almost.

"I've got it now," she said, ticking up through gears with her foot and leaning forward into the wind.

O'Rourke nodded and rubbed his head.

The highway crossed a high pass above Sinaia, and by the time Kate reached the summit she had worked things out between her and the machine.

"Stop here!" yelled O'Rourke, pointing to a narrow gravel shoulder on the other side of the road.

Kate nodded, swerved, realized that she hadn't really practiced with the brake yet . . . where was it? . . . but found it and applied it hard enough that their skid did not take them over the edge. Quite. The bike had spun around during their deceleration phase, and when the dust and flying gravel dissipated, they were facing back downhill and O'Rourke and the sidecar were hanging out over treetops and rocks.

He took his goggles off slowly and rubbed grit out of his eyes. "I just wanted to admire the view," he said softly over the idling engine.

Kate had to admit that the view was worth stopping for. To the north and west the Bucegi Range of the Carpathians blended into the snow-peaked Făgăraş Range which curved south just where the horizon became murky. The highest foothills below the snowfields were spotted with sturdy juniper and dwarf firs, the middle regions glowed green with pine and fir, the lower hills were mottled white with birch, and the valleys miles below were dappled with the dying leaf colors of oak, elder, elm, and sumac. Clouds were boiling in from the north and the west, but the sun was still bright enough to send their shadows sliding down limestone ridges to the tree-filled valleys below. Except for a glimpse of the briefest stretch of road behind them, there was no sight of man. None. Not smokestack or rooftop or smog or aircraft or microwave antenna for as far as Kate could see to the west and south. In a country contemptuous of all environmental standards, this was the first time she had seen the real beauty of the earth.

"It's beautiful," she said, hating herself for mouthing the cliché but not knowing what else to say. "What's that bright green plant up high? Near the juniper trees below the snow?''

''I think it's called *zimbru*,'' said O'Rourke. He leaned over the edge of the sidecar and looked down. ''Say, could you engage the brake, let the clutch out just a little, and ease us a bit forward . . . toward the road?''

Kate did so. She liked the percolating of the oversized engine and the feel of the motorcycle between her legs. Sunlight glinted off the tarnished chrome of the handlebars.

''Thanks,'' said O'Rourke and cleared his throat. He turned and pointed to the southwest. ''The Argeş River and Vlad's castle is out that way.''

''How far?''

''For a bird, maybe a hundred klicks. Sixty, maybe seventy miles. By road . . .'' He chewed his lip. ''Probably about eight hours of driving.''

Kate glanced at him. ''We're not wrong, Mike. It's Sighi-şoara tonight.''

He looked at her and then nodded. ''What do you say we find a better place to park up on the summit, get the bike away from the road, and eat lunch?''

There had been bread and cheese at the monastery, and enough bottles of wine to make all of Transylvania drunk. O'Rourke had explained that the monks still grew vineyards and bottled wine for the local region. It was a way to help pay expenses. Kate had loaded three bottles under the seat of the sidecar and left fifty American dollars in a kitchen drawer.

The cheese was good, the bread was stale but delicious, and the wine was excellent. They had no glasses but Kate did not mind swigging directly from the bottle. She drank only a bit; she was, after all, driving. The last of the sunlight before the clouds won the aerial battle warmed her skin and brought back sensuous thoughts of the previous day and night.

''Do you have a plan?'' said O'Rourke, leaning back against a tree and chewing on a tough strand of crust.

''Hmm? What?'' Kate felt like someone had thrown cold water on her.

"A plan," said O'Rourke. "For when we catch up to the *strigoi*."

Kate set her chin. "Get Joshua back," she said tightly. "Then get out of the country."

O'Rourke chewed slowly, swallowed, and nodded. "I won't even ask about part two," he said. "But how do we achieve part one? If the baby is really their new prince or whatever, I don't think they'll want to give him up."

"I know that," said Kate. The clouds now obscured the sun. A cold wind blew down from the snowfields above them.

"So . . ." O'Rourke opened his hands.

"I think we can negotiate," said Kate.

O'Rourke frowned slightly. "With what?"

She nodded toward her travel bag. "I've brought samples of the hemoglobin substitute I was giving Joshua. It should allow the *strigoi* to break their addiction to whole human blood and still allow the J-virus to work on their immune systems."

"Yes," said O'Rourke, "but why would they want to go on methadone when they enjoy heroin?"

Kate looked out at the now shadowed valley. "I don't know. Do you have any better suggestions?"

"These are the people who killed Tom and your friend Julie," said O'Rourke, his voice very low.

"I *know* that!" Kate did not mean for her voice to be so sharp.

He nodded. "I know you know that. What I mean is, did you come just to get Joshua, or is revenge on your agenda?"

Kate turned her face back to him. "I don't know. I don't think so. The medical research . . . the breakthrough potential of this retrovirus . . ." She looked down and touched her breast where it ached. "I just want Joshua back."

O'Rourke slid closer and put his arm around her. "We're a strange choice for the dynamic duo," he whispered.

She looked up, not understanding.

"Caped crimefighters. Superheroes. Batman and Robin?"

"What do you mean?" The ache in her chest subsided slightly.

"You said that you shot that intruder the first time he entered your home in Colorado," said O'Rourke. "The *strigoi*. But you didn't kill him."

"I *tried* to," said Kate. "His body rejuvenated because of—"

"I know. I know." The pressure of O'Rourke's arm was reassuring, not condescending. "What I mean is that you haven't killed anyone yet. But you might have to if we keep going on this quest. Will you do it?"

"Yes," Kate said flatly. "If Joshua's life and liberty depend on it." *Or yours*, she added silently, looking at his eyes.

O'Rourke finished his bread and drank some wine. For a giddy moment Kate wondered how many times this man . . . this lover of hers . . . had said Mass, had prepared the Eucharist for Communion. She shook her head.

"I won't kill anyone," he said softly. "Not even to save the person most dear to me in the world. Not even if your life depended on it, Kate."

Kate saw the sadness in him. "But—"

"I've killed people, Kate. Even in Vietnam, where none of the usual reasons made sense anymore, there was always a good reason to kill. To stay alive. To keep your buddies alive. Because you were attacked. Because you were scared . . ." He looked down at his hands. "None of the reasons are good enough, Kate. Not anymore. Not for me."

For the first time since she had met the priest . . . ex-priest . . . she did not know what to say.

He tried to smile. "You've gone on this mission with the worst choice for a partner that you could have made, Kate. At least if killing people is going to be called for." He took a breath. "And I think it is."

Kate's gaze was very steady. "Are you sure these . . . these *strigoi* are people?"

His head moved almost imperceptibly back and forth. "No. But I wasn't sure that the shadows in Vietnam were human either. They were gooks."

"But that was different."

"Maybe," said O'Rourke and began cleaning up their

modest picnic site. "But even if the *strigoi* have become so alien from human emotions that they're another species . . . which I won't believe until I see more evidence . . . it's not enough. Not for me."

Kate stood and brushed off her skirt. She pulled a jacket on over her sweater. The wind was colder now, the sky grayer. The brief return to autumn was over and winter was blowing down from the Carpathians.

"But you'll help me find Joshua," she said.

"Oh, yes."

"And you'll help me get him out of this . . . country."

"Yes," he said. He did not have to remind her of the police, the military, the border guards, the informants, the air force, the *Securitate* . . . all obeying the orders of those who took orders from the *strigoi*.

"That's all I ask," Kate said honestly. She touched his arm. "We'd better get moving if we have another hundred miles or so before we get to Sighişoara."

"The main highway is faster," said O'Rourke. He hesitated. "Did you want to continue driving for a while?"

Kate paused for only a second. "Yes," she said. "Yes, I do."

The road down from the pass was a series of hair-raising switchbacks, but Kate had got the hang of handling the bike now, and used the compression of the lower gears to keep the brakes from overheating. O'Rourke had double-checked the gas tank and thought they would have enough to get to Braşov, but the uncertainty made Kate nervous.

There was no traffic at all on this steep stretch of the highway and Kate saw only a handful of cottages set far back in the pine trees. Then they were in the outskirts of Sinaia and the homes grew more frequent and larger, obviously country houses for the privileged *Nomenclature*—those party *apparatchiks* and smiled-upon bureaucrats who earned extra perks from the state. Sinaia itself looked like a typical Eastern European resort town—large old hotels and estates which had been fine places a century earlier and which had received little maintenance since, signs to winter sports facilities where a "ski lift" would involve ropes and the occasional T-bar, and a newer, larger section of town featuring Stalinist apartments and heavy industry pouring pollution into the mountain valley.

But the scenery above the town could not be compromised by socialist ugliness. On either side of Sinaia and the busy Highway 1 that ran through it, the Bucegi Mountains rose in almost absurd relief, leaping skyward to bare peaks whose summits reached 7,000 feet. Kate's home—her ex-home—in the foothills above Boulder had been at 7,000 feet, and the peaks of the Rockies to the west had risen to almost 14,000 feet, but these Bucegi Mountains were much more dramatic, rising vertically as they did from the Prahova River Valley that was not far above sea level. The result, Kate thought, glancing up at the scenery while winding the motorcycle through truck traffic exiting from what looked like a steel mill, was a mountain scene that looked the way the nineteenth-century painter Bierstadt only *wanted* the Rockies to look: vertical, craggy, the summits lost in clouds and mist.

Kate had been to the Swiss Alps before, and the scenery here rivaled anything she had seen there. It was just the gray people shuffling along the highway, the empty shops, the decaying estates, the disintegrating apartment buildings, and the filthy industry pouring black smoke at the mountains that reminded her she was in an environment that no self-respecting Swiss would tolerate for an hour.

There was no gas station in Sinaia, and Kate pressed on toward Braşov thirty miles to the north. The road continued to follow the river, with cliffs and breathtaking views on either side. Kate was not looking at the view. When the truck traffic thinned out, she throttled back so that she could be heard. "O'Rourke," she shouted. When he looked up from whatever thoughts he was lost in, she went on. "Why don't you trust Lucian?"

He leaned closer as they rumbled past a closed-down Byzantine Orthodox church and followed the highway around a long bend in the river. "At first it was just instinct. Something . . . something not right."

"And then?" said Kate. Clouds continued to pour between the mountains to the west, but occasional shafts of sunlight would illuminate the valley and the narrow river.

"And then I checked on something when I went back to the U.S. Before I went to Colorado and . . . before I saw you in the hospital there. Do you remember telling me that Lucian said he'd learned his idiomatic English during a couple of visits to the States? When he'd gone with his parents?"

Kate nodded and maneuvered to miss a Gypsy wagon and a small herd of sheep. She swerved back to the right lane just as a logging truck roared by in the opposite direction. It was half a mile before they escaped its blue exhaust fumes. "So?" she said.

"So I called my friend's office in Washington . . . Senator Harlen from Illinois? . . . and Jim promised to check on it for me. Just look at the visa records and so forth. But he didn't get back to me before you and I left for Romania."

Kate didn't understand. "So you didn't learn anything?"

"I told him to contact the embassy in Bucharest when he did get the records and have them leave word with the Franciscan headquarters there," O'Rourke shouted over the engine. "They'd gotten the message when I spoke to Father Stoicescu the other morning. The morning after Lucian showed us the bodies of his parents and the thing in the tank at the medical school."

Kate glanced at him but said nothing. The valley was widening ahead.

"Visa records show that Lucian visited the United States four times in the last fifteen years. The first time he was only ten. The last time was in late autumn of 1989, just two years ago." O'Rourke paused a minute. "He didn't go with his parents any of those times. Each time he came alone and was sponsored by the World Market and Development Research Foundation."

Kate shook her head. The vibration and engine roar were giving her a headache. "I never heard of it."

"I have," said O'Rourke. "They called my superior in the Chicago archdiocese almost two years ago and asked if the Church would suggest someone to go on a fact-finding trip to Romania that the foundation was sponsoring. The archbishop chose me." He leaned up out of the sidecar so that Kate could hear better. "The foundation was started by the billionaire Vernor Deacon Trent. Lucian went to the States four times at the invitation of Trent's group . . . or perhaps at the old man's personal invitation."

Kate found a wide enough spot in the shoulder to pull over and did so. The river rushed past to their right. "You're saying that Lucian *knows* Trent? And that Trent is probably the leader of the *strigoi* Family? Maybe even a direct descendant of Vlad Ţepeş?"

O'Rourke did not blink. "I'm just telling you what Senator Harlen's office found out."

"What does it prove?"

He shrugged. "At the very least it proves that Lucian was lying to you when he said he traveled to the States with his parents. At the worst—"

"It says that Lucian is *strigoi*," said Kate. "But he showed us that blood test . . ."

O'Rourke made a face. "I thought he went to rather great pains to disprove something we hadn't even suggested. Blood tests can be faked, Kate. You of all people should know that. Did you watch carefully when he did the test?"

"Yes. But the slides or samples could have been switched when I was distracted." A heavy truck rumbled past. Kate waited for the roar to fade. "If he's *strigoi*, why did he shelter us and take us to Şnagov Island to see part of the Ceremony and—" She took a deep breath and let it out. "It would be an easy way for the *strigoi* to keep tabs on us, wouldn't it?"

O'Rourke said nothing.

Kate shook her head. "It still doesn't make sense. Why did Lucian run away when the *Securitate* or whoever it was were chasing us in Bucharest? And why would he allow us to be separated like we are if his role was to keep tabs on us?"

"I don't think we have any real understanding of the power struggles going on here," said O'Rourke. "We've got the government versus the protesters versus the miners versus the intellectuals, and the *strigoi* seem to be pulling most of the strings on each side. Maybe they're fighting among themselves, I don't know."

Kate angrily stepped off the bike and looked out at the river. She had liked Lucian . . . *still* liked him. How could her instincts have been so wrong? "It doesn't matter," she said aloud. "Lucian doesn't know where we are and we don't know where he is. We won't see him again. If his job was to keep track of us, they probably fired him." *Or worse*.

O'Rourke had uncoiled himself from the sidecar and was checking the gas tank. There was a fuel gauge on the narrow console between the handlebars, but it had no needle and the glass was broken. "We need gas," he said. "Do you want to drive us into Braşov?"

"No," said Kate.

They got no gas in Braşov.

Foreigners in Romania could not—at least theoretically—buy gas at the regular pumps using Romanian *lei*. Laws still required tourists to use their own hard currency to purchase petrol vouchers at hotels, the few car rental agencies, and Office of National Tourism outlets—each voucher good for two liters—and to exchange these for gas at special ComTourist pumps set aside at the few-and-far-between gas stations.

That was the theory. In practice, O'Rourke explained, the ComTourist pumps usually sat idle while the gas station manager waved tourists to the front of the inevitable line at the regular pumps. This involved hateful stares from the people in the long lines while the time-consuming voucher paperwork was done, as well as baksheesh to the person whose job it was to pump the gas (*never* the manager of the station and all too frequently a woman in six layers of coats and stained coveralls).

Braşov itself was a once-beautiful medieval city which had been covered with industry, Stalinist apartment tracts, half-

finished Ceauşescu-started construction, abandoned systematization projects, and even more industry like barnacles on
a sunken ship. It may have been possible to find some streets
or vistas of former beauty, but Kate and O'Rourke certainly
did not during their ride down the busy Calea Bucureştilor
and Calea Făgăraşului boulevards in search of the Sibiu/Sighi-
şoara highway and the gas stations the map promised.

One of the gas stations was closed and derelict, windows
broken and pumps vandalized. The other, just past the turnoff
from the boulevard to the Sibiu/Sighişoara highway, had a
line that stretched more than a mile back into the city proper.

"*Merde*," whispered O'Rourke. Then, "We can't wait.
We'll have to try the ComTourist pump."

A fat man in stained coveralls came out to squint at them.
Kate decided to hunker down in the sidecar and be invisible
while O'Rourke handled things; few things were more con-
spicuous in Romania than a take-charge Western female.

"*Da?*" said the manager, wiping his hands on a grease-
black rag. "*Pot sa te ajut?*"

"*Ja*," said O'Rourke, his demeanor suddenly self-assured
and a bit arrogant. "*Sprechen Sie Deutsch? Ah . . . vorbiţi
germana?*"

"*Nu*," said the man. Behind them a woman in several
layers of jackets pumped gas into the first car in a line that
stretched literally out of sight. Everyone was watching the
exchange by the ComTourist pump.

"*Scheiss*," said O'Rourke, obviously disgusted. He turned
to Kate. "*Er spricht kein Deutsch.*" He turned back to the
manager and raised his voice. "Ah . . . *de benzină* . . . ah
. . . *Faceţi plinul, vă rog.*"

Kate knew enough Romanian to catch the "Fill 'er up,
please."

The manager looked at her, then turned back to O'Rourke.
"*Chitanta? Cupon pentru benzină?*"

O'Rourke at first looked blank and then nodded and pulled
an American twenty-dollar bill out of his pocket. The manager
took it but did not look happy. Nor did he unlock the heavy
padlock on the gas pump. He held up one grease-black finger

and said, "Please . . . you . . . to stay . . . here," and went back into the tiny station.

"Uh-oh," said Kate.

O'Rourke said nothing. He got back on the bike, gunned the engine to life, and drove off slowly. Eyes watched from the cars in line as they headed back into town. "Dumb, dumb, dumb," O'Rourke was saying to himself.

"Aren't we going the wrong way?" asked Kate.

"Yes." He drove back to the main boulevard, swung right at a traffic circle, and accelerated out into the truck traffic heading southwest. A road sign said RIŞNOV 13 KM.

"Do we want to go to Rişnov?" called Kate over the roar and rattle.

"No."

"Do we have enough gas to get to Sighişoara?"

"No."

Kate asked no more questions. In the outskirts of Braşov another highway branched northwest and O'Rourke swung onto it. A kilometer marker said FĂGĂRAŞ. O'Rourke pulled over and they studied the map. "If we'd kept going on the Sibiu/Sighişoara road, that fat toad could have sent the police right after us," he said. "At least now they might look south before checking north. Damn."

"Don't blame yourself," said Kate. "We had to get gas."

O'Rourke shook his head angrily. "Running out of gas is a way of life in this country. Dacias have little pumps built in under the hood so people can transfer a liter or two to someone who's broken down. Everyone carries liter jars in their trunks. I was an idiot."

"No, you weren't," said Kate. "You were just thinking in American terms. Run low on gas, stop at a gas station. So was I."

O'Rourke smoothed the map on the edge of her windscreen and pointed. "I think we can get there this way. See . . . stay on Highway One here until this village . . . here, Şercaia about fifteen klicks this side of Făgăraş . . . and then take this smaller road up to Highway Thirteen, then straight to Sighişoara."

Kate studied the thin red line between the two highways. "That road would be in poorer condition than the cow path we took over the mountains."

"Yeah . . . and less traveled. But there aren't any high passes that way. Worth a try?"

"Do we have a choice?" said Kate.

"Not really."

"Let's go for it," she said, hearing an echo of Lucian in the slang. "Maybe we'll be lucky and find another gas station."

They were not lucky. The motorcycle ran out of gas about six miles north of Şercaia on the mud and gravel road that was a fat red artery on the map. There had been no traffic since they had left the main highway and very few houses except for one huge collective farm, but now they could see a single home a quarter of a mile or so ahead, set back only slightly from the road behind a fence laced with dried wisteria vines. Kate got out and walked while O'Rourke pushed the heavy bike and sidecar along the road for a distance.

"To heck with it," he said at last, rocking the bike to get it through muddy ruts. "Let's hope they have a liter jar of *benzină*."

An old woman stood outside the gate and watched them approach. "*Bună dimineaţa!*" said O'Rourke.

"*Bună ziua,*" the old woman replied. Kate noticed that she had said "good afternoon" rather than morning. She glanced at her watch. It was almost one P.M.

"*Vorbiţi engleză? Germana? Franceza? Maghiar? Roman?*" said O'Rourke, standing casually.

The old woman continued to stare, occasionally working her toothless gums in what might have been a smile.

"No matter," he said, smiling boyishly. "*Imi puteţi spune, vă rog, unde este e cea mai apropiabă staţie de benzină?*"

The old woman blinked at him and raised empty hands. She appeared nervous.

"*Simtem doar turişti,*" said O'Rourke reassuringly. "*Noi*

călătorim prin Transilvania . . ." He grinned and pointed to the motorcycle down the highway. ". . . *'de benzină.*"

When the woman spoke, her voice was like old metal rasping on metal. *"Eşti însetat?"*

O'Rourke blinked and turned to Kate. "Are you thirsty?"

Kate did not have to think about it. "Yes," she said. She smiled at the old woman. *"Da! Mulţumesc foarte mult!"*

They followed her through the muddy compound and into the home.

The house was small, the porch where they sat much smaller, and the old woman's daughter or granddaughter who joined them was so tiny that she made Kate feel grossly oversize. The old woman stood in the doorway speaking in her raspy, rapid-fire dialect while the daughter or granddaughter ran back and forth, fluffing pillows on the narrow divan for them, waving them to their seats, then rushing in and out of the room bringing glasses, a bottle of Scotch, cups, saucers, and a carafe of coffee.

The younger woman also spoke no German, French, English, Hungarian, or Gypsy dialect, so they all tried to communicate in Romanian, which led to much embarrassment and laughter, especially after the Scotch glasses were refilled. They held more than the diminutive coffee cups.

Through pidgin Romanian they ascertained that the old woman was named Ana, the younger one Marina, that they had no *benzină* here, on the farm, but that Marina's husband would be home soon and would be happy to give them two liters of petrol, which should be enough to get the motorcycle to Făgăraş or Sighişoara or Braşov or wherever they wanted to go. Marina poured more coffee and then more Scotch. Ana stood in the door and beamed toothlessly.

Marina asked in slow, careful Romanian whether they were staying in Bucharest, how did they like Romania, were they hungry, what were farms like in America, had they seen the tourist sights yet, and would they like some chocolate? Without waiting for an answer she jumped up and ran into the other room. The radio, which had been playing softly, came on much louder; a moment later Marina returned with small chocolate biscuits that Kate guessed had been saved for a special occasion.

O'Rourke and Kate munched the biscuits, sipped the coffee, said *"Este foarte bine"* to compliment the food and drink, and asked again when Marina's husband might be getting home. Would it be long?

"Nu, nu," said Marina, smiling and nodding. *"Approximativ zece minute."*

O'Rourke smiled at her and said to Kate, "Can we wait ten minutes?"

Suddenly Kate did not want to. She rose, bowing and thanking the two women. Ana stood smiling and blinking in the doorway as Kate moved toward it.

They heard the helicopter first. O'Rourke grabbed her hand and they ran out into the small yard just as the red and white machine roared in over the leafless trees and barn. When it passed, another, smaller chopper, black, looking all bubble and skids, buzzed in over the farmhouse like a furious hornet.

Kate and O'Rourke looked once at Ana and Marina standing in the doorway, fingers to their mouths, and then the two Americans ran for the road.

Police cars and military vehicles blocked the road a hundred yards away in each direction. Men in black cradled automatic weapons as they encircled the farmhouse. Even from a distance, Kate could hear radios squawking and men shouting. She and O'Rourke skidded to a halt on the gravel road, looking wildly around.

The two helicopters returned, one hovering above them while the larger Jet Ranger circled, hovered, and settled onto its skids fifteen yards away. The blast from the rotors threw dust and gravel over O'Rourke and Kate.

She pivoted, thought about running toward the barn, saw the black-clad figures already there, saw more of them moving through the yard and up the road. The black helicopter buzzed above them, darting back and forth.

"Marina turned the radio up so we wouldn't hear the phone

call," said O'Rourke. "Or the trucks coming. Goddamn her." He gripped Kate's hand. "I'm sorry."

The door of the Jet Ranger opened; three men jumped out and walked quickly toward them. O'Rourke whispered the name of the short man: Radu Fortuna. The second man was the dark-eyed stranger Kate had seen twice before—once in her son's bedroom, once on the night they tried to kill her. The third man was Lucian.

Radu Fortuna stopped three feet from them and smiled. He had a slight gap between his strong front teeth. "I think you have created much mischiefs, yes?" He smiled at O'Rourke, shook his head, and made a clucking sound. "Well, the time for mischiefs is over." He nodded and the men in black jogged forward, pinning O'Rourke's arms, grabbing Kate's wrists. She wished Lucian would come closer so she could spit in his face.

He looked at her with no expression and kept his distance.

Radu Fortuna snapped something at one of the men and he jogged back to the house and gave something to Ana and Marina. Fortuna smiled at Kate. "In this country, Madame, one out of every four peoples works for the secret police. Here we are all either the . . . how do you say it? . . . the informed or the informed on."

Radu Fortuna nodded. Kate and O'Rourke were suddenly grabbed and half-dragged, half-carried toward the waiting helicopter.

Chapter Thirty-three

ROMANIA from the air was beautiful. The helicopter stayed low, below a thousand feet, following the upper regions of the Olt River northwest and then swinging northwest up a broad valley. Kate saw a ribbon of highway below, sparsely traveled, and thought it must be the highway from Braşov to Sighişoara. The valley gave way to a high plateau which was still green in places, relatively free of trees except where thick copses grew on hilltops, and ridged with passes connecting the snowclad Făgăraş and Bucegi ranges in the south to the unnamed mountain wilderness stretching as far north as Kate could see. The helicopter wove its way up the ascending plateau, often flying past tumbledown castles, huge stone abbeys that looked as if no one had visited for centuries, and medieval keeps that sat atop hilltops and crags which dominated the valley below. There were few farms in the valley and those few were collective monstrosities that seemed to be nothing more than a collection of long barns and stone buildings. Villages were small and scarce. The rest of the scenery was forest, mountain slopes, steep canyons boiling with low clouds, and ancient ruins. It was dramatic and beautiful.

Kate Neuman did not give a good goddamn about the scenery.

She and O'Rourke sat on a padded bench in the rear of the

Jet Ranger cabin, their wrists still tied uncomfortably behind them. No one had tightened their seat belts, and the updrafts, thermals, crosswinds, and other vagaries of small aircraft travel jostled them and left them lurching uncomfortably. Kate especially hated the nauseating feeling when the helicopter dropped suddenly and she lifted a bit off her seat. She had always hated roller coasters.

They did not talk. The sound of the jet engine and rotors was simply too loud to carry on a conversation even if anyone had wanted to. Radu Fortuna sat in the front right seat where a copilot would normally sit, Lucian was belted into a jump seat behind the pilot, facing backward, and the dark man whom Kate thought of only as the intruder sat between O'Rourke and her. The man was firmly strapped in. Lucian was looking out the window to his right with a calm, almost distracted expression. Kate tried not to look at him. Her mind was rushing but it found no answers, no clever plans, and very few branches of hope to cling to.

The helicopter banked left, Kate gasped as she slid helplessly against the *strigoi* intruder—he smelled of musk and sweat—and then they were rushing down a narrower valley with higher peaks on either side. A thin ribbon of highway ran along another river below. The roar of the engine and rotors made Kate's headache almost intolerable. Her left arm, still bandaged and aching, throbbed in unison with her migraine.

Radu Fortuna was wearing a communications headphone, and now he slid one of his earphones off, put his hand over the mike, twisted in his seat, and shouted, "Sighişoara."

Kate looked out and ahead with dull eyes.

The town was like a fairy tale city: perched on a small mountain between taller ones, bound about with high stone walls and battlements, its steep hillsides pocked with crenellated towers, steep slate roofs, cobblestone streets, covered walkways, and tall tan and yellow homes that had been built almost a thousand years earlier.

Then the chopper banked and Kate caught a glimpse of the socialist reality of "new Sighişoara." Industry on the outskirts of town, a single highway lined with cheap cinderblock structures, and a few *Nomenclature* estates sitting fat and arrogant on opposing hillsides. But unlike so much else in Romania, this intrusion of postwar ugliness made no real dent in the atmosphere of the medieval city proper. The highest hill was all Old City, and the Old City must appear much as it had when Vlad Ţepeş' father first rode into it and established his headquarters there in 1431.

The helicopter banked again and this time Kate saw the military vehicles along the roads, the police cars at the road-blocks, and the almost total absence of vehicles within the city.

"You see, it would not have been too easy for uninvited peoples to visit us tonight," shouted Radu Fortuna. "Yes?" Kate did not answer and he put the earphones back on and said something to the pilot.

They came in over the Old City on the hill, and the towers, red tile roofs, narrow streets, tiny courtyards, and steep stair-ways became larger and more real. Kate saw that Sighişoara proper had been laid out within its protective walls, and although steps and a few winding roads connected it to the larger village below, both the wall and the Old City remained intact. They flew over the wall, banked sharply around a tower with a large clockface, slowed with a suddenness that almost sent Kate lurching off the bench, and then settled with a jar, a slight rising again, and then a solid thump as the machine lost its ability to fly. The pilot threw switches while Lucian and Radu Fortuna were out of the machine and moving away in a crouching run. The second helicopter, the strange little bubble-cockpitted black machine, buzzed angrily over-head and disappeared behind the tower.

The *strigoi* in the middle shoved Kate out and then O'Rourke. Kate almost tripped and landed face first on the sharp cobblestones, but the man's strong hand seized her roughly by the upper arm and pulled her upright.

They had landed in a grassy area near the edge of the fortifications, a small square looking down on the Old City walls which offered a view of the New City below, a river, and the wooded hills across the valley. Behind them, ancient Sighişoara stacked its steep-roofed homes up the mountainside. Kate saw a church spire through the trees above them. She tried to see everything, to get her bearings now, in case she escaped and needed to know which way to run.

She did not know which way to run.

Lucian took a step in her direction as if he were going to say something. If he had come any closer, she would have kicked him, but he paused and then turned away, walking to a waiting car and talking to the swarthy man. Radu Fortuna came up to her, saw the direction and intensity of her gaze, and said, "Oh, you think that your friend is a part of our Family, eh? No, no, no." He shook his head and showed his broad grin. "The young student works for money, just as so many do in our country. He has served his purpose."

Fortuna snapped his fingers and the dark man handed Lucian a thick wad of Romanian bills.

He sold Joshua and me out for lei, thought Kate. She felt physically ill.

The waiting car was neither Dacia nor Mercedes, but some intermediate level of German car. Lucian took the money, got in the backseat, and did not look out again as the driver started the car and drove out of sight under the courtyard arch.

"Come," said Radu Fortuna. There were several of the security guards in black in the square now and they took Kate and O'Rourke by the arm and led them after the briskly striding Fortuna.

They came out of the square into a smaller open area, a sort of corner park, and then strode down the cobblestoned hill only a hundred feet or so to the massive clock tower Kate had seen from the air. The hands on the clockface sixty feet above them were frozen.

Fortuna led them past the small main door that had a tiny sign which said MUSEUM, down some stone stairs, through a thick door which was opened as he approached, through a narrower second door, down another flight of worn stone steps, and into a cellar lit only by two naked 20-watt bulbs.

"Ion!" snapped Fortuna.

The intruder—*He and his men killed Tom and Julie! He threw me off a cliff!*—stepped forward and lifted a heavy wood-and-iron trapdoor set in the stone floor. The opening was a square into blackness.

Radu Fortuna smiled and beckoned Kate forward. "Come, come. You have traveled a long way in search of our hospitality. Now enjoy it." He nodded and the guards pushed her forward and lowered her into the darkness, her arms still tied behind her and protesting in pain.

There was an almost vertical stairway of wooden steps, but her foot missed it and she dropped three or four feet to a stone floor. The impact knocked the wind out of her and she could do nothing but roll to one side as O'Rourke was tossed in after her.

Radu Fortuna stood above them, his face and shoulders a silhouette in the open trapdoor. "Our tower has a wonderful view, our modest museum a fascinating collection. But I think you will not, perhaps, have time to enjoy these things, yes? But do make the most of your final moments together."

He stepped back and the trapdoor slammed down with a noise that Kate would not have believed if she had not heard it. There came the sound of a bolt sliding and clicking above.

The darkness was not quite absolute: there was the dimmest of dim glows, a light so faint as to be almost illusory, around the edge of the trapdoor. She fought her way to a sitting position and raised her face to the promise of light.

There were voices and laughter above. Heavy boots trod on the trapdoor itself and then scuffed across stone. A laugh came from farther away and for several minutes there was no sound at all, although Kate sensed someone up there, waiting, guarding. She twisted toward a slight stirring near her. "Mike?"

"Yeah." His voice sounded pained. He had hit harder than she had. Kate wondered if his artificial leg had been damaged.

"Are you all right, O'Rourke?"

"Yeah." He took deep breaths in the darkness. "How about you, Neuman?"

She nodded, realized he could not see her, and said, "Yes." Her nose was running and she craned to wipe it on her shoulder. Her wrists were still tied very tightly behind her; she could barely feel her hands now.

"We fucked up," whispered the priest.

Kate said nothing. She wiggled closer until she could feel his right arm tied back. She moved until they were back to back, her hands reaching for his wrists. She had some idea of untying his bonds while he did the same for her, but she found unrelenting plastic there, clipped together with a snap like a hospital bracelet.

"It's no use," he whispered. "Cops use these plastic restraints in the States. You can't break them or untie them. You can't even cut them with scissors. They've got a special shears that cuts them off."

Kate folded her fingers into fists. "What are they going to do to us?" She realized how stupid the question was even as she had to say it.

O'Rourke leaned closer. It was cold and damp in the pit and his warmth was welcome. "Well, didn't Lucian say that none of the *strigoi* drank human blood until the last night of the Ceremony?"

"No," whispered Kate. "He said that legends had it that the young prince who was being invested didn't drink blood until the fourth night . . . the last night." She laughed out loud, a strange and somewhat frightening sound in the darkness. "Although I'd say that the veracity of some of the things Lucian told us might be a little suspect. Jesus . . ." Her laughter died.

"On the other hand," O'Rourke whispered, his voice low and steady as if to calm her, "it does seem he knows a bit more about the *strigoi* than he let on. Maybe his information *is* accurate."

Kate tried to laugh again but her mouth was suddenly too dry, her throat too constricted. She forced saliva into her mouth and licked her lips. "I'm sorry I got you into this, O'Rourke."

"Kate, you don't have to—"

"No, listen. Please. I'm sorry I got you into this, but I swear I'll get us out of it. And Joshua."

O'Rourke said nothing. Suddenly a scrabbling was audible from several directions.

"Oh, shit," breathed Kate, her skin crawling. "Rats." She and O'Rourke huddled closer, their backs together and knees drawn up. Clumsily, with almost no feeling in their fingers as circulation ceased, they reached behind and between themselves and held hands in the darkness.

Time became unmeasurable except for the growing pressure in Kate's bladder. She half-dozed, felt O'Rourke sag against her in his own state of dull exhaustion, and awoke only when the pressure to urinate became more urgent. She closed her eyes and prayed to no one in particular that someone would come and let them out before she had to wet her skirt or crawl into a corner and try to pull her underwear down.

The darkness was too deep to reveal any detail, but they had moved around enough to know that the pit was just that, a pit about ten feet by ten feet. There seemed to be no straw, no chains, no iron bracelets complete with dangling skeletons on the wall as far as they could tell from kicking out with their feet, only cold, wet stone and the occasional scurry of rats in the corners. *I hope they're only rats.*

Finally she could stand it no longer and whispered to O'Rourke, "Excuse me." She hobbled into the corner that seemed to have had the least sound of rodent toenails on stone, squatted, managed to get her skirt up and underpants down, and urinated. The sound of her water on the stone seemed very loud.

"There doesn't seem to be any toilet paper," she said aloud.

O'Rourke chuckled in the dark. "I'll call housekeeping."

Kate managed to get everything rearranged and crawled back to the center of the pit on her knees, feeling damp, uncomfortable, a little embarrassed, and infinitely relieved.

She leaned against O'Rourke and rested her head on his shoulder. "Something will happen," she whispered.

"Yes." He kissed her on the cheek and she felt the comfortable rasp of his beard. If she nestled just right, she could feel his heartbeat.

Kate had dozed off when the trapdoor slammed up with a noise that made her heart freeze. She crashed out of a dream.

God, this is real.

The dim light from the 20-watt bulb was as bright as sunlight in their pained and dark-adapted eyes. Kate squinted up through tears at the silhouette of the man named Ion.

"You are to say good-bye to the other," Ion said in heavily accented English. "You see one the other no more."

Two men came down and dragged O'Rourke up and out.

Kate screamed and stood then, shouting at them, berating them, trying not to weep but weeping anyway. Two men in black came down the steep stairs and she kicked at them. One of them kicked her back, his heavy boots sending shock waves down her shin.

They lifted her roughly by arms that had gone beyond pins and needles to stilettos of pain. Kate was almost sick then, almost threw up as they lifted her up and out of the pit. She did not know if the nausea was coming from the pain, terror, anger, or from pure relief at being taken out of the pit.

Radu Fortuna was standing there. His dark eyes gleamed. "He wants to see you first, woman." He raised a hairy hand and lifted the back of it toward her. "No, do not speak. If you say anything to anger me, I will take a needle and deep-sea fishing line and sew your lips shut. You may speak only when He asks you a question. Do you understand?" He had not lowered his large hand.

Kate nodded.

"Good," said Radu Fortuna. He snapped his fingers. "Ion, take her up to the house. Father wishes to meet the woman."

Chapter Thirty-four

I T was night outside and the streets were absolutely empty. They took Kate to a tall old house on the corner not far from the clock tower. An elaborate sign hung over the single door in front. Kate glanced up and saw that it was a golden dragon curling almost in a circle, its talons extended and mouth gaping. Inside, the place looked like an abandoned restaurant or wine cellar. Cobwebs connected the dark bar counter to low beams.

The man named Ion walked ahead of her up the stairway while one of the nameless *strigoi* in black followed, occasionally pushing her when she faltered on the steep steps. The wooden stairs were so old that they were worn down in the middle. The carpet on the third-floor landing had been walked on until any color or pattern in it was long since lost.

On the third-floor landing, Ion removed a blunt shears from his pocket and clipped the plastic restraint free from her wrists. Kate raised her hands and tried to flex her fingers while hiding her agony from the two men.

"You speak not unless Father asks question," said Ion, repeating Radu Fortuna's admonition. The intruder's eyes seemed black. "You understand, yes?"

Kate nodded. Despite her best efforts, her eyes had filled with tears at the pain in her hands.

Ion smiled and opened the door.

* * *

It was not a large room and it was lit by only two candles. There was a bed near the tiny windows against the east wall and Kate could see a bundled figure in it.

One of the shadows moved then and Kate jumped as she saw two huge men in opposite corners. They were gigantic— at least six-foot-four or -five and massive—and their shaved heads gleamed in the weak light. Each wore black clothes and a long mustache. The closer of the two gestured for her to approach the bed. There was a single chair set near it.

Kate went closer and stood behind the chair. She tried to see the man lying under the covers as if she were just a doctor assessing a patient for the first time: only his head and shoulders and yellowed fingers were above the covers; he looked to be in his mid to late eighties; he was almost bald except for long strands of white hair which fanned out from above his ears and lay across the linen pillow; his face was heavily lined, liver-spotted, and gaunt to the point of emacia- tion, with sunken eyes and the sharp turtle's beak mouth of the very old or very sick; his nose, underlip, cheeks, and chin were protuberant, the jaw prognathous; air rasped in and out of his open mouth with the terrible cadence of Cheyne-Stokes breathing and the breath was sour—Kate could smell it from three feet away—as was often the case with people who had been fasting so long that the body was metabolizing needed tissue; he still had his teeth.

Kate stood there, unable to think diagnostically, barely able to think at all. She had seen a younger version of this face not long before: in Vienna's Kunsthistoriches Museum, in a portrait of Vlad Ţepeş on loan from Castle Ambras' "Monster Gallery."

Then the terrible breathing stopped and the old man opened his eyes like an owl awakening at the sound of prey.

Kate stood very still and resisted the impulse to flee. Her fingers, still pulsing with the pain of renewed circulation, grew white again as she gripped the back of the chair, her fingernails gouging splinters.

For several minutes the two looked at one another. Kate

noticed his eyes: how large and dark and commanding they were. Then his fingers flexed above the blankets and Kate noticed his nails were two inches long at least, and yellowed to the color of old parchment. The silence stretched.

The old man said something in what sounded like Turkish or Persian. The words emerged softly, like the half-heard crawl of large insects in rotten wood.

Kate did not understand and said nothing.

The old man blinked slowly, licked his thin, cracked lips with a white tongue that seemed far too long, and whispered, *"Cum te numesti?"*

Kate understood this simple Romanian. "I am Doctor Kate Neuman," she said, amazed that her voice was as steady as it was. "Who are you?"

He ignored the question. *"Doctorul Neuman,"* he whispered to himself and Kate felt her flesh crawl at the sound of her name in his mouth.

She wondered if the old man was rational, or if Alzheimer's had wreaked as much havoc on his mind as the years had to his body.

He licked his lips again and Kate thought of a lizard she had once seen sunning itself in the Tortugas. "Are you the Doctor Neuman the hematologist from the Centers for Disease Control?" he whispered in unaccented English.

Kate blinked her surprise. "Yes."

The old man nodded. The turtle beak turned up in the smallest of smiles. "I prided myself in knowing most of the major blood specialists in the country." He closed his eyes for a long moment and Kate thought that perhaps he had gone back to sleep, but then his voice rattled again. "Are you comfortable here, Doctor Neuman?"

Kate had no idea what "here" meant—Romania? His house? The pit in the clock tower?—but she knew her answer. "No," she said flatly. "My child, my friend, and I have been kidnapped, I've been assaulted by thugs, and they're keeping me against my will right now. If . . . *When* the American Embassy hears about this, there will be a major international incident. Unless . . . unless we are released immediately."

The old man nodded, his eyes still closed. It was hard to tell if he had heard. "Do you know me, Doctor Neuman?"

Kate hesitated. "You're Vernor Deacon Trent." It was not quite a statement.

"I was Vernor Deacon Trent." The old man coughed with the sound of stones rattling in something hollow. "An indulgence, that name. After a while one feels that time and space are barriers to memory. Always a mistake."

One of the bald men in the shadows approached, lifted the old man's head and shoulders with infinite tenderness, and helped him drink water from a small glass. Finished, the huge man returned to the shadows.

"One of the young Dobrins," whispered the old man. "Their ancestors were very helpful when . . . but never mind. What do you think will happen to you, your child, and the priest you traveled with, Doctor Neuman?"

Kate opened her mouth to speak but a sudden terror gripped her bowels and throat. She had to sit down. "I don't know."

The old man's head nodded imperceptibly. "I will tell you. Tomorrow night, Doctor Neuman, your adopted son . . . my true son . . . will become the prince and heir apparent of a rather unique Family. Tomorrow night the child will be given the name Vlad and will taste the Sacrament. And then the family will disperse to a hundred-some cities in twenty-some nations, and the heir will grow to manhood here while his . . . uncle . . . will manage the vast and varied affairs of the Family while he waits for me to die. Is there anything else you would like to know, Doctor Neuman?"

The old man's voice had grown progressively weaker but his eyes were fierce.

"Why?" she whispered.

"Why what, Doctor Neuman?"

Kate leaned closer and also whispered. "Why this insane ritual? Why the exercise in perversion? I know about your so-called Sacrament. I know about your family disease. I can cure it, Mr. Trent . . . cure it while offering you a substitute for the human blood you have had to steal. I can cure you while offering you a chance to help humanity rather than prey on it.''

The old man's head turned then, slowly, like a clockwork mannikin. His eyes did not blink. "Tell me," he whispered.

Kate felt a surge of hope. She kept her voice calm and professional even while the thrill in her grew. *I have something to barter for our lives. All of our lives.*

She told him then: about the J-retrovirus, about Chandra's studies, about the hope the applied retrovirus held out for curing AIDS and cancer, and, finally, about the success of human hemoglobin substitute with Joshua.

". . . and it works," she concluded. "It provides the building materials necessary for the retrovirus to maintain its immunoreconstructive role without having to consume whole blood. With frequent doses, the hemoglobin substitute can be administered intravenously so that the hormonal and mood-altering effects of the blood-absorption mutation organ can be moderated, if not bypassed altogether.'' She stopped, out of breath and terrified that she had gotten too technical and lost the old man. "What I mean to say," she said, heart pounding, "is that I *brought* some of this experimental blood substitute with me. Your men took my bag, but I have medical supplies in it . . . several vials of the artificial hemoglobin that I tested on Joshua."

He blinked now, slowly, and when he looked at her again his eyes were tired. "Somatogen."

It was Kate's turn to blink. "What?"

"Somatogen," said the old man, shifting slightly to find a more comfortable position. "It is a biotech firm in your own city of Boulder, Colorado. You should know it."

"Yes." Kate's voice was weak.

"Oh, it is not one of my corporations. I do not even own a majority of its stock. But I . . . we . . . the more progressive members of the Family . . . have been monitoring its research on artificial hemoglobin. You are probably aware of DNX Corporation and Alliance Pharmaceutical. They have announced their breakthroughs, although a bit prematurely perhaps . . . but Somatogen will make its announcement at the

Tenth Annual Hambrecht and Quist Lifesciences Conference in San Francisco in January of the new year.''

Kate stared at the old man.

He raised a white eyebrow. "Do you think the Family would be uninterested in such research? Do you think that all of us live in Eastern Europe and keep orphanages stocked for our needs?'' There came a rattling, rasping sound that might have been a cough or a laugh. "No, Doctor Neuman, I am aware of your miracle cure. I have tried the prototypes and they work . . . after a fashion. Most of all, I am aware of the commercial applications for it.'' He smiled. "Did you know, Doctor Neuman, that the market for safe transfusions in the United States alone would be over two billion dollars a year . . . and that is now, while the AIDS epidemic is in its early stages?'' He coughed or laughed again. "No, Doctor Neuman, it is not the addiction of blood that is so hard to break . . .''

Kate sat back in her rough chair. Her body felt boneless, nerveless.

"What is it, then?''

The old man lifted a single finger with its long yellow nail. "The addiction to power, Doctor Neuman. The addiction to license. The addiction to the taste of violence without consequence. Did you bring a cure for that in your travel bag?''

Kate stared at him but no longer saw him. There was a long silence which she was only dimly aware of. *If I stand up and run now I might make it to the door of the room. If I make it out the door, the others might not be waiting on the landing. If I make it out of the building* . . . At that second she saw all of Romania as a giant black extension of the lightless pit she had spent the last six or seven hours in. A pit with sides too steep to climb; a pit with police and military and customs people and an air force, all following orders to find her and kill her. Beyond Romania she saw the reach of the *strigoi* like a long black arm, as boneless as a tentacle but with no end to its reach, and the hand on that arm had razor claws instead of fingernails. *If I magically escaped with*

Joshua, how long would it be until I awoke in the night to find a stranger in black in my room . . . in my child's room? How many would they send after me? They would never stop. Never.

"What . . ." Kate stopped and cleared her throat. "What is going to happen to Father O'Rourke and me?"

The old man did not open his eyes again. His voice was vague, dreamy. "Tomorrow night you will be taken to a sacred place, you and the priest. The Family will be there. Young Vlad will be there. At the proper time, you and the priest will be impaled upon two stakes of gold. Then the new prince's uncle . . . Uncle Radu . . . our new leader in all things . . . will open your femoral artery."

There was a ringing in Kate's ears and her vision clouded with dark spots.

"You will feed your child first," whispered the old man. "And then you will feed the Family."

For several minutes the old man did not appear to be breathing at all, but then the tortured rasping began again. He was asleep. Kate did not stir until the door opened. Radu Fortuna beckoned the *strigoi* named Ion into the room, her hands were bound in front of her, and she was taken immediately back to the pit in the basement of the clock tower.

O'Rourke was not there. She did not see him again that night. Whatever ceremony the *strigoi* held there in Sighişoara on that cold October midnight, they held it without Kate's presence or understanding.

Late in the unrelieved darkness of the next morning, they came for her.

Chapter Thirty-five

KATE had never been comfortable in the dark. As a child she had used a night-light until she was ten years old; even as an adult she preferred a tiny plug-in light in the bathroom or hallway—anything to lessen the darkness.

The pit was absolute darkness. The single 20-watt bulb in the basement above her must have been turned off since not even the faintest glow crept around the cracks in the trapdoor. Even though it was dark up there, she sensed that one of the *strigoi* was up there. She could not hear him, but she *felt* a presence there. It was not reassuring.

It seemed like hours passed and Kate knew that sunrise must have come, but the darkness and stench and scrabbling did not change. At other times she felt that time was not moving at all, that it had been only minutes since she had been returned to the pit. The next minute she would be sure that the next day had already come and gone, that Joshua had already been initiated into the clan of blood drinkers.

No, it will be my blood he drinks first. I will be there.

Kate dozed only once and awoke with a rat creeping across her skirt and bare legs. She did not scream, but her body rippled with revulsion in the seconds after she had flung the thing across the pit. *It* screamed as it hit the wall.

By any sane measurement of mood, Kate knew, this should be the most despondent few hours of her life. Her realization that there could be no real escape for Joshua, O'Rourke, and her, that the *strigois'* reach was too long, their evil too powerful, should have sent her spiraling into hopelessness and despair.

It did not.

In those black hours in the pit, Kate found all of her external identity stripped away: honored scholar, doctor, respected researcher, wife, former wife, lover, mother. What remained had nothing to do with identity, with *who* she was, but everything to do with *what* she was.

Kate Neuman was a woman who was not about to go gently into that good night. She was not about to surrender the man she loved—the realization that she loved Mike O'Rourke was like a light slowly growing brighter in the dark—nor the child she had sworn to protect. It did not matter that the *strigois'* power was almost beyond imagining. It did not matter that she had no secret weapon left after the old man's dismissal of her "miracle cure"; it did not matter that no new plan had occurred to her yet there in the lightless pit. She would think of something. And if she did not think of something, she would act without thinking in the faith that the mere fact of *acting* would change the set of variables.

So let the *strigoi* do their worst. Fuck them.

When they opened the trapdoor to take her away an eternity later, she was smiling.

Kate had not wept in the pit, but the sunlight outside, as weak and watery as it was, made her eyes brim over. She could not wipe them away because her hands were still tied. The plastic binding was the same, but they had secured her arms in front of her after her interview with the old man the night before and not so tightly as to cut off circulation this time.

Ion and two smaller men, all of them wearing the kind of cheap, baggy suits which seemed the hallmark of Eastern Europe, led her outside to a waiting Mercedes. A second black car sat farther down the hill. The wind was cold and from the north. Radu Fortuna was standing in the middle of the street with his arms folded, looking quite pleased with himself.

Kate glanced at her watch. It was 1:40 P.M. The early afternoon offered the kind of ebbing light that warned of winter's approach. *Am I really never going to see another season? Another sunrise? Are all of the experiences remaining to me to be suffered in the next twelve hours . . . and then nothing?* Kate shook her head and pushed the thoughts away before they filled her chest with panic. She was pleased to feel that just underneath the fluttering surface of terror remained the iron core of resolve she had found in the darkness.

"I hope you sleeped . . . no, slept? . . . yes, slept well last night," beamed Radu Fortuna.

Kate just stared at him. Suddenly her attention was drawn to four men walking up the cobblestone street from the direction of another stone tower beyond the grassy area. One of the men was Mike O'Rourke. Kate first saw that he was limping; then, as the four men drew closer, she realized that he was being supported by two of the *strigoi* guards. Even from thirty feet away she could see that his face was bruised, one eye was swollen shut, and his lips were puffy and discolored.

O'Rourke saw her, smiled through his swollen lips, and raised his bound hands in a salute. The guards opened the rear door to a second Mercedes and began shoving the ex-priest into the car. O'Rourke's gaze never left her.

"Mike!" she shouted, being restrained now by her own *strigoi* thugs. "I love you!"

O'Rourke was crammed in the backseat of the car, doors slammed, and the vehicle moved away, passing under the arched gateway of the Old City and out of sight down the steep and narrow street. Kate did not know if O'Rourke had heard her.

Radu Fortuna chuckled and nudged Ion. "How very touching," laughed Fortuna. "How deeply moving."

Kate wheeled on him. "Why did you beat him?"

Radu Fortuna said nothing, but Ion evidently felt he could

add to the mirth of the moment. "The idiot priest, he have not-real leg. We do not know this. When men come last night to take him out of cell to see Father, idiot priest hit Andrei and Nicolae over head with leg he take off. He try to leave. Nicolae unconscious. Andrei and three others do not like and hit. Hit for long time and . . ."

"Shut up, Ion," snapped Radu Fortuna, no longer smiling. Ion shut up.

So Mike also saw the old man.

One of the *strigoi* guards opened the back door of the idling Mercedes. Kate made a mental note that if she somehow got out of this alive, she would never buy one of these goddamn cars.

"Well, I wish you good trip," said Radu Fortuna, standing by the open door while one of the thugs shoved her inside.

"Where am I going?" She was disappointed to see Ion going around the car to slide in the backseat with her. The *strigoi* thug with a scar above his left eye slipped behind the wheel while the other thug stood just outside.

Radu Fortuna opened his hands in a dismissive gesture. "You wish to see Ceremony, yes? You have, I think, come a long way for this privilege. Tonight you have privilege." He grinned at her and she saw a certain resemblance between Fortuna's gap-toothed smile and the incessant TV images of Saddam Hussein from the previous winter and spring: both men's facial expressions did not involve their eyes. Radu Fortuna's eyes were as dead as black glass. Only the mouth muscles went through the motion of human emotions.

"Well," he continued, voice still brimming with humor, "I think maybe we must say our good-byes now. I will see you tonight, yes, but there will be many peoples there and you may be too busy for chitchat. Bye bye." He slapped his palm on the roof of the car, the other *strigoi* thug slid in next to her so she was sandwiched between Ion and this one with his garlic breath, Radu Fortuna slammed the door, and the Mercedes glided away, drove under the arch of the wall, down the hill past homes that were old in the Middle Ages, and out of Sighişoara.

* * *

They turned right onto a narrow highway. Kate looked past Ion and saw the white sign: MEDIAŞ 36 KM, SIBIU 91 KM. She closed her eyes and tried to remember the map she and O'Rourke had been referring to for several days. If the series of highways they had been on constituted a rough circle, ignoring the mountains and countless diversions, then she imagined traveling counterclockwise with Bucharest the starting point at the six o'clock position. Tîrgovişte was not on the circumference of the circle but just beneath the center where the hands were attached. Braşov would be at the three o'clock position, Sighişoara at the twelve, and Sibiu would be somewhere around the nine.

Where was the castle on the Argeş? Somewhere between the nine and Tîrgovişte near the center. Would Sibiu be on the road to the Argeş castle? It didn't seem likely. She and O'Rourke must have guessed wrong about Vlad Ţepeş' castle being important to the ceremony. Sibiu was their probable destination.

How many miles until I reach the place where I will die? Less than sixty miles. Kate wiped her moist palms on her dark skirt. Suddenly her stomach growled.

Ion glanced at her and did not hide his smirk. "You do not like the breakfast?"

There had been no breakfast, no food the night before. Kate tried to remember the last thing she had eaten, and the memory of the chocolate biscuits she had shared with the women, Ana and Marina, made her dizzy with nausea.

There were few other cars on the road today, and those few were almost driven off the road as the *strigoi* driver honked at them and overtook them at what seemed breakneck speed for such a rough and winding road. The Mercedes slowed for nothing but animals, but even flocks of sheep were sent scurrying.

Kate thought that the Transylvanian countryside that she was watching pass by so quickly must be beautiful in the summer: high green meadows, thick forests rising into areas unscarred by roads, crumbling abbeys on hilltops, the onion domes of Orthodox churches visible in tiny villages down along the river, and the colorfully dressed peasant farmers and Gypsies working in fields. But even in October the weight of winter now lay on the land like a gray pall. The trees were black stripes against gray rock, the peasants walking with heads down along the highway or staring from muddy fields were gray faces in black wool, and the few villages seemed to be studies in gray stone and black wood.

Both the driver and the young *strigoi* to her right were smoking and there seemed to be no ventilation in the car. She could smell the sweat-and-urine reek of the men, and the odor of garlic from the young one to her right seemed stronger every mile. There was no silence during the ride. The driver was talking with either Ion or the young man all the way, each of them speaking in such rapid-fire Romanian that she could not understand any of it. They all laughed a lot. Frequently she caught their glances toward her just before or after a laugh. Although the words were gibberish to her, she knew the tone and arrogance very well: it was the swaggering self-assurance of the not-terribly-intelligent male bully in a situation with a woman he knew he controlled. Kate had heard these same tones of conversation, seen the same leers and glances, and suffered the same laughter as a girl in the company of older boys, as a student with sexist teachers, as a young doctor with fellow interns out to prove something, and as a divorced woman on her own. She knew these sounds well.

"You know there will be big party tonight," said Ion, setting his huge hand on her knee. "You are invite . . . you are special guest." He translated for his cronies and the smelly air was filled with their laughter.

Ion's hand slid up the inside of her leg until Kate clamped her tied wrists against her thigh and stopped it. Ion said something and the men laughed again. He removed his hand and lit a cigarette.

If Kate had been sitting by one of the doors, she would have waited until the Mercedes slowed—which it did only occasionally—and then thrown herself from the car. The road here was cracked concrete or pitted asphalt, the shoulder alongside it almost nonexistent, but jumping would be preferable to sitting here like a fat steer being driven to the slaughterhouse.

But the men crowded her on either side and she knew that she could not get the doors opened before they shoved her back in her center seat.

They passed through the city of Mediaş, much larger than Sighişoara, but Kate had little impression of it except for factories, more factories, littered railyards, a terrible stench that may have come from one of the many petroleum or textile plants, and the glimpse of a single church spire, very tall, rising above the industrial towers like a black ghost from the past. Then they were in the country again and following Highway 14 toward Sibiu.

She noticed a strange thing leaving Mediaş. A factory shift must have let out and there were scores, hundreds, of workers standing along the highway leaving the ugly town. Traffic was backed up along a section of the road that was unpaved and these men, black with soot and grease, would step in front of the Dacias and other cars, wave their arms imperiously, palms down, as if they were ordering the automobiles to stop. Kate realized that it was a Romanian version of the upraised hitchhiker's thumb.

The men did not try to wave down the Mercedes. Kate leaned forward and even raised her bound hands so that she could be seen, but the workers looked down and away from the black car. Some stepped back from the road almost fearfully.

They left the town behind and Kate settled back in her seat. She felt sick with hunger, thirst, and a level of fear she had never imagined.

A few miles out of town, Ion set his thick fingers on her leg again. He said something to the young *strigoi* to her right and this time the laughter in the smoke-filled car was strained with a new tone.

"My friend," said Ion, leaning so close that Kate could see bits of food caught between his teeth, "says he has never fucked an American woman."

Kate said nothing. She imagined her body made of razors.

Ion said something else and rubbed his hand up her leg again. When she tried to stop him, he slapped away her wrists. Ion said something to the garlic-smelling man; a moment later this one set his left hand on her right thigh.

Kate closed her eyes and tried to remember the self-defense classes she had taken at the Boulder Rec Center years before. All she could remember was the laconic comment Tom had made when she returned home from the exercises, feeling bruised but powerful: "Kat," he had said, "the bad news is what my daddy taught me—namely, a good big guy can always beat the shit out of a good little guy. I'm afraid that even when you get good at all this kicking and gouging stuff, you'll always be a little guy. So carry Mace. Learn to use the gun I keep in the closet." He had hugged her then. "Or just stick close to me, kid."

Kate opened her eyes. The driver was glancing back over his shoulder. His face was flushed.

Ion pointed to a gravel road leading away from the highway to a small copse of white trees. The driver nodded and turned off the highway. A single Dacia passed them and then the road was empty. The Mercedes' suspension absorbed the ruts and bumps as they crawled their way a hundred yards to the grove of trees and an old house or barn that had once stood there. Nothing remained now but stones and the collapsed roof.

Ion's fingers slid up her thighs to her crotch. He poked at her through the thin cotton of her underpants.

When I count to three, I will claw his eyes. I will sink my nails in and pull his eyes from their sockets. Let it end here if it has to. She curled her fingers, feeling her unkempt nails and wishing they were longer. *One . . . two . . .*

As if reading her mind, Ion slapped her in the face. It had seemed a casual movement, almost languorous, but the force of the big man's hand knocked her back into the seat cushions and made her almost lose consciousness. She tasted blood in her mouth and nose. When she was fully aware of where she was and what was happening, she was stretched half across the seat, the garlic-smelling, pockmarked man had gotten out and gone around to stand behind Ion in the open door, and Ion was shoving up her skirt and pulling off her pants. Ion was half standing, half leaning in the car. His weight was on her lower legs. She had no leverage to kick; no chance to squirm away. The driver was turned fully in his seat now, his arms hanging over the leather seatback and his fingers flexing the way she had seen men's hands do at prizefights and football games.

Ion snapped something at the other two and then smirked at her. "I tell them, we take the turns. Three times for the each of us. One time for each of your holes . . . yes?" He reached into his coat pocket, removed a pair of shears, cut through the plastic that bound her wrists and handed the shears to the driver. He said something and garlic-breath laughed eagerly.

"I tell him," translated Ion, "if you struggle, to cut your nose off." His wet lips curled up. "But I say, he hold you down while he is to do it so that I am not interrupted." Ion unbuttoned his pants and lowered them with a violent tug. He spit on one hand and rubbed his half-erect and uncircumcised penis vigorously while his other hand spread her thighs apart.

I am not here. This is not me.

The *strigoi* called Ion leaned over and breathed in her face. "I remember . . . you try to kill me, bitch . . . now I fuck you to death." His mouth opened wide and descended on hers. His tongue was like moist sandpaper against her closed lips. She could feel his wet member thrusting against her thighs and groin.

Kate was concentrating so hard on not being there, on feeling and sensing nothing, that the sharp sound at first seemed remote, unrelated to anything. It came again, like the crack of a branch being snapped, and Kate opened her eyes. Ion pulled his mouth away. He was not quite inside her, but his face was sagging in the slack, alarmed vacuity that some men show at the second of orgasm. There was another crack and the garlic-smelling *strigoi* behind Ion seemed to throw himself away from the open car door.

The driver shouted something, the branch cracked again, glass shattered and sprayed, and the shears fell to the carpet near Kate's right shoulder.

She reacted in less than a second, twisting, swinging her right arm over Ion's forearm, seizing the open shears and slashing up and to the left in a single movement that could not be blocked. She felt the blade slice through cheek muscle and rattle along teeth. Ion screamed and spit blood onto the black leather upholstery. All the while, his hips continued to move against her, his penis batting against her crotch.

Kate shoved backward, lifted her knees, got her feet on Ion's shoulders, and shoved him out the door. She clambered backward but the other door was locked.

Ion was bellowing, staggering for balance as his lowered pants fell below his knees. The *strigoi* clamped his hand to his cheek, squeezed shut the flap of sliced skin and muscle that ran from his ear to his mouth, spat blood, and said, "I kill you now."

"No," said a voice behind him.

Ion whirled. Lucian stepped into Kate's line of vision, raised a black pistol with a very long barrel, and shot Ion in the face from three feet away.

Chapter Thirty-six

LUCIAN walked to the open door of the Mercedes and Kate set her back against the locked door and held the shears in front of her, her thumb tight on the top of the blades. She was gasping, trying not to hyperventilate even while her lungs demanded more air.

"Kate," said Lucian, lowering the long-barreled pistol and holding his hand out.

Kate clenched her teeth and lifted the shears like a knife. "Stay away. Don't touch me."

Lucian nodded and stepped back. He reached into the grass below the car, came up with her underpants, and set them carefully on the rear seat. "I'll be out here," he said softly.

Kate sat watching, the shears still raised, while Lucian dragged the body of the driver out, then returned for the other two. She pulled on her pants, her body still rippling with disgust and shock, and then peered out the car door before getting out.

Lucian had moved the bodies to the far side of the car, near the collapsed barn. The pistol was tucked in his belt but there was an ax in his hands. "Kate, come look at this."

She leaned against the car a moment. She was shivering and her mind refused to focus. Colors seemed to shift and part of her still wanted to scream or weep, or both.

"Kate, please come look." Lucian was kneeling by the body of the driver.

She approached slowly, the shears by her side. The sight of the driver lying there still twitching triggered some medical part of her mind and she knelt next to the man, her fingers probing the neck for a pulse. There was none. The driver's hands and legs still twitched.

"I shot him in the throat and the forehead," Lucian said emotionlessly. "Wouldn't you agree that he should be dead?"

Kate stared at the young medical student as if seeing him for the first time.

Lucian touched the twitching fingers. "It's the virus that refuses to die, Kate. Even now it's sealing off the wounds, coagulation working at an impossible rate. The virus is direct-ing a surfeit of oxygen to the brain even as body temperature drops to that of a corpse."

Kate felt for the nonexistent pulse again. She was surprised to hear her own voice. "It can't send blood to the brain. His heart has stopped."

Lucian nodded and set three fingers deep into the driver's solar plexus. "Feel here. No? All right . . . but the shadow organ, the blood-absorption mutation, is taking over minimal circulation chores. The virus wants to live. This man is clini-cally dead, Kate. But if he receives whole blood within the next forty-eight hours or so, the body will rebuild. There'll be no brain damage . . . or at least minimal. This . . . thing . . . will be walking again if the *strigoi* find him and supply the blood. Stand back."

Kate stood up and moved away as Lucian spread his legs, hefted the ax, and brought it down in a single vicious arc. Blood sprayed and the driver's head was separated from his body.

"Oh, Jesus . . ." said Kate and turned away. She went and leaned against the Mercedes as Lucian did the same to Ion and the younger *strigoi*.

Lucian had dragged the headless corpses into the tumble-down shack. Now he picked up the heads one by one, carried them to the copse of trees, and tossed them far into the weeds. He took clumps of dried grass, rubbed blood from his pantlegs and boots, and walked back to the car. Kate stood rubbing her arms, the shears unnoticed in her right hand. Lucian took them away from her and threw them into the high grass. "Stand right here," he said softly, moving her away from the car.

He opened the door on the driver's side, brushed shattered glass from the slick leather, started the car, and drove the Mercedes under the tumbled roof of the shed. When he came out he pulled the ax from the soft dirt where he had buried the blade, hefted it, and walked to Kate. "I had to leave my car down the road and cross the field on foot. I kept the trees between me and the car. Come."

He started to take her hand but Kate pulled back. Lucian nodded and started off down the lane. Kate waited a minute and then followed.

The white Dacia was much like the blue Dacia that Lucian had driven in Bucharest. It squeaked, rattled, and smoked the same, and there was no second gear. Kate settled back in the cracked vinyl seat and let Lucian drive her west and south.

"It was a temptation to take the Mercedes," he was saying. "Everyone would have recognized it as a *strigoi* car and left us alone. But it would have been too visible from the air . . . and everyone would remember which way we went."

"You followed me," said Kate. It was not exactly a question.

Lucian nodded. "They drove me to Bucharest, I got my car, my father's target pistol, the ax, and binoculars and drove straight back. I saw them drive the priest east. They must be going to the castle by way of Braşov and Piteşti."

"The castle?" Words seemed strange in Kate's mouth. Her mind kept replaying the moments of the rape, the helpless feeling as he pinned her down, the sense of becoming someone and something else than herself . . .

"Vlad's castle on the Argeş River," said Lucian. "It's where tonight's ceremony is. They drove the priest the west way; they were taking you via Sibiu and Calimaneşti. It's just habit, in case they were followed. I only followed your car." He glanced at her.

Kate looked him in the eye for the first time. "You betrayed us."

Lucian glanced back at the road where a Gypsy wagon was weaving ahead of him. He honked, passed the wagon, dodged some sheep, and looked back at her. "No, Kate. I never did . . ."

She clenched her fists. "You were working for them. For all I know, you're *still* working for them."

Lucian took a breath. "Kate, you saw me kill those three—"

"You said yourself that the *strigoi* fight among themselves!" She had not meant to shout. "Factions! You may be with them and against them at the same time. You *betrayed* us. Lied to us. Informed on us."

Lucian was nodding. "I had to . . . to keep you both alive. The *strigoi* knew you were coming. As long as I kept tabs on you, they were reassured . . ."

"You're one of them," whispered Kate.

"You *know* I'm not!" snapped Lucian. "That's why I ran the assay test."

"Blood tests can be faked."

Lucian pulled the Dacia to the side of the road and turned toward her. "Kate, I've been fighting the *strigoi* since I was a child. My adopted parents died fighting them."

"Adopted parents?" Kate remembered the old poet with his elegant manners, his gracious wife; she remembered the two bloodless corpses on the slab in the medical school morgue.

Lucian nodded. "I was an orphan. I was adopted by them when I was four. My parents were killed because of the medical experiments they were doing on *strigoi* . . . trying to isolate the retrovirus."

Kate shook her head. "Your father was a poet, not a doctor. I met him, remember?"

Lucian did not blink. "My foster father was a poet. My

foster *mother* was director of the State Virology Research Institute from nineteen sixty-five until nineteen eighty-seven. She was the reason I went to medical school. To learn about the *strigoi*. To learn how to destroy them but to isolate the retrovirus so that it could be used—"

"The thing in the tank," whispered Kate.

Lucian nodded. "Not the first. We needed to experiment to see how the *strigoi* survive what should be mortal wounds. Mother worked for years to isolate the virus." Lucian turned and squeezed the steering wheel until his fingers turned white. "We never had the proper equipment . . . access to the proper journals." He looked away out his window. A truck roared by on the highway.

Kate shook her head slowly. "But you worked for the *strigoi* . . ."

"As a . . . what do you call them in your James Bond movies? A double agent. A mole. A flunky who observed things that had to be observed."

Kate squinted at him. Her head hurt terribly. "You went to the United States. Not with your parents, but as a guest of Vernor Trent's institute."

Lucian was nodding with her words. "And to West Germany. And once to France. I ran errands for several of the more powerful Family members. The *strigoi* trusted me as a messenger. They helped pay for my medical schooling so that I could work with them on the human blood substitute they were helping to research in America and elsewhere."

Kate folded her arms and moved away from him. "*Why* would they trust you?"

He stopped talking and looked at her for a silent moment. "Because my biological parents were *strigoi*," he said at last.

"But you said . . ."

He nodded. "I am not *strigoi*. That is true. Remember, Kate, it's a very rare double recessive. Most of the J-virus positive who mate have normal children. The regression is toward the norm ninety-eight percent of the time. Otherwise the world would be overrun by *strigoi*. And usually, when the *strigoi* have normal children, they do what normal parents in Romania do with retarded children, or diseased children, or malformed children . . .''

"They abandon them," whispered Kate. She rubbed her temples. "So your foster mother and father found you, adopted you . . ."

"No," said Lucian, his voice so soft she could hardly hear him. "I was taken out of the orphanage and placed with Mother and Father by someone who hates the Family more than you or I do. By someone who had decided to act against them. I've worked for this person and for our shared goal of destroying the *strigoi* family for most of my life."

"Who is it?" said Kate.

Lucian shook his head. "This is the only thing I cannot tell you, Kate. I have given my word of honor never to reveal my mentor's identity."

"But there is no Order of the Dragon?" said Kate.

Lucian smiled. "Only me. And the person who has sponsored me." The smile faded. "And Mother and Father until the *strigoi* destroyed them."

Kate looked askance at him. "Why would they trust you after they discovered your foster parents?"

Lucian had bitten his lip. "Because I informed on them. I had to. It was just a matter of weeks until they would have been discovered. We . . . I had to go to the *strigoi* so that I would be beyond suspicion. The stakes were too high this summer to allow everything to be destroyed at the last minute."

"What stakes?" said Kate. "You mean Joshua? You helped me adopt him and then you helped the *strigoi* steal him back."

Lucian shook his head. "My hope was that you would find the secret of the retrovirus before they found you. You did."

Kate lost it then, flying across the seat at Lucian, pounding at his chest with her fists. "They *killed* Tom and Julie, you lying son of a bitch! They killed them and burned my house and took my baby and . . . *goddamn* it!" Only when her fingers clawed toward his eyes did he restrain her wrists.

"Kate," he whispered, "it had to be. Just as the death of my parents had to be. The stakes are too high."

She pulled away from him and threw herself against the far door. "*What* stakes? What are you talking about?"

Lucian put the car in gear and pulled out onto the empty highway. "The destruction of the *strigoi* Family," he said. "All of them. Tonight."

The stone kilometer marker read COPŞA MICA—8 KM. The road wound along the Tirvana Mare River through iso-lated uplands with no farmhouses, no villages, and no traffic except for the occasional rubber-wheeled cart. The clouds were low and a cold wind blew leaves across the narrow road and slammed against the Dacia like invisible fists.

"Tell me," demanded Kate.

Lucian did not take his eyes off the road. "It would be foolish, Kate. There is little chance that they will come after us today . . . they won't notice you're missing for several hours . . . and we'll be far away from here by then. Still, if we were caught . . ."

"Tell me," said Kate. Her voice held an imperative that she had honed through long hours in emergency rooms, op-erating rooms, and conference rooms.

Lucian glanced at her. "Really, it would be stupid to—"

"Tell me." Her tone left no choice in the matter.

Lucian licked his lips and smoothed back his spikey hair-cut. "It's arranged, Kate. Tonight the *strigoi* Family is going to die. All of them."

"How?" Kate said flatly.

Lucian shook his head but kept talking. "They're gathering at the castle on the Argeş . . . Poienari Citadel, it's called . . . the ancient keep that Vlad rebuilt more than five hundred years ago. It's been arranged . . . they won't survive the ceremony."

"How has it been arranged?" Her voice showed her disbe-lief.

"The citadel has been abandoned and shunned since the

days of Vlad," said Lucian. "The locals still fear it. The government ignored it. The tourist bureau led the few tourists to fake 'Castle Draculas' like Bran Castle near Braşov rather than acknowledge the real site on the Argeş River."

"So?" said Kate.

"So this ceremony has been anticipated for years. Ceauşescu began reconstruction of Poienari Citadel more than three years ago. The new government has finished it, despite the economic collapse. The *strigoi* demanded it." He paused and looked at her, then went on. "Explosives were planted there during the reconstruction." He let out a deep breath. "They're timed to go off tonight during the Ceremony. The entire mountain is wired. None of the *strigoi* will leave alive."

Kate folded her arms. "You're lying again."

He seemed startled at her attitude. "No, Kate, I swear . . ."

"You have to be lying. The *strigoi* would never allow someone access to one of their Ceremony sites like that. Also, their security people would sweep the place before the Ceremony. They're cruel bastards, but they're not idiots."

They were entering the valley town of Copşa Mica. It was an industrial town unlike anything Kate had ever seen: the streets were black with soot, the houses were black, the people walking by were gray and black, and tall smokestacks belched out more pollution. Lucian pulled the car into a rutted area beside the railroad tracks. "Kate," he said, "it's true. I swear it."

She stared at him.

He sighed. "The construction was authorized by the *strigoi* Family leaders, was paid for primarily by Vernor Deacon Trent's foundation, and was carried out by Radu Fortuna's construction company."

Kate's arms were still folded across her chest. "And you're saying that Fortuna just happened to ignore your mythical bombs being planted. Or is it going to be done the way they tried to kill Hitler . . . one *strigoi* turncoat with a bomb in his briefcase?"

Lucian gripped her arms and then released them quickly

when he felt her stiffen up. "I'm sorry. Listen, Kate . . . Fortuna almost never visited the site. Most of the work was done by Hungarian artisans. During my summers I worked as a supervisor on the project . . ." He stopped when he saw her look of disbelief. "The *strigoi* trusted me, Kate. I had been an international courier as a teenager. I was ambitious and greedy and showed loyalty only to those with the power to help me. And I had help . . ." He stopped.

"Your mystery mentor," Kate said sarcastically.

"Yes."

"And the bomb was set in place while no one was looking."

"It's not a single bomb, Kate. The two main towers of Vlad's citadel were rebuilt, as were the main hall, the south battlements, the old approach bridge, and the east battlements, where the actual ceremony will be held tonight. They're all loaded with explosives and wired with separate timers. The entire mountaintop is coming off."

Kate held her cold stare but she felt her heart rate accelerate. "The *strigoi* security people will find it."

Lucian shook his head. "They've been over all of the sites a dozen times. The explosives are sealed in the actual construction. Even the timing devices have been mortared up and shut away. They haven't found anything and they won't. There's no way to disarm it. If the *strigoi* are there tonight, they'll be destroyed."

"With Joshua," said Kate. "And O'Rourke."

Lucian touched her hand. "I'm sorry, Kate. I'd hoped they might bring the baby with you today. But they must be flying him down tonight in the helicopter with Radu Fortuna and the other VIPs."

Kate pulled her hand away. "You're lying there, Lucian. You didn't think Joshua would be in the car with me. You wouldn't have rescued us if he were. You *need* him there tonight, so the ceremony will proceed. So the assassination will proceed."

He looked away and she knew then that he was lying about wanting to save Joshua, but telling the truth about the explosives. Her arms and legs literally ran cold at the thought. Outside, gray shadows moved through the industrial filth of Copşa Mica.

"Kate," Lucian said softly, not turning to look at her, "you have to understand that there have only been three of these Investiture Ceremonies in the past five hundred years. There will never be a better time. The entire Family will be there . . . all the *strigoi* who are important enough to count."

Kate nodded. "And my baby and an ex-priest who never hurt anyone are a small price to pay for that chance to assassinate them."

Lucian wheeled and his eyes were wide. "*Yes*! A hundred babies and a hundred priests are a small price!" He took her by the shoulders and shook her. "Do you realize how many centuries my people have been *enslaved* by these monsters, Kate? Do you know how many babies and priests and ordinary people have died horribly because of their cruelty? Can you imagine a nation which has never taken a breath outside the shadow of totalitarian madness?" His voice was shaking. His entire body was shaking.

Lucian let go of her arms and put the car in gear. "It doesn't matter what you think, Kate. It will happen tonight. I'm sorry about Joshua . . . I truly am. And O'Rourke. They will be martyrs just as my adoptive parents were." He drove slowly down the highway through the black city.

"Where are we going?" she said dully.

"We'll change to Highway Fourteen B here in Copşa Mica," he said. "Then north on E Eighty-one to Cluj-Napoca by nightfall, and then west to Oradea and the Hungarian border."

"How will we get across?"

Lucian smiled. "I have ways better than your Gypsy smugglers. We'll be in Budapest by tomorrow night."

"And Joshua will be dead."

He looked at her. "Yes. Would you rather he be a full-fledged *strigoi*? He'll drink human blood tonight, Kate. But it will not turn him into one of them. It will all end tonight."

She leaned across and seized the steering wheel. Startled,

Lucian pulled into an empty market area near the factory gates. No one was in the broad, cinderblock area. The road west went on to the right. The road south to Sibiu and the citadel branched left just behind them. The sky rained black snow on everything.

"You know that Joshua can be saved from that," she said. "With transfusions of the human blood substitute, his immune-deficiency disease can be alleviated but the shadow organ never has to be involved. He won t build a dependency on human blood . . . human life. The artificial hemoglobin will be like insulin to him, nothing more. His body could give us the cure for cancer, for AIDS, and he never has to be *strigoi*."

Lucian touched her cheek. "It's too late, Kate."

She swooned then, allowing her eyes to slide up under her fluttering lids and sliding off the vinyl seat against the door.

"Kate!" Lucian leaned across and lifted her lolling head.

Kate slipped the target pistol out of his belt and set the muzzle against his chest. "Sit back, Lucian."

"Kate, for Christ's sake . . ."

"Sit back," she snapped.

He did so, setting his hands on the steering wheel. "You're not going to shoot me."

She waited until he looked at her so that he could see her eyes. "I won't kill you, Lucian. But I will shoot you. In the leg. Away from the femoral artery, but smashing a major bone. So you won't come after me."

"Come after you? To where?"

"I'm going to get Joshua."

Lucian laughed. It was a thin sound. "Kate, let me explain something to you, all right?"

She said nothing.

"It's not just the explosives or the usual *strigoi* security," he said into the silence. "This is the important night. *Strigoi* from all over the world who were not at the first three nights will be there tonight. It's like Easter to ardent Christians. There will be at least five hundred people up there. All of them will have brought their own guards."

Kate held the pistol steady.

Lucian ran his hand through his hair again. "Kate, we couldn't even get there. There is only one road to the citadel on the Argeş . . . it's Highway Seven-C and it makes this lousy road look like one of your American Interstates by comparison. Highway Seven-C is closed in the Făgăraş Mountains to the north of the castle because of early snows and rock slides. It's only open in late June to early August, and even then you risk your life on that road. Even the *strigoi* are flying or taking the highway through Braşov or Sibiu."

Kate's finger was on the trigger.

Lucian held both hands in front of him, asking for time with his palms. "To the north of the citadel the road is closed and there are hundreds of troops stationed there because of the big hydroelectric project on the Argeş River above the castle."

"The *strigoi* have to get there," said Kate.

Lucian nodded. "They'll drive up from Bucharest and Rîmnícu Vîlcea. Yes. But the highway will be closed miles below the citadel. There will be roadblocks and security checks from the town of Curtea de Argeş on. No one who is not *strigoi* could get through."

"How close could I get before the roadblocks?" asked Kate.

Lucian shrugged. "How the hell do I know? The village of Căpăţîneni is only four or five kilometers below the castle."

"If I get that far," said Kate, "I could walk the last couple of miles."

"*Scuzaţi-mă, Domnul Politişt, puteţi să-mi arataţi cum să ajung Poienari Citadel?*" said Lucian in a falsetto. "*Mă duc la plimbare.*"

"What?" said Kate. "What about the citadel?"

"Nothing," said Lucian. "I'm just imagining you asking directions and telling the *strigoi* guards that you're just going for a walk." He shook his head slowly. "You couldn't get to the citadel, Kate. If you did, they'd just take you and make you part of their fucking Sacrament. There's no way you could get the baby away."

Kate did not lower the pistol. "Perhaps it would be worth it just to make sure that they did not turn him into a full-fledged *strigoi*."

He frowned at her. "You mean kill the child before they make him drink? But why, Kate? The Ceremony starts a little before midnight. The *strigoi* are a prompt race. The Investiture Ceremony is scheduled to take about an hour and a half. The explosives go off at twelve twenty-five. Chances are that they will not have gotten to the so-called Sacrament part of the Ceremony before . . . before it happens."

Kate nodded her understanding. "Get out of the car, Lucian. I don't know who to trust or what to believe anymore, but I know that I'm grateful for what you did an hour ago. He . . . they . . ." Her hand started to shake and she steadied it on her knee. The muzzle of the pistol was still pointed at Lucian's chest. "If you promise not to come after me, I'll just leave you here. You go on to Hungary."

Lucian opened the door and stepped out. The road was empty except for a Gypsy wagon rumbling by. The sway-backed black horse pulling the black wagon may have been any color under the soot that coated him. The children's faces staring out from under the dark gray canvas were streaked with sooty rivulets where tears had muddied the grime on their cheeks. Their hands were black.

"Kate," said Lucian, his voice sad, "why?"

"Don't worry. You said yourself that when they catch me they'll just make me part of their Ceremony. They won't take time to interrogate me. At any rate, I could stand anything until . . . when? Twelve twenty-five?"

Lucian gripped the top of the car door. "But *why*?"

Kate lowered the pistol. "I don't know. I just know that I'm not leaving Joshua or O'Rourke there. Good-bye, Lucian." She slid over, closed the door, put the car in gear, and made a U-turn on the empty highway to head back to the intersection where Highway 14 ran south to Sibiu. The windshield was already so dusted with the rubber ash and soot in the air that she had to turn on the windshield wipers. They clawed back and forth with a sound of fingernails on glass.

Lucian had jogged across the street while she was making the turn. Now he put both hands out the way she had seen hitchhikers do in Mediaş. He switched to an upraised thumb as she came up to the sooty stop sign.

"Thanks, babe," he said as he slid into the passenger seat. "I thought I'd never get a ride."

Kate held the pistol in her lap. "Don't try to stop me, Lucian."

He held up three fingers. "I won't. I swear. Scout's honor."

"Then why—"

He shrugged and settled back in the tattered seat, his knees high. "Hey, Kate, did you know that before we shot Ceauşescu we tried to electrocute him?"

Kate started to speak and then realized that this was one of Lucian's dumb jokes. "No," she said. "I didn't know that."

"Yeah," said Lucian, "but even though we pulled the switch a dozen times, the electricity never hurt him. Afterward, while the firing squad was hunting for bullets, we asked him why the electricity didn't work. You know what he said?"

"No."

"*Látjátok, mindig is rossz vezető voltam.*"

Kate waited.

"He said, 'You see, I always was a bad leader/conductor.' Get it? *Vezető* means leader, but also, like, semiconductor. Get it?"

Kate shook her head. "You don't have to go with me on this, Lucian."

He spread his fingers and settled lower in the seat. "Hey, why not. It's easier to follow. I always was a lousy *vezető*."

Kate turned right onto Highway 14. Black letters were just visible on a gray-sooted sign: SIBIU 43 KM. RÎMNÍCU VÎLCEA 150 KM.

Once out of the smoke and soot of Copşa Mică, Kate turned off the wipers but had to turn on the lights. Despite the early hour, it was getting dark.

Dreams of Blood and Iron

If there is any fate more ignominious than to be a patriarch without power in the grip of one's own family, I do not wish to imagine it. Events proceed, although it is apparent that my final act for the Family shall be styled as mere ceremonial pawn in the power machinations of Radu Fortuna.

Radu. I think of my brother Radu, the boy with the long lashes who became the beloved of more than one sultan. The boy who grew up to wrestle the throne from me through treachery and guile. The people called him Radu the Handsome and welcomed his soft ways after my stern years as their liege lord.

The idiots.

I knew Radu as the brainless, spineless little Sodomite he was. Sultan Mehmed had no difficulty controlling Wallachia and Transylvania with Radu as his puppet: God knows that the Sultan had had his hand up this particular puppet enough times.

I, Wladislaus Dragwylya, had beaten the Turks more decisively than any Christian ruler in history, had sent the Sultan cowering back to Constantinople, and had won the liberty of my people. But my people deserted me.

The Sultan had left his play toy, Radu, in Wallachia to woo my boyars away from me, to undermine their liege oaths. At this, Radu was successful in the dark closets of diplomacy

*where he and the Sultan had failed on the daylight battlefields.
Now that I had vouchsafed the freedom of the Seven Cities
through the spilling of my own blood, the boyars of these
German strongholds turned against me and made secret pact
with the serpent Radu.*

*By midsummer of 1462, my position had become, as the
politicians now phrase it, untenable. I had beaten the Turks
everywhere I had found them, but behind me my army had
melted away like sugar in the mouth of a child. I took my few
and most loyal boyars, my fiercest and best-trained troops,
and fled. I fled to my castle keep on the Argeş River.*

*Here is the folk legend that tells of my final hours at Castle
Dracula.*

*The Turks were approaching by night, setting up their
cannonades on the high fields near the village of Poenari on
the bluffs across the Argeş. In the morning they would storm
my citadel. Then, as the folktales have it, a certain relative
of mine who had been taken by the Turks years before, remembering my many kindnesses to him and his love of family,
climbed to a high spot and fired a warning arrow through the
only lighted window in my tower. Legend has it that the arrow
was so well-aimed that it snuffed the candle by which my
concubine was reading.*

*She was alone in the room, goes the tale. When she read
the appended warning of the Turkish attack, she woke me,
told me in hysterical tones that she would rather have her
body eaten by the fish in the Argeş than be touched by the
Turks, and then threw herself from the battlements to the river
a thousand feet below. To this day, the river there is known
as Rîul Doamnei—the Princess's River—in tribute to this
tale.*

This false tale.

*In truth, there was no relative, no warning arrow, and no
selfless suicide. Here is the truth:*

*We had watched from the citadel for two days as Radu and
the Turks advanced to Poenari and to the bluffs beyond. For
another two days we had suffered their cannonade, although
their cherrywood guns did little damage; I had ordered the*

towers rebuilt with too many layers of brick and stone to fall to such a minor pounding.

Still, we knew that on the morrow Radu's cavalry would cross the Argeş and swing up the valley to the hills behind the keep, while the Turkish foot soldiers, stupid and stolid as ambulatory tree trunks, would die by the hundreds while ascending the cliffs to the citadel walls. But they would win. Our forces were too small, the keep too isolated on its crag to allow any eventual outcome except the defeat of Lord Dracula. That night I was deep in preparations for my escape when my concubine, Voica by name, demanded my time to have an argument. Women have no sense of timing; when they wish to argue, they must argue, and it does not matter what events of real importance are taking place.

Voica and I walked the darkened battlements while she went on in a tearful voice. The issue was not the attacking Turks nor the threat of my treacherous brother Radu, but the future of our sons, Vlad and Mihnea.

I should say here that I loved Voica, at least as much as it is possible for a leader of men and nations to love a woman. She was small, dark of eye and skin but usually light of heart, and she did my bidding in all things. Until this night.

Of our two boys, Mihnea had been born normal enough, but his one-year-old younger sibling, Vlad, had the wasting sickness that had plagued my father and me. Vlad had received the secret Sacrament only days before. His health shone now in his eyes and I knew that the boy would be like his father in requiring the Sacrament throughout his life.

It was on this night, of all nights, that Voica chose to protest that our child would be brought up this way. I pointed out that neither the babe nor I had a choice in the matter: if he were to survive, he would have to drink. This upset Voica. Her mother had been a secret drinker. Indeed, her mother had been tried and destroyed as a witch, and I first met Voica when she was brought before my court to face a similar fate. But Voica had never tasted the Sacrament. Instead of ordering her burned or impaled, I took her into my palace, gave her my affection, and allowed her to bear my children. And now *she thanked me by striding the battlements, on the very night the campfires of Radu and the Turks were visible across the black river valley, and demanding that young Vlad be allowed to grow up without the Sacrament. She called it blasphemy. She called it witchcraft. She called me* strigoi *like her mother.*

I reasoned with her for several minutes, but the hour was drawing near when we would have to leave. I pronounced the conversation finished.

Voica had always been an overly emotional and dramatic woman. It was probably that as much as her mother's habit of drinking the blood of corpses which had brought Voica to my court in chains. Now she surrendered to her sense of drama and leapt to the parapet, threatening to throw herself and our two babes in her arms into the void below if I did not give in to her wishes.

Tired of her histrionics, in a press to leave before the moon rose, I jumped to the top of the low wall and wrestled the children away from her. She lost her balance then. For a second I thought it was part of her melodrama, but then I saw the true terror in her face and, shifting Vlad to the arm which held Mihnea, I held out my hand to steady her.

Our fingertips touched. She fell backward without a sound, disappearing into the darkness of the chasm like a mermaid diving to greater depths. One of her slippers remained behind on the wet stone. I kept that slipper for three centuries, losing it only when I had to flee a burning building in Paris during a minor revolution.

I took the children that night and left everyone else in the castle behind. Their loyalty meant nothing to me. They meant nothing to me.

One of the reasons I had chosen Poenari Citadel for my own was that it was built atop two faults in the rock which led down more than a thousand feet to the cave which held the underground river. The first fault was only ten inches wide, but it served as a well for fresh water even during siege. The second fault was, with a little help from artisans who died with the boyars who rebuilt Castle Dracula on that long-ago Easter Sunday in 1456, large enough for a man to descend, hanging on to iron cables and rungs as he did so.

Below, in the secret cave that ran out to the Argeş more than a mile above the citadel hill, the seven Dobrin brothers were waiting with horses shod backward to confuse those who would track us. The Dobrins took me up the trackless valley, then led me across secret passes and dangerous snowfields of the Făgăraş peaks to the north. If it had not been midsummer, even that retreat into Transylvania would have been closed off.

When I descended into Transylvania proper in the mountain wilds south of Braşov, I called for a rabbit-skin parchment and deeded all the land north and west, as far as our eyes could see, to the stolid Dobrin brothers. None of the rulers who followed me in Wallachia, Transylvania, and now Romania have defied that order. Even Ceauşescu, with his collectivization and systematization frenzy, left this one parcel of private land untouched by this socialist madness.

That is the true story, although I cannot imagine that anyone cares. Not even the Family, who have forgotten to honor and obey their patriarch, even though most of them are the descendants of the young Vlad I saved from death that night.

My half-dream state is broken by the sound of arriving Family members. In a moment they will come up the stairs to bathe me and dress me in fine linen vestments and drape the chain of the Order of the Dragon around my neck.

One final Ceremony. One final act as patriarch.

Chapter Thirty-seven

KATE and Lucian drove through Sibiu in the failing light: Sibiu where medieval lanes opened onto cobblestone squares surrounded by homes and buildings with sleepy-eyed rooftop windows.

They drove down the Olt River Valley as the late-afternoon glow faded to gray twilight. The highway wound along the river between steep canyon walls. One minute the road would be broad, smoothly asphalted, with a gravel shoulder, and the next they would be bouncing through a mile of muddy ruts where some roadwork had been started and abandoned months or even years before.

They skirted the industrial town of Rîmnícu Vîlcea. The Dacia needed petrol and the only gas station they passed had a line at least an hour long. Lucian said that he knew a black-market gas depot on the east edge of town and they stopped to change drivers. Few Romanian women drove cars; if they were important enough to travel by car, they tended to be chauffeured. Lucian slid behind the wheel, left the highway just beyond the city limits, and bought five liter-bottles of petrol out of the back of a lorry parked near an old tunnel.

Later, Kate was to think of how the simple act of changing drivers sealed their respective fates.

* * *

Just beyond Rîmníca Vîlcea on the road leading southeast to Piteşti, Lucian turned left onto tiny Highway 73C and followed it through a few dimly lighted villages into the darkness of the Carpathians. They encountered the first road-block fifteen kilometers farther on, right where the road diverged in a village named Tigveni toward either Curtea de Argeş to the east or Suici to the north.

"Shit," said Lucian. They had just topped the rise coming out of the village when he saw the lights, the military vehicles, and two black Mercedes stopped at the checkpoint. Lucian doused the Dacia's already weak lights, made a U-turn, and drove back into the village, turning down a dark sidestreet that was little more than an alley. Tigveni may have held a hundred people in its eight or ten homes, but tonight, even though it was not yet eight P.M., the town was dark and silent.

"What now?" whispered Kate, knowing that it was silly to whisper but doing so anyway. The target pistol was in the low console between their two front seats.

Lucian's face was just visible. "It's another fourteen kilometers to the town of Curtea de Argeş," he said. "Then twenty-three kilometers north up the valley to the citadel."

"More than twenty miles," whispered Kate. "We can't walk from here."

Lucian rubbed his cheek. "When I worked on the citadel, I had to drive to Rîmnícu Vîlcea regularly to pick up materials and workers. Occasionally the bridge outside of town here would be washed out by storms." He slapped the steering wheel. "Hang on, babe."

With the headlights still out, Lucian bumped the Dacia down a rutted sidestreet, across what appeared to be a meadow, and then settled into two ruts that ran along a river. Kate heard frogs and insects from the darkness under the trees and for a moment she could imagine that summer was coming rather than dying.

The Dacia halted under the trees on a wide stretch of gravel alongside the river and Lucian killed the engine. Two hundred meters to their left, the spotlights of the military roadblock lit the night.

"They're stopping cars at the one-lane bridge," whispered Lucian. As they watched, another limousine approached the roadblock, flashlights flicked on, and Kate could see the gleam of the soldiers' helmets as they stepped up to the car, checked it, and then saluted and let it pass.

"We should have taken the Mercedes," she whispered.

Lucian grinned. "Yeah. We look so *strigoi*, don't we? Did you bring your identity papers?"

Kate glanced at her watch. Four hours to go twenty miles. "What next?"

Lucian pointed at the river. It was at least a hundred feet wide here, but it looked shallow. Reflected light from the distant searchlights gleamed on numerous ripples.

"We'll never cross here without them seeing us or hearing us," hissed Kate. "Isn't there another place? Farther from the road?"

Lucian shrugged. "I don't know of any. This is where the locals used to reroute traffic when the bridge was out." He looked to his left. "Hear their music? Somebody in one of the trucks has a radio going."

"Yes, but all they have to do is *look* this way."

Lucian cranked his window down and leaned out. "The trees overhang here for most of the way. It's dark near the banks." He turned and looked at Kate. "You call, Kate."

She hesitated only a second. "Go."

Lucian started the car. The four-cylinder motor sounded like a jet engine to Kate. Lucian put the car in first and edged out into the river. Within seconds the water was up to the car's hubcaps, then to the bottom of their doors, then rising along the fender. The Dacia rocked and bumped.

"We're shipping water," whispered Kate, lifting her feet from the dribbling floorboards. Lucian kept one hand on the wheel and one on the stick shift and jostled them forward.

Suddenly the right front wheel dipped, something smacked the bottom of the car hard, and the engine stalled. They sat there in the middle of the river, the current lapping halfway to the windows, and tried not to breathe too loudly.

The music from the two military trucks was a loud, Gypsy beat. Lucian pulled the choke out and set his hand on the ignition keys.

"No!" Kate said aloud and stopped his hand just as he was turning the keys.

A limousine had glided up to the roadblock. The music stopped. In the sudden silence they could hear the questions of the three soldiers and even soft replies from the car. The beam from one of the bright searchlights atop the truck jostled, lost its focus on the Mercedes, and stabbed out onto the river. A moment later the limousine rolled on, the searchlights were aimed lower, and the music started up again.

Lucian turned the ignition key.

Please God, prayed Kate to a God she had never really believed in, *don't let the coil or the spark plugs or the other things Tom used to try to explain to me be wet or broken. Amen.*

The Dacia started. Lucian rocked it carefully forward and back, freed the wheel from the hole, and drove on to the opposite bank. Kate felt her skin and muscles beginning to unclench when they were half a mile down the rutted lane and out of sight of the roadblock because of thick trees and the hill. She had not known that one's body physically awaits the impact of bullets.

"OK," breathed Lucian as he bounced the Dacia back onto the narrow highway. "I don't know what the fuck we'll do when we get to Curtea de Argeş, but, hey . . . the name of the game is improvise, right?"

They bypassed Curtea de Argeş and two roadblocks they could see in the distance by driving north up the railroad line that ran along the west side of the Argeş River. "O'Rourke's idea," said Kate.

They had a flat which Kate helped change by the light of the few stars now shining between high clouds. The spare was so patched and so threadbare that she could not imagine it getting them much farther. *There isn't much farther to go,* she assured herself. *Fifteen kilometers. This tire will make it.*

If you're not planning on coming back, another part of her mind answered.

A kilometer farther and the rail line diverged west through tunnels into the Fâgâraş Mountains. Kate went out on foot until she found two overgrown ruts in the darkness and they bounced east down the old access road until they reached a two-plank bridge over the river and Highway 7C that ran past the citadel.

Lucian got out of the car and Kate joined him. The highway was quiet here but they had seen traffic earlier. To the east and west, foothills rose to mountains lost in the night and clouds. To the north, the valley visibly narrowed until it made Kate think of a narrowly opened door. Into darkness.

Lucian pointed toward an orange glow against the clouds low above the peaks ahead. "They have the ceremony site lit up already." He glanced at his watch. "It's ten-fifteen. Time sure flies when you're having fun."

Kate felt like pounding her fists on the car roof. Instead she touched Lucian's arm. "We can't keep creeping along like this. How do we get there quickly?"

He grinned at her. "What do you say we just drive? Maybe they don't have any roadblocks this close."

"How close are we?"

He looked toward the black doorway in the mountains. "Three miles. Four."

Kate stepped out onto the highway. "I don't see any spotlights like at the other roadblocks."

Lucian nodded. "Maybe we're past them all. Maybe there's nothing between us and the citadel but valet parking for the *strigoi*."

Kate tried to smile but found that she was on the verge of crying instead. She walked over to Lucian and put her arms around him.

"What, babe?" he whispered.

She shook her head, feeling how soft his cheek was. "Thank you, Lucian. Thank you for . . . stopping him . . . today." Her throat was too tight for her to say more.

Lucian patted her awkwardly on the back. Kate smiled

through incipient tears at the thought of how young he was, how filled with energy. She kissed him on the cheek and stepped back. "OK, let's go find that valet parking."

There was a roadblock less than two miles ahead. No searchlights or military trucks here, two black *strigoi* vans pulled out from the woods behind them while a black Mercedes and some sort of armored vehicle became visible around a bend in the road ahead.

Lucian hit the breaks and the Dacia wallowed to a stop between the two barriers. "Damn," he whispered.

There were no back lanes here, no friendly railroad grades, no obvious ways out. The *strigoi* had set this trap well: the sides of the road dropped steeply six or eight feet on each side, the river ran by beyond the ditch to their left, and the canyon wall was to their right.

Searchlights snapped on from the armored car and the grimy windshield of the Dacia became opaque with white light. Kate blinked and shielded her eyes, but the intensity of the glare was like a physical assault.

Someone hailed them with the bullhorn.

"They want us to drive slowly to them," whispered Lucian. He was grinning broadly and waving at the unseen figures behind the spotlight. "They want us to keep our hands in sight."

Kate lifted her hands to the dash. Lucian kept both of his on top of the steering wheel. He put the car in gear and began edging slowly toward the Mercedes and armored car a hundred feet ahead.

The bullhorn barked in Romanian again.

"They want us to stop and get out of the car," said Lucian. He stopped. "I don't really want to stop and talk to these guys, do you?"

"No," said Kate.

"Shall we go for it?" Lucian was grinning in all sincerity now.

"Go for it," said Kate. Her heart was pounding so fiercely that her chest ached. The white light filled the world.

"Okay, babe." He shifted his right hand, touched her hand, and then slammed the car into gear while flooring the accelerator.

The Dacia lurched, almost stalled, and then whined into motion. The bullhorn barked again. Lucian smiled and waved. *Maybe they recognize him*, was Kate's thought. Then the shooting began.

Lucian jerked the car to the right as if they were going to try to get behind the armored car, the searchlight lost them for a second, Kate saw the slightest gap between Mercedes and armored vehicle the same instant Lucian shifted to third gear and aimed for it, and then the windshield disappeared in a thousand flakes, Kate covered her eyes, bullets pounded across the hood, roof, and fenders, there was a terrific impact that slammed her against the door, and then Lucian was steering hard to keep them on the road. He turned the headlights on to show empty highway ahead and then the blazing white light was back in their rearview mirror and rear window. That window exploded inward, Kate felt something tug at her left heel and something else pass between her upraised arm and her ribs, and then they were around the bend in the road and accelerating again, weaving wildly as they did so.

"We made it!" screamed Kate, not believing it even as she shouted. She knew that most of the exhilaration she felt was a pure adrenaline high but she did not care. Lucian grunted something and fought the wheel.

The spare on the right front wheel gave way then with a pop louder than the gunfire had been, the Dacia slewed right, Lucian fought it left, and then they were sideways and flipping down the road. Kate threw her arms over her head, felt her knees bang the underside of the dash, and then she was watching through the broken windshield as the road, sky, road, and sky alternated past.

The Dacia rolled a final time, came to a stop on its wheels, and then slid sideways down a thirty-foot bank into the river.

The old car did not go fully into the water but stopped upside down and wedged between a boulder and a tree with the hood underwater and the left wheel spinning. The right wheel was only tattered rubber on a twisted rim. Kate realized that she was seeing all this from outside the car and she sat up, braced herself on a rock the size of her head, and looked at the Dacia upside down, its headlights under the water.

"Lucian!" She ran to the other side of the vehicle, found him half pinned under the driver's seat that had come out of its brackets and fallen on him, and—ignoring every rule she had learned as an emergency room intern—pulled him from the wreckage. There was no sound of pursuit yet from the highway above them.

"Lucian," she whispered, dragging him to the shelter of trees downstream. "We made it. We got past them."

"Yeah," he grunted.

She laid him against the roots of the largest tree and scrambled back to the wreckage, feeling around for the pistol. She could not find it, but she came up with the binoculars that had been in the backseat. She put the leather strap around her neck and waded back to Lucian, listening hard. Still no sound of the vehicles.

Lucian was sitting up and was inhaling deeply as if to catch his breath after having the wind knocked out of him. She knelt next to him. "I think I'm all right. My God, what a mess. Are you all right, Lucian?" His face was very white in the dim light.

He steadied himself with one hand against the tree. "Not really," he said. "I think I'm going to lie down a minute."

She heard the armored car shifting gears and moving down the road toward them. A spotlight stabbed into the water two hundred yards away. "No, come on, we have to get across the river and into the woods there," she hissed in his ear. "Come on, Lucian." She lifted him to a sitting position and pulled her hands away thick with something.

"Just . . . rest a minute," he muttered. "*Am o durere aici*, Kate. Uh . . . I mean, I have a pain right here. *Mă doare pieptul.*" He touched his chest.

Kate pulled him forward and ripped away the tatters of his shirt. As far as she could tell in the darkness, there were four large entry wounds high on his back, two near or above the spine, and another entry wound low and to the right. She felt his chest and stomach but found only one exit wound. It was very large and hemorrhaging badly.

"Ah, Lucian," she whispered and used his tattered shirt as a compression bandage. "Ah, Lucian . . ."

"Tired," whispered Lucian. "*Mă simt obosit.*"

"We'll rest here," she whispered, cradling him and stroking his brow with her free hand. She felt him nod against her. The armored car was almost above them now. She smelled the diesel stink of its exhaust.

"Babe," whispered Lucian, his voice urgent, "I forgot to tell you something."

"It's all right," crooned Kate, holding the crude bandage in place. The bundle was soaked with his blood and she could hear the bubbling. It was what they had called a sucking chest wound in the emergency room. Only the most immediate and extensive care could save someone with a sucking chest wound. "It's all right," she whispered, rocking him.

"Good," said Lucian in a relieved voice, and died.

She felt him go. She felt the energy and consciousness and spark go out of him like air from a ripped balloon. If she had been religious, she would have thought that she felt his soul leave him.

Kate knew CPR. She knew mouth-to-mouth. She knew a dozen high-tech resuscitation techniques and a dozen basic ones. She knew that none of them would help Lucian now. She set her fingers on his eyelids, closed them, kissed them, and lowered him gently to the moss of the riverbank.

The armored car was chugging back and forth along the highway like some smelly dragon. Another vehicle had joined it and there were shouts back and forth. The searchlight swept the river thirty yards below, then twenty yards above where she crouched. Kate realized that the smashed Dacia was under a slight overhang of a boulder here and that they must have left a trail of tattered rubber and smashed metal for two hundred feet down the highway but evidently no major sign of where they went off the road.

It would not take them long. The searchlight was sweeping

in a frenzied arc now and more voices were shouting up and down the highway.

Kate touched Lucian's cooling hand a final time and moved away along the riverbank, staying under the trees, freezing when footsteps pounded or searchlights stabbed through the bare branches. Two hundred yards upstream she stopped, gasping, and then pushed out into the water. The river was only four or five feet deep here but it was very fast and very, very cold. Kate gasped and kept wading, her shoes sliding across smooth rocks on the river bottom.

There were shouts from downstream and searchlights converged on the wreck of the Dacia. If Kate slipped now, the current would take her downstream to the light in seconds. She did not slip. By the time she reached the far side of the river, her legs were numb and her teeth were chattering uncontrollably. She ignored it and clawed toward the shallows.

More searchlights flicked across the river now. One slid over her just as she pulled herself from the water. It moved back immediately as if feeling for her, but she was crawling through the high reeds and mud toward the trees. There was an infinity of forest on this side of the water, stretching a half a mile or more between the river and the black hills. All dark. No roads here. No lights.

The sound of shots came across the water. They were shooting at her. Kate ignored it, stood, and staggered into the woods. There was just enough starlight there for her to check her watch. It was still working. It was ten twenty-seven.

She could see light far up the canyon, but the citadel was still two or three miles away according to Lucian. Staying deep within the protective screen of trees, Kate turned north and began walking.

Chapter Thirty-eight

IT took Kate an hour to walk to the lights, and the lights were only another village, not the citadel itself. She stayed in the trees, looked across the river at the tiny village busy with military traffic, police, and spotlighted roadblocks, and thought: *Lucian mentioned this place . . . Căpăţîneni. The citadel should be less than a mile north.* But the river twisted under a bridge beyond the village, the highway ran along the west side of the river beyond that point, and the surrounding bluffs hid the citadel from sight. Kate could see an orange glow against the low clouds, but it seemed impossibly distant, impossibly high.

She glanced at her watch: 11:34. She would never travel that mile and climb that mountain in time. Lucian had said that there were steps switchbacking up the mountain crag to the citadel—1400 steps. Kate tried to convert that to feet and height. A thousand feet above the river? At least. Exhausted, she leaned against a tree and concentrated on not weeping.

There was a shuffling, snorting sound to her left and Kate froze, then crouched with her fists clenched. She had no weapon, only the old binoculars strung around her neck. The sound came again and Kate slipped forward through the trees.

In a meadow between the river and the forested hillside, a single Gypsy wagon sat alone. A small campfire had burned down to embers. Beyond the wagon, a white horse cropped the dry grass. It was a huge horse with hooves as big as Kate's head. It lifted its head, made a whoofing noise like a sneeze, and began grazing again. The sound of its massive teeth crunching grass was very clear in the cold night air. There was no other sound.

Yes, thought Kate.

She circled around through the trees, staying low and setting her feet with care. Occasionally bullhorn sounds or the sound of shouts would drift across the river from the village. Once Kate froze into immobility as a black helicopter roared down the canyon just above the river, going from south to north. Then the machine was out of sight around the bluff and Kate began stalking the horse again. Her heart pounded as she moved out of the shelter of the trees and slid through the high grass.

The white horse raised its head and watched her with curious eyes.

"Shhh," Kate whispered uselessly as she came up next to the horse, keeping it between the quiet Gypsy wagon and herself. "Shhh." She patted its neck and noticed that its rope halter was tied to a longer rope staked down eight or ten feet closer to the wagon. "Shit," she breathed to herself.

The stake had been driven deep. Kate crouched, could not free it, shifted her position, put her back into it, and pulled the long peg free. The horse moved away slightly, eyes wide at her exertions. Kate coiled the rope and hurried to the animal, patting its neck and whispering reassurances.

A hand fell on Kate's shoulder while a knife blade came around to her throat. A cracked voice whispered something in a language neither Romanian nor English. Kate blinked as the blade moved away. She turned.

The Gypsy woman may have been Kate's age but she looked twenty years older. Even in the dim light, Kate could see the wrinkles, the sagging cheeks, and the missing teeth. She and the woman were dressed alike in black skirt and dark sweater. The knife the woman held was barely larger than a dagger, but it had felt very sharp against Kate's neck.

"You . . . American woman?" said the Gypsy. Her voice

seemed far too loud to Kate. Trucks moved toward the high-way bridge behind her. "You come in Romania with Voivoda Cioaba?"

Kate felt her knees go weak. "Yes," she whispered back.

"Come with *preot*? Priest?"

Kate nodded.

The woman grabbed Kate's sweater, bunched it in her strong fist, shoved Kate backward in the grass, and brought the knife up to Kate's face. "You mother of *strigoi*." The last word was a hiss.

Kate moved her head slowly back and forth an inch from the tip of the knife. "I hate the *strigoi*. I came to destroy them."

The woman squinted at her.

"They took my baby," whispered Kate.

The Gypsy blinked. The knife did not move. "*Strigoi* take many Gypsy babies. Many hundreds of *ani* . . . years. They take Gypsy babies to drink. Now they take Gypsy babies to sell to Americans."

Kate had nothing to say to that.

The woman moved the knife away and knelt in the grass. The horse continued to graze nearby, ignoring them. "I come here because entire families of *Romany* brought here this week. Soldiers have . . . in soldier place near dam. My hus-band and daughter are there. I with sister in Hungary. Soldiers will not let people up road here. I think *strigoi* will be using *Romany* tonight. Yes?"

Kate thought about the ceremony. She and O'Rourke were to provide what Radu Fortuna had called the Sacrament, their blood, for Joshua and the *strigoi* VIPs. What was to feed the hundreds of *strigoi* guests?

"Yes," said Kate. "I think the *strigoi* will kill them to-night."

The Gypsy woman clenched her fists. "You do some-thing?"

Kate took a breath. "Yes."

"You kill them somehow? American smart bomb, like with Saddam Hussein?"

Kate did not smile. "Yes."

The Gypsy woman looked skeptical but got to her feet and helped Kate up. "Good. You want horse?"

Kate chewed her lip and looked at the highway. Military trucks and police vehicles moved back and forth in regular patrols. The hillside on this side of the river was wooded, but too steep to ride a horse on. On the other side of the road, the river stretched to the shale cliffs on the opposite shore.

"I have to try to get up there to the citadel . . ."

The Gypsy woman shook her head. "Not road." She pointed to the forest behind her. "Old trail there. Almost gone. Go back to days of Vlad Ţepeş . . ." The woman stopped, spat, and warded off the evil eye with two fingers raised toward the glow to the north. She walked over to the horse, said something sharp to it, set the dagger in the belt of her skirt, and cupped her hands in what Kate realized was an invitation to mount the animal.

Kate did so, although not gracefully. She rode sometimes in Colorado, but never on a horse this large. Her bruised thighs ached just straddling its back.

"Come," said the woman and lifted the coiled rope to lead the horse toward the forest.

Kate looked at her watch. It was 11:46.

There seemed to be no trail, but the woman led the horse through the trees and the horse seemed to know where he was going. Kate had to hunker over and cling to the animal's neck at times to avoid being swept off by branches.

The road, if the vaguest hint of trail between the trees could be called a road, cut behind the bluff and rose steeply above the valley floor. Kate realized that the highway below wound a mile or so along the river to the citadel, but this way would shorten that distance by at least half.

Two-thirds of the way up the mountain, the woman took out her dagger, cut the rope, handed the short end to Kate, and said, "I go down now. Go to dam near Bilea Lac. If my man and daughter not freed, I join them." She hesitated a second and handed Kate the short knife. Kate stuck it in her belt, feeling the absurdity of her little dagger against several hundred *strigoi* and their armies.

The Gypsy woman paused and lifted a weathered hand. Kate clasped it in a palm-over-palm handshake, and then the Gypsy woman was gone with only the slightest rustle of her black skirt.

Kate gripped the short rope in one hand, wound some mane around her other hand, bent low over the horse's neck, dug her heels in the animal's side, and whispered, "Go . . . please go."

The huge beast continued lumbering up a trail that Kate could not even see.

It was one minute before midnight when they came out of the forest along the high ridge and Kate could look down and across at Castle Dracula on its crag.

It was more impressive and fantastic than she could have imagined: two of the five tall towers had been completely rebuilt, the fortified crag was connected to the rest of the mountain only by a long bridge—possibly a drawbridge—over a deep fissure, the center hall and the battlement terraces were ablaze with torchlight, people in black and red robes milled along the hundred yards of rocky crag, along the battlements, and filled the terrace at the farthest end of the citadel. Torches wound down along the steep stairway which zigzagged through the bare trees, south into the forest, then down to the meadows more than a thousand feet below. Kate could see a veritable parking lot of dark limousines down there, as well as *strigoi* guards pacing in the torchlight. A grassy area on a lower crag a couple of hundred yards along the stairway below the citadel obviously had been cleared of trees and Kate could see Radu Fortuna's helicopter at rest there, a single pilot or guard lounging by its skids. "Slick, slick," Kate whispered to herself. All along the upper path, into the citadel, and along the north edge of the rebuilt structure, sharpened stakes six feet high gleamed in the torchlight.

She slid off the horse, tied it to a branch behind a boulder, and crawled forward to peer at the castle through her binoculars.

One of the lens tubes had cracked and filled with water, but the other amplified the scene. From her vantage point on the hill above and a little northwest of the citadel, Kate could see the guards on the drawbridge, the guards near the busy entrance to the citadel, the guards around the north edge of the battlements, and the scene on the terrace farthest from the entrance.

Torchlights flickered there on hundreds of faces and silk robes. A space had been cleared on the highest area of the terrace, right where the battlements and south walls dropped a sheer thousand feet to the river and boulders below. In that lighted space, Kate could see Vernor Deacon Trent on a small throne near the battlement edge. The old man was dressed in an elaborate red and black robe and looked like a wizened mummy propped up for display. There were two tall metal stakes set into the stone in that cleared area: one was empty, Mike O'Rourke was tied to the other.

Kate's heart froze when she saw him. They had dressed Mike in a parody of his priest outfit—black clothes, tall white collar, a crucifix made of thorns hung upside down from a vine necklace—and he had a black blindfold on. His hands were tied behind the stake.

Radu Fortuna stood in front of the crowd, resplendent in a pure red silk robe that outshone the old man's. Kate had eyes only for the silk-wrapped bundle in Fortuna's arms.

The binoculars were shaking and she had to steady them on a branch. Joshua's face was quite clear, pale and feverish looking in the torchlight. On the table between Fortuna and O'Rourke, four golden chalices sat on white linen. The group was chanting softly. Fortuna was saying something.

Kate lowered the binoculars and looked at her watch. 12:05. *Lucian said the timers were set to go off at 12:25.* She was less than a hundred yards from her child and lover, but she might as well have been a light-year away. *Strigoi* guards in black watched the approach, lounged on the bridge, stood at the citadel entrance, and were lined around the rear of the crowd on the broad terrace. The crowd itself would keep her away from the ceremony. Her watch shifted to 12:06.

Kate flung the binoculars from her, clambered over the boulder, and began lowering herself into the fissure that separated her ridge from the citadel crag. The rocks were slippery. *Slick*, she thought. Fifty feet down and the fissure narrowed to a rocky crevasse that dropped another eighty or a hundred feet like the inside of a ragged chimney. It was only five feet across here and from the reflected lights from the torches above, Kate could see a fairly flat rock.

She did not think. She jumped.

Her cheap Romanian shoes scrabbled on stone and she realized that she was missing part of a heel. *Shot off when we ran the roadblock.* She was sliding back toward the narrow abyss.

In a technique that Tom had taught her during one of their few joint rock-climbing exercises, she spread-eagled herself on the steep rock face, bringing her entire body to a friction point.

She quit sliding.

A hundred feet to her right, the bridge rose above the fissure, connecting the stairway and path to the citadel. Guards paced back and forth on the echoing timbers.

Kate began edging right, finding handholds and footholds more by faith than by vision or feel. Once a rock came loose and she held her breath while pebbles rattled down into the fissure that was at least thirty feet wide here. The sound of sliding rock seemed terribly loud to her, but none of the shadows on the walkway above stopped or shouted.

Kate moved under the bridge, clambering over lashed timbers the size of trees. She could climb up here, but that would avail her nothing. She could hear the footsteps of the guards twenty feet above her, listen to the chanting of the hundreds of *strigoi*.

Kate kept clambering right, always keeping three points in contact with the rock the way Tom had taught her, until suddenly the rough rocks ended and she was staring out at the river canyon itself.

Under Kate's right foot now, the cliff fell away for a thousand feet into darkness. Torchlight illuminated only snatches of the stone wall ahead of her, but she realized that the south wall of the citadel along this face rose directly from the stone of the mountain.

This end of the castle was not broad, a hundred and twenty feet at most, but the wall was sheer, seeming to overhang at places, and torches crackled on the battlements above. The stones here were part of the original structure, chipped and eroded in places, cracked by ice, and overgrown by weeds and even small shrubs in places. *Vegetable holds*, Tom had called such plant growth on a cliff face. *Don't use them.*

Kate saw immediately that if she started sliding at any point along this traverse, she would not stop until she slid off the wall into the void above the canyon. She looked at her watch. 12:14.

Just time enough to get to the terrace in time for the end.

She shook her head. Without looking down, without looking back, Kate edged her way out onto the vertical wall of Castle Dracula and began the traverse in a steady crablike motion.

Chapter Thirty-nine

THE graduation exercise of Kate's short-lived climbing experience with Tom had been the climb of the Third Flatiron, a giant limestone slab that lifted above Boulder like a piece of broken sidewalk tilted on end. That climb had taken most of a Saturday morning; Kate figured that she had five minutes maximum to make this traverse.

There were more footholds and handholds on the castle wall than there had been on the Flatiron. Kate continued sliding to her right, slowing frequently but never completely stopping. She remembered from climbing with Tom and from watching Tom climb that sometimes speed itself substituted for friction, the very act of moving quickly over rock allowing one to cling like a fly where there was not enough friction to hold one on if the climber stopped.

Kate did not stop.

Fifty feet out and the pitch of the wall increased, becoming true vertical and worse than vertical in places. The torches above shed some light here, but what might look like a promising foothold often turned out to be a millimeter-thin ledge of rotting rock, an apparently sturdy handhold would become a weed with two-inch roots. But Kate kept moving, climbing when she had to get above some obstacle, reluctantly dropping lower when she had to pass under an overhang or avoid a smooth stretch of stone. At one point she felt the hilt of the

432

silly little dagger cutting into her waist, but it was too dangerous to leverage her body in such a way she could get at the
knife to throw it away. She left it poking her and continued
moving.

Her mistake was thinking that it would be faster halfway
across to follow a four-inch ledge of soil where ice had fis-
sured the stone. For a moment it was, and then the ledge slid
away with the noise of sand collapsing and she was sliding
down the wall with no points in full contact, no handholds,
and the toes of her cheap shoes rattling uselessly against
stone.

Kate closed her eyes and curled her fingers into claws. Her
right hand slammed into a narrow ledge where a block of
stone had been displaced an inch by some forgotten earthquake, three of her fingernails snapped off, but she kept her
fingers curled and hung on, all of her weight supported by
three fingers of her numb right hand.

Kate slapped the wall with her left hand, but there were no
handholds. Her toes scrabbled without finding a crack or
ledge. Finally she remembered Tom's technique of wedging
the toes and palm and just finding a friction point to balance
gravity.

She pulled her knees up, forced her feet against the near-
vertical stone, pressed her left palm tightly against rock, and
was able to lift some of the weight from her cramping right
hand. She was panting so loudly now that she was afraid they
would hear her on the terrace twenty-five feet above, but no
sounds came down to her except the crackle of torches and
the incessant chanting, rising to some peak now. She did not
turn her head to look at her watch.

The friction point would not hold for long. Two feet to the
right of her tiny handhold, another stone jutted farther out,
offering a hypothetical hold for both hands. Cracks four feet
below that should serve for her feet. If she could only shift
her left hand across her body . . .

She could not. Any movement of her palm or arm put all
of her weight on the bruised fingers of her right hand. Her
toes were slipping and she did not have enough grip anywhere

to lift her feet again. The only thing she could do was let go of her one hold and try to scrabble the two feet to her right.

One, she thought, *two* . . . her legs were beginning a sewing-machine shake, her fingers were surrendering the grip . . . *fuck it*. Kate shifted her hand, slipped, kept all four points in touch as she scrabbled to her right, slipped again . . . *too far*! . . . and then caught one of the "toeholds" as she started to slide past it. It was deep enough for eight fingers to wedge full length between the stone. She set her chin against the tiny fissure and gasped into it. A bat exploded from the hole, its leathery wings brushing her face. Kate did not even consider letting go.

I could stay here a few minutes. Rest.

The hell you can. Move!

She opened her eyes. Another thirty feet should put her where she wanted to be under the edge of the terrace where the ceremony chanted on. She carefully turned her head and looked at her watch.

12:19. She did not have time for the rest of the traverse.

What if my watch is slow? Kate shook with sudden giggles until she used her wrist to wipe her nose and bring her out of the hysterics. Her arms were shaking again.

She looked above her, picked out a route from crack to crack, stone to stone, and began climbing.

Kate came up over the battlements less than twenty feet from where she wanted to be. All eyes were on Radu Fortuna, who was holding Joshua above him like an offering. A *strigoi* with a black hood stood next to Mike O'Rourke with a curved blade lifted to the ex-priest's throat. The chanting was very loud.

Grunting despite herself, Kate leveraged her body up and over the last stone block and swung her scraped and bleeding legs off the battlement and onto a low ledge that ran along the inside of the wall. She did not take time to feel relief at being off the cliff face.

Heads turned her way. Some of the chanting halted. But

Radu Fortuna and the man who called himself Vernor Deacon Trent were too intent on the ceremony to turn their heads.

Before anyone else could move, Kate sprinted toward Fortuna. Her legs, shaky from the traverse, almost went out from under her once but she gritted her teeth and covered the last ten feet in a flat run. She did not pause to think what she must look like to the hundreds of assembled *strigoi*—this wild-eyed woman coming over the castle wall, her face still smudged with Lucian's blood, her hands bleeding, her clothes ripped and in disarray.

Vernor Deacon Trent saw her first, his heavy-lidded eyes widening, one hand rising from the carved arm of the heavy chair, and Radu Fortuna turned and saw her a second later.

Not in time.

Kate hit Fortuna hard with her shoulder, slamming into his rib cage and hearing the air whoosh out of him. He dropped Joshua.

Kate caught the baby and backed away. Joshua was not much heavier than when he had been kidnapped; his skin was pasty, his eyes too wide, too dark, and terrified. He began to wail.

The *strigoi* were assembled row on row. Now black and red cowls were shoved back, guards shouted and pushed forward from the rear wall fifty feet across the terrace, there were screams and curses from the crowd, and hands reached for Kate and the baby. She glanced at her watch. 12:20.

Kate hurriedly backed to the low ledge, leaped on it seconds before Radu Fortuna reached her, and then jumped to the lower ledge of the crenellated battlement wall.

Radu Fortuna and the others slid to a stop three feet from the wall.

Kate calmly stepped up on the higher stone and held Joshua out over the edge with both arms, her bruised and bleeding fingers tight under his tiny arms. The outer layer of red silk fell away, fluttering on the wind blowing up the castle wall.

"Not a step!" she shouted. "Or I drop him."

Chapter Forty

"Y OU crazy American cunt," hissed Radu Fortuna, his face close enough that Kate could see the white spittle at the corners of his mouth, "you can't believe we are going to let you and the child go."

"No," said Kate. She suddenly felt very calm. This is where all of her efforts had brought her. This is where she had to be. Joshua had quit wailing and fidgeted only slightly in her hands. His tiny feet were bare and she remembered all the times they had played this-little-piggy together before bedtime. He was looking at her with wide eyes.

"Give us the child," ordered Fortuna, taking another step closer.

"If you don't get back," said Kate, "I drop him." She tossed Joshua slightly, catching him firmly under the arms. But not before the crowd of reverent *strigoi* gasped.

Radu Fortuna took a step back. The crowd was too dense and pressing to allow any more room. He turned and said something in rapid-fire Romanian to Vernor Deacon Trent. The old man had stepped off his throne and was just another face in the crowd.

"Doctor," Vernor Deacon Trent said to her, "there is no purpose to this."

"Yes," said Kate, "there is." She could not see her watch.

Three minutes remaining perhaps. Not enough time for anything. But she would go ahead.

Vernor Deacon Trent shrugged. Two huge bodyguards were plucking at his sleeve in some haste, as if Kate's very presence were a threat. "If you are going to jump, jump," said the old man, and turned away.

Kate licked her battered lips. "Release him." She had to nod in the direction she meant.

Radu Fortuna turned slowly. "The priest?" He laughed out loud. "All this to save your lover?" He spat and looked behind him. A dozen *strigoi* guards had rifles or automatic weapons aimed at Kate's face. If they fired, Joshua would drop with her.

Kate's arms were very tired from holding the baby out above the darkness.

"Release him," said Kate. "Release him and I will step down and give you the child."

Radu Fortuna sneered. "No."

Kate turned and looked down. It would be a long fall. She shifted her wrist so that she could see her watch. 12:22. Too late. She wondered if she and the baby would feel anything.

"Yes," said Vernor Deacon Trent from deep in the crowd in his shaky, old man's voice. "Release the priest."

"*Nu!*" shouted Radu Fortuna. "I forbid it!"

Vernor Deacon Trent's face seemed to Kate to shift then, from something merely old and worn-out to something powerful and not quite human. "*Release him!*" bellowed the old man, and there was no trace of weakness in his voice this time.

Radu Fortuna blinked as if he had been slapped. He gestured weakly to the executioner who stood next to O'Rourke at the stake. The long knife cut the ropes that bound the priest.

O'Rourke took off his blindfold, rubbed his wrists, and looked at her. "Kate, I don't—"

"Shut up, Mike," she said, her voice soft. The only other sound was the crackling of torches. "Just go."

"But I—"

"Just go, my darling." She nodded toward the bridge and the steps leaving the castle. "Go down the trail . . . past the slick, all right? Past the slick and down to the bend we can see from here. Take one of the torches out when you get there and wave it back and forth so we can see that you are there. Then I will give the baby back to them."

"Let it be so," Radu Fortuna said in English and then in Romanian.

O'Rourke hesitated only a second. Nodding, saying nothing, he stepped down from the sacrificial dais, went around the table laid out with chalices, and made his way through the *strigoi*. He was limping, but his damaged prosthesis obviously still worked. The dense crowd parted for him; one guard spat as he passed, but no one interfered.

Kate leaned out farther and hugged the baby to her side. Anyone rushing her would send both of them plunging. If she were shot, the impact would knock her off. Joshua began crying softly, his pudgy hands gripping the wool of her sweater. He babbled syllables and Kate was sure that she heard "Mommy."

"Hand us the child and we will let you go," Radu Fortuna said smoothly, extending his arms.

Kate hunted for Vernor Deacon Trent but the old face was no longer visible in the crowd. "You won't let me go," Kate said tiredly.

"*Goddamn you, woman!*" exploded Fortuna. "Of course we will not fucking let you go! Nor the fucking priest! Even if he leaves this mountain, we will find him, return him, and drink his fucking blood! *Now give me the child!*"

Kate held Joshua out over the abyss with straight arms. The pain tore at her muscles and shoulder sockets, but the movement froze Fortuna in his tirade.

She could see her watch. 12:25. She closed her eyes.

The white light, when it came, was a surprise. The noise was very loud.

The Bell Jet Ranger helicopter just cleared the west tower and seemed to skim the east tower, its searchlight was on and flashing across the crowd, blinding the *strigoi* and Kate as well. The helicopter slewed sideways, seemed to be about to land in the middle of the *strigoi* throng, and sent the crowd shoving back toward the far wall, the wind of the machine's rotors pelting them with dust, gravel, and grit thrown up from the terrace. The chalices on the long table were blown off as red and white vestments fluttered and linens lifted into the sky like streams of toilet paper in a high wind.

Radu Fortuna screamed a curse that was lost in the incredible rotor noise. Guards tried to press forward and left their weapons in the crush of the retreating *strigoi* mob.

Kate caught the briefest glimpse of O'Rourke on the left side of the helicopter's steel and Plexiglas bubble, his face intent as he obviously wrestled with the controls, and then she was holding on to the baby with one arm and flailing to keep her balance with her right arm as the rotor wind threatened to tumble her off the wall into the canyon.

Radu Fortuna lunged forward and seized her ankle. Joshua screamed at the avalanche of light and noise.

The helicopter pivoted, its skids six feet above Kate, and the entire machine moved sideways out over the canyon as if sliding on an invisible layer of ice. The rotor blast almost threw Kate back onto Radu Fortuna. The *strigoi* shielded his eyes with one hand and pulled at her ankle with the other. Several guards pushed through the mob.

The helicopter slid back toward Kate, the machine rocking like a rowboat in rough waves. Kate ducked as the slick's right skid bobbed where her head had been a second before. She started to rise and then ducked again as the door that O'Rourke had left open on the right side of the machine swung wider and almost took her head off. The rotor noise and gale was beyond belief.

Radu Fortuna snarled and grabbed the collar of her sweater. Kate did not look back as she swung her right elbow back, hard, into his teeth. His hand released her collar.

Kate stood up quickly while the door was open, leaned out over the emptiness, and set her baby in the right seat. O'Rourke shouted something she could not hear, lifted his right hand from the stick to reach across and keep Joshua from sliding out, had to return his hand to the controls, and bobbed the helicopter down and to the left to keep the baby from rolling out.

Kate pinwheeled her arms, could not catch her balance, and leaped as hard and as far as she could out into the abyss.

Chapter Forty-one

THE helicopter was already sliding back toward the castle and Kate hit the right skid hard, her arms going over it, her chin snapping down, her breasts feeling as if she had been slammed by a baseball bat, and the wind going out of her in a rush. She hung on.

The door on the right side was still swinging open and shut, and O'Rourke was working the controls, trying to hover without allowing Joshua to tumble out. The helicopter wheeled right. Kate glanced over her shoulder and saw *strigoi* guards raise their machine guns in the hailstorm of grit and dust.

"*Nu!*" screamed Radu Fortuna. He stepped up onto the wall.

Kate tried to scream at O'Rourke to move left, but the ex-priest was obviously too busy trying to control the machine and keep the rotor from slamming into the tower or battlements. The helicopter slid another eight feet to the right as if on invisible rails, Radu Fortuna reached up, grabbed the open door, and stepped easily onto the skid.

O'Rourke glanced left, saw the shadow of the man leaning in, and banked the helicopter steeply to the left. Kate's fingers slid off the fuselage but she clung to the skid and the metal strut holding the skid in place. Under her shoes, the vertical face of the castle wall suddenly upended and seemed to swing sideways as the chopper first dove, then rose again, always tilting a bit to the left so that Joshua would not tumble out.

Kate swung her leg up onto the strut and kicked Radu Fortuna's ankles out from under him before he could step into the cabin.

Fortuna fell forward and swung out on the door, his legs hanging free. Kate released her secure handhold, balanced forward on the skid as if doing a forward roll on a tubular balance beam, and got her left hand in the open cabin doorway. There was a ridge there and she locked her fingers around it and pulled herself to one knee on the slippery skid.

O'Rourke leveled the helicopter sixty or seventy feet above the castle terrace. A score of muzzles were lifted toward them, but no one fired because of the baby and Radu Fortuna.

With the helicopter level, the door swung inward and Fortuna's stocky body slammed into Kate, squeezing her against the doorframe but not giving her enough room to pull herself into the cabin. His strong left hand seized her by the throat and began squeezing.

They were both standing on the bobbing skid now. Their weight tipped the machine sickeningly to the right, and Kate felt Joshua's small form strike her back. If she and Fortuna went off now, the baby would come with them. She tried to twist out of the *strigoi*'s grasp but the chopper tilted left, his weight fell against her, and he freed his right hand to complete his choking. His thumbs closed over her windpipe and Kate knew that he could break her neck in a second.

The helicopter bobbed slightly, a space opened between their bodies, and Kate pulled the Gypsy's dagger from her belt and plunged it through Fortuna's flapping vestments into his stomach.

The blade did not go deep. Kate's leverage was too restricted and Fortuna's robes too thick. But the pain and shock stopped Radu Fortuna's thumbs from closing on her neck. Kate released her grip on the inside of the door and pushed the knife farther in, knowing precisely where the largest bundle of nerve fibers was.

Radu Fortuna roared, pulled his hands from her throat, and

wrestled the knife away from her, pulling it from its shallow cut. O'Rourke banked the hovering machine to the left at precisely the right instant, Kate leaned far back onto the seat over Joshua's wailing form, lifted her legs, and kicked Fortuna off the skid.

She swung her legs in, held the baby tight against the back of the seat, and leaned out the flapping door to watch Fortuna fall. Several hundred white faces stared up from red and black cowls, all of them watching while the short man, arms swinging and legs extended as gracefully as a sky diver's, did two complete somersaults in the air and then fell, faceup, with all limbs extended for the final sixty feet. Directly onto the metal stake that had been reserved for Kate.

The crowd of *strigoi* raised their hands as blood spattered their robes and faces. Two of the guards began to fire short bursts.

"Go!" screamed Kate, slamming the banging door shut. "Higher!" Her watch said 12:26 and thirty seconds.

Something banged against the fuselage behind them, but O'Rourke ignored it, twisted something on the stick in his right hand, lifted a lever in his left hand, kicked at rudder pedals, and the Jet Ranger's engine whined higher. They banked to the left and started climbing away from the citadel and the muzzle flashes.

Kate looked down, realized that the castle was now on the other side, saw something dark far below—*like a giant bat*— its shadow rippling across the river for the briefest second, and then she raised her wrist again, looked at her watch, and shouted above the engine roar to O'Rourke. "What time is it?"

He glanced toward her incredulously. "You expect me to take my hand off the collective to tell you—"

"*What is the fucking time?*" she screamed, realizing that she sounded a little hysterical even to herself.

O'Rourke blinked, freed his left hand for a second, and said, "My watch says twelve twenty-fi—"

The world exploded beneath them and around them.

Chapter Forty-two

$\mathbf{A}$T the last second O'Rourke swung the helicopter around, still in its climb, to face the shock wave, and that probably saved their lives. Instead of being swatted out of the sky like a fleeing insect, the Bell Jet Ranger rose on the blast like a leaf above a roaring fire. The ride was vertical, faster than any elevator Kate had ever been on, and the view below was not something she would soon forget.

Poenari Citadel—Castle Dracula—exploded in a score of places, gigantic mushrooms of flame rising a thousand feet above the crag the castle was built on. More explosions ripped through the woods, the stairway, the grassy area where the helicopter had been parked, and the stairway to the valley below. An instant later a second series of explosions seemed to erupt from the cliff wall itself.

The west tower of the citadel became a billion fragments of shrapnel flying ahead of the blossoming orange ball of flame, but the east tower seemed to rise like some medieval space shuttle, much of the upper battlements seemingly intact and balancing on a tail of pure flame. Then the illusion dissolved as the tower flew apart in ten-ton fragments and fell onto the screaming *strigoi* crowded on the terrace. The terrace itself was rocked with explosions that sent flame a hundred yards out over the river valley.

If there were any human forms left on the east and north

sections of the crag that held the citadel, they were not visible as more explosions opened cracks in what little brick and stone that remained. The terrace section of the castle separated itself from the rubble of the main keep and tumbled a thousand feet into the valley, its cloud of dust adding to the pall of smoke and haze that filled the entire width of the canyon.

The trees within a hundred yards of the former citadel had burst into flame, the fire jumping to their crowns in seconds, and a great wind seemed to be whipping thick trunks back and forth like reeds.

Kate saw all this in the few seconds of their vertical elevator ride. She cradled the screaming Joshua tighter as the helicopter reached the top of its arc and prepared to drop straight down into that conflagration. She had no seat belt on and she and the baby rose six inches off the seat as the helicopter reached its apogee.

"Hang on!" O'Rourke yelled uselessly, and then he threw the stick in his right hand hard to the left, kicked his right rudder pedal, and squeezed the throttle wide open. The roar of the jet turbine became louder than the explosions and landslides two thousand feet below them.

They could not recover in the fifteen hundred feet of altitude they had above the blazing ruins of the citadel. O'Rourke obviously did not try to. He put the helicopter's nose down and dove it into the canyon. The turbine screamed louder, alarms went off on the console in front of both him and Kate, and the wind slammed at the not-quite-latched door inches from Joshua's face. Kate held the baby tight and watched the river rise toward them at a terrifying rate.

O'Rourke set both his good leg and artificial one hard against the pedals, gripped the stick in both hands, and began easing the machine out of its bucking, screaming dive. Kate felt the heat of the burning mountain as they hurtled past it, and then the canyon walls were whipping by on both sides, the river rising to fill the soot-streaked windscreen in front of them. Kate closed her eyes for a second.

When she opened them, they were hurtling along in level flight thirty feet above the Argeş, heading south. Kate saw trucks and lights on the riverbank to her left and realized that it was the spot where the Dacia had crashed. The spot where she had left Lucian. She closed her eyes again. *Good-bye, my friend. There will be no more orphans used to feed the strigois' thirst.* Joshua stirred in her arms and she patted the baby's back. *With luck . . . just a little luck . . . there will be no more AIDS babies.*

O'Rourke was clicking off alarms, snapping toggles on a panel between them. He glanced to his right. "Are you all right?"

Kate started to answer but began laughing instead. She put her free hand up to stop the giggles but ended up just snuffling and giggling into her wrist. O'Rourke frowned for a second, but then began laughing himself.

When they could stop, Kate shifted the baby to her right arm and touched his shoulder with her left hand. "Are they going to shoot us down now? The air force or something?"

O'Rourke let go of the stick for a moment to take a headset from a bracket and slip it over his head. He tapped the microphone and then lifted the right earphone. "Nope. I don't think so. Romania has one of those air forces that doesn't like to fly at night." He threw toggles on the console and she could hear a beeping from the earphones near her head. O'Rourke gestured and she set them on.

"Hear me better now?" he asked. The engine roar and rotor noise was a distant thing, his voice clear in her headphones.

She nodded.

He banked to the right and gained altitude over the foothills. Kate realized that they had already covered all the ground that it had taken Lucian and her hours to drive through the Transylvanian hills between Rîmnícu Vîlcea and Curtea de Argeş. She settled back in the seat, found a shoulder harness, and buckled herself in. Joshua was breathing easily, dozing off. Kate shook her head.

"This kind of aircraft carries a transponder," O'Rourke said through the intercom. "I suspect that no one in Romania would mess with this particular helicopter even if we buzzed the capital." They continued to climb. High peaks were ahead but they were already flying higher than the snowcapped summits.

"Do we have enough gas to get out of here?" she asked into the little microphone. O'Rourke would know that "here" meant Romania.

He smiled at her. His eye was still swollen almost shut and his lips were a mess from the beating they had given him, but he looked happy. "If I find even the slightest tail wind, we'll have enough gas to land in downtown Budapest," he said. "Which side of the river would you prefer, Buda or Pest?"

"You choose," Kate whispered into the microphone. "I've made enough decisions for one day."

O'Rourke nodded and concentrated on the controls.

"Mike," she said a minute later. She was gently rocking Joshua, feeling the baby's warm breath on her cheek. "Lucian is dead."

"I'm sorry," he said. "Do you want to tell me about it? And how you managed all this?"

"In a while," said Kate. "But tell me something first . . . do you know anything about Lucian's mentor?"

"Mentor? No." His voice was puzzled.

"It wasn't you?"

"No, Kate."

She rubbed her hand across her baby's head. His hair had grown. He was blowing bubbles in his sleep. *New cure for colic*, she thought irrelevantly. *Take the baby for a helicopter ride*. "Could it have been the Church . . . sponsoring Lucian in his fight against the *strigoi*, I mean?"

O'Rourke thought a minute. "No, I don't think so. I think I would have heard about it if the Church had been actively involved like that. The best the Church could do was tend to the victims all these years. I'm sorry, Kate . . . is this mentor thing important?"

"Perhaps not," said Kate. They were flying through scattered clouds now, still climbing. The instrument lights were red. O'Rourke fiddled with something and a heater came on. The sound and feel of the warm air was soothing to Kate, like being a child again, out on a ride in her parents' car at night with the heater fan blowing gently. Despite the adrenaline still surging through her body, Kate actually felt sleepy.

"There is something important we have to talk about, though," she said. She did not add the "us."

O'Rourke nodded. She looked his way and saw him smiling at her. "I look forward to talking about that," he said softly.

Joshua made the kind of vaguely troubled noise that babies make while dreaming, and Kate rocked him gently. Suddenly they came out of the cloud layer and it seemed to her that the tops of the clouds were like a sea and they were a submarine rising to the surface . . . and above it. The cloud tops gleamed beneath them as far as she could see in each direction. There was no sense now of national boundaries, or of nations, of the darkness that lay below those clouds. Kate would not mind staying above these clouds for a while. She rocked the baby, crooning very softly, and watched out the window as they leveled off and flew northwest.

"I've got the tail wind we needed," said O'Rourke. "And I'm pretty sure the NavStar system is working right. We'll be following the Danube for part of the way."

Kate nodded in a distracted way. She had just realized how bright the stars were up here in this moonless sky, so bright that they turned the cloud tops into a milky ocean of subtle white hues.

O'Rourke was holding the stick with his left hand now, turning a radio dial with his right. When he had found the channel he wanted, Kate reached over and gently took his hand.

Not speaking, still holding hands, they flew west under the canopy of stars.

Epilogue

*When they opened my grave on Şnagov Island, they found it
empty. That was in 1932. In the winter of 1476, I had briefly
regained the throne of Transylvania, but my enemies were
legion and they would not cease their attempts until I was
dead.*

*That winter, surrounded and outnumbered by foes, I was
driven into the swamps near Şnagov by those who would have
my head. Instead, they found my headless and mangled body
in the marshes there. They identified me by my royal clothes
and by the signet ring bearing the sign of the Order of the
Dragon on my finger.*

*I had taken only one loyal boyar ally in my flight to the
marshes. He was loyal, but not terribly smart. He was my
general size and build.*

*It was to be the first time I left Transylvania with one of
my sons. It was not the last.*

*I admit that I was not sure whether I would stay at the
citadel for the denouement. That morning, being outfitted in
my clumsy robes and flown south in the machine, I decided
that I would. I was very tired. If my body would not die of its
own accord, I would give it peace by other means.*

*But when the woman showed up, the irony of the situation
appealed to me. I supposed dear young Lucian had violated*

his orders and interceded to save her. I had half expected him to. Sometimes it is best to allow fate to play the last hand.

I had only met Lucian the two times I brought him to the United States to receive his instructions, but I will not forget him. At first the boy refused to believe that he was one of my sons, but I showed him the photographs of his mother, taken of course before she fled from me to return to her homeland. I showed Lucian the documents that proved that it had been Radu Fortuna who had killed his real mother and placed him in an orphanage. I told him that he was lucky, that most pure-strigoi couples put their "normal" offspring to death.

Lucian's zeal served us well. He joined the Order of the Dragon. He never doubted my motives of purifying the Family of its decadent branches. He understood my sincerity in finding a scientific answer to the family disease.

Which may be another reason that I did not stay for the final act. The morning of the ceremony, I had injected myself with the serum the woman doctor had brought all that way only to lose in Sighişoara. By evening I could feel the change. It was like the Sacrament without the hormonal ragings that had so tired me out over the ages. By the time the absurd woman pulled herself over the parapets of our citadel, I felt centuries younger. My long disgust at what Radu Fortuna and the others of his ilk have done to my Family—not to mention the people of my nation—was burning in my gut like the flames of pure anger I had not felt for many years.

So, in the end, I decided not to stay for the end.

The Dobrins whisked me through the crowd to the secret exit in the basement of the main hall. The German elevator I had installed there worked efficiently, as do all things German. I must admit that I thought of the tons of explosives set in the walls we were descending through. I thought of the Czech, Hungarian, and German engineers I had brought in to set those charges over the past two years, and about how their bones were now mixing with the new mortar there. The irony was inescapable, but we were running late and the Dobrins' obvious anxiety did not allow me to enjoy an old man's love of irony.

There were no horses waiting in the cave this time, only the golf cart and the third Dobrin brother. It took less than a minute to race down the paved tunnel to the river exit, but we only had a minute or two.

The black OH-6 Loach helicopter was where I had directed it to be, the engine warmed, the rotors turning, the fourth Dobrin brother at the controls. We were away in thirty seconds. It was almost not in time. The entire mountain came apart above us as we roared up the canyon toward Sighişoara and home. I must admit, I have always enjoyed fireworks, and this may be the best show I have attended.

In the weeks and months since that night, I find that the hemoglobin substitute has other effects beyond renewing my capacity to enjoy life. It reduces the amount I dream almost to zero. This is not an unwelcome thing.

I have thought about the child of mine who was taken that night. At first I considered retrieving him, of raising him the way I raised Vlad and Mihnea. But then I remembered what potential he holds and I have decided to let the woman doctor raise him and learn from him.

I have been a source of terror to my people and employees many times in my long life. I know now that I would have welcomed being a savior to my people. Perhaps, through this child . . . just perhaps.

Meanwhile, I am considering returning to the States, or at least the civilized part of Europe, to be closer to the laboratories making my hemoglobin substitute. It occurred to me recently that Japan is a place I have never lived. It is an intriguing place, filled with the energy and business that is the lifeblood I feed on now.

In the meantime, I have given up thoughts of dying soon. Such thoughts were the products of illness, age, and bad dreams. I no longer have the bad dreams.

Perhaps I will live forever.

ACKNOWLEDGMENTS

The author would like to thank the following people for their invaluable help in the preparation for this novel:

In Romania:
    My sincere thanks to the poet Emil Manu, and to his wife and family for their wonderful hospitality. A special thanks to Lucian and Joanne Manu for their friendship, insights, and for a peek into a Bucharest most tourists do not see. Also, a sincere *multumesc foarte mult* to Marius from ONT and to Ana Manole and her sister in the village of Ciofringeni for their kindness to strangers.

In the USA:
    I would like to thank Gahan Wilson for the pleasant dinner conversation and the copy of his 1977 *Playboy* article, "Dracula Country." It was the single best source for tracking down the real Castle Dracula. My thanks also to Keith Nightenhelser of Depauw University for sharing the research of Robert Cochran and Laszlo Kurti on the "politics of joking" in Romania and Eastern Europe. I would also like to thank Dana Gall for the Romanian instruction and Rodica Varna for keeping me out of a Bucharest hotel which had its walls shot out.
    A special thanks to Byron Preiss and Richard Curtis for

making me write about Dracula in the first place. And thank you to Chris Pepe at Putnam's for her patience and enthusiasm.

In the USA, Romania, Hungary, and Austria:

An inadequate but sincere thanks to Claudia Logerquist for her research, linguistic skills, stamina, courage, and spirit of adventure.

Finally, I would like to acknowledge my debt to Radu R. Florescu and Raymond T. McNally, authors of *Dracula: Prince of Many Faces, In Search of Dracula*, and other works. Their writings have almost single-handedly renewed interest in the historical Vlad Dracula, and I recommend their books to the interested reader. (One caveat for the serious Dracula-seeker, however—the caption under the photograph of the only extant bust of Vlad Ţepeş on p. 170 of *Dracula: Prince of Many Faces* says that the statue is to be found in the village of Copitineni [sic]. In truth, the bust is to be found not in the shadow of Castle Dracula in Căpăţîneni, but across from the old palace grounds in Tîrgovişte some 100 km. away.)

Thanks to the research of these men and other scholars, I can say that all of the memories I ascribe to Vlad Dracula in this book, with the possible exception of the Sacrament, are true.